No Control

Shannon K. Butcher

FOREVER

NEW YORK   BOSTON

Copyright © 2008 by Shannon K. Butcher
All rights reserved. Except as permitted under the U.S. Copyright Act of 1976, no part of this publication may be reproduced, distributed, or transmitted in any form or by any means, or stored in a database or retrieval system, without the prior written permission of the publisher.

Cover design by Dale Fiorello

Forever
Hachette Book Group USA
237 Park Avenue
New York, NY 10017
Visit our Web site at www.HachetteBookGroupUSA.com

Forever is an imprint of Grand Central Publishing. The Forever name and logo is a trademark of Hachette Book Group USA, Inc.

Printed in the United States of America

First Printing: February 2008

10 9 8 7 6 5 4 3 2 1

For my parents, who nurtured my creativity, taught me the joy of hard work, and showed me every day of my childhood what true love is really all about.
Miss you, Mom.

ACKNOWLEDGMENTS

I have a lot of people to thank for helping me make this book so much better than it would have been otherwise: my agent, Nephele Tempest, my editor, Michele Bidelspach, and my beta readers, Dyann, Julie, Karen, Michelle, Sara, Sherry and Tonia. Your efforts, input, and encouragement are an invaluable help to me, and I can't thank you enough.

PROLOGUE

---·❖·---

Armenia

Lana Hancock prayed for a swift death. The hood over her head made it hard to breathe, as did the smell of her friends' bodies. Through a tiny slit in her hood that her captors didn't know was there, she could see Bethany's lifeless eyes staring at her.

Lana tried to turn away, but even the smallest movement sent pain screaming through her broken limbs. The man who had broken them, Boris, came back into the cave, and she knew this was the end. Whatever her abductors told Boris to do, he did. She'd heard them order him to kill her right before they left, and she'd been lying here, waiting for the end, for what seemed like days.

She was going to miss her family. Her friends. Her fiancé.

She wanted to see her nephew grow up and spoil him with loud presents that would drive her sister crazy. The little drum set Lana had bought him for his birthday was tucked in her closet. She hoped they'd find it and give it to him when her family cleaned out her apartment.

Boris pulled out his gun and crossed the dusty cave to

where Lana lay. He was a skinny man with bright blue eyes and dimples that made her stomach turn. A sadistic killer shouldn't have dimples.

His booted feet stopped only inches from her face. Part of her was afraid, but most of her was simply grateful he was using the gun instead of the pipe again. At least this way would be fast. She hoped.

She saw a shadow cross the mouth of the cave, then another and another. Maybe her abductors were back to watch it happen. Maybe she was hallucinating. Lana couldn't bring herself to care. She was too tired. Too weak.

He reached down and ripped at the tape that was holding her hood closed around her neck. The movement caused broken bones to grind, and her dry scream echoed against the cave walls.

She must have passed out, because when she opened her eyes, her killer was looking down at her with a concerned frown, patting her cheek as if to revive her. When he saw she was awake again, he nodded once as if satisfied and stood up again. Apparently, he didn't want to kill her if she was unconscious.

His gun aimed for her head, thank God. Like with the others he'd killed, it would be a head shot. Quick and painless.

A thick arm appeared from nowhere and wrapped around Boris's head, pulling it back while a second arm sliced his throat open with a knife. Blood spewed from the man's neck, and his gun clattered to the hard ground.

Lana tried to figure out what was happening, but she couldn't move her head. Couldn't keep her eyes open.

"We've got to get you out of here," said a deep, tight voice she'd heard somewhere before.

Pain sliced through her, and she realized she was being lifted. Her broken legs dangled painfully over a man's arms, but she kept herself from screaming. She couldn't alert her captors that she was escaping.

Lana forced her eyes open just as he carried her out of the cave. Light seared her retinas, but she welcomed it. Light meant freedom—something she thought she'd never again experience.

He laid her down and spoke in a quiet voice to someone nearby. "She's the only one alive."

"Not for long, she isn't," said a second man. "And not if they find out she made it out alive."

Lana's body throbbed in time with each beat of her heart. He was right. She wasn't going to last much longer. She could feel herself growing weaker by the second. Maybe she was bleeding somewhere.

At least she wasn't going to die in that cave.

"Our team took down three of them."

"How many were there?"

"I don't know. I only saw two, and not closely enough to ID them. I got orders from that skinny bastard, Boris. There could be another dozen for all I know."

"You took care of Boris?"

"Yes."

"Our men are in the hills. They'll find anyone who got away," said the second man.

"They'd better."

Lana wasn't sure what that meant, but she knew she should. What they were saying meant something to her, but her brain was too foggy to figure it out. She was using all her strength just to keep from screaming.

If she screamed, they could find her.

A shadow fell over her face, and Lana looked up into the face of Miles Gentry—the man her abductors had hired to bomb a U.S. elementary school.

Lana couldn't breathe. She wasn't safe. Not with him. He was a monster—a man willing to kill children for money.

He must have seen her fear, because he smoothed her matted hair back from her face and said, "Shh. It's okay. I'm a U.S. soldier. I'm not going to hurt you."

Liar! Lana tried to pull away from his touch, but her body wouldn't move, wouldn't cooperate.

"Back off, Caleb. You're scaring her," said the second man.

Caleb, or Miles, or whoever he was moved away. Behind him, from high in the rocky hillside, she could see twin flashes of sunlight reflecting off glass. Binoculars.

With a painful stab of clarity, she realized she was being watched.

She tried to tell the men, but her lips were swollen and stuck together with dried blood and she couldn't seem to form a coherent word.

The wind kicked up and dust choked her lungs. She tried not to cough. Someone pulled a sheet over her head to keep the dust out. It didn't help. She couldn't keep from coughing, and as soon as she did—as soon as her broken ribs shifted—the pain ricocheted inside her until all she could do was gasp for air.

All the pain and going without food or water for days

was too much. She had to give up and let go. She couldn't take any more.

Lana's mind shut down, and she welcomed the oblivion as it came to claim her.

CHAPTER ONE

———— ❦ ————

Columbia, Missouri, eighteen months later

Caleb Stone had no business being this close to the woman he'd nearly killed eighteen months ago. Just the thought of having to face Lana Hancock again made him break out in a cold sweat. This assignment was going to be as much fun as taking a bullet in the gut.

Lana's office at the First Light Foundation was nestled in the middle of a run-down line of small one-story leased office spaces, between a walk-in clinic and a print shop. The long prefab building was cheaply constructed and badly in need of a fresh coat of paint. Early morning sun filtered through the line of trees adorning the front of the parking lot. It was late July in central Missouri, and even with the shade the decorative trees offered, Caleb's car was already beginning to grow uncomfortably warm.

He didn't shift to crack a window or turn on the air. With all the mistakes he'd made, he figured he was headed for hell, anyway. Might as well get used to the climate.

Another car pulled into the lot and parked. It was Lana Hancock's white Saturn.

Caleb's body tensed and his stomach flooded with acid. This was not going to be fun.

She got out of her Saturn, putting Caleb no more than fifty feet away from her. It was too damn close, and every corner of his soul screamed for him to back away slowly before she got hurt again. But backing away wasn't an option. Colonel Monroe had ordered him to come here. The bastard.

If Caleb had thought for one second that Lana was in danger, he would have been the first one in line to play human shield, but that wasn't the case. Monroe was just being paranoid over a bit of random chatter the CIA had intercepted. Monroe was worried that the Swarm was back, but that couldn't be true. That particular terrorist group was gone. Caleb had been on the team that took them out six months ago. They'd made sure no one survived.

Monroe was convinced something was going on, so here Caleb was, up close and personal with the only living reminder of the worst three days of his life. Lana Hancock.

She looked a lot different now than she had the last time Caleb had seen her. She still had the same rich brown hair, but it no longer fell down her back, tangled and matted with blood. She'd cropped it shorter so that it swung in a shiny wave that ended just above her shoulders. Her face was no longer swollen or bruised from repeated beatings, and he found himself staring at her, drinking her in, trying to replace this new, healthy image of her with the horrible one he'd held in his head for too many months. He hadn't been able to tell when she'd been lying unconscious in that army hospital bed, but now he could see how pretty she was, and that the fullness of her mouth hadn't been totally due to swelling.

A man pulled his Honda into the lot and waved at Lana. She smiled and waved back, and Caleb caught a glimpse of deep twin dimples in her cheeks. He'd never seen her smile before, and until now he hadn't realized what he'd been missing. The only expressions he'd seen on her face were ones of terror and pain. He'd stayed by her bedside for three long days and even longer nights, and neither the terror nor the pain had lessened. When he'd been forced back to work, every day he'd expected to hear that she had died, but that word never came.

Even though he'd kept tabs on her recovery, this was the first time he'd seen her since, and watching her walk around was like witnessing a miracle. It soothed him and eased some of the tension that had been growing in him ever since he'd been ordered to come here.

Caleb watched with a mixture of respect and awe as she crossed the hot asphalt to her office. Her walk was smooth and steady, her hips swaying slightly beneath her faded jeans. If he hadn't known for a fact that it had taken her months to learn how to walk again, he'd never have believed it by watching her move. There was nothing hesitant in her stride, no hitch of pain or jarring movement. She was all rolling grace and swaying strength.

Her functional white T-shirt and matching tennis shoes were completely without frills, and there wasn't a single glitter of jewelry on her body or a speck of makeup on her face. She used a green canvas backpack instead of a purse, and that looked like it had seen better days. But even without the bells and whistles, even though she was nothing like the glamorous women he usually dated, she still had more pull on him than all the women he'd known combined.

And if that wasn't fate's way of slugging him in the gut for fucking up, he didn't know what was. No matter how much she appealed to him, she'd probably rather spit on him than look at him. Which was probably safest for both of them.

Caleb forced his breathing to even out into a steady rhythm while he willed his heart to slow its pounding pace. He'd known that seeing her again would affect him, but until now, he hadn't realized just how strongly. He'd never known anyone who'd come back after being that close to dying, and he'd known a lot of strong, highly motivated men.

Lana was one hell of a woman. If only he'd met her under other circumstances, things might have been a lot different between them.

If only. Caleb squashed that line of thinking before it could gain a foothold. If onlys could get a man killed.

⚜

Lana hadn't even had time to pour a cup of coffee before the first crisis of the day hit. She rubbed her temples in an effort to stave off the tension headache that was growing by leaps and bounds with every passing hour. But headache or not, she had a fundraiser coming up in two weeks and it wasn't going to plan itself. "Are you sure he said *canceled*?" she asked Stacie Cramer, her assistant and friend.

Stacie was a petite, consistently well-dressed woman who was quick to smile even though life's tragedies had tried to strip away her sense of humor. She was old enough to need reading glasses but young enough to resent them, so more often than not, they hung on a beaded chain around her neck, ignored.

She squinted at the message pad, holding it out at arm's length. "His exact words were, 'Tell Lana-darling that I simply must go to Milan. My muse has left me, the bitch, and I will surely find her there, whoring herself out to other men.'"

"Great," said Lana. "So now that His Artistic Majesty, Armand, has abandoned us, the rest of the artists are going to see our fundraiser as more of an obligation than an honor."

"That's what I was worried about," said Stacie.

"I should have forced him to sign a contract like the rest of the artists."

"You tried and he refused, remember?"

Lana sighed, trying to release some of her frustration. She was putting on this fundraiser for a good cause, so couldn't fate just cut her a freaking break for once? "How many artists have committed to donating their work so far?"

"Twelve. Sutter canceled this morning before signing his contract."

"So, the word that Armand has canceled is already out." Lana stifled a curse before it spilled from her lips. If she let it out, Stacie would give her one of those motherly frowns of disappointment, and Lana didn't need any more of those in her life than she already had.

Getting her foundation, First Light, off the ground had been both more difficult and more rewarding than she'd ever imagined. Of course, it wasn't technically off the ground yet, but it was close—almost hovering. The art auction would breathe enough monetary life into the foundation to help her hire another permanent staff member, which would free up Lana's time to work on expanding First Light's reach.

The focus of First Light was simple: to give kids a safe place to go after school and during the summer months so they wouldn't be as tempted to occupy themselves with drugs and violence. She gave them art and music and games to keep them busy in the hopes that there would be no time for the other stuff. They also offered help with homework, organized sports, and worked one-on-one with some of the more troubled or at-risk kids. Dozens of local volunteers gave their time and talents to help her make this happen, and she was proud of the work she'd done, even though it wasn't nearly enough.

Her family thought she was wasting her life on a lost cause. She had no business doing something so stressful and financially risky in her "fragile" state—as if she hadn't been strong and healthy for months now. Her mother didn't understand why Lana felt the need to get involved when it would only put her in contact with troubled kids. Why did she want that burden?

Then again, Madeline Hancock had never met Eddie—one of the men who was on a similar physical therapy schedule with Lana. He'd been a narcotics officer before a ten-year-old boy's bullet had shattered his femur, basically ending his career. Not only had Eddie forgiven the boy, he'd adopted the orphan, and now Eddie spent his time going from school to school talking to kids about everything from drugs to sex to gangs.

Lana had been so inspired by Eddie's passion for helping kids, and so desperate for a reason to get up in the morning, that she decided to join the cause. She didn't care if her parents approved. She was doing what she thought was right, and even if she helped only a handful of kids, it was enough for her.

She'd done good. Maybe not much, but some. If this art auction went well, she'd be able to do even more. Maybe she'd be able to move her work into St. Louis or other, smaller cities. Maybe she'd even get to travel enough that no one could be able to predict her movements. She'd be free from always looking over her shoulder, wondering if whoever she'd seen on that hillside in Armenia was still watching her.

She would give almost anything for that kind of freedom.

Certainly, if that person wanted her dead, she'd already be six feet under. She was silly to keep worrying about nothing. Life was finally getting better. Why couldn't she just accept that gift and move on?

An almost paranoid sort of anxiety pulled at her, but she forced it away with a cheerful smile that probably looked as fake as it felt. "What's the status with finding an auctioneer?"

Stacie's shoulders slumped, wrinkling her perfectly pressed blouse. "I've called six, and none of them are willing to donate their time."

That tension headache grew a little tenser and achier. She hadn't been sleeping well, not that it was anything new.

"I'll see what I can do with the rest of the auctioneers on our list," Lana said. "I can make some money available if I put off the electric bill a few days. That might be enough to tempt someone, especially if I give them a prime advertising spot in the auction book."

Stacie nodded and peered down at her paper again, squinting. "I'll make the adjustments to the auction listings courtesy of Armand. The layout for the auction book is nearly done. We should be able to send it to the printers as soon as we hire an auctioneer. They said it would take three days to print, so there's still time."

"That's something, at least," said Lana, pushing her slippery hair behind her ears so she could rub her temples to ease the throbbing. Two more weeks until the auction and then she could relax. "I'll get onto our website tonight and post the updated artist list. I'll deal with finding an auctioneer today, or I'll sign myself up for a class and do the damn thing myself."

"And when will you find time to take a class—even a one-day class? You're already working seventy-hour weeks. Maybe more. What about going to the youth center? The whole reason you started this foundation was to help the kids, and you haven't seen them in days. They miss you."

"I'll find a way to fit that in, too."

"You can't do it all." Stacie gave Lana her best maternal frown.

"I'm not trying to do it all. I just want to get through this auction without emptying out the foundation's bank account. Every hour I put in is one I don't have to pay someone else to do."

"If it helps, you don't need to pay me this month."

Lana snorted. "You work for next to nothing. If I can't afford to pay you, then we're in big trouble."

"I checked the books. You've been without a paycheck for three months."

Lana winced. She didn't hide the financial records from Stacie, but there wasn't usually a need. Stacie hated anything to do with numbers. She'd been a pampered executive's wife most of her adult life and had never had to so much as lift a calculator. Until her husband and son were killed in a car accident. That had ended Stacie's days of pampering.

"I won't take another paycheck until you do," insisted Stacie.

"I'm fine."

Stacie arched a brow. "Liar."

Lana felt a smile play at her lips, and she gave in to it. "You're not supposed to call your boss a liar."

"For what I make, I've got to find my fringe benefits where I can," teased Stacie. "I mean it, Lana. You can't run yourself into debt to keep this place going."

"I'm not in debt." Yet. But man, was it close. She had enough to pay her bills this month and buy some groceries, but that was it. After that, she had no idea what she would do.

"Uh-huh. When's the last time you bought yourself a new pair of shoes, or even a new shirt? I swear I see you in the same clothes every week. And that backpack you use as a purse is ghastly."

"I'm clean. I'm decent. That's enough. Besides, I set the dress code around here, so lay off."

Stacie shook her head, making her bun slide around on the back of her head. Lana had no idea how she kept the thing in place, but it had never fallen. "Just don't stretch yourself too thin. I know you want to make this work, but without you, it won't. If you go pushing yourself too hard, you'll end up broke and sick, and our health insurance plan sucks."

"What health insurance plan?"

"Exactly my point."

Lana held up her hands in an effort to ward off any more mothering. She got enough of that on the weekends as it was. "Okay. I'll be good."

"Good," said Stacie as she rose to her feet and straightened a stack of papers into a file folder. "Then you'll be leaving with me tonight. No more staying late."

Lana was saved from having to lie to Stacie by the jingling of the bell on the office door.

She squinted against the sun as the tinted-glass door swung open. The transition from dim to bright light still brought back a rioting swirl of emotions, the same way that some scents brought back vivid memories. It had been a long time since she'd been carried out of that cave into the sunlight, but she had never forgotten the way it felt to know she'd been rescued from her nightmare. Even though her body had been bleeding, broken, and knotted with pain, her heart had soared with the knowledge of her freedom. Every time she saw the sun, she was reminded of that joy all over again. She welcomed the light, reveled in the fact that she was alive and free enough to enjoy it.

That brief feeling of freedom was short-lived, however, because as soon as she saw who'd walked in, she knew she was in trouble.

Caleb Stone.

Lana would have known him anywhere, whether he went by Caleb or, as she'd first come to know him, as

Miles Gentry, amoral mercenary and demolitions expert for hire.

He was a huge man—not just tall, but big everywhere—and nearly overpowering just standing there a few feet away. He was well over six feet and a whole heaping pile of muscles over two hundred pounds. His thick legs were braced apart, and his hands were fisted at his sides as if he were expecting a physical blow.

Shock stilled her mouth, and her pen fell from her hand onto the floor. Her heart squeezed hard, and dread flooded her system. He couldn't be here. This had to be some kind of sick joke—a trick of her mind. Another nightmare.

"Ma'am," he greeted her in that deep, soothing voice of his.

This was no nightmare, or rather it was, but she wasn't asleep. This was real. He was here, torturing her all over again, bringing back those first few days when her world had been only pain and the sound of his voice. He'd been beside her, demanding that she live, compelling her not to give up. She was too weak to do anything but listen, too confused to do anything but obey his commands, and because of that—because of him—she'd lived.

Sometimes she still hated him for that.

Lana struggled to remain calm. He was watching her expectantly, waiting for a response to his greeting. What could she say? She wanted to scream at him to leave, to drive her fists into that solid body of his until he'd never dare show his face again.

She swallowed hard to ease her constricted vocal cords. "What the hell do you want?" she asked him in a biting tone that had Stacie's thin eyebrows lifting.

Caleb's mouth tightened, and he flicked a glance toward Stacie. "Is there someplace private we can talk?"

"No," she said, not sure if she could keep her cool without Stacie there to back her up, and she did not want this man to see her lose that frail composure. She detested the fact that he already knew just how weak she could be.

She could see something close to pity in his dark eyes, and she had to look away. She didn't want his pity. She wanted nothing from him but his absence.

"It's important," he told her. "I'm under orders to speak with you."

If listening was the quickest way to get him to leave, then that's what she'd do. "Start talking. I'm a busy woman."

"Privately," he added.

"Lana? Do you know this man?" asked Stacie in an uneasy tone.

Stacie's hand was on the phone, and Lana didn't need two guesses to figure out she was ready to call for help. The last thing she needed was to have Stacie panic and call the police. It was best—fastest—if Lana sucked it up and got rid of Caleb quietly without any interference.

Lana gave Caleb a hard stare. "Stay right there," she ordered as she took Stacie by the arm and led her back to the storeroom at the back of the office.

The small room contained several shelves of office supplies and their photocopier. It was stuffy and cramped, but Lana shut the door anyway.

"Who is he?" asked Stacie.

"He's the soldier who pulled me out of that cave in Armenia."

Stacie's eyes lit with a bad case of hero worship. "You didn't tell me he was so handsome."

"I wasn't exactly thinking about that at the time." She'd been too busy writhing in pain.

Stacie's mouth turned down in a pained frown. "Sorry. That was insensitive of me."

Lana waved the remark away. "Don't worry about it. Handsome or not, I'll get rid of him soon enough."

"He saved your life and you act like you don't want to see him? I don't get it."

Lana hadn't told anyone that he was also the man who had witnessed her torture and done little to stop it. He'd been undercover, trying to figure out which elementary school the terrorist group was planning to attack. He couldn't break cover to save her or any of the other Americans with her. If he'd done that, hundreds of children could have died.

She understood that his hands were tied, and if he'd been able to ask her if she was willing to suffer to save those kids, she would have agreed without hesitation. But that didn't mean she wanted to see him again and relive that horror and pain.

Her life was finally getting better. Not good, but tolerable. She couldn't handle any setbacks right now—couldn't stand to be reminded of everything those three days had cost her.

"It's complicated," said Lana, nearly choking on the understatement.

"Why is he here?"

"I have no idea, but I'm sure he'll tell me as soon as we're alone." That thought was enough to make her skin grow cold with apprehension. She did not want to be alone with him. That would have been too much like being back in that hospital bed, drowning in pain and fear with him at her side as her only lifeline. She couldn't go back to that dark place. Not ever.

"He doesn't look like he wants to be here," said Stacie.

"That's because he's not an idiot."

"Do you want me to get rid of him for you?"

"If I thought you could, I would let you, but I don't think that's going to work. I'll let him have his say and then he'll leave."

"I have a couple of errands to run," offered Stacie. "If you're sure you want to be alone with him."

Lana didn't want to, but she guessed from the stubborn set of Caleb's jaw that he wasn't going to go away until he'd had his say. The sooner she got rid of him, the better. "You go ahead," she told Stacie. "I'll be fine."

Lana led Stacie out of the storage room. Caleb was still there, right where she'd left him. He looked at her with a solemn expression, and Lana had to turn away. She didn't know how she was going to get through the next five minutes, but she knew she would. Her recovery had taught her that lesson over and over again.

Stacie made a hasty exit out the front door, and Lana went straight for some coffee. There was no way she was going to be able to face this man without the support of caffeine. She poured a cup and turned to go back to her desk, nearly running right into the wall of his chest. "Damn it! Don't go sneaking up on me like that."

"Sorry, ma'am." He backed away a step, but she still felt overwhelmed. The man knew how to take up space in a room.

Lana cringed at being called *ma'am* again. That was what people called her mother, and she didn't want anyone treating her like her mother. "It's Lana."

"Lana," he repeated, and to her amazement, that was much worse. Hearing that deep voice saying her name flooded her with bleak memories of torment and terror. She was thrown back to those horrible days in the hospital where there was only pain and the sound of his voice speaking her name. She could feel the tearing agony of her body trying to rip away her sanity. She could smell the hospital stink, her own blood, and the warmth of his skin. She could see only blackness—a hungry mouth waiting to swallow her whole.

Lana felt a familiar wave of panic head toward her. She couldn't do this. She couldn't go back there and live in that nightmare for even one more second. She was forced to relive it every night, but it was broad daylight, and she was supposed to be safe in the light. She couldn't let the fear invade her days, too. She wouldn't have anything left if that happened.

Her coffee was stripped from her hands before she could spill it on herself. A warm hand grasped her elbow, steadying her. "Sit down," he said, easing her into a chair.

Lana sat, unable to do anything else. She clawed at the memories, fighting them back, trying desperately to force her body to remember she was safe. In her office. With plenty of light. Nothing could hurt her here.

"Please . . . please leave." She was begging him. There was no pride in her words, no dignity, but she didn't care. She *needed* him to leave and take all those memories with him.

"I can't." His voice sounded strained, thick. "I swear to you that if I wasn't under orders to be here, I'd turn around and never bother you again. But I can't do that."

Lana found the strength to pull herself out of that spiraling void of the past. She opened her eyes, realizing that she'd started crying and her face was wet with tears. Those tears were just one more reason to hate Caleb Stone.

Lana wished she had the energy to hate him, because hating him would have made things a whole lot easier. She liked to think that if he hadn't been such a noble freaking hero, she would have hated him for what he'd done.

"Just say what you want and get out," she told him, angrily swiping the wetness from her cheeks.

Caleb's mouth hardened into a grim line. "I'm afraid it's not going to be that simple."

"You've got three minutes to simplify it, and then I'm calling the police."

His voice was gentle, almost apologetic. "My boss thinks you might be in danger."

Panic tightened her insides until she could barely breathe. This was all supposed to be over. "Why?"

"There's been some chatter, conversations we've intercepted that have happened between some very bad people. Your name was mentioned. More than once."

Had someone figured out what she'd seen in Armenia? Had they found the slit in her hood and realized what it meant? "What did they say?"

"Nothing incriminating, or we'd have already taken action. My boss was still concerned. He sent me here to see if you'd remembered anything new or could think of a reason why someone would want to hurt you."

"There never was a reason for them to hurt me. People like them don't need one. Do they?"

Caleb's jaw tightened, and a violent light glinted in his dark eyes. "You're right. They don't."

She hated asking, but she had to know. "Do you think I'm in danger?"

He stared right into her eyes. "If I did, no one would have had to force me to come here. They wouldn't have been able to stop me."

"So I am safe." *Please, God, let him say yes.*

"Until I am sure, I'm sticking close enough to protect you, just in case."

Her knees went a little weak, and she was glad she was already sitting. She gathered her anger, because it was so much more comfortable than the fear that was crawling around in her gut. "I don't want you here, and I'm not interested in your protection. Besides, since when do average civilians get personal military bodyguards?"

"You're special."

"Why?"

"My boss thinks you're hiding something."

They didn't know. She was still safe. Her family was safe. "He and his men interrogated me for five days after I woke up. I'll tell you what I told them. I didn't hear anything of military value in Armenia, because I don't speak the language. I couldn't have seen anything, because there was a hood over my head." She uttered the lie like a politician, smoothly and without a blink. "I can't help you, so please. Get. The. Fuck. Out."

He was leaning his big body over her, hovering in a way that made her feel crowded and shielded all at once. "You're not going to make this easy on me, are you?"

She looked up at him, unable to see his expression with the bright fluorescent lights shining behind his head. "Can you think of a single reason why I should?"

"No, ma'am. Not one. But that doesn't change the fact that I was ordered to come here, protect you, and convince you to cooperate or stay here until you do."

"You're going to have a long, boring road to retirement, then. I don't have anything to say to you, and I never will."

CHAPTER TWO

Forget the bullet in the gut. Caleb was willing to take a bullet in the balls if it meant he never had to see Lana cry again. Those tears had torn at his heart like rusted razor wire. It was the kind of torture military training couldn't teach a man to resist. It had taken every last scrap of willpower he had to keep from pulling her into his arms. And wouldn't *that* have been a fun time for her? Who was he to think he could comfort a woman, when most of her problems could rightfully be placed squarely on his shoulders?

Damn Monroe for his hand in this. He had to have known what it would do to Lana to be forced to face Caleb again. He had to have known what it would do to Caleb, too. The bastard.

Caleb pulled a chair into the farthest corner of the office and tried to disappear—no small feat for a man his size. He'd refused to leave, and she refused to acknowledge he was there. For now, the stalemate was the best he could hope for. Maybe once she got over the shock of seeing him, she'd be willing to listen. Until then, Caleb would just have to be patient and keep his eyes open.

❦

Not ten minutes after Lana had finally managed to push Caleb's silent presence out of her mind, her ex-fiancé, Oran Sinclair, came striding into her office. He moved with the arrogant confidence of a man who was sure that everyone around him was watching and enjoying the view. Lana's stomach twisted at the sight of him, sending up a flare of anger and disgust—anger that he'd come waltzing in here like he owned the place, and disgust that she hadn't come to know him for the selfish man he was before he broke her heart.

He was just as handsome now as he had been when she'd fallen in love with him during her sophomore year at MU. With his perfectly trimmed blond hair and those all-American, camera-friendly good looks, he'd swept her off her feet. She'd been too young then to realize that she'd only land on her ass a few years later.

So much for true love.

Oran straightened his power tie and gave her a disarming smile—the one he used when posing for the press after a successful trial.

He gave Caleb a speculative glance as he strode over to her desk. "Lana," he greeted, taking her hand from her side when she didn't offer it.

His fingers were cold and a little clammy, as if he was nervous, which was ridiculous, because Oran hadn't been nervous a day in his life. He fed on pressure, bloomed under stress—like some sort of exotic fungus.

Lana pulled away from Oran's grip a little too fast, giving away her dislike for the man. Caleb saw it and stood

from his seat, taking a warning step forward. She gave
Caleb a small shake of her head, and although his frown
was grim, he stayed on his side of the room.

"Who's your friend?" asked Oran with a nod toward
Caleb.

"He's not my friend. Just ignore him. That's what I'm
trying to do."

Oran's smile widened, and a touch of victory lit his
eyes.

"What do you want, Oran?" she demanded. "Trolling
for campaign contributions for that lofty political career
you've had your eye on?"

He gave her a handsome smile that crinkled the corners
of his flashing blue eyes. "Nothing like that, darling. I
haven't heard from you since Easter. Why haven't you
returned my calls?"

"Because I have nothing to say to you. Mom never
should have invited you to dinner."

"She's worried about you."

Nothing new there.

He continued, "She told me how strapped you are for
cash these days. I wanted to discuss what I could do for
you."

Warning bells gonged in Lana's head. Oran never did
anything outside of his own self-interest. "No, thanks," she
said and sat down, dismissing him without explanation.

"You didn't even hear me out," he said, pulling up a
chair too near her own.

"Don't need to. Whatever it is, I'm not interested."

"Not even if I told you that I'm willing to fund your
foundation for the next five years?"

Lana's hand stilled its scribbling and she looked up. He

wore that same disarming smile that had made her give her heart away to him so easily six years ago. The same one that would win votes.

His offer of funding sounded too good to be true. Oran was not a generous man. "You only give to charity when the press is watching. If I actually believed you, I might listen, but I know better."

He reached out toward her, and it was all she could do not to flinch away and draw Caleb's attention. She hated having an audience for this. It was hard enough without one.

His fingers settled against her cheek in a mockery of a caring touch. "You look tired. You're working too hard, Lana. I know how much this place means to you, and I want to help."

"Why?" she asked, knowing she'd regret being pulled into his world—a world where nothing else mattered beyond his political aspirations. She had to remember that.

"Would you believe I want to help because I care about you?" he asked, sounding sincere.

"No."

He gave a self-deprecating smile that reeked of long hours of practice in front of a mirror. "I didn't think so. I know things didn't end well between us, and I just wanted you to know how badly I feel about that. I should have been more understanding."

Out of the corner of her eye, she could see Caleb watching them without even the pretense of trying to give them privacy.

Lovely. As if she hadn't had enough awkwardness today.

"You told me that I was no good to you in a wheelchair,

Oran. You told me that a woman who might not be able to give you children just wasn't an option for you. Tell me how you could have been any *less* understanding."

Oran threw a quick, questioning glance at Caleb, then lowered his voice. "I was an ass. I'm sorry, Lana. I want a chance to make it up to you."

"By helping fund my foundation?" she asked in disbelief.

"By giving us another shot. You and I were good together."

"Apparently not good enough for you to stick around. You dumped me before I was even out of the hospital!"

Caleb surged to his feet, and from over Oran's shoulder, she pinned Caleb with a hard glare. "You stay out of this. It's none of your business."

"Who is he?" asked Oran. "Can you send him away so we can talk in private?"

"Send him away?" she nearly screeched. "That is so like you, Oran. Everyone is your servant to be ordered around as you please."

"I'm not going anywhere," said Caleb in a warning growl. His dark eyes were fixed on Lana, daring her to try to get him to leave. As if she needed to cause any more of a scene than she already was with Oran.

"Just ignore him," Lana told Oran. "He doesn't live here, so he can't vote against you."

"I'm hurt that you think that's all I care about," said Oran.

"I *know* that's all you care about." She jabbed a finger hard into Oran's chest. "You couldn't wait to unload the burden of having a handicapped woman hanging around your neck. I've told you over and over that it's over between us. Period. What makes you think I'd give you another chance?"

"Because if you do, I'll make sure the First Light Foundation doesn't fold. I know how important it is to you."

He knew it and was using it to shameless advantage. If she had even the slightest reason to believe him, she might be tempted to play along, but she knew better. "Are you saying you want to buy my forgiveness?"

"I know better than to try to do that. All I want is for you to see how sorry I am for the way I treated you."

"Why now? Why not six months ago, when I was struggling to get the foundation started? Did you just now realize what a complete asshole you were? Or did one of your campaign managers run the numbers and find out that I'm a better attachment than Brittney?"

A guilty flush rose up from under his collar.

"You do remember her, right?" asked Lana. "Brittney? The woman you're supposed to marry?"

"She can never be to me what you were. My first love." His fingers stroked along her jaw, and Lana pushed his hand away with a hard shove.

From the corner of her eye, she saw Caleb's big hands tighten into fists, but he stayed put.

Lana wanted to snort at Oran's ludicrous statement. Once upon a time, his comment would have made her go sappy, but that was a lifetime ago. "Then perhaps you shouldn't marry her."

"That's what I was hoping you'd say. Somewhere deep down, you know we belong together." He reached for her again, but Lana leaned away and he took the hint, letting his hand drop.

"What I know is that the only person you've ever

truly loved is yourself. I don't care how much money you're offering the foundation, it's not enough to buy my forgiveness."

"Then what about your time? All I want is another chance. Come have dinner with me. Just dinner." His voice was coaxing.

"Why do you keep asking me out? Didn't you just get engaged?"

"It's not working out," he said.

"What happened? Did Brittney use the wrong fork while dining with the governor?"

"Don't be ridiculous. I've just been doing a lot of soul-searching and realized that you're the woman I want. If that means supporting your chosen career, then that's what I'll do." He made it sound like he would be making a sacrifice to let her do her job.

Lana had a flash of insight and decided to test her theory. "What if I want to quit my job?"

"You love it too much. I wouldn't want you to do that, darling."

"Why not?" she asked sweetly.

"You're doing good work. The press loves you. Why on earth would you want to quit?"

The press. That was it. Lana had been the focus of several major news articles lately, and Oran wanted a piece of the coverage. "We're done here, Oran. See yourself out."

Lana went back to her work, trying to focus on the page in front of her. The words made no sense, but she stared at them as if they held the meaning of life.

How could she have ever believed he loved her? It was so clear to her now that that emotion was beyond him. He was just one more foolish mistake she'd made.

"Don't do this, Lana." That gentle, caring tone he used nearly killed her. He was offering her everything she wanted, but she knew it was an illusion. No matter how much she loved him, he'd never be able to love her back the way she wanted. Needed.

"I'm not doing anything," said Lana. "I didn't ask you to come here. I didn't ask anything of you at all. But now I am asking you to leave."

Caleb took a step forward, scowling, looking hugely intimidating. Oran didn't seem to notice the threat, but then, he didn't know what Caleb was capable of the way she did. She'd seen him kill the man who'd beaten and tortured her. In fact, he made killing look frighteningly easy.

"I don't want to leave things like this. You and I can have a future together. Come back to me and let me prove it."

"There is no future for us. You ruined any chance of that when you abandoned me when I needed you most."

"I told you I'm sorry. Can't we move past it?"

"It's too late for that," said Lana.

"The lady asked you to leave," said Caleb, his voice low and steady. He was still several feet away, but no less threatening because of it. "You should do so."

"Who the hell are you, anyway?" asked Oran, his nose twitching as if he smelled something bad.

Lana wasn't quick enough to think of a reason for Caleb to be here.

"I'm the man who's going to help you find the door if you can't do it on your own," said Caleb. His voice was even, calm.

Oran looked up and down Caleb's big body. "Do you work with Lana?"

"Yes," said Caleb at the same time Lana said, "No."

Oran looked between them, his photogenic smile nowhere to be found. "Think about what I said, Lana. I'll give you some time to think things over, and then I'll be back for your answer."

"It will be the same as it is has been for months. The same as it is now. You might as well not waste your time," she told him.

Oran just shrugged and pasted on his look-at-me smile as he headed for the door, just in case someone outside was watching. "We'll see. One of these days you may decide you need me again."

"When I did need you, you walked away. I'll never make that mistake again."

❧

Caleb had learned at a young age that he had to control his temper, because he'd always been bigger and stronger than the other kids. Without that patience and self-control, he would have hurt people, and those traits had always served him well until today.

As he watched Oran walk away, he wished that he'd slammed his fist right into Oran's handsome nose. Blacking both of that asshole's eyes would have been fun. Therapeutic.

He couldn't believe that Oran had been stupid enough to dump Lana. And the thought of him doing it while she was still weak and vulnerable made Caleb clench his fists against the urge to hit something.

"Does he always come around here like that?" asked Caleb.

Lana's face was still tight with anger, which was now aimed directly at him. Caleb had kept quiet, trying to stay out of her personal business, but he just couldn't keep quiet any longer. Not after that.

"Eventually, he'll get the point."

Caleb didn't like the idea of her hanging around with scum like Oran. Not that it was any of his concern. She was a grown woman and could make as many bad choices as she wanted. Heaven knew he'd made plenty of his own.

"He's an ass," said Caleb. "If it's any consolation, you were lucky not to have been stuck with him."

Lana let out a deep breath and looked back down at her work. "I know that now."

But she hadn't known it when he dumped her, was the obvious subtext.

Caleb clenched his fists again and tried to remind himself that he wasn't here to inflict violence on Lana's ex-fiancé, no matter how appealing the idea was.

❧

It was time for Lana to go home, and Caleb was still sitting there. Stacie had left a couple of hours ago, giving Lana that maternal frown that could make her feel like she was nine years old. She'd scolded Lana for working too hard and then left, saying she'd be in early in the morning.

Lana glanced over at Caleb. He'd hardly moved all day. He intervened when Oran wouldn't leave. He ate the burgers Stacie had brought him, thanking her politely for thinking of him. He used the bathroom at the back of the office a couple times, but other than that, he hadn't moved.

Lana felt him watching her, but every time she looked up, he was never looking her way. She wished he had been, because then she could have scolded him for that and maybe even worked up the nerve to call the police and have him hauled off for stalking or something.

Like that would work. They'd get one glimpse of his military record and likely take him out for drinks or invite him to date their sisters. That was just the kind of thing Lana had come to expect from fate where her life was concerned.

Caleb was watching the street outside. Sometimes he'd scribble something on a little notebook he carried. She had no idea what he was doing, but it was clear that it was taking up all his concentration. She used the opportunity to just look at him.

His black hair had been a little longer in Armenia. It was still long enough to defy military regulations, but then again, he was special. He did things like pretend to be a criminal in order to infiltrate a terrorist group. He couldn't go around looking like GI Joe and expect to be accepted as scum by scum.

His skin was deeply tanned, with a few paler lines of scar tissue on both his hands and face that showed where his dangerous career had damaged his body.

His face wasn't as handsome as it was simply . . . powerful. Intense. His jaw was wide and bold, covered in five-o'clock shadow that accentuated the sharp, masculine angles. His eyes were a deep, rich black. Only the faintest slivers of golden brown gave away where his pupils started and his irises ended. She remembered them in vivid detail. They were the first thing she'd seen when she'd opened her eyes in the hospital and knew she was going to live.

Lana didn't want to like him, and she sure as hell didn't want him sticking around, but she couldn't keep herself from respecting him. He'd done something she wasn't sure she could ever do. He'd held the fate of innocents in his hands and chosen who would live and who would die.

She didn't envy him that responsibility.

"Are you sleeping here tonight?" he asked her without turning around. Night had fallen outside, and he was looking at her in the mirrorlike reflection of the tinted windows.

Lana felt her face heat as she realized that he'd been watching her watch him. "No. I'm just about done. Feel free to tell your boss you tortured me, or whatever, to get me to talk, but I just didn't have anything to say. I wouldn't want him to think any less of you for failing."

"Who says I've failed? I'm a patient man, Lana."

Lana swallowed a vile curse by force of habit, even though Stacie wasn't here to hear her. "I'm not letting you in tomorrow. That's final. You want to sit outside in the parking lot and bake, that's fine, but you're not coming in here where it's all cool and comfy."

He gave her a shrug of indifference. "I've been hotter places than here."

He probably had, too. He'd probably climbed frozen mountains and swum crocodile-infested rivers, and crossed scorching deserts with no water, and jumped over tall buildings in a single leap. He was a freaking hero.

He'd saved hundreds of lives. He could probably walk on water if he tried.

Why couldn't he just go away and leave her in peace? Her life was bad enough without the constant reminder of what she'd suffered.

And if any of the terrorists who had escaped justice found out he was here, they might figure out she'd seen them. Having Caleb here was like putting a giant neon sign over her head, reading, "Witness here. Come get her."

She needed him to go. Now. Before any more attention was drawn her way.

"I'm going home. Don't try to follow me, or I'll call the police."

"I have my orders," was all he said.

"Screw your orders. Stalking is a crime, buddy."

He looked completely unconcerned by her threat, and that's when Lana knew the ugly truth. No matter where she went or what she did, he was going to be there. He wasn't going away until she told him what he wanted to hear, and there was no way she was going to do that. Not if she wanted to live.

❦

Caleb sat in his car outside Lana's nearly deserted apartment building. He hadn't even bothered to ask her to let him in so he could check the place out. He knew what the answer would be, and he really didn't want to give her the chance to scream at him.

From what he could tell from the outside, the place was run-down and badly in need of repair. Closer to the highway, several similar buildings had been polished up and remodeled, but not this one. It looked like it had been built in the seventies and not much had been done since then. There weren't even many cars in the lot, just her Saturn, his car, and an ancient Taurus that looked like its tires had rotted into the concrete.

Trees grew up all around the apartment building, shielding it from the noise and stink of the highway. As beautiful as they were, they were also an excellent source of concealment for anyone who might want to get into Lana's apartment. She had a ground-level unit with plenty of windows to climb through—windows that also happened to be on the side facing the thick growth of trees. It wouldn't have taken a genius to find a way in. Hell, a kid could have done it without putting down his Game Boy.

After he was sure she was asleep, he'd get out of his car and scout the place more closely to see if his first impressions of security here were accurate, but he didn't want to scare her by snooping around while she was still awake to watch.

Caleb's belly growled in hunger, but he ignored it. He had some MREs in his duffel and he'd break one out later, but not until the lights in Lana's apartment went out. It was nearly ten, and he hoped she'd get some rest soon. She looked like she could use it.

A few minutes later, Lana's face peeked out from between the slats of her cheap blinds. She was too far away for him to make out much more than the shape of her head, but somehow he got the feeling that she was scowling at him.

Caleb sighed. Not much he could do to change her opinion of him. As it was, she'd already shocked him by not calling the police. No matter how tough she wanted to sound, he could tell the idea of him sitting out in the heat bothered her. She didn't want him to suffer. How ironic.

Caleb's gut twisted in a slow roll of regret. Wishing things had been different never made them so, and even if he had to go back and live that nightmare all over again, he wouldn't have done anything differently.

Except maybe he wouldn't have gone to Lana's hospital room. Seeing her suffer like that had slain something inside him—some innocent little piece of his soul that believed in fairness, justice.

Of course, had he not gone there, he'd never have been able to live with himself. There were just some things a man didn't do, and walking away from a dying woman that he'd helped kill was one of them.

The blinds cracked open again, and a minute later, Lana came stomping out of her apartment. She carried a plate of food in one hand and a glass of water in the other. By the time she'd gotten to his car, he'd rolled down the window.

Lana shoved the food at him. "Here," was all she said.

Caleb took the food and thanked her, but she was already stomping off again. He thought he heard her mutter something about hoping he'd choke.

Caleb stared at the plate in amusement. She'd made spaghetti for him.

The door of her apartment slammed shut, and Caleb couldn't help but smile. She didn't like him, she had every reason to hate him, yet she couldn't stand to let him go hungry—couldn't stand the thought of him baking in the hot sun.

Maybe there was still hope for this mission yet.

Caleb wolfed down the meal, grateful for real food when faced with the option of a lukewarm MRE instead. He'd had enough of those to last him a lifetime.

When he'd cleaned the last noodle from the plate, he figured he had just been handed the best excuse he could think of to get a look inside her home. He had to return her dishes.

Caleb pocketed one of his wireless mini-cams and made his way up the concrete stairs that led to the sidewalk that ran along the apartment building. One of the security lights was out, casting the trees behind her unit into deep shadows. Decorative bushes sat in thick clumps beneath her windows, and they were in desperate need of a haircut. He was too big to make much use of a hiding place like that, but a lot of people wouldn't be. All they'd have to do was sit there and wait to break in after she'd left her apartment, then wait inside for her to return. She'd never even suspect she was walking into a trap.

But none of that bothered him nearly as much as her front door. It was a flimsy piece of construction with a lock that wouldn't have taken him twenty seconds to bypass. Even an amateur would have had no trouble getting through that door. A stiff wind could do the job.

Caleb didn't have time to knock before the door was opened. Lana stepped out onto her welcome mat, blocking his path, a clear sign he was not welcome inside.

"I brought you back your dishes. The food was great. Thanks."

Lana gave a grudging nod and took the dirty plate and glass. "Please tell me you're not going to stay out there all night."

"Sorry, but I'm under or—"

"Orders. Yes, I know. And I've got a lot of work to do. At least go where I can't see you watching me. You're making me nervous, and I can't get anything done." It was the weariness in her tone that nearly had him backing off. She looked exhausted, with dark smudges under her blue eyes and a tired droop to her shoulders.

"I can't leave you alone, but I'll try to keep out of your hair."

"Whatever," she said, but it sounded like she was admitting defeat, and he hated that he'd pushed a strong woman like Lana that far.

She turned to go back into her apartment, and Caleb knew he had one more job to do before he could let her go. "Would it be okay if I used your bathroom?"

He could tell she wanted to say no, but there was that look in her eyes again—the one that told him she didn't like the idea of him suffering. She let out a long, weary sigh. "Go ahead."

She held the door open for him, and he had to nearly touch her to squeeze past. He caught her scent as he passed, and something deep in his chest tightened. He remembered that scent; under the sterile, sickly stench of the hospital, she had smelled the same way. Like honeysuckle and miracles, like spring and second chances.

That scent had haunted him last spring when flowers had started to bloom and he'd caught a whiff of honeysuckle. He'd remember Lana lying in the hospital bed and wish that he could have saved her, too.

If only.

Caleb shoved the thought away and took in her small apartment with one sweeping glance. It was like countless other rental places, with white walls, matted gray-brown carpet, and cracked vinyl floors. There was an open living/kitchen area that took up most of the apartment and a single bedroom and bathroom off to one side. A sturdy plaid couch in front of a tiny TV filled most of the living area, with heavy wooden bookcases filling the rest. The shelves nearly bowed under the weight of dozens of travel books, as well as thick guides on fundraising and how to build your own business.

The walls were decorated with sketches where other people used photographs. The art was good—lifelike enough that it captured the emotion and personality of each subject. A much older version of Lana, which Caleb guessed was her mother, was holding a newborn who still wore the tiny hospital band on his chubby wrist. Pride filled the older woman's face, and Caleb swore he could almost see the tears of joy running down her cheeks. Another sketch showed a teenage girl in a soccer uniform holding a trophy while a crowd of other girls hoisted her high overhead. Cheers and praise were frozen on their lips, and it was easy to imagine the sound they had made. Another sketch was of a man in his sixties, pruning shears in hand, tending a rosebush. The look of contentment on his face was nearly palpable, and the roses were so intricately drawn that Caleb was sure he would feel the velvet texture of rose petals if he ran his finger over the paper. He had to force himself not to keep staring at the artwork and move on.

On the small dining table sat an outdated PC and piles of bills and paperwork. The kitchen counters were nearly bare, with the exception of a coffee pot and a toaster sitting out, ready to use.

Caleb made quick use of the bathroom and came back out. Lana was at the sink washing the dishes, and he took the opportunity to mount the minuscule wireless camera on the frame above her bathroom door. No one was getting in through her front windows or door without him seeing it. When no one came through, he could prove to Monroe that Lana wasn't in danger and get out of this blasted assignment. Anyone who wanted to do Lana harm could walk right in here and do it. Once Monroe saw how easy it would be to get to her, he'd be satisfied that she was safe. Anything that was going to happen would have already happened by now.

Or maybe that was just wishful thinking on Caleb's part. Maybe he wanted to believe she was safe too much.

"Thanks," he told her.

"You're welcome." Perfect politeness, but Lana didn't turn around. The line of her back was straight and stiff. He needed no further reminder that she didn't want him here. The least he could do was get out and leave her in peace.

"Don't forget to lock the door when I leave."

She turned then, and Caleb thought he saw fear flitter over her eyes for just a split second before it vanished. "I never forget to lock the door."

CHAPTER THREE

———⚜———

Denny Nelson jumped when his cell phone rang, causing beer bottles to topple over and crash onto his kitchen floor.

He'd been waiting for this call for so long he was beginning to think his new boss had forgotten him.

"Hello," Denny answered, hoping he didn't sound as drunk as he felt.

"I have a job for you," said the man on the other end of the phone. His voice was creepy—a metallic monotone that was artificial and emotionless. It sounded like a robot was talking, but Denny knew better. The man just didn't want Denny to recognize his voice, which was fine with him. The less contact he had with his boss, the better.

"I'm ready," Denny said, scrambling for a notebook and pen.

"Go to Meg's Diner. In the restroom, behind the prophylactic machine, you'll find instructions for the job I want you to do. When you're finished, go home, turn on your porch light, and wait for my call."

Denny felt the spidery legs of paranoia crawling up his back. "You can see my house?"

"I can see everything you do. Remember that."

Denny swallowed a lump of fear and peered out of his kitchen window. It was too dark to see anything out there, but suddenly he could feel his boss's eyes on him. He needed another beer. Bad. "What's the pay?"

"Same as it was for the last job," said the robot voice.

"What if that's not enough?"

"We both know it is. Your father's debts increase daily. I'm sure you'd like to start paying them off before the interest rate increases to broken bones."

Denny shoved that thought out of his mind before he got sick. He'd seen what the men who held his dad's debt had done to him before they'd finally killed him. Denny had no fondness for the man, but he didn't wish that kind of punishment on anyone. Especially himself. "Okay. I can be at Meg's in fifteen minutes."

Denny opened the fridge and pulled out a beer to settle his nerves.

"Good boy. I knew you'd make the right decision."

Denny tightened his jaw over the caustic words that wanted to spew out. He was twenty-two, hardly a boy, yet his boss insisted on saying that every time they made a deal. It was enough to make a man crazy.

"And Dennis?"

Not Denny, Dennis. He hated that, too. "Yeah?"

"You've had enough beer tonight."

❦

Caleb was getting angrier by the minute. It was after one in the morning, and Lana's lights were still burning bright. He opened his laptop and pulled up the image from the camera he'd planted. Along the far edge of the image, he saw Lana sitting at her computer, working. Her body was slumped with fatigue, but her fingers continued to fly over the keyboard. He heard the buzz of some infomercial in the background spewing something about building better abs. Beside her sat a steaming cup of coffee that she must have just poured.

He wanted to bust into her apartment and demand that she go to bed, but he didn't dare. He wasn't ready to let her know about the camera he'd planted, nor was it really any of his business. If she wanted to work herself sick, he just had to live with it.

Caleb closed his laptop before he could change his mind about barging into her life.

His dashboard clock read one-eighteen. The perfect time to call in and report to Monroe. Waking his CO up from a nice, cozy bed with the missus was the perfect way for Caleb to let him know just how much he was enjoying this job.

The colonel picked it up on the first ring, and there was no hint of sleep in his voice. The bastard.

"Monroe," greeted the colonel in a terse voice.

"Sir, it's Stone."

"About time you called. Report."

"I'm at her place." Caleb didn't use Lana's name, on the off chance that someone would monitor the call. Even though they'd taken every precaution to secure his cell phone, there was always new technology out there that could thwart their efforts and countersurveillance.

Caleb could hear the smile in Monroe's voice. "That's quick work. The closer you are to her, the safer she'll be."

"It's not like that, sir. I'm outside. In my car."

"Grant would have already been in the woman's bed."

"I am not Grant," growled Caleb, hating the thought of another man in her bed more than he should have.

"Sitting outside isn't good enough. Do whatever you have to do to stick by her side. She knows something she didn't tell us when we debriefed her. Find out what it is."

Anger swirled in Caleb's gut. He didn't like the colonel implying that she'd lied, even though he knew that it was a possibility. "How do you know there's anything to find out, sir?"

"Just a hunch."

Fuck your hunch, is what Caleb wanted to say, but he bit back the remark and showed the colonel the respect he deserved. "I'll feel her out and see if I can get her to talk, but I'm not going to go dragging up bad memories if I don't think there's anything to be gained by it. She doesn't need me to force her to relive her torture."

"Would you prefer to see her dead, son?"

Caleb snarled, and his hand tightened around the phone until he heard the plastic groan in protest. "Of course not," he bit out.

"Then you damn well better find out what she's hiding. I never did buy her story that she didn't hear or see anything over those three days."

"You spent five days interrogating her. Are you saying that our men aren't good enough to break one weak, bedridden woman?"

"We thought we had the whole story, son. We were wrong." There was no smugness in Monroe's tone, only the heavy weight of responsibility.

"How do you know that?"

"If we weren't wrong, then why is her name being

tossed about by men we know were linked to the Swarm before we took them down? Men they hired to do some of their dirty work?"

Caleb had no answers. "The good news is that if she did witness something, then we got all the terrorists that day. If any of them survived, they would have already tried to capture or kill her."

"Not necessarily. They might have thought she was dead. Lord knows she looked dead when you pulled her out."

Caleb's mind filled with that horrible image of her broken, bleeding body, the way he'd pulled the sheet over her head to keep the dust from choking her. The memory alone was enough to nearly send him into a rage. He held on to his temper by a thin thread. "So why now? Why haven't they come after her sometime in the past eighteen months?"

"It took her six months before she could even walk again. It took another six months before she was able to take care of herself and move out of her parents' home to live on her own. She's only recently gotten any sort of media attention for her foundation, and I think that's what did it. Her name started popping up on the CIA transcripts right after that big news article that plastered her face on the front page of the local paper. If there's anyone out there who wants her eliminated as a witness, they might not have even realized she was still alive until recently."

That made too much sense for Caleb's peace of mind. "I want to get her into protective custody."

Monroe sighed. "You can try to talk her into it, son, but she's been refusing it ever since she regained consciousness."

"I don't care," said Caleb. "We should make her. Even if she isn't hiding anything, someone might think she is. That alone puts her in danger."

"If she doesn't want to go into hiding, I won't force her. It wouldn't work anyway without her cooperation, and I'm not willing to waste resources like that. Convince her to give in if you can, but any woman who can live through what she did has got to be about as stubborn as God can make her."

"That stubbornness is going to make this job ten times harder," said Caleb. "Since this is going to take a while, you might as well send in my replacement. She'll be more comfortable with someone she can trust. Lots of them, just to be safe."

"Sorry, Stone. Can't do that. All my men are tied up at the moment."

Caleb felt his patience pulling into thin shreds. His words hissed out from between his clenched teeth. "Then drag in someone else's men, sir."

"You're already there and know the situation. She knows you. You're the best man for the job, and she deserves the best, don't you think?"

"Stop trying to manipulate me, damn it. It won't work."

"Who said anything about manipulating you? I'm just stating a fact. You're the best man for the job."

"I doubt she thinks so. It's got to be hell for her to have to see me again." He knew it was. He'd made her cry, damn it.

"Maybe that will convince her to cooperate faster, just to get you out of her life. Stay put. I'll send someone else if and when I can."

With that, Monroe cut the connection and left Caleb writhing in frustration. Lana needed someone else to watch out for her—someone who wouldn't remind her of how she nearly died. Someone she could trust not to get her hurt again.

❧

Bedtime was always the worst time of the day for Lana. She put it off a little longer each night, but it was nearly two in the morning, and after the dose of sleeping pills she'd taken so she wouldn't remember her dreams, she was too exhausted to put off the inevitable.

Lana turned on every light in her bedroom until it glowed with brightness. It helped ease the fear that clawed at her belly, but only a little. Caleb showing up and unearthing all those memories was going to make her nightmares worse. She was sure of it. She wanted to scream at him or put a gun to his head or whatever it took to make him leave, but in her heart, she knew it was too late. Even if he left now, the damage was done. The memories Caleb had stirred caused a wound to reopen, and she was going to have to go through the long, torturous process of letting it heal. Again.

Lana lay on her bed and curled up into a tight ball as she struggled not to cave in under the weight of her fear. This shouldn't be happening. Not now. Not after all this time and all her effort to make something of the shattered remains of her life. To forget what had happened.

She'd worked so hard to get to this point. She'd sacrificed everything—her career, her fiancé, her friends, her money, and any hope of ever having a normal life. All of that was gone, ripped away by the three longest, most horrible days in her life. And still, she hadn't let it beat her. She'd fought and struggled and forced herself to endure the pain of rehabilitation so that she could survive and do something meaningful with her life.

And now it was all spinning out of control, caving in around her. It was so fucking unfair that she choked on the rage welling up in her throat. She wanted to lash out and break something, but she didn't dare. Her control was stretched too thin to allow her to let go for even a moment. She had to get a grip on herself. There was too much work to do and not enough time or manpower to get it done. She feared that if her foundation crashed and burned, she'd lose her last reason to keep going, to keep fighting off the pressure to give in to her terror and let it consume her.

It was a dark temptation to just let go. As close as she was hovering to the limits of her sanity, it wouldn't be hard to go over the edge. Just a short fall. She could collapse in on herself and let the world go away. She'd almost done it once after the doctors had told her she'd never walk again, probably never have children because the beatings had damaged her too badly. She could do it again and let the calm, black numbness embrace her.

It was so tempting she felt herself slip that much closer before she pulled herself back, shocked that she'd even consider giving in. People needed her. The kids needed her. She couldn't let them down. She'd fight this threat with every ounce of effort she had left in her. There wasn't much strength left after all the fighting she'd already done, but she had to try. It was the only way she could live with herself.

CHAPTER FOUR

———— ❧ ————

In her nightmares it was always dark. Choking, thick darkness that crawled into her nose and mouth and filled her lungs with clotted, oily air. She couldn't see, but she could feel the cold metal pipe hammering against her ribs until they cracked. She could hear her own screams, high-pitched and gurgling wetly with the blood that filled her mouth. She was bound, helpless. She couldn't fight. She couldn't even move. Hard plastic bindings sliced through the skin on her wrists as she struggled to crawl away. It was futile. Her legs had been broken in so many places she couldn't even climb to her knees.

Pain swamped her body, a bone-deep, writhing, living pain that clawed through her blood with every terrified beat of her heart. She didn't believe that she could endure this much pain without dying. It didn't seem possible, but that was just one more cruel torture they had devised to punish her. They wanted her pain; they reveled in it.

They laughed when she screamed.

They were laughing now, and she realized in some distant sliver of her mind that remained sheltered and sane that it must mean she was screaming, even though she didn't know she had been. She'd screamed so much for so long that it almost seemed as natural as breathing. But she didn't want to give them that pleasure, so she tried to be quiet. She tried to calm herself enough to pull in a decent breath. Her lungs were burning, and her heart was pounding way too hard. She couldn't think. She couldn't breathe. She panicked as the cold blackness closed in around her, swallowing her whole.

She couldn't fight it. She wasn't strong enough. She'd been worn down too hard for too long, and there was no strength left to fight it anymore.

Then she felt Caleb's hand wrap around hers, a rough warmth of skin-to-skin contact. The heat tore through her, lashing out at the cold black claws of terror that were tugging her down. She focused on that warmth, knowing it had saved her before and it could again. She couldn't die if he was here. Not if he was here.

Caleb's low, insistent voice pulled her from her nightmare. "Wake up, Lana. Come on. Wake up, honey. You're safe."

Her body trembled, but her breathing slowed until she could pull in a full breath before it was hastily forced from her lungs. She was dimly aware of Caleb's low, calming voice muttering hushed tones of comfort against her temple. She felt his hard, hot body surrounding her. He was rocking her back and forth like a child, stroking her back with one hand while his other was clutched inside her death grip.

She could smell his skin, a hot, masculine scent, and remembered it from the day he'd carried her out of the cave into the sunlight. He'd saved her. She was safe.

Lana shuddered and relaxed against him. She was too

tired to fight, but she didn't have to now. He was here and she could rest. He wouldn't let her die.

❧

Caleb had risked his life countless times. He'd jumped from planes in the dead of night into enemy territory. He'd infiltrated buildings full of men bristling with weapons and hatred. He'd fought his way through war zones and felt bullets fly by so close they burned his skin. But he'd never known true terror until he heard Lana's screams coming through the microphone on the camera he'd planted in her apartment.

Adrenaline flooded his body, and he'd busted open her front door, weapon in hand, before she had time to pull in a breath for her second scream. He raced to her bedroom to find it was brightly lit, every one of the many lamps blazing.

It took him only a brief instant to realize no one was in there with her and that she was just dreaming. Although *just dreaming* wasn't the right way to put what she was going through.

Her body writhed on the bed, wrapped in a cocoon of sheets and blankets. Sweat poured off her, wetting her hair and the collar of her oversized sleep shirt. Her head was thrown back, and her neck was stretched at an extreme angle, as if she were trying to get away from something.

Horrible, wailing sounds of terror welled from her mouth, and her face was streaked with tears.

Caleb pulled her into his arms, covers and all, trying to wake her. He shook her and called her name, but she was too caught up in the nightmare to hear him. Frantically, he tried to drag her back into consciousness, squeezing her hand while he rocked her in his lap.

Something he'd done must have helped, because she started to calm down. Her harsh breathing evened out, and she curled against him. "Caleb." Her voice was groggy and rough from the strain of screaming. "Please don't leave me again."

Caleb wasn't sure he heard her right. She sounded like she was still half-asleep. She'd asked him to stay, which meant she couldn't be thinking straight. But her words were too alluring for him to refuse. Maybe he was just hearing what he wanted to hear, but for now, that was enough.

He ran his hands over her bare arms and down her back, letting himself imagine that she actually wanted his comfort. She was still bathed in sweat, and as she relaxed, he could feel her skin roughen with cold. Caleb didn't even stop to think how she'd react if she were awake. He just arranged her on the bed, pulled up the covers to her neck, and moved his body against hers to keep her warm. Maybe she wouldn't thank him for the intimacy when she was awake, but in her sleep, she wiggled closer to him, seeking his warmth. After a few minutes, she was sleeping peacefully.

Caleb let out a long breath and held her tight. Adrenaline subsided, leaving him shaking harder than he had since he went on his first real op before he was even old enough to drink legally.

Her head was tucked under his chin, and he could feel her breath fanning out across his neck. Her tears left cool, wet spots on his T-shirt. The honeysuckle scent of her skin wafted between them, and Caleb dragged it into his lungs, praying it would calm his frayed nerves.

She was safe. Plagued with nightmares likely caused by PTSD, but safe.

Caleb cupped the back of her head in his palm while the other hand smoothed down her delicate spine over and over. She fit against him perfectly, and the feel of her soft curves under his hands was like coming home. For about half a second, he nearly allowed himself to think of her as a woman, all sweet and soft in his arms. But then he ruthlessly slaughtered that thought and cursed himself for being such a selfish ass.

It wasn't enough that he'd nearly killed her, or that he now had to come back into her life and make her re-live her past—he had to heap on a full serving of dick-centered lust to go with it.

God, how could he be such a low-life scum?

He closed his eyes in regret, wishing that there wasn't a huge canyon of ugly past between them. It would have been so nice to allow himself to think of her as a woman rather than an assignment. He would have shucked his jeans and T-shirt, crawled under those covers with her, stripped her naked, and warmed her with the most primi-tive of methods. If the rest of her skin was as silky as her arms, it would be like stroking sunshine when he touched her. The urge to find out was almost too much to bear, but Caleb held back. She deserved his restraint. She deserved a hell of a lot more, but right now, restraint was all he had to offer.

Her lips pressed against his throat. Caleb's body clenched in a fit of pure animal lust. His jeans became un-comfortable, and his blood prowled in hot pulses through his veins. His fingers curled into soft flesh, and until then, he hadn't realized her hip was under his palm. Somehow, his hand had snaked under her blankets without his permission and was resting on her nearly naked flesh. Only a narrow strip of her cotton panties separated his hand from her skin. He relaxed his grip, and his fingertips grazed over her skin as he did so, causing his stomach muscles to tighten.

God, she was so soft and smelled sweet and womanly against him. He'd always had a good sense of smell, and he knew that for the rest of his life, he'd remember just how she smelled right now, lying all warm and trusting and sleeping in his arms.

Her fingers slid up his chest and curled over the collar of his shirt. She had elegant hands. He remembered that from the hours he'd spent holding them, willing her to live. He probably knew the texture of her skin better than he knew his own, and her fragile bones were so slender that he could hardly feel them laced between his fingers.

He had no right getting this close to her. Hell, he could probably roll over in his sleep and hurt her without even trying.

She let out a sigh, which moved her lips and breath over his throat in a soft caress.

Caleb's eyes slid shut, and he pushed his mind away from the physical feelings of his body. He'd spent years learning to ignore pain, fatigue, and hunger. Certainly he could ignore his lust.

Slowly, with so much effort it was almost humorous, Caleb untangled his body from Lana's. If he stayed here holding her, he'd do something he'd regret. There was not a single doubt in his mind.

❦

Lana woke up slowly, fighting off the grogginess that often plagued her after a rough night. She stretched and rolled over onto a patch of pillow that held a subtle, masculine scent—a scent that brought back the memory of her dream last night. For the first time in months, she'd had a good dream—one in which Caleb had driven away her nightmares and held her in his arms. For a while, she'd felt like a normal woman with normal desires.

She'd actually been happy, and it had been so long since she'd last been happy, she'd forgotten what that felt like.

The grogginess faded, but the scent of Caleb's skin was still on the pillow. It hadn't just been a dream. He'd actually been there.

Which meant he'd seen her at her worst, locked inside her nightmares.

Humiliation filled her stomach until she wanted to vomit. He'd seen her in her lowest, most vulnerable state, helpless and screaming over things that were no longer real—things that were all in her head. Surely he'd think she was a total mental case now, which, she supposed, wasn't far from the truth.

Her cheeks burned with shame, and she briefly thought about calling in sick so she wouldn't have to go to work. She couldn't face him today, not after last night. She'd die of humiliation.

She heard the gurgle of her coffee pot, and a few seconds later she smelled it brewing. He was still here, in her apartment. There was no avoiding him, even if she called in sick. She had to face him one way or another. Preferably after she'd showered and brushed her teeth.

Lana pushed out of bed and raced to the bathroom too fast for him to stop her from getting there safely. Fifteen minutes later, she was clean and dreading seeing him even more than before. She should have gotten her humiliation over with first and enjoyed her shower.

Lana wrapped herself in a plaid flannel robe she'd permanently borrowed from her father and bravely stepped out of the bathroom. He was sitting on her kitchen counter next to the coffee pot, reading her newspaper. He wore a white cotton T-shirt that blazed in comparison against the deeply tanned skin of his throat and arms. He looked up from the paper as she padded into the kitchen, suddenly feeling indecent wearing only a thin layer of body lotion and her father's huge bathrobe.

"Coffee?" he asked, watching her with solemn black eyes.

Lana nodded, not trusting herself to speak when those feelings of shame were starting to swell again upon the sight of him.

"I hope you don't mind that I helped myself to your paper."

"No. Of course not. I rarely have time to read it anymore, anyway."

He slid off the counter and stood to his full height. He seemed to fill the kitchen with his large presence, nearly blocking out the overhead fluorescent lighting.

The memory of him carrying her out into the sun flashed in her mind, so potent and powerful that it made her sway. Lana gripped the counter behind her to steady herself and felt Caleb's hands wrap around her upper arms. His fingers were hard, hot bands that completely encircled her biceps, making her feel vulnerable and protected all at the same time. She had no idea how he did that, and it kept putting her off balance.

"You need to eat something. You had a rough night."

Lana blinked up at him, trying to make sense of his words. "Rough?"

"The nightmares," he said in a bleak, harsh tone.

She felt her face heat with embarrassment. "I'm sorry you had to see that. They're not usually so bad," she lied.

Rage flared in his eyes and tightened his jaw. His cheeks darkened with anger, and his hands tightened slightly around her arms. "Bullshit."

Lana shrugged, feeling the strength of his grip around her arms. She couldn't think straight when he was touching her. "Think what you like. It's none of your business, anyway."

He cursed a low, violent word. "I'll take care of the door if you give me your landlord's name and number."

"The door?" Lana hadn't even noticed until he'd said something that her front door was lying in two splintered pieces against the hole it had once fit into. "You did that? With or without the help of a battering ram?"

"Sorry. I heard you screaming and I thought—"

"It doesn't matter what you thought. This never should have happened, and it wouldn't have if you'd left like I asked you to."

"What would you have done last night if I hadn't been here?" he demanded.

"The same thing I do every night. Get through it." She wished the words back into her mouth the second she saw his face darken.

"You mean you have those nightmares every night?" He was so close she could see the golden brown flecks in his black eyes nestled against his pupils.

"It's none of your business. Can't you get that through your head? I don't want your help."

His jaw bunched under the force of his clenched teeth. He released her arms and turned around, but not before she saw the look of hurt that crossed his hard features. The cloth of his shirt stretched to contain the thick layers of muscle over his ribs and along his spine. Lana's mouth went dry, and she couldn't help but stare. He was such a powerfully built man, yet when he touched her, he was achingly gentle.

Lana rubbed her arms, trying to hold in the heat of his touch. Whether or not she wanted him here, there was something soothing in his touch—something that calmed the parts of her soul that were constantly screaming in fear.

He turned back around a moment later, looking solemn and calm once more. His gaze fell to her hands, which were still futilely trying to hold the memory of his touch. "Did I hurt you?"

She let her arms fall hastily to her sides and felt that embarrassed flush rise up her throat again. "No."

He took her arm and shoved the loose sleeve of her robe up to her shoulder. There was not a sign that he'd even touched her. Not even a pink mark of irritation, just pale, naked skin.

His nostrils flared, and his fingertips just barely grazed along her arm.

Lana shivered in a purely feminine reaction, and Caleb's gaze shot up to meet hers. She was sure he could see every bit of her feelings about him in her face—every bit of solace his touch gave her, every sliver of calm he offered, every single horrible memory he dredged up with his presence. He just kept looking, making her feel stripped bare of all her secrets.

Those golden slivers in his eyes widened, outlining the sudden dilation of his pupils. Then his thick black lashes lowered, veiling his eyes as he went about the job of checking her other arm for damage.

When he was satisfied that she was whole, he stepped back, and in that single step, he put an entire world of distance between them. His emotions vanished, and he donned the mask of professionalism so easily it left Lana reeling, wondering if she'd seen anything at all in his eyes.

❦

Caleb slugged down his coffee, poured another cup, and finished that one off, too. Even though it burned all the way down, it was much cooler than the blood pumping through his veins.

God, he wanted Lana.

He knew he shouldn't want her. He figured his attraction to her was just a cruel joke of fate, but he wasn't laughing.

It was all he could do not to rip that oversized robe off her and run his hands over every bit of the naked skin beneath. And he knew for a fact that she'd been naked under that robe, too. He could smell her body all warm from her shower, the lotion she'd smoothed onto her skin, and the subtle, womanly scent that was all her own.

When he'd touched her, she'd blushed. He wasn't sure whether it was out of anger or embarrassment or desire, but he knew which he wanted it to be. He'd wanted to part the lapels of that droopy robe and see just how far down her chest that blush went. He'd bet his last dollar that it would go all the way down to cover her small, high breasts and her tight little nipples.

He congratulated himself for being strong and not jumping her. It hadn't been easy to resist her when he'd known she'd just as soon slit his throat as speak to him, but now that he had a sliver of doubt about her feelings toward him—a faint hope that she might feel even a tenth of the desire he did—it was going to be impossible.

CHAPTER FIVE

———— ❧ ————

Lana's landlord, Mr. Simmons, showed up just before Lana left for work. Caleb stayed behind to deal with her broken door rather than leave her apartment open and unguarded.

Mr. Simmons was a potbellied man in his sixties with a ring of white hair orbiting the back of his bald head. He greeted Caleb with a firm handshake and a smile. "Good to see Lana's found herself a man."

Caleb saw no point in correcting Mr. Simmons. "Been a long time for her, huh?"

Mr. Simmons went around to the back of his truck and began loosening the ropes that held Lana's new door in place. "I'm not the kind to snoop, but I try to keep an eye on the little lady, seeing as how she's all alone out here. I've never seen her with a man before you."

A fierce little spurt of satisfaction made Caleb smile. He hopped up into the back of the truck and finished freeing the door. "It's good to know someone's been watching out for her."

Mr. Simmons shook his white head. "She doesn't make it easy, that's for sure. I keep telling her she should move back home with her folks again until she's well enough to be on her own."

Caleb lifted the pre-hung door out of the truck and eased it onto the ground. "What do you mean? She seems healthy enough to me."

"Oh, her body is fine, I'm talking about the rest of her." Mr. Simmons tapped his temple. "The poor girl needs therapy. I've seen the same kind of thing in a couple of my buddies who fought in 'Nam. I don't know a lot about what happened to her, but I know it had to have been bad."

Caleb turned away before Mr. Simmons could see the look of anger he felt on his face. The idea of Lana suffering the same way war veterans did made a lot of sense. Too much for his peace of mind. "What makes you say that?"

"You're the one who broke down the door trying to get to her. I figure you heard the screams."

Helpless rage clenched his gut at the reminder of those screams. He picked up the heavy door by himself, needing a physical outlet to vent some of his anger. "I did."

Mr. Simmons nodded and followed Caleb with a tool-box in hand. "It's why I had to move her out to this empty building. She was in one of the units I'd just renovated, but her neighbors kept complaining about the noise. We had the cops out here six times in three weeks. I tried to get her to go back home, or to get some help, but she refused, so I put her out here in this building that I've emptied so it can be renovated next. Once the renovation is done, though . . ."

"She'll have to leave."

Mr. Simmons nodded. "I hate to kick the girl out, but I

have to make a living. I've already put off the renovation longer than I should have, trying to give her some time to heal, but apparently it hasn't helped."

Caleb set the new door against the outside wall of Lana's apartment and surveyed the old one lying in pieces. "No, it hasn't."

"You planning on moving in with her, maybe? Maybe it's nosy of me to ask, but I figure that if she's got someone there at night, maybe her nightmares wouldn't be so bad."

The idea of being able to help Lana with something as simple as his presence was a strong lure, but Caleb knew it was just wishful thinking. Even if she did let him into her life in such an intimate way, chances were his presence would just make things worse by reminding her of what had happened.

Then again, she had quieted last night when he'd held her. Maybe the old man wasn't completely wrong. "Lana's a bit independent," said Caleb.

Mr. Simmons let out a bark of laughter that made the shirt over his potbelly gape open around the buttons. "That's like saying the sun's a bit bright."

"I guess you do know her pretty well, huh?"

Mr. Simmons pulled out a crowbar and went to work pulling the frame off the doorway. "About as well as anyone, I suppose. She doesn't have a lot of people in her life, from what I've seen. Her folks go to church with me, and her father worries about her something fierce. He's told me a little bit about what she's gone through, but I don't think even he knows the whole story."

"She's trying to protect him from the truth," said Caleb before he thought better. Instinctively, he knew it was true.

Lana was not the type of woman to dump her problems onto her friends and family. She'd shoulder the burden herself rather than bring them down with her.

Caleb wondered if she'd even told them enough to allow them to help her.

"Hell of a thing for a father, though—to want to help your little girl, but not know how," said Mr. Simmons.

Caleb needed to know how much Lana had shared with her family. Maybe that was the key to finding out if she was hiding something or if she was in danger. "How much do you know about what happened to her?"

Mr. Simmons lowered the crowbar and ripped off a section of molding with his rough hands. "Just what her father told me one night after a few beers. She went to Armenia with some do-good group that was hoping to help out there. She was supposed to teach art classes to kids or something. I'm not exactly sure. Something went wrong, and she was taken hostage by a terrorist group. They held her and a bunch of other Americans for three days, beat her up pretty bad, but she was the lucky one. The others all died."

The facts were right, but only in the same way as it was a fact that the ocean was wet. It was a hell of a lot more than that, but Caleb didn't feel the need to expand on what the man knew. "I'm not sure she'd agree about being the lucky one."

Mr. Simmons gave a slow, grim nod. "That's just what my buddy who survived 'Nam said."

❧

Lana saw Stacie's car in the parking lot and knew she'd lost the race again. Man, but that woman got into work early. One of these days, Lana was going to win their contest to see who could show up first, but only if she didn't sleep at all.

Lana parked her car and went into the office, expecting to smell coffee brewing and hear Stacie singing off tune along with her MP3 player. Instead, the office was silent. The lights were all out. Papers littered the floor.

The place looked like it had been ransacked.

Lana stood there in shocked silence, trying to understand what she saw. Then she heard a low moan coming from the bathroom at the back of the office and her shock turned to terror. She raced back to the bathroom to find Stacie lying on the floor. Blood soaked her crisp yellow shirt and pooled under her slim body. More blood trickled from a small wound on her head.

Lana cried out in anguish as she bent down to see if Stacie was still alive. At Lana's touch, she moaned again but didn't move. Panic seized Lana's heart, and a flood of fears and memories flickered through her mind until her brain was clogged with a jumble of horrible images of blood and pain. Somewhere in the back of her mind, she heard herself chanting, "No, no, no."

"Lana?" whispered Stacie, pulling Lana out of her frozen panic and spurring her into action.

"I'm here, sweetie. Don't move. I'll be right back." Lana sprinted for the cordless phone, ripped her T-shirt over her head, and dialed 911.

The emergency operator picked up while Lana was folding her shirt into a thick pad, her voice calm in the midst of the chaos. "Nine-one-one. Please state your emergency."

"I need an ambulance. My friend's been hurt. Shot, I think." Her voice was tight with fear, but clear enough to make out, thank God. She repeated the address and threw the phone down despite the operator's request that she stay on the line.

Lana pressed the folded T-shirt against the wound in Stacie's side, making her hiss in pain.

"I know it hurts," she told Stacie. "I'm sorry, sweetie, but I've got to stop the bleeding."

Slowly, Stacie started to come around. Her skin was ghostly pale, her voice weak. "I told him he could take whatever he wanted. I wouldn't have tried to stop him. He didn't have to shoot me."

Lana's heart broke open, bleeding tears of guilt. "Shhh. Try not to talk."

"There wasn't anything here worth stealing," said Stacie in a pained voice.

"I know, sweetie. I know. Just lie still."

It seemed to take an eternity for the ambulance to arrive. Sirens wailed in the distance, coming ever closer, but not close enough. Lana willed them to hurry as she watched blood seep slowly through her T-shirt, turning it red.

A few moments later, the door swung open with a merry tinkle of bells. "Back here," she shouted.

A pair of EMTs came hustling back, loaded down with gear. Lana backed out of the bathroom to give them room to work. She just stood there, her hands and clothes covered in blood, watching them work. She was helpless, trapped, out of control.

Her friend was dying, and there was nothing Lana could do.

❧

Caleb saw the flashing lights in front of Lana's office while he was stuck at a traffic light. There were several police cars. An ambulance.

Panic iced over his insides, and he felt himself slip into battle mode—that space where time slowed down and emotions were put on hold. He couldn't let himself feel anything right now. Not until he knew Lana was safe.

The light turned green, but all the entrances to Lana's office building were blocked by patrol cars. Caleb drove his car over the curb and parked in the grass on a steep incline. He had just jumped out of his car when he saw them wheel a gurney out of Lana's office. A woman's slim body was on it. She was wheeled out feet first, and for a moment, all Caleb could see was blood.

That cold inside him hardened and began to splinter.

A swarm of cops had gathered, and the sound of radio communication buzzed in the air. A policeman stepped in his path, but Caleb just shoved him out of his way without a thought. "Lana!" he roared.

Nearly every head turned, but Caleb didn't care. He raced toward the gurney. "Lana!"

He was close enough now to see them loading Stacie onto the ambulance. Not Lana. Stacie. A second later, Lana came out of the office. She was shirtless, wearing only a modest bra, and blood soaked her jeans from the knees down, but her walk was smooth, and Caleb knew then that it wasn't her blood.

That ice inside him shattered. He hadn't failed Lana again. She was alive.

She stood there, brittle with tension and deathly pale, smeared with blood. He saw her try to straighten her spine and lift her chin—saw her try to regain her composure—but it wasn't fooling him. Inside she was sobbing.

Caleb crossed the space between them, ignoring repeated questions about his business here from the surrounding officers. None of them dared to stop him physically. He reached Lana and, without asking permission, took her into his arms.

"Caleb, I—" Her voice broke, so he saved her pride.

"Just hush and let me hold you a minute," he told her. Her arms wrapped around him in a tentative hug, and then she gripped him hard as if afraid he'd let go.

He just held her, her lithe body pressed fully against his from chest to knees. He felt the soft mounds of her breasts flatten against his ribs and the warm rush of her breath over his skin. Her mouth was nestled just above his heart, and he could hear low, fervent words spilling from her lips, even though he couldn't kick his brain into functioning enough to understand them.

He bowed his head over hers, pressing his lips against the top of her head to mumble incoherent, soothing words into the silky strands. She smelled so good. And she was safe.

Lana shuddered against him as if soaking up his heat, and it was all Caleb could do not to pick her up and carry her off somewhere private where she could cry in peace while he held her.

She sniffed and pulled away enough that there was room for air to swirl between their bodies. Sweat had gathered along Caleb's ribs, and it cooled as it evaporated in the slow morning breeze.

Lana wiped her face with her hands and then wiped her hands on her thighs. Dried blood stained the skin between her fingers. Her nose was pink, and her blue eyes were luminous from her tears. Caleb just stared into her eyes, losing himself in their blue depths. It was like flying over a tropical ocean, seeing the varying shades of blue as the depth of the water changed. Her irises went from the palest silver blue near her pupils to a deep indigo around the rim. Her lashes were a thick black fringe that needed no help from cosmetics to add to their lushness.

Caleb realized he was still holding her. He took a deep breath and pulled his hands away quickly, like ripping a bandage off of hairy skin. Not touching her hurt a hell of a lot worse, though.

She gathered herself, and Caleb began to realize they had an audience. Mostly men.

Caleb stripped his shirt off and pulled it over Lana's head to cover her breasts. As lovely as the sight was, he didn't like sharing it with the other officers present.

She snaked her arms through the sleeves. "Thanks. I had to use my shirt as a bandage. There was so much blood." Her voice broke, but she held together.

Caleb's gut twisted at the pain vibrating in her tone. He pulled her back up against him, unable to let her stand there and hurt without offering his comfort. His touch. Lana didn't resist, and he knew then just how desperate she had to be if she was willing to take comfort from him.

"We're not finished interviewing Miss Hancock," said a detective, whose role was given away by his inexpensive suit and tie. His hazel eyes roamed over Caleb as if categorizing him in an instant. He had a muscular build and the kind of posture that told Caleb he knew how to use it. The name on his badge read Jacob Hart.

"I told you everything I know," she said as if she'd already repeated it twenty times. "I came in, saw the place was a wreck, heard Stacie in the bathroom, then . . ." Her voice broke again, but she pulled in a deep breath and continued on. "I called nine-one-one, and then you showed up."

"Did Stacie say anything?" asked the detective.

"Just something about how she would have let him take whatever he wanted. He didn't have to shoot her." She turned to Caleb. "Someone shot Stacie."

Caleb smoothed a hand over her shiny brown hair. "I know, honey. It's going to be okay."

"I should have been there earlier."

"You couldn't have stopped him, either, Lana."

"No, but if I'd shown up earlier—"

"Then you'd be the one lying on that gurney right now, miss," said Detective Hart, gently.

Lana's eyes darted toward the concrete, but not before Caleb could read the thought that passed through them— one that he'd had a thousand times while sitting next to Lana's hospital bed. She would have done anything to trade places with Stacie.

"I need to go to the hospital," she said.

"Of course, but we have just a few more questions," said the detective.

Caleb felt Lana's body tighten, and the urge to protect her—even from a few questions—was overwhelming.

"That's enough questions for now," stated Caleb in the voice he used to command other men.

"I'm afraid we have to go over this just one more time," said the detective, unfazed.

Caleb took a step forward and put on his intimidation face. He didn't use it often, since his size was usually more than enough to get nearly anyone to cooperate, but on the rare occasions that he needed to, he knew how to make another man back down. This was just one of those occasions.

He gave the detective a smile that was mostly just a baring of teeth and dropped his voice until the detective had to strain to hear him. "I'm taking Lana to the hospital to check on her friend. You may speak to her later today, if she's up to it. If not, she'll talk with you again tomorrow."

The detective's eyes slid to the dog tags hanging over Caleb's bare chest, then to the tattoo on his arm. "Active duty?" he asked.

"I'm on leave," he lied.

A flash of keen intelligence lit up Detective Hart's eyes. "You're both free to go as long as you stay in town. We'll finish here and let you know when you're allowed back in the building."

"Thank you," said Lana.

Caleb was pretty sure that thanking him was a bit premature. Whatever Detective Hart was, he wasn't stupid, and he was letting them go, which meant he had another plan for getting the information he wanted.

CHAPTER SIX

————— ❦ —————

Jacob Hart wrote down the name and number he'd read off Caleb's dog tags. He still had a few buddies in the army that could help him use that bit of information to figure out who this giant was. His gut told him that he had nothing to do with the shooting this morning, but it also told him that something more was going on here than just a simple robbery gone bad.

Nothing of value had been touched. The little metal box containing a few bucks of petty cash was sitting out in plain sight. The CD player by the coffee pot was untouched, as was the MP3 player on one of the desks. The only thing that had been rummaged through was paperwork, and something about that nagged at him.

Jacob went back into the office, careful not to get in the way of the officers and techs collecting evidence. One of the men was sawing away a section of drywall to retrieve the spent round. With any luck, it would be in good enough shape for a ballistics match—assuming they had anything to match it to.

Jacob let his vision blur and just stared at the scene. White paper nearly carpeted the floor. It was everywhere. On each of the two desks was a stack of spiral notebooks.

Why were they still stacked when everything else was a mess? Had the ladies who worked here left them like that?

Jacob wrote down the question so he'd remember to ask it later.

"Hey, Jacob," said one of the uniformed officers. "Found something."

Jacob crossed the room, trying not to step on any of the trash. "What?"

The officer held up a little bit of plastic and metal. It almost looked like a broken piece of circuitry from the inside of a computer or something. It was thin, black, and no larger than the tip of his little finger. Jacob snapped on a rubber glove and took the tiny thing. A slim, short wire poked out of the back, and next to it was a thin adhesive pad. "Where did you find it?"

The officer motioned to the picture hanging behind the coffee pot. It was one of those cheesy motivational posters that offices everywhere used. This one showed a picture of an astronaut floating in space high above the earth, all alone. The caption read, "Courage."

"On the poster?" asked Jacob.

"On the frame, along the top."

Where it wouldn't be noticed. Jacob took another look at the device and suddenly knew what it was. A listening device.

Interesting.

❧

Lana hated hospitals. They made her want to curl up into herself, or run away or throw up, or maybe all three at the same time. The sterile stink burned her nose, but she ignored it. Stacie had been taken into surgery immediately upon her arrival. That had been three hours earlier, and Lana was wearing a hole in the carpet of the waiting area.

Caleb had disappeared a few minutes ago and Lana tried not to freak out. Ever since she'd seen him walking toward her this morning, bellowing her name like he was afraid something had happened to her, Lana had been grateful that he'd come barging back into her life. She couldn't stand the thought of facing this alone, and there was no way she was going to call her family. Not after what had happened to Stacie. Caleb's arrival being followed closely by the shooting couldn't be a coincidence. Whoever had escaped Caleb's men in Armenia had found her. It was safest if she kept as much distance as possible between herself and everyone she loved.

Caleb came back bearing a steaming cup of coffee and some cheese crackers from the vending machine. He didn't bother to try to make her sit down or be calm like her mother would have. He let her walk out her worry and frustration without scolding her for fidgeting.

Lana took the coffee but turned down the crackers. "Thanks."

"Is there something I can get you to eat? Worry and coffee on an empty stomach aren't such a good thing."

"Maybe in a little while."

Caleb nodded. He didn't ask her any stupid questions like whether she was okay. He just stayed there, silent and strong, ready to support her in any way she wanted.

It was such a precious gift it nearly made her start crying again.

He didn't know her, but he seemed to somehow know just what she needed. Then again, in his line of work, maybe this was normal for him.

On the way to the hospital, he'd pulled a clean shirt from the luggage in his car and covered his bare chest. She still wore his old shirt, which hung loosely on her but kept her from causing a scandal in the gift shop. The scent of his skin was with her constantly now, somehow helping to ease some of her tension.

He sat down to watch her pace, and after a few minutes, finally, Lana felt like resting herself. She sat down next to him and sipped her coffee. Caleb's arm draped over the back of her chair without touching her—offering support without forcing it on her. She could lean back and let him touch her or stay upright and know he wouldn't push.

She wanted to lean back into his embrace, and she didn't even care that it made her weak to need his touch. She was at her limit and would do whatever it took to be strong for Stacie, even if it meant taking comfort from a man she should have distanced herself from.

They sat in silence, his strong arm so near, her body frozen in indecision. He didn't ask anything of her, nor did he try to push her. He let her take what she needed.

"Oh, my God!" wailed a voice that made Lana flinch. She turned to see who had just walked into the waiting room, praying it was someone else's mother.

No such luck.

Madeline Hancock raced across the room, streaks of mascara running down her cheeks. Her dark hair was just starting to turn noticeably gray, and even though she was past fifty, she had the skin of a woman half her age. Madeline was a crier. She always had been, and every time Lana cried, she knew she took one step closer to becoming just like her mother. It was enough to make Lana want to have her tear ducts surgically closed.

"Baby, are you okay?" asked Madeline. "You're covered in blood."

Lana decided not to go into detail about how the blood got there. That would only cause more problems. "I'm fine, Mom. It's not mine. What are you doing here?"

"It's all over the news. They said someone was shot and then showed your office building. I called your office and kept calling until the police answered and told me you were safe." Madeline pulled Lana in for a tight hug, and despite knowing how this scare would make her mother overreact, a hug from Mom felt good. "Sit down, honey. You shouldn't be on your feet at a time like this."

"My feet are fine."

"Nonsense. I know how much your legs ache when you overdo. Sit."

Lana pulled in a deep breath in an effort not to take off her mother's head with the scathing remarks leaping behind her sealed lips.

"I bet you haven't eaten anything today, either. Let me take you home and make you some nice soup."

"Stacie is in surgery and you want me to go have soup?" Lana asked her mother.

"You have to keep your strength up if you want to be of any use to her at all."

"My strength is fine. I don't need to sit and I don't need soup. Just stop, okay?"

Madeline gave Lana a disapproving frown that made

Lana feel like a child. "You're upset. You'll feel better if you just rest for a while."

"I'll feel better if you just leave. Let me deal with this on my own. Please, Mom."

Madeline pretended not to hear the plea in Lana's voice. "You should have called me earlier. You need a cell phone, Lana. You had me scared half to death."

Lana realized that her mother's fear was driving her now, and she couldn't blame her for being worried. Lana might have been the one hurt in Armenia, but Madeline had to watch her suffer through a mother's eyes. That couldn't have been easy. "We've talked about this. I can't afford one right now."

"Then let me buy you one."

Lana closed her eyes in an effort to gather her patience. "Mom, please. Not now. Stacie is in surgery, and I just can't deal with you, too."

The hurt look on Mom's face made Lana feel like she'd just kicked a dog. "No one's asking you to *deal* with me. I came here to support you."

"I'm fine. You should go home and make sure Dad knows I'm okay."

Madeline patted Lana's arm. "You can come with me. After a scare like this, you should come stay with us for a few days."

It had taken Lana months to get out of the house the last time, and she wasn't strong enough for that kind of battle again. As far as her mother was concerned, Lana should just come live at home permanently, because she was too weak to live on her own. "Thank you, but I'll be fine."

"Nonsense. You shouldn't have to be alone at a time like this."

"I'm not," said Lana before she could stop the words from coming out of her mouth. Too late now.

Lana motioned to where Caleb sat a few feet away watching them silently. "Mom, this is Caleb. He's a friend of mine." A lie, but a necessary one. She couldn't let her mother get involved. It wasn't safe.

Madeline's blue eyes narrowed. "A friend or a boyfriend?"

Caleb stood up to his impressive height and stepped over to them, offering Madeline his hand. "Just a friend, ma'am. It's nice to meet you."

Madeline's expression turned from skeptical to speculative, and Lana realized her mistake. If Mom couldn't control Lana's life, a husband was the next best candidate. That's why she hadn't given up hope that Lana and Oran would patch things up.

Lana was sure that in Madeline's eyes, Caleb had gone from friend to boyfriend to husband in the blink of an eye.

"You should come over for dinner tonight," invited Madeline.

"Mom, now isn't a good time," said Lana. "I need to be here for Stacie."

"When she's better, then," replied Madeline, still addressing Caleb. "You can come over and meet the family. We'll have a cookout, and Lana's father can show off his new roses."

"That would be nice, ma'am," said Caleb.

"No promises, Mom," said Lana before Caleb could make any. He had no idea what he was dealing with—

that in Madeline's mind, they were probably already engaged by now. "Maybe after the fundraiser I'll have some time."

"You should make time for your family, Lana. We're all you have now."

That was not true. She also had Stacie and the foundation. And the kids. "This isn't the time. I'll call you later, as soon as we know about Stacie's condition."

"It sounds like you're asking me to leave."

Lana pulled in a deep breath. Aside from the fact that she really couldn't deal with her mother's well-intended interference, the less she was around her family, the safer they'd be. She couldn't forget that. "I am. I'll be fine. There's no sense in you spending your day here. You hardly even know Stacie."

"I'm not here for her, Lana. I'm here for you."

Lana wanted to say that she didn't need her, but that was too cruel and hurtful. Instead she settled for, "Caleb is here with me. I'll be fine."

As if trying to help her prove it, Caleb looped his thick arm over her shoulders and pulled her against his side. "I'll keep an eye on her for you," he told Madeline.

Lana was too shocked to move. She just stood there, soaking in his heat. And it felt good being inside his embrace. Too good. Caleb's comfort was something she could get used to in a hurry, and that was a dangerous thing to her hard-won independence.

Madeline looked from Lana to Caleb, and that speculative light flared in her eyes. "I suppose you two have this handled. You'll call if you need me?"

Lana nodded. "I promise."

Madeline hugged Lana, making Caleb step back and

take his warm comfort with him. It felt strange being swept from one set of arms to another, and Lana gave herself permission to enjoy something so rare.

Madeline repeated the motherly hug with Caleb, who took it like a man, smiling down indulgently at the top of Madeline's head. "You take good care of my baby girl," she told Caleb in a firm tone.

"Yes, ma'am." He gave her a solemn nod.

"Call me tonight or I'm coming to stay at your place. A mother can only take so much worry," said Madeline.

"I will, Mom. See you later."

Madeline left, wiping a new set of tears from her cheeks, and infuriatingly, Lana felt an answering sting in her own eyes. Despite Madeline's interference, Lana loved her.

"Something tells me that there isn't a force on this planet that would keep that woman away if you needed her," said Caleb.

"Be careful," warned Lana. "She was looking at you like you were prime son-in-law material."

Lana expected a look of surprise or horror to cross his face, but instead he just gave her a level stare. "You think?"

"I know."

"She doesn't know who I am, does she?"

"It's best that way. Mom wouldn't be able to handle the truth."

He opened his mouth to say something, but before he had time, a man in rumpled scrubs pushed through the double doors, heading straight for Lana.

She surged toward him, her fingers twisting together with nerves. "How is she?"

"Are you family?" asked the man.

"The closest thing Stacie's got. She works for me."

That seemed enough to satisfy him, and he ran an elegant surgeon's hand through his messy hair. "She's going to be okay. There was some bleeding, but we got it under control."

"Can I see her?"

"She's still in recovery. When we move her to a room in a few hours, then you can see her."

Lana felt hot tears of relief well up in her eyes, and she blinked hard to hold them back. "Thank you for saving her."

The surgeon gave her a charming smile. "It's what I do. Now, you look like you could use a bit of cleanup yourself," he said, looking down at her bloody jeans. "Go home and get a shower, get a meal. Come back in four hours. No sooner."

"I'd rather stay," she told him.

The surgeon's mouth flattened. "How do you think she's going to feel if she wakes up to see you covered in her blood?"

Lana hadn't thought about it that way. She just hadn't wanted to leave Stacie alone.

"There's nothing you can do for her now. Go home." He looked up at Caleb for support. "She really should go home and clean up."

Lana almost told him that she'd make up her own mind, but she didn't have the energy for a pointless squabble. "Will you call if she wakes up?"

"If that's what it will take to get you to leave, sure."

Lana gave him her number and left the hospital

with Caleb by her side. "She's going to be okay," Lana repeated.

"Yes, she is," Caleb agreed.

"I almost killed her."

He glanced down at her, a fierce frown on his face. "This isn't your fault. You can't think like that."

Lana swallowed hard to dislodge the lump of guilt in her throat. "She's my employee. My responsibility."

"She's a grown woman who makes her own decisions. You can't control her any more than you could those terrorists."

Lana flinched as if she'd been hit. "I don't want to control her."

"You can't hold yourself responsible for something out of your control," said Caleb.

"What if it wasn't out of my control? What if I caused this?"

Caleb pulled her to a halt. The summer heat beat down on her head, and out here in the sun, she could see those golden chips in Caleb's eyes clearly. He had amazing eyes. So dark they were black in all but the brightest light, where they were a rich, mink brown.

"How could you have caused this?" he asked. "Did you ask that guy to shoot her?"

"No."

"Then explain to me how this is your fault."

Lana's eyes slid away from his. She didn't want him to see her thoughts—didn't want him to know that she was hiding something from him. "I don't know."

"Bullshit. What aren't you telling me?" he demanded.

"I'm just being paranoid," she said.

"Paranoid is just another word for cautious if there's a reason for it. Is there a reason for it, Lana?"

"You tell me. You're the one who showed up telling me I might be in danger."

"I'm not going to let anything happen to you."

"Our history together proves otherwise."

He jerked as if she'd slapped him, and then his face went hard. Expressionless. "Hate me all you want. I'm still not going anywhere."

❦

They had to stop by the apartment-complex office to pick up the keys to Lana's new door, but Caleb was pleased by the sturdy steel barrier and deadbolt. At least this door would take some effort to break through. Her windows were another story, but he'd take what he could get.

Caleb pocketed the spare key, which Lana didn't even notice. It was just one more sign how thinly she'd been stretched today. He waited for her to start the shower before he called Monroe.

"We had an incident today," he told the colonel.

"I heard. Seems Detective Jacob Hart has done a little snooping into your records."

"What did you let him see?"

"The public stuff. The honors and commendations. I think he's got a crush."

Caleb gave an amused grunt. "I'm sure. Be careful with that one. He's smart."

Monroe offered a noise of acknowledgment. "I heard about the woman being shot. Did she make it?"

"Yes, sir. We're going back to the hospital to see her soon."

"Find out what happened. The police weren't able to get much out of her."

"I'll try. She took a blow to the head, so I don't know how much she'll remember," said Caleb. "One thing is for sure. That shooting was no coincidence."

Monroe grunted in agreement. "There's something else you should know."

"What?"

"Her office was bugged."

"What?" growled Caleb, feeling his muscles tighten.

"It wasn't cheap tech, either. Professional stuff."

"Ah, hell."

"How do you want to proceed?" asked Monroe.

"I have some names of people she works with who need background checks. A list of license-plate numbers from cars that drove by her office too many times. I'd like to see if Stacie has any background of her own that might be to blame for her shooting."

"Send the info via e-mail and I'll take care of it."

❧

Lana regretted losing the comfort of Caleb's shirt, but it didn't make sense for her to keep it now that she had her own clothes to wear. After she showered and dressed, she folded it back up, tossed her bloody jeans in the trash—no way was she ever wearing them again—and went out into the living room.

Caleb had rummaged in her fridge and thrown together some sandwiches. "I thought you might want to eat."

"Thanks." She grabbed a plate and went to the living room to sit down. There wasn't enough room for a table in her kitchen, and she'd gotten so used to eating in front of the TV that she hardly thought about it anymore.

Caleb followed her and sat on the other end of the couch. She placed his shirt between them. "Thanks for the loan."

"One of those blasted cops should have done the same thing. Guess they just liked looking a little too much."

His big body was sprawled out, his long legs crossed at the ankle. Tight denim covered his thick thighs, and it was all Lana could do not to stare.

She hadn't so much as had a spark of attraction for anyone since Armenia. There was simply nothing left of her to spare on a relationship. But as she stared at him, she felt something long dead come back to life—some deeply feminine part of her that took notice of things like thick, powerful legs. She should have been too worried about Stacie to even think such thoughts, a realization that doused her little spurt of longing with a dose of guilt.

Lana finished eating. "I need to get back to the hospital. Can you take me to get my car? The police are probably finished blocking off the parking lot by now."

"Are you sure you don't want a nap or something? The doc said it would be a few hours."

Lana looked up at him. "Is that what you did when I was in the hospital? Did you go home and sleep? Because to me, it felt like you were there the whole time."

Caleb looked away and took a drink of water. It was a delay tactic, and she knew it.

"I didn't realize you knew I'd been there," he said.

"I heard you. Saw you." She'd felt his hand stroke hers

so she knew she wasn't alone even when she'd been too weak to open her eyes.

"You saw me?"

She nodded. "Once. After you'd shaved." Miles Gentry had a bushy beard that obscured much of his face, but Caleb's jaw was smooth, only shadowed by the midnight stubble just beneath his skin. Just like it was right now.

"You remember seeing me even though you were full of pain meds and barely conscious?"

She wished those drugs had done a better job of obscuring her memory. Her life would have been a lot easier if she didn't have those memories of him caring about her to muddy the waters. Hatred was so much easier.

"I have a good memory for faces, and yours stuck, because at that moment, I hated you," she admitted quietly.

Caleb's mouth hardened and his voice went gruff. "That makes two of us."

Lana heard the sound of self-loathing in his tone, and she knew he was thinking about the seven people that died beside her in that cave. She knew because she spent a lot of time thinking about them, too, wondering why she was still alive and they weren't. What made her so special?

"Survivor's guilt" was what the doctors called it, but naming it didn't make it any easier to live with. Didn't make it go away.

"Why didn't you just let me die?" she asked in a whisper.

"Because I couldn't. I'd lost everyone else in that cave. I didn't want to lose you, too. You were all so young, trying to do good. I should have found a way to save everyone."

What could she say to a confession like that? Words held no value, so she reached out her hand and placed it on his much larger one in an attempt to offer what comfort she could. The blind leading the blind, maybe, but it was all she had to offer.

His hand was deeply tanned, in contrast to her sun-deprived skin, and so incredibly warm. Little scars dotted the flesh here and there but didn't detract from their masculine beauty. She imagined he'd earned every one of those scars fighting to protect others. Maybe there was even one there to mark the day he pulled her out of that cave after killing the man who had hurt her.

From the depth of his silence, she sensed his guilt, his suffering, and she didn't want that for him. Maybe things hadn't worked out so well for her, but it wasn't his fault. She knew in her heart he was a good man. A noble hero. He'd saved countless others, and she couldn't stand to watch him suffer, no matter how many bad memories his presence unearthed.

She had to swallow to relax her throat before she could speak. "There's something I've been wondering for a long time, and whenever I asked, Monroe and his men dodged the question."

"I'll tell you if I can," he said. "There are a lot of things I can't talk about, but I'll tell you the truth, even if it's just that I can't tell you anything."

"Why us?" she asked him. "Why was my group targeted? We weren't in hostile territory. We weren't doing any antiterrorist work. We were just a group of young people trying to make a small difference in the lives of a few women and children. I don't understand why we were taken."

Caleb pulled in a deep breath and stayed silent as if trying to find the right words. "The people who took you were out to prove themselves. They were trying to gain entry into a terrorist group, and that video that they took of the torture and killing was their audition tape, so to speak. It wouldn't have made any difference to them what you were doing there. All they wanted was an easy target—a group of several innocents they could use to earn their bones."

"So we were just in the wrong place at the wrong time?"

"I'm afraid there's not much more to it than that. It was bad luck that you were there, but if it hadn't been you, it would have been someone else."

"This group, are they the ones Monroe called the Swarm?"

Caleb nodded. "I'm surprised he told you that much."

"I think he thought I was going to die, so it wouldn't really matter," she told him. "He never told me what they want, though."

"Money. Power. There's nothing altruistic about them. They aren't fighting for some noble cause. They kill whoever they need to to get what they want. In much of the world, fear *is* power. People will do nearly anything to protect those they love. The Swarm knew that and used it as they would any other tool."

"You're telling me they're into torturing and killing people for money?"

"In most cases, yes. In your case it was for status. Prestige. Acceptance."

"So if they were all about money and power, then what were they doing targeting children?"

He paused as if deciding what to tell her, or maybe what not to tell her. "Sometimes the only way to get someone to cooperate—to give them information or help they need—is to threaten to take away the only thing that means more to a person than their honor or integrity."

"Their child," guessed Lana.

Caleb nodded. "It happens more often than anyone would like to believe. Sometimes we get a chance to stop it, but most of the time, people take the safer route where their children are concerned."

"They give in."

"Wouldn't you?" he asked.

She thought about her nephew, about her sister and her parents. There wasn't much she wouldn't do to protect them, be it honorable or not. "Your job . . . it's a lot harder than anyone knows, isn't it?"

He shrugged his wide shoulders as if it didn't matter how he felt about it. It was his job.

"I'm glad you do it," she said. "If you hadn't been there, I'd have died, too."

"I should have done a better job of protecting you and the others. I should have found a way to save them all."

"I was there, remember. I know the kind of evil you were up against. You did the best you could—the only thing you could."

She toyed with the soft fabric of his folded shirt, feeling restless and edgy. She didn't like dealing with the past, but she knew there was something she had to tell him. She owed him that much. "For a long time, I hated you for what you did. I know it wasn't fair, and that you were only doing your job, but you were an easy target, and I needed that anger to fuel my recovery—to give me the strength to keep going."

His eyes closed as if he was in pain. "Lana, please. We don't have to talk about this."

"No. You need to know." She had to get rid of this burden. Her life was too heavy to keep carrying it around, too. "I pushed myself to recover so that I could walk up to you one day and tell you how much I hated you for letting them hurt me. I thought about it all the time—how shocked you'd be. How humiliated and guilty you'd feel. Some days, it was the only thing that got me through physical therapy."

Her anger was the only thing holding her together then. She could barely stand living like that, but if she hadn't had that hatred and the goal it gave her, she was sure she would have given up. Her recovery had been nearly as painful as her torture.

Lana pushed those bleak memories aside. "And then you were here. And I had the chance to live out my fantasy and tell you how much I hated you."

"Why didn't you?" he asked. There was no accusation in his voice, just gentle curiosity.

"Because it would have been a lie. I hate what happened and I hate thinking about it, but for what it's worth, I don't hate you. Not anymore."

His hand turned over, and he laced his thick fingers through hers. "You have no idea how much that means to me."

❧

Caleb felt like he'd been handed a rare gift. She didn't hate him anymore. It was more than he'd ever hoped to hear her say.

She tidied up the kitchen while he just sat there in stunned silence. She didn't hate him.

Caleb's chest swelled with hope, and some unseen burden he'd been carrying lightened until he felt ten years younger. He hadn't realized until now just how much her opinion of him mattered. He should have been scared by how much it mattered, knowing that if he cared what she thought, he was already in trouble. But instead, he was too grateful for the gift she'd given him.

She didn't hate him. It was a long way from trust, but it was a start.

CHAPTER SEVEN

———— ❧ ————

Denny knew better than to let the call roll over to voice mail. Again. His boss had called three times, and until now, Denny hadn't been drunk enough to answer.

"What a naughty boy you are," said that emotionless robot voice.

"I didn't know anyone was going to come into work that early."

"You should have handled the situation better. Now the police are crawling all over the place, patrolling her office every twenty minutes."

"I know," he said, propping his pounding head in his hand. He'd fucked up big-time. He'd panicked when that lady came in. He hadn't meant to shoot her, but the damn gun had gone off, and then there was all that blood.

Denny swallowed hard to keep from puking.

"Did you find what I was looking for?" asked the robot.

"No. Nothing like that. Just business stuff. There was a flyer that had some photos of kids on it, but no drawings."

"And you checked everywhere?"

Denny considered lying, but the thought that his boss

might figure it out, on top of him botching the job, was just too frightening. Bruce had come by today and told him he had a week to pay up his dad's debt. He hadn't said anything else, but the baseball bat propped up in the back of Bruce's convertible had done plenty of talking for him.

"I couldn't get to one of the file cabinets in back. The lady walked in before I finished."

"You can't go back now. The police will interfere."

"I'm sorry I screwed up. It won't happen again."

"I know," said his boss, but whether it was in response to his first statement or his second, Denny had no idea. That was less than comforting.

"What do you want me to do now?"

"I'm not sure I can trust you any longer."

Desperation clawed inside Denny's sour stomach. "Please give me another chance. I swear I won't fuck up this time."

Silence stretched out for a long time, making Denny squirm.

"There is one more thing I need you to do, but it is considerably more dangerous than your last job."

Nothing was more dangerous than facing Bruce again without money in hand. "Anything. I'll do it."

He could almost hear the smile in the metallic voice. "Good boy."

❧

Stacie was pale but smiling when Lana was finally allowed to see her. They shared a teary hug that Lana was careful not to put too much force behind. Stacie's normally perfect makeup was smudged in some places and missing in others, and rather than a crisp blouse, she wore a droopy hospital gown.

"How are you feeling?" asked Lana.

"Like I've been shot," joked Stacie. "But they tell me I'll live."

"Have the police been bothering you?"

"Not much. They had a few questions, but there was so little I could tell them they just gave up and went away."

Lana felt Caleb's presence as he stepped up behind her. He said, "I'm sorry to have to ask you more questions, but I really need to have you tell us what you saw."

Stacie leaned her head back on the pillow. "Not much. I unlocked the door, turned on the lights, and a man came out of the back room where we keep all the files and office supplies. He pointed a gun at me, told me to get into the bathroom, so I did."

"Did you see his face?"

"He wore a mask, but I could see enough skin around his eyes and mouth to tell he had coloring about like yours, Caleb. He was youngish. His eyes were bloodshot like maybe he was on drugs."

"How young?"

"No wrinkles yet, and there was this . . . wildness about his eyes that make me think he was new to the whole armed-robbery experience. I'd guess midtwenties, but it's hard to be sure."

"So then what happened?" asked Caleb.

"I went into the bathroom like he said. I backed in, keeping my eyes on that gun. I guess I wasn't fast enough, because he shoved me. I started to fall and reached for him to catch my balance—which was a stupid reflex.

That's when the gun went off. I hit my head on the sink, or maybe the toilet. That's all I remember until Lana showed up." Stacie smiled at her. "They said you saved my life— that if I'd gone much longer without help I would have bled to death. Thank you."

"Don't thank me. If it weren't for me, you'd never have been there in the first place. You'd have been working in an office with decent security."

"Don't be ridiculous. You didn't invite that robber in. He made his choices all on his own."

Caleb's voice was gentle but insistent. "Is there anything else you can remember? The sound of his voice? The way he smelled? Something he said?"

"Sorry," said Stacie. Her eyes drooped heavily and she gave a big yawn. "I wish I could help more. Now you see why the police stopped bothering me so fast."

Lana saw Stacie was wilting. "We'll get out of your hair so you can get your rest. Is there anything you need?"

Stacie's eyes shut as if she just couldn't keep them open any longer. "Just promise me you'll go see the kids and meet our new volunteer. I know you're busy, but I told them I'd get you out there this week, one way or another. Don't make me a liar."

"I'll go," agreed Lana.

"Now?"

"Right now." It was almost six, and most of the kids would be gone. The center closed at seven, so going tonight would ensure a quick visit, and then she could get back to work. There was a lot to catch up on, and Stacie was in no condition to help.

Lana was on her own.

꠸

Lana had Caleb park behind the youth center and took him in the back entrance. Caleb followed her in through the employees' door she had to use a card key to open. They went down a long hall lined with office doors.

This part of the building was made up of offices, storage and utility areas, and a small break room. Down the long hall were restrooms and double doors that led into the gymnasium and craft area.

Most of the offices were empty, but that was going to change once they had better funding. This building would become the headquarters for the First Light Foundation, filled with people like herself who were passionate about making a difference in kids' lives.

"Why don't you keep your office here?" asked Caleb. "You'd be safer around more people."

"The lease on the other office isn't up yet, but Stacie and I will move when it is." Maybe sooner, now.

"How many people work for you?"

"Four, including Stacie. The rest are volunteers."

"Do you do background checks on those volunteers?"

"Absolutely. I'd never let them near the kids without one. Plus we have strict rules for our volunteers as another layer of protection for the kids."

"That's good. Smart."

Peggy, one of Lana's employees, was still working when Lana and Caleb walked by.

"Hey, Lana," she called from her desk. "Hold on a sec."

Lana stepped into the woman's office, feeling Caleb's

bulk right behind her. Peggy's office was a chaotic mess, but Lana didn't feel the need to say a thing. As long as Peggy kept bringing in the volunteers, she could raise livestock in here for all Lana cared.

"How is Stacie?" Peggy asked. Concern lined her wide face, looking odd on her. Lana was too used to seeing her smile.

"She's doing okay. A little weak, but they said she'll pull through. She's a fighter."

"I'm going to go see her tomorrow before work if you think she'll be up to it."

"I'm sure she'd love to see you."

Peggy eyed Caleb. "Who's this?"

"A friend of mine visiting from out of town."

"Ma'am," greeted Caleb in a deep drawl.

Peggy smiled and blushed. She was a happily married mother of four, grandmother of ten, but with all his muscles and that quiet confidence, Caleb was the kind of man a woman enjoyed watching no matter how old she was.

"Care to join the ranks of volunteers?" asked Peggy.

Lana explained, "She's in charge of recruiting our volunteers. Watch out, or she'll have you slaving away before you know what's happened."

"I'd be happy to help out while I'm here if I can," offered Caleb.

"Sold. I'll hold you to it," said Peggy. "Speaking of volunteers, we have a new one. She's a little upper-crust, but I think she'll be great once the kids break her out of her shell. I'd like you to meet her if you have the time. She's here now."

"Sure," said Lana. "Just let me duck into the little girls'

room and I'll be right there. Do you mind showing Caleb around for a minute?"

Peggy grinned wider. "My pleasure."

Caleb offered the older woman his thick arm. "Shall we?"

Lana watched them walk down the hall. Caleb's steps were slow and careful in deference to Peggy's aged gait. He said something low that Lana couldn't hear and had Peggy laughing before they'd disappeared through the double doors.

Lana went into the bathroom and found herself anxious to get back to Caleb's side. She wasn't sure how it had happened, or when, but she was getting used to having him around.

She scolded herself for being so foolish. Caleb couldn't stay. He had a job to do and as soon as he was convinced she knew nothing, he'd leave.

Lana flushed the toilet and opened the stall door. Standing there, not ten feet away, alone in the bathroom with her, was the woman who had ordered Lana's death.

CHAPTER EIGHT

❧

The killer was tall, maybe three or four inches taller than Lana. And beautiful—elegant in her tailored suit and expensive jewelry.

"I'm your new volunteer, Kara McIntire," she said. She smiled and reached out her hand for Lana to shake.

Lana couldn't move. Couldn't breathe. Time crawled by, suffocating her more with every passing second. Her heart still pounded, her blood still moved in painfully sluggish pulses through her body, but it didn't matter. She was already dead. Kara had found her, and it was all over. She was going to die on a dirty bathroom floor with help only a shout away.

But Lana couldn't shout. Her lungs burned from lack of oxygen, but she couldn't drag in any air—just like in her nightmares.

"Are you okay?" asked Kara in a mockery of concern.

A sliver of doubt stabbed at Lana, getting her attention. Maybe she was hallucinating. Certainly a killer wouldn't walk up and introduce herself. Not unless she was toying with Lana.

Or testing her.

Kara couldn't know that Lana had seen her face. No

one knew, which was why she was still alive after eighteen months. If Lana could fool Kara into believing it, maybe Kara would let her live. What use could there be in killing her and risking getting caught when all Kara had to do was walk away knowing her secret was safe? All Lana had to do was pretend Kara was a stranger and she might live.

Reach out and shake her hand. That's what she was supposed to do now.

"Do you need help?" Kara asked, taking a step forward.

Lana barely stifled a flinch. "Sorry. I thought I was going to get sick again for a minute there."

"You're sick?"

"Just a stomach bug," she lied. "I'm feeling a little better now."

A smile brightened Kara's face, and she extended her hand again. "That's good to hear. I've been looking forward to meeting you. Everyone around here loves you."

Lana couldn't bring herself to touch Kara. She wasn't strong enough to touch her and not scream. So, she said, "Haven't washed my hands yet," and proceeded to do just that, taking her time.

Her fingers were trembling, and she prayed Kara hadn't seen it. "So, you're our new volunteer?"

"That's right. Just signed on this week. I've heard so much about your work I had to come help out."

Lana's hands were more than clean. She was starting to look foolish, so she turned off the water and dried them. "Do you live nearby?"

"Just down the road. Well, it's my mother's house, but I decided to move back after she died."

"I'm sorry for your loss." Lana was sure the words didn't sound sincere. She was too stunned by the fact that this killer had a mother to put any feeling into her voice.

Kara shrugged. "Death is just part of life."

She would know. She'd caused enough of it.

Lana shoved her hands into her pockets to ward off any more of Kara's attempts to shake. "What do you do for a living?"

"I'm a day trader. You know, stocks and options?"

Liar! Lana wanted to scream and lash out at her for what she'd done, but she managed to hold her tongue. "Sounds exciting."

"It has its moments. I think working with the kids will be even more . . . rewarding, though. Don't you think?"

No way was Lana letting her spend any time alone with the kids. The thought made her skin crawl. "Peggy explained our rules to you, right?"

"You mean how I'm not allowed to do any activities with the children for at least three months?"

"That's right. You can help set up and clean up, but we have to be strict about screening out the weirdos."

"I thought that's what the background check was for."

"It is. We're just careful."

"That's good to know. You wouldn't want any unpleasantness."

Too late for that.

Kara cocked her head to one side. "You look familiar. Have we met?"

Lana felt acid rise in her throat. She had to get out of here. "No. I don't think so."

"I could have sworn I've seen you somewhere before."

"Probably in the newspapers."

Lana reached for the door, but Kara was faster. Their hands collided near the handle, and Kara's were reptile cold.

Her voice was elegant and warm. "It's such a thrill to be here. I'm sure you and I will be spending lots of time together."

Over Lana's dead body. Maybe literally.

This was too much. Lana needed to get away and think for a minute—decide what to do.

She let Kara open the door for her rather than risk contact again. When she came out, Caleb was waiting for her. As soon as he saw her, he frowned and stepped forward.

"You okay?" he asked.

"Fine."

"You don't look fine."

Behind Caleb, Kara was talking with Peggy. The older woman smiled at something Kara said and Kara put a hand on Peggy's shoulder.

Lana pulled her eyes away. She couldn't stand to watch that killer touch her friend.

She had to get away and think. Pull herself together. Caleb was watching her too closely. He was going to see something was wrong and give her away. She couldn't let that happen.

"I'm worried about Stacie. I need to call her. I'm going back to one of the offices to use the phone."

"Want me to tag along?"

"No. I'll be back in a few minutes," said Lana.

She wasn't sure an eternity would be long enough to calm her down, but she had to try.

Caleb gave her a solemn nod. "Don't be long, or I'm coming to find you."

Great. Like she didn't have enough pressure.

"Wait here," she told him and retreated back to the offices. Lana found the first empty office she could and locked herself inside.

Kara was here at First Light.

Panic started to close in around her, blocking off her air. She slid to the floor, hugging her knees to her chest, trying to take up as little space as possible. Maybe if she was small enough, Kara wouldn't find her.

She was panting. Nearly hyperventilating. A low, terrified whimper fell from her lips with every rapid breath.

What if Kara could hear her? What if she was on the other side of the door, listening?

Lana clamped her mouth closed and sucked in air through her nose. She scrambled away from the door to the farthest corner of the office. She huddled there, hugging herself and rocking. She had no idea how long she was there, but slowly, she got control over her panic, and her breathing started to even out.

She had to think.

From the time Lana had seen that flash of sunlight reflecting off binoculars on the hillside outside of the cave in Armenia, she knew someone might find her. She didn't know who had been watching her then, but she did now. The only protection she could devise was based on a short conversation she'd overheard while in the cave.

"Do you want me to kill his wife, too?" asked one of Kara's goons.

"No," she answered. *"She knows nothing. Killing her would only draw attention we don't need."*

If Lana pretended to know nothing, could that save her life as it had saved that unknown woman? Could it keep her family safe?

She had to believe so. It was the only thing she could think to grasp a hold of. The only glimmer of hope she could find.

Sure, she could tell Caleb. Maybe he'd even be able to get rid of Kara forever. But what good would that do when the other three men she'd seen found out Kara was gone? They'd know she'd identified Kara and realize she'd seen them, too. They'd come after her.

They'd come after her family.

Her parents and sister were listed in the phone book. Anyone with an Internet connection could find out where they lived and retaliate. If Lana said a thing, she was sure that whether she lived or died, her family would suffer. She had to protect them, and the only way to do that was to keep her mouth shut.

Staying silent had worked for eighteen months. Everyone she loved was still safe. It would continue to work. She had to believe that. She couldn't face the possibility that she would fail. She'd find a way to smile at Kara if that's what it took. She'd shake her hand. Hug her. Whatever it took, she'd do it. It was the only way.

Once Kara believed that Lana knew nothing, she'd go away. Everyone would be safe, and this nightmare would finally be over for good.

Lana pushed her trembling body to her feet and pulled in a deep breath. She wiped the tears off her face, straightened her clothes, squared her shoulders, and went to face her enemy.

❧

Caleb had just decided to hunt Lana down when she came back into the gymnasium. Something was definitely wrong. She was pale, and even from here he could see her shaking. He watched as Lana took a few deep breaths like he used to do when he'd first learned how to parachute out of airplanes.

Caleb excused himself from Peggy and went to Lana. Up close, he could see a fine layer of sweat along her hairline and goose bumps on her arms. Without thinking, he rubbed his hands up and down her arms to warm her. "Is Stacie okay? You looked a little freaked out."

"She's fine."

"Then what's wrong?"

"I'm fine."

"You don't look fine." He pressed his wrist to her forehead to see if she was fevered. She was cool and clammy.

She swatted him away and plastered a fake, dimpleless smile on her mouth. "I'm not sick. It's just been a long day."

"Let me take you home." Where he could take care of her.

"In a little while. I want to play with the kids first."

One of the younger children saw her and squealed, racing over to give her a hug. "Lana's back!" shouted several of the other kids as they, too, saw her.

Lana's fake smile turned genuine, and her dimples returned as she soaked up the attention of about ten kids.

Hugs all around, they finally backed up enough to let her walk into the room.

"You gonna give us art class today?" asked a boy about seven years old. He wore a stained shirt and jeans with too many holes. His hands were covered in smudges of green marker, some of which had transferred to his face where he'd touched it.

"Not today, Jeremy. It's too late to start a class, but I'd love to see your latest drawings."

Jeremy grinned and raced off to the wall that was lined with coat racks and small lockers, and started digging for his papers.

After a few minutes of excited chatting and an art show by Jeremy, the kids thinned out. They went back to their basketball games and coloring books. Two adults who'd been watching the mob of kids came over. One was a man in his late thirties, and the other was a strikingly beautiful woman. The man would have been handsome if anger hadn't shaped his face into a sour mask. He was heavily muscled but moved awkwardly, as if he wasn't used to his own body. His arms swung out at his sides, sticking out like there just wasn't room for them to hang against his body with all that muscle in the way. He looked at Lana with frankly sexual interest, tainted with the anger of repeated rejections. Caleb sized him up swiftly and decided to keep a close eye on this man. Between his bulk and attitude, he was a possible threat to Lana.

The woman was nearly six feet tall and simply gorgeous. Her golden blond hair was pulled back in a sleek twist of some kind, and she wore an outfit that looked like it had been stripped from a first lady, complete with pearls. She wore a subtle floral perfume that probably cost more per ounce than gold. The legs peeking out under her skirt were shapely and long, and even though she was likely nearing forty, she still had the kind of beauty that could turn men's heads.

There was something familiar about her that Caleb couldn't place, and he worked his brain to remember.

"Who's your friend?" asked the woman, giving Caleb a thorough perusal.

He felt Lana tense beside him and shot her a quick glance. That plastic, dimple-less smile was bright on her face, but her eyes were too wide. "This is my friend Caleb. Caleb, meet Kara McIntire and Phil Macy. Volunteers."

Phil held out a beefy hand in greeting. "New boyfriend, Lana?" He squeezed Caleb's hand hard, entering one of the older, more childish pissing contests around. Caleb smiled as he squeezed back hard enough to make the bones in Phil's hand shift. Phil relented with a grimace and put his hand behind his back, likely to massage it.

Caleb nodded his head toward the woman but didn't offer to shake hands, because she didn't seem inclined to, either. "Ma'am. Nice to meet you."

"The pleasure is entirely mine," purred Kara in a rich voice that matched her elegant attire.

"We heard about Stacie," said Phil. "How is she?"

"She'll recover, but it's going to take a while," said Lana.

Kara offered a gentle smile. "I hardly got a chance to know her, but I could tell we were going to be good friends."

"She'll be back in a couple weeks, I'm sure. I'll tell her you were thinking about her next time I talk to her," offered Lana.

"That would be lovely," said Kara, dismissing the topic of Stacie with a wave of her hand. Her eyes roamed up and down Caleb's body in a blatant show of admiration. "I'm looking forward to seeing you again," she said, then walked away in a lovely swing of hips. Phil wasn't far behind, panting after her.

Lana stood there, motionless, breathing a little too rapidly as if relieved.

Caleb stepped in front of her, blocking her from the rest of the room. He bent his knees and tilted up her chin so she couldn't escape eye contact. For a moment, he was distracted by the startling beauty of her blue eyes fringed by dark lashes. "Has Phil been bothering you, Lana?"

He saw her face shut down. No warmth, no anger. Just the neutral mask of a mannequin. "No."

"I can speak with him. Make sure he knows to leave you alone. I promise when we're done chatting he won't go within twenty feet of you."

"Don't you dare. He's harmless and I don't want your interference."

"I'm not so sure about that, especially not after what happened to Stacie."

"*You* don't have to be sure."

"Promise me that if he bothers you, you'll let me know."

She hesitated for a moment as if she was going to say something different, but what came out was, "Okay. I promise that if Phil bothers me, I'll tell you."

Caleb gave a nod, but he wasn't satisfied at all. There was something she wasn't saying, but he had no idea what. He hated not being able to read her beneath that artificial expression.

She walked off to join the kids who were coloring at the table. Caleb hung back and watched as she chatted with them, sometimes picking up a crayon or marker to help them color. One of the little girls asked her to draw a puppy, and Lana smiled indulgently. "Here, sit right beside me and draw what I draw," said Lana to the girl.

The little girl watched Lana's paper as if waiting for a miracle to appear, but Lana hesitated. The pencil in her hand quivered as her hand shook and she closed her eyes in defeat. "My hand is tired. How about I use yours?"

The girl nodded happily as Lana put the child on her lap and guided the chubby little hand over the paper. The puppy they drew was lopsided, but the girl ran off squealing with pride to show it to her big brother, who was playing basketball.

Caleb looked back at Lana and saw the pain of loss on her face. He remembered those sketches in her apartment—how lifelike they were—and wondered if something had happened to her hands to make her unable to draw. Her left hand had been broken in Armenia, but her right had only been a little bruised. He knew because he'd spent hours holding her hand, praying that she'd live.

Before he realized what he was doing, Caleb had gone to her and wrapped his hands over her slim shoulders. She felt delicate under his fingers, but Caleb knew that was an illusion. Lana Hancock was made of tempered steel.

She was stiff under his grip, but she didn't flinch away.

"You look beat. Let me take you home," he offered.

He felt her sigh, her shoulders rising and falling with the long breath. "I should go back to the office, clean up the mess, see what can be salvaged."

"You're exhausted. Let it go for tonight."

"I wish I could, but there's so damn much to do, and now, with Stacie in the hospital—"

"Let it go tonight and I'll lend a hand tomorrow. I'm not Stacie, but maybe I can help."

She turned around and leaned back so she could look up at him. She had the oddest look on her face—a mix of hope and desperation that made his heart ache with the need to hold her and make her life a happy place. "I wish you could, Caleb. You have no idea how much."

CHAPTER NINE

———— ❧ ————

Kara's hand shook with excitement as she dialed Marcus Lark. She wasn't sure if he was going to be pleased or angry that Caleb Stone was in town, but both prospects were thrilling, each in its own way.

"Hello, love," came Marcus's deep voice from over a thousand miles away.

Kara let a shiver course over her body at the sound of his voice. "I miss you," she told him.

"Of course you do. I was hoping you'd be home soon."

He hadn't said he missed her, but Kara refused to pout. Marcus wasn't a man given to affection or empty words. He was a man of action, and Kara was determined to prove to him that she was the kind of woman who could be his equal, the kind of woman who wouldn't turn squeamish in the face of hardship.

"I was making you a gift."

An interested lilt colored his tone. "Oh? What sort of gift?"

"A video. Would you like to hear a sample?"

At his silence, she pressed play and held the phone near the speaker on her laptop. Lana's terrified screams shrieked from the speakers, and the image of her body writhing in imagined pain filled the screen. Marcus was going to love it.

"You've finished the job, then, I take it."

He thought those screams meant Lana was dead. Kara did pout then. She'd worked hard to collect all this footage and meld it together in a seamless montage of Lana's suffering. It was a gift from the heart and yet still not enough for him.

Nothing she did for him was ever enough. That had to change. She couldn't let him send her out on her own again. She would never go back to that life.

"I saw her today. Spoke to her."

"You're not there to toy with her."

"I planned to finish it tonight," she told him, unable to keep the sharpness from her tone. He'd punish her for that when she got home, but she'd learned to like that, too.

"I told you not to call until it was done."

"I thought you would want to know that there's been a development. Caleb Stone came to town. He's with her now."

There was a long pause and the sound of grating teeth coming from the phone. "It's too late, then. You'll never get to her now. Come home. We need to talk."

Icy fear lanced through her body. She knew that tone. Marcus was more than simply mad, he was enraged. She'd failed him, and he was going to send her away. "I can still do it. I swear."

"How do you plan to kill her without getting caught?"

"You have no faith in me."

"Too much is at stake. We allowed Caleb and his men to destroy the Swarm so they would leave us alone. If

Caleb finds out that any of the old members survived, it will start a hunt. It's much easier to do business when none of his kind are watching us. I will not let you compromise that advantage."

"I won't. I would never do anything like that to you." Surely she'd proved her loyalty to him by now.

"How can you possibly prevent it if you proceed now? If anything happens to the girl, it will be obvious who did it."

"No. I'm being careful. I've hired help that can't be linked back to us."

"To me, you mean."

"Yes. Of course, to you."

"You are expendable," he reminded her in a cruel tone.

And that cruelty hurt. She loved him so much. All she ever wanted was to make him happy, to be by his side and feel like she belonged there. "I know."

The heat left his voice. It dropped to a low, seductive tone. "Come home to me, love. We'll figure out what to do together."

"I can't let you down like that. I'll finish what I started. You'll see I can do it. Just give me a little time."

Another long pause had her sweating. She knew that if he ordered her to come home, she would go. She would do anything for him, even if it meant letting him vent his anger on her. It wasn't his fault she made him so angry.

"Fine. But if you do anything to compromise me, don't bother coming back. I'll find you."

❖

Lana slid under the cool sheets and stared at the ceiling. The fan twirled lazily overhead, sending a breeze over her arms and face. With all the lights in the room on and the heat of summer outside, the fan was the only thing keeping the room comfortable.

Lana should have been too wired to sleep after a day like today, but instead she was exhausted. Even the fear of dreaming couldn't keep her from her bed. The worry that Caleb would bust in again made her hesitate, but she couldn't do anything to drive him away. He was still sitting outside in his car after stuffing her full of food and driving her home.

She wasn't sure how she'd managed to get the food down, but she did. It was all part of the act. Nothing was wrong. He might as well leave, although she wasn't so sure she wanted him to go anymore.

At least she knew he could protect himself if Kara came after him.

Lana wondered if Kara recognized Caleb as Miles Gentry. More important, she wondered if he'd recognized Kara—if he knew she was the woman who'd run the operation in Armenia, the woman who had ordered Lana's death.

Lana wasn't sure that Caleb and Kara had ever actually met, since Kara's goon had served as the go-between as well as the muscle. Lana had seen her only once, but that had been enough. Fear had imprinted her face on Lana's memory the way nothing else could.

Tonight Lana had been watching both Kara and Caleb closely, and she didn't think that either one of them recognized the other. If so, they hid it well.

All this subterfuge made Lana's head ache. She

couldn't keep up with all the lies, and it was wearing her thin. If it hadn't been for Caleb's support today at the hospital, she didn't think she would have made it through.

He hadn't hovered or pushed her. He'd just been there, ready to help in whatever way she needed. Lana wasn't used to that kind of treatment. Her family's idea of helping was either babying her to the point where she wasn't even allowed to feed herself or pushing her to lay all her pain and grief out in the open so she could "heal." Neither one worked for her, but there was something about Caleb's quiet support that made her burdens feel lighter.

Maybe fate hadn't sent him back into her life to torture her, after all.

Then again, maybe this was fate's way of giving her something only to rip it away later. Like her ex-fiancé, or her drawing, or her feeling of security. She had to remember that Caleb wasn't going to become a permanent fixture. She couldn't come to depend on him too much, because, unlike what she believed she'd had with Oran, Lana knew that Caleb's presence was only temporary. The more temporary, the better—the safer—for everyone.

❧

Caleb stretched out as much as he could in his rental car and downloaded the data from the mini-cam in Lana's apartment. The break-in at her office bothered him, and not just because Stacie had been hurt, or because it could have just as easily been Lana who'd shown up to work first. It bothered him because there was nothing of value to steal, and any robber worth his salt would have broken in to either the walk-in clinic for a possible score of pain meds or the print shop, which was full of expensive computer equipment. So if the break-in wasn't for the sake of robbery, then it was for something else. The perp had definitely been looking for something. What could Lana have in her office that someone would want? And what did it have to do with what happened in Armenia, if anything? Even if the Swarm had somehow survived and was still operating, the only thing they'd want is Lana's death—proof that no one could escape their grasp. Whoever had broken in had wanted something more. What could they possibly think she was hiding at work? It didn't make any sense inside the framework the Swarm operated in.

His laptop chimed, indicating the data stored on the camera was ready to view. Caleb pulled up the image of Lana's apartment during the time they'd been gone today and scanned through it in fast motion, looking for anything unusual. About seven hours into the footage, Lana's new front door opened, and someone who was covered from head to toe in black came in. He was fairly tall, nearly six feet, with a thin build. He moved confidently as he swept into the apartment, heading straight for Lana's bookshelves. He pulled out a book and leafed through it, looking carefully at each page. Caleb couldn't read the title or see what the intruder was looking at.

After he finished looking at the book, he went to the far wall, unscrewed the faceplate on the electrical outlet, and pulled something out of the hole. Something else went back in, the faceplate was put back on, and the man left the apartment as easily as he'd come in.

The whole section of footage covered maybe a minute, and Caleb realized that he'd just seen a pro at work. Whoever that man was, he knew what he was doing. And he was listening to every word Lana said.

Caleb's stomach iced over, and he felt himself slipping into that adrenaline-altered state that prepared him for battle, stretching out each second into an endless eternity. By the time he reached Lana's apartment, he knew exactly what he needed to do to get her out of her bugged house safely without letting whoever was listening, and possibly watching her, know.

CHAPTER TEN

━━━━❖━━━━

Lana had just changed into a comfy pair of short pajamas when she saw Caleb striding toward her apartment. There was a strange look on his face that she'd never seen him wear before. It was fierce, determined, without a hint of mercy anywhere.

He knocked once before she got the door unlocked and opened it for him. "What is it?"

Caleb didn't wait for her to step aside to let him in, he just moved forward, crowding her with his big body. "I'm sorry, baby," he said in a low, fervent voice. "I couldn't stay away. I need you too much."

Lana blinked in confusion and opened her mouth to ask him what the hell he was talking about when his mouth covered hers in a kiss, silencing her. His arms slid around her, and she heard the front door being kicked shut.

Lana went stiff with shock for about two seconds before all her questions faded away. She hadn't been kissed since before she left for Armenia. She'd forgotten how wonderful it was. That flush of heat, that spurt of excitement shooting through her limbs, that heavy, languid warmth that made her go weak in a really nice way. She was hungry for it. Her body took over and decided that this was a good thing. Very good.

She had no clue why Caleb was kissing her, but she didn't care. She drank it in, starved for the contact of a man after being alone so long. And not just any man. Caleb. A hero with a body that that was carved by the hand of God for a woman's pleasure. He was strength personified, and she felt all those masculine ridges pressing against her body. It was enough to make a woman melt and give herself up to whatever he had in mind, no matter how insane.

His tongue teased her mouth open and she gave him entry, sighing with pleasure at his boldness. One wide hand pressed against the small of her back, holding her tight to his hard body while the other hand cradled her head, guiding her so he could nibble his way to her ear. Everything he did felt right and she wanted more—wanted to kiss him back so he'd never stop. She tried to kiss his mouth, but he held her immobile.

In a quiet, breathless voice, he said, "You're being watched. Play along."

Her brain stuttered trying to make sense of what he said, but finally gave up. There was no sense to be made. Her whole world narrowed to the few square inches where his bare skin touched hers—his fingertips sliding under the hem of her pajama shirt, the press of his lips along the edge of her ear. She'd never felt anything so completely right in her life, and nothing else mattered.

Her heart pumped hard, heating her blood, making her feel both powerful and weak at the same time. Lana went up on tiptoe and guided his mouth back to hers, where it belonged. A rough, pleased male rumble vibrated against her breasts, making her nipples harden.

"Shower," he whispered against her mouth.

"What?"

"I need to get you into the shower." He sounded tense. Desperate. When her feet didn't move fast enough, he picked her up and carried her into the bathroom, then set her down to turn on the water.

Lana didn't understand why he needed the shower, but she wasn't sure she cared. Without his touch fogging her brain, her head had cleared enough to ask him, "Caleb, what are you—" but then he pulled her back up against his big body and silenced her with another scorching kiss. His fingers clenched against her hips, and she could feel the hard length of his erection pressing into her belly.

Lana's mouth went dry at the proof of his desire for her. She couldn't remember the last time she felt desired, and she'd never felt it quite like that before. The man was definitely built in perfect proportion—big everywhere.

He stripped his shirt off over his head, giving Lana access to the sprawling width of his bare chest. Dark hair accentuated the deep ridges of his muscles, which his clothing had partially concealed. Her hands couldn't resist the lure of all that naked male skin, and she trailed her fingertips lightly over his pecs and down his ribs. Caleb shuddered, and his dark eyes shut tight as if he were trying to focus.

He grabbed her wandering hands and held them hostage as he tested the temperature of the water. A second later, Lana was lifted into the tub, and he pulled the curtain closed behind them. He maneuvered her under the pounding stream of water, dousing her from head to toe despite her clothing.

She surrendered to his strange treatment, allowing her hands to slide up over his thick shoulders and back down along the muscles of his spine. Needy little noises were rising up in her throat, and there was nothing she could do to stop them. He felt too good. Tasted too good.

Lana's hands encountered his clothing, and she looked down to see he still wore his jeans, which had turned dark with moisture, and his heavy boots.

Something about this picture wasn't right, but Lana's brain was too busy dealing with a sudden dose of lust poisoning to care. She tugged her wet PJ shirt over her head, boldly displaying her naked breasts.

Caleb let out a low, pained groan, and his fingers clenched against her hips. "I don't know how much more I can take," he whispered so softly she barely heard it over the pounding of water on the tiles.

"A lot more, I hope," she told him and pressed her breasts against his muscled body. The springy hair rasped lightly over her nipples, sending shockwaves of current racing along her nerves. She felt her body heat further until the warm water felt cool against her skin.

His fingers plunged into her wet hair, and he bent down to whisper in her ear. "We have to stop now or I'm not going to be able to."

"Then don't."

"They might be watching, and if things are going to go any farther, I'd rather not have an audience."

Lana had no idea what he was talking about. "Watching?"

Her voice wasn't as quiet as his had been, and he si-

lenced her with his mouth. Lana parted her lips and made
a demanding foray with her tongue. She felt Caleb's muscles trembling with effort, and after a moment, he pulled
away from her mouth. Lana tried to follow him, but he
used his body to pin her against the cool tile.

She shuddered as she felt the weight of his body hot
along her front and the hard tiles cold against her back.
Her wrists were captured tight in one of his big hands, and
even as slippery as the water made their skin, she couldn't
break away to touch him.

He gave her a stern look, but his eyes were black with
need. "Listen!" he whispered urgently. "I need you to
listen."

Without his mouth on hers driving her stupid, sanity
started to return. Something was wrong. He was trying to
tell her something was wrong.

Lana stopped fighting against his hold.

Caleb let out a relieved sigh and leaned near her ear
again, still holding her body immobile. "Your house is
bugged. The water is covering our voices, but we need to
get out without them knowing we know."

Fear made blood drain from Lana's limbs until she was
hardly strong enough to stand. Her house was bugged.
Oh, God.

Caleb must have seen that she'd finally come to her
senses, because his grip on her hands relaxed. "I'm going
to get you out of here—I just need you to follow my
lead."

Lana gave him a shaky nod.

"Damn!" said Caleb loud enough to be heard over the
water. "I forgot the condoms."

"Forgot them?" she asked. Her voice was perfect—all rough with unquenched desire and frustration.

"It's okay, baby. I'll make it up to you," he gave her an open-mouthed kiss just under her ear.

Lana's body arched against him despite her orders to stay still. "How are you going to do that?"

"How about a nice getaway. Hotel room with room service. Champagne. Giant tub big enough for two."

"What is it with you and sex in the shower?"

"I like you nice and wet," he said in a deep, sexy tone.

Lana felt something low in her belly clench tight against a wave of lust. Caleb's grip tightened again, and it wasn't until she felt it that she realized she'd tried to get free to touch him again. She wanted to run her hands over his body until she convinced him to strip naked and slide hot and thick inside her.

Caleb's voice shook when he asked, "Is it a deal?"

"Room service and champagne?" she asked, trying to sound petulant, and failing. There was too much need in her voice, and she couldn't do anything about it.

"You bet, baby. Anything you want."

"Including you?"

"Especially me."

❧

Moving his body away from Lana's had been one of the hardest things Caleb had ever done. He backed away slowly, feeling the caress of her tight little nipples over his skin. He couldn't stop himself from letting out a nearly silent hiss of pleasure.

He was shaking with unsatisfied lust. It pumped hot

and hard through his veins, luring him to finish what his ingenious lie had started. The plan had seemed simple enough—get Lana to pretend to have sex with him in the shower while he used the water to cover their conversation, as well as possibly shorting out any bugs that might be on her clothing.

Not that she was wearing much. Just a tiny little shirt and matching shorts that showed off legs so shapely he barely even noticed the surgical scars. She wore no bra or panties underneath, just smooth, hot skin that shivered under his touch.

That part hadn't been acting. In fact, he didn't think that anything she'd done had been an act until the very last. Lana wanted him, and the knowledge was enough to bring Caleb to his knees. If the history between them hadn't been so full of land mines, he would have taken her without hesitation. He would have pinned her against the tile and filled her up until they were both too wild to care that the water had run cold. He would have tried to give her the kind of pleasure that erased past pain, or at least dulled the memory of it. When she stripped her shirt off and bared her sweet, pink-tipped breasts, Caleb nearly lost his resolve not to do just that. It had been a close thing, and he knew that if he watched her getting out of the shower, he'd be a goner.

Caleb dunked his head under the spray, making sure enough water went into his eyes to keep him blind. A moment later he heard her say, "Here's a towel."

Caleb shut off the water. She was wrapped in a thick towel, her dark hair dripping water onto her slender shoulders. Her lips were a bit puffy and her eyes a bit wide, but her chin was high and she showed no sign of fear. Caleb admired the hell out of her for that courage. Not just any woman could stand there calmly after just finding out that her house was bugged.

"I'll throw some clothes on and be out in a sec," she told him.

Caleb did the best he could to dry off his soaked jeans and pulled his shirt back on. He gathered up her tooth-brush, her hairbrush, and a few toiletries he thought she'd need, and by the time he had, she was dressed and waiting for him.

She gave him an impatient wave of her hand, and he hoped that anyone watching wouldn't be able to see the way it shook. "Let's go."

CHAPTER ELEVEN

Lana sat in the car unable to speak. She'd made such a complete fool of herself coming on to Caleb like that. How could she have been so stupid not to see that he was just playing a role? He played Caleb the seducer as easily and convincingly as he'd played Miles Gentry, amoral mercenary.

How could she not have thought about the possibility that her house was bugged?

Lana wondered how long she'd been without privacy. Had Kara heard her screams at night? Seen her writhing on the bed? Did her screams still make her smile?

Lana shoved the questions away before they made her sick. She could never go back there now. She had no home.

Caleb scribbled something on a notepad and handed it to her as he drove out of the parking lot.

Don't say anything. Your clothes may be bugged.

Lana felt her neck tighten another notch, making her head throb. Was this nightmare ever going to end? Did she have to give up her life and disappear before she'd be free? And if that was the cost of freedom, did she even want it?

She'd spent enough hours thinking about that very thing to know that she didn't. She would never again be caged, trapped like she had been in that cave. She was going to live free, or die trying. Period.

Caleb pulled into the nearest drugstore and parked away from the clump of cars nestled near the door. He reached into the backseat, fumbled in a bag, and pulled out something about the size and shape of a cell phone. He pushed a couple buttons and a line of three LEDs lit up. He reached over and ran the device over her backpack turned purse. The little lights flickered, and Caleb pulled a complicated knife out of his damp jeans. He slit open the lining in one of the pockets and pried out a listening device no larger than a button on her shirt.

Lana's stomach cramped, and it was all she could do not to let out a hoarse cry of frustration. She carried that backpack with her everywhere, which meant they'd listened to every word she'd said—at work, at home, even in the hospital with Stacie. She felt betrayed. Violated.

Thank God she'd never told anyone what she'd seen in Armenia. Anyone who shared her secret would be dead right now, and it would have been her fault.

Caleb continued running the device over her purse, then her shoes. He found two more bugs. When he motioned for her to lift her arms, Lana thought he'd lost his mind. At least until the little lights went off when he ran the thing along the underwire of her bra.

Lana choked down her rage, unfastened the bra, and slipped it out through her sleeve.

Caleb gave her that look all men have when they see a woman remove her bra without taking off her shirt—the one that kids get when they see a new magic trick. She handed him the lacy bit of fabric, and he used his knife to cut open the casing that held the underwire. Another tiny listening device slid into his wide palm. He offered her the bra, but she refused. There was no way that was going back on her body.

He took all the little bits of plastic and metal and folded them into a makeshift envelope he made out of a piece of paper.

"I'll be right back with those condoms," he said and got out of the car, locking the doors behind him.

Lana sat there in the dark parking lot, feeling trapped. What else didn't she know about besides the bugs? Had her food been tampered with? What about her office? Was it bugged, too? Could Kara just hear her, or had she also been watching her? Was it just Kara or had the others found her, too? She hadn't seen them, but that didn't mean anything.

Lana felt her stomach tighten painfully, and she took slow, deep breaths in an effort to keep her dinner down.

What was she going to do? She couldn't go back to her apartment, and she sure wasn't going to go live with her parents again. As much as her folks would love having her there to fuss over, Lana couldn't stand the thought of bringing any possible harm to them, even if she could tolerate the fussing.

If her apartment had been bugged, maybe her parents' house was, too. Not that it would do any good. Her parents knew nothing. And she'd stopped drawing altogether now. Her hand would only sketch those faces, and if anyone saw, that could get her and anyone else around her killed.

Even Caleb.

Lana buried her face in her hands, riding the wave of humiliation and regret his name caused to swell inside her. She had to find some way to make him leave. Kara would never believe Lana knew nothing if he continued to stay. Her only hope was to continue to pretend she knew nothing until Caleb believed her and left. Until she'd lied to herself so long she started to believe it, too.

He came out of the drugstore, walking toward her in a long, easy stride. Lana couldn't help but stare and admire his strength as he moved. The tight denim of his still-damp jeans did nothing to hide the flexing bulges of his thighs, nor did the thin knit of his black T-shirt disguise the thick layers of muscles over his chest and ribs. He was built along a grand scale that would make it impossible to hide his bulk under regular clothing. Not that she'd ever want him to hide from her. She liked looking too much. He radiated strength and power with every breath, and Lana felt herself wondering if he was completely invincible. He certainly looked like it.

He got in the car and just watched her with those dark, solemn eyes. He didn't seem in a hurry to speak or do anything until she acted first. Maybe he was just trying to be polite, since she'd humiliated herself so thoroughly.

"We're clear," he told her.

"What?"

"I got rid of the bugs. Hopefully it will take whoever's listening a while to realize that no one spends that much time on the makeup aisle of a drugstore."

"And then what?"

"And then whoever is listening will know that we know. They'll either plant more or rely on whatever bugs they have planted elsewhere."

"Like in my office?"

"Probably. And your car. I'll call in a team to sweep for them, but in the meantime, be careful of what you say."

She gave him a shaky nod.

He started the car, and a few minutes later they were gliding along the buzz of traffic on I-70. "Where are we going?"

"A hotel." He glanced over for a second, and in the flash of oncoming headlights, she could see the grim set of his jaw.

Lana felt her body tighten at the memory of what he'd said about room service and a big tub. Too bad it had all been a lie.

"Do you want to talk about it?" he asked her.

She didn't need to ask him what *it* was. *It* was the giant pink elephant in the car with them, weighing her down with embarrassment. *It* was the way she'd melted in his arms and acted like the biggest hussy ever. *It* was the fact that she'd do just about anything to get back to the point where he was kissing her and she'd thought it was real. Where she wasn't thinking about danger for the first time in more than a year.

"No," she told him in a firm, unyielding tone.

Caleb nodded and drove in silence for a couple minutes. "Then I guess we're up to the topic of the bugs. I don't suppose you know who planted them."

"I have no clue."

He sighed as if he didn't quite believe her. "Is there any chance that you accidentally left your backpack at home one day, giving them a chance to sew a bug in the lining?"

"No. I keep my life in there. Copies of my work files,

photos of my family, my sketch pad. I never go anywhere without it."

"That's what I was afraid of. You know what that means, don't you?"

Lana's stomach gave a sickening twist. "It means that the bug was planted by someone I know."

Caleb looked over at her with narrowed eyes. "I suppose that could be true, but I was actually thinking that it meant that whoever planted the bugs did it while you were asleep."

Cold little legs of fear scampered down her back. She hadn't thought about that, though it made perfect sense.

"Why would you think that someone you know did this?" he asked quietly.

Oh, crap. She hadn't realized at the time she said it how strange it would sound to him. Of course he wouldn't expect her to think the bugs had been planted by someone she knew, unless she knew more than she was letting on. Damn, this lying stuff was hard. She couldn't keep up with all the little strands of truth that dangled around, just waiting to be pulled on so her lie would unravel.

Lana gathered her wits and shrugged. "I don't think that. I was just guessing."

"Uh-huh. Just guessing. What aren't you telling me?"

"Nothing."

Caleb's mouth flattened, losing that fullness that had been so soft and warm against her lips. She found herself hoping that they'd be forced to pretend to be lovers again. It was the only way she could see a man like him kissing her.

"I can't help you if you lie to me."

"You can't help me at all. I'm fine."

"Bullshit. You're scared to death, but not about the news that someone's been in your apartment while you were sleeping. I'd think something like that would creep you out more than it has. Why is that, Lana?"

"I *am* scared."

"Yes, but no more than you have been since I came to town. You've been living in fear, and I'll be damned if I know why you won't let me help."

"You can't help."

"Only because you won't be honest with me. At least not about this."

"What's that supposed to mean?"

"It means that the only honesty you've given me since I showed up was in your shower tonight. You weren't lying then, by God."

"No, but you were." Her voice was quiet, barely audible over the hum of traffic.

Caleb's hands tightened on the wheel. "I let things go too far. I'm sorry about that."

"Forget it. I have."

"Another lie for the pile?"

Lana turned away and looked out the window, watching buildings slide by in the darkness. Maybe she should just disappear. Someone else could take over the foundation, and she could just go away where no one would find her. Not even Caleb. Who knows, maybe she'd start some new life and find a little happiness. She didn't need much to be happy. A decent job, a few friends, a place to go home where she'd feel safe. It wasn't much to ask for.

Caleb pulled the car into a hotel and parked. "I know that you have no reason to trust me, but I promise you that

I can help. Whatever it is you're dealing with, you're not alone."

And that was the problem. If she'd been alone, it would have been easy. It was all those people she cared about that chained her to her lies, her secrets. She couldn't let them get hurt. But rather than explain that to him, Lana just nodded and got out of the car.

⊰⊱

Kara wiped a drop of blood from the video screen, so she could see Caleb's image clearly. The small office at the back of the drugstore was cramped and hot, but it was the only place where she could view the security-camera footage. It showed her all too clearly how easily Caleb had thwarted her.

He'd stripped all of Kara's toys from Lana and left them sitting next to a bottle of cheap perfume. Not fair. If she hadn't already been planning to kill him, this stunt would have been enough to convince her.

Marcus was right. Caleb's presence was going to make getting to Lana much harder. Kara had promised Marcus she'd finish this tonight, but she didn't even have a clue where Lana was. Not in her apartment, certainly. All of those cameras and microphones were still in place, and no one was home.

Kara kicked the corpse of the security guard in frustration. He fell from the chair onto the floor in a squishy heap, with his pants still around his ankles. His wife was going to be pissed when they found him like this, but that was his fault for being so easy to seduce.

With her rubber gloves carefully in place, Kara removed

the VCR tape from the outdated surveillance equipment, making sure her entrance into the store wouldn't be found by the police. She was going to have to face Marcus with her failure to kill Lana tonight, but there was no way she was going to do it from behind bars. That's what Dennis was for.

❧

Caleb went into the bathroom of their hotel room and stripped out of his wet jeans. He needed a few minutes away from Lana to gather his thoughts. Ever since the fiasco in the shower, he hadn't been able to think straight. How could he think about anything else but the way she'd tasted, the sweet little sounds she'd made when he'd kissed her? The scent of her need rising up with the steam of the shower? Five years from now, he'd probably still be thinking about it, wishing he'd gone farther while cursing himself for having gone too far as it was. Her taste was in his memory now—the scent of her hunger for him.

Caleb tossed his jeans over the shower curtain rod to dry. This shower was bigger than Lana's. They'd fit in here a lot easier. He'd have lots of room to maneuver when he braced her against the wall to thrust up inside her, and the endless supply of hot water would give him plenty of time to make her come over and over.

Lana would let him. He knew it without a doubt. Her reaction to him had been honest—maybe the only honest thing about her. It was almost as if she needed the connection to another human, as if she was starved for affection. Or maybe just pleasure. There had been dark times in his life when he'd sought out female company just to drive away the guilt and fear and loneliness. Maybe this was one of those dark times for Lana. Maybe he could ease her pain, if only for a little while.

Caleb gritted his teeth and pushed away the temptation. He was trying to justify seducing her, and there was simply no justification. She was his assignment. He had to keep his dick out of it.

Like that was going to happen.

His wet boxers did nothing to stave off his erection, but getting the clammy material off was a considerable chore with the added obstacle. He took his time, trying to think about something else, something completely unsexy—anything else to ease his lust.

It took a while, but he finally got himself under control.

Caleb stormed out of the bathroom ready to do whatever it took to get her to tell him what was going on. He would use coercion or scare tactics or whatever he had to to get her to talk. He wasn't going to let his guilt or sympathy for her get in the way of his job.

But she had fallen asleep while he'd been working himself up to interrogating her, and all those good intentions went out the window. She hadn't even taken off her shoes. She was just lying there across the blankets on one of the beds, her chest rising and falling in the rhythm of sleep.

Caleb sighed and tried to fight back all the softness that seeing her like that brought up in him. There was no place in his life for softness right now, but despite his best efforts, he failed to feel anything else.

He slipped her shoes off her feet, but she didn't stir. He pulled the blankets down on one side of the double bed and slid her under them. She made sleepy sounds of protest but didn't wake. She must have just been at the end of her strength. It had been a long day and he was glad she was getting some rest. Maybe it would make her more reasonable—make her see that she could trust him.

Maybe it would just make her that much more stubborn and silent.

Caleb went back into the bathroom, turned on the shower, and dialed Monroe. "Yes," he answered.

"You were right."

Smug satisfaction hung in Monroe's voice. "Is that so? What am I right about this time?"

Caleb bit back an insult he would have flung at anyone but a superior officer. "She's hiding something."

"What?"

"I don't know. She just let something slip tonight. Her house was bugged, and so was her purse. Her first thought was that they'd been planted by someone she knew."

"Interesting."

"Exactly. I called her on it and she clammed up."

"What are your plans for getting her to talk?"

"Push her until she breaks." He hated the idea, but he had to protect her.

"Sorry, son, but playing bad cop isn't going to work for you. Not with her. We tried that approach for hours. Just made her more stubborn. I suggest a more . . . subtle approach."

Caleb did not like the sound of this. "Subtle?"

"Gentle. Coaxing."

"You mean seduce her."

"Seduce her. Fuck her. Whatever gets the job done."

"You're a bastard, sir."

Monroe laughed. "I remember David saying the same thing to me a few months ago. He's expecting his first child, by the way. Did you know?"

Caleb had found out just before he came here. David had offered him a job with his new security company. He'd never seen David happier, and it was about damn time. The man had suffered long enough. "I did."

"Maybe you and Lana—"

"Don't you dare finish that sentence, sir."

Monroe just chuckled and moved on. "I'll send Grant out to clear the bugs from her apartment, car, and office. It sounds like you could use some help, and Grant's good with the ladies."

Caleb wasn't sure whether to thank Monroe for the help or try to reach through and slug him for sending the biggest womanizer on the face of the planet. Then again, maybe that was a good thing, too. Grant had a way with women that boggled the mind. If anyone could convince Lana to talk, it'd be Grant.

Of course, Caleb would have to kill Grant if he touched her, but that couldn't be helped.

"If Grant was available, why didn't you send him here in the first place?" So Caleb would never have had to know what it was like to kiss Lana.

"To piss you off. Obviously. At least that's what you'll tell yourself anyway, so it works for me."

Caleb stayed silent. Barely.

"Let me know what you find out," ordered Monroe. "Grant will be there tomorrow. I'll enjoy pulling him out of whoever's bed he's in."

Monroe hung up, and Caleb stood there in the bathroom a long time. He didn't want Grant to come. He loved Grant like a brother and had spent more time with him in the past few years than he had alone, but that didn't change the way he felt. Once Grant was here, any chance he had with Lana was gone. Grant would toss her a wink and a smile, and they'd be naked together within an hour. And when Grant left her, she wouldn't even frown. He had the magic touch, and he'd used it on countless women, leaving all of them smiling.

Lana would just be one more, but at least she'd be safe. That's what really mattered.

⤞⤝

"I have another job for you," said the metallic voice Denny had grown to hate.

He grabbed a pen in his shaking hand. "I'm ready."

"I've left directions in your mailbox. I want you to go to the address listed and pick up a package for me."

"What's in it?"

"Do you really want to know?" asked the robot.

No. No he did not. This shit was way deeper than he'd signed up for. "I can't—"

"You can and will. Bruce is coming for a visit tomorrow. I made sure of it."

Denny felt his beer coming back up into his throat, and he swallowed hard to keep it down. "I'll find another way to get the money."

"In time for Bruce's visit?"

Shit. Denny saw the image of his father's body flare in his mind. The bastard had looked like hamburger—all that blood against fish-belly white skin. No way was Denny gonna let that happen to him. What the hell did he care what his boss wanted him to do? There wasn't a damn person in the whole world he cared about enough to let Bruce take that bat to him.

"Fine. I'll do it, but you're paying double."

He could almost hear the grating smile in that metallic voice. "You're a good boy, Dennis. A very good boy."

CHAPTER TWELVE

*I*t was dark, but Lana could see just enough through the tiny slit in her hood to make out the bodies of her colleagues, her friends, lying lifeless on the floor of the cave. The stench of death filled the dank hole in the ground until there was no air left to breathe. Terror choked her lungs as she realized that she was the only one left—the only victim left alive.

Boris stepped over the leg of one of the dead and set up a video camera. They always filmed the beatings, the torture, the killing.

Lana tried to scream for help, but the air was too thick, and it wouldn't pass through her throat. She tried to curl into a ball to protect herself from what was to come, but her broken body wouldn't respond. She was frozen, trapped without any means of escape. Everything had been taken from her—her freedom, her dignity, her control. She had nothing left to fight with.

The man picked up the heavy pipe he'd beat her with yesterday and came toward her. Small flecks of blood dotted the pipe's gray surface. Her blood? Allen's? Bethany's? They had been the last ones to die.

Lana heard the muffled thud of her killer's combat boots

on the dirt floor. The emotionless eye of a video camera sat silently, watching as the man came nearer. He rolled his shoulders as if warming up so he wouldn't strain a muscle. Lana almost wished she hadn't been able to see. Maybe blindness would have been easier. Not knowing what was coming.

She closed her eyes, testing the theory, but the terrifying blackness was worse.

She opened them again just as the pipe came down on her legs.

Pain roared through her system, sending her brain a jumble of signals she couldn't understand. Her limbs twitched in automatic response, but she had no control.

"Enough!" came a harsh command. Miles Gentry. He leaned against the wall in an impassive stance, but his bearded face was hidden in shadow. She couldn't see him clearly.

Lana struggled to breathe. It was all she could do, and even that was an effort. Her body was on fire, flooding her with searing waves of agony. One on top of another, so close together there wasn't time to breathe in between.

"You kill her and you'll have to go hunting for more leverage. Not smart," said Miles.

The man with the pipe turned around. "It's not about leverage. Boss says we're in the group now. We're done with her."

Miles pushed away from the wall with a bulge of strength. "What if I want her?"

The man scoffed. "She's no good for that now."

Miles shrugged. "Depends on whether you like screamers or not."

"*Suit yourself,*" he said, handing Miles the pipe. "*Just finish her when you're finished with her.*"

He left the cave. Miles switched off the camera and came near her. She could see his face clearly now—a hard mask of suppressed rage. Lana tried to curl up, but nothing moved.

Miles leaned down close to her, looking like he ached to say something. He reached out a hand, but Lana whimpered, knowing that wherever he touched her, it was going to hurt. His hand halted in midair and curled into a fist. She prayed he'd be quick and release her from her pain. She gathered the little strength she had left, begging him to kill her, "Please." It was hardly even a sound. Her lips were stuck together with dried blood, muffling the word.

Through the tiny split in her hood, she saw his expression harden further, and then he stood with a jerk. Miles shoved the pipe under the pile of dead bodies, effectively hiding it, and left her alone.

He was gone for only a blink of time before the man with the pipe was back. Somehow he'd figured out where it was. He lifted it over his head and smiled, and Lana watched as the blood-flecked metal sped toward her.

❧

Caleb woke as soon as Lana started whimpering. He threw the sheet back, crossed the small space between the double beds, and sat down next to her. He'd left the bathroom light on so she wouldn't be disoriented if she woke up in the middle of the night, and a soft glow lit one side of her face. She was sweating and shaking, curled up in a tight ball.

Something deep inside Caleb split open, filling him with a mixture of grief and self-loathing. He should have saved her. He should have found a way to prevent the beatings she suffered. He wasn't sure how, and he'd spent a lot of sleepless nights trying to figure out how he could have done things differently, but he knew a better man would have found a way.

He gave her shoulder a shake, hoping to wake her up before the nightmare got any worse. At his touch, her whimpers deepened into agonized moans. Her whole body vibrated with tension.

"Wake up, Lana. Come back to me," he coaxed in the gentlest voice he could find beneath all his anger.

Her breathing sped, and she flailed her arms as if trying to fight him off. Caleb feared that if he restrained them, it would only frighten her more, so he let her hit him, welcoming the blows. He deserved so much worse.

"Come on, Lana. It's only a dream. Wake up."

Her eyelids fluttered and finally opened. Terror was plain on her face, and he saw her trying to sort out the reality of him sitting there from her nightmare.

Caleb smoothed her hair back from her sweaty forehead with one hand while he stroked the inside of her wrist with the other. She went stiff for a moment, then slowly relaxed as the dream lost its grasp. Her breathing was still labored, and he could feel her pulse speeding beneath his fingers.

She closed her eyes for a moment and pulled in a deep breath.

"You okay?" he asked, knowing what a stupid question it was. Of course she wasn't okay. No one who lived with nightmares like she had was okay.

"Just give me a minute."

Caleb did. He sat silently, but nothing could have pried him away from her. He kept stroking her hair because he simply couldn't not do it. He had to touch her—to convince himself she was safe.

A few moments later, she sat up and slid out from under the covers on the far side of the bed. Away from him. She went into the bathroom and shut the door. He heard the water run, then turn off.

She came out but kept her eyes carefully off of him. "Did I . . . did I make much noise? Wake anyone?"

Caleb stood, his heart aching for her shredded pride. "No. I woke you up before you could."

She gave him a quick glance, then looked away, staring at the cheap art print over his bed. "Thanks. I'd hate to get us kicked out."

"I wouldn't let that happen," he assured her. "You don't have to worry about it."

She let out a sharp, humorless laugh. "Easier said."

Caleb stood up slowly and went to her. Light from the bathroom cast her face in shadows, but his night vision was good enough that he could still see the humiliation staining her cheeks. He longed to see her smile again—a real smile with deep twin dimples.

He knew it was a mistake to touch her, but he couldn't help himself. His hands settled on her shoulders and smoothed down her arms, reveling in the feel of her bare skin below the short sleeves of her T-shirt. A shiver went through her, but he couldn't tell if it was because she didn't want him touching her or because she liked it too much. "Do you want to tell me about the dream?" he asked.

Her expression tightened, and he thought she was

going to shut him out, but instead, she pulled away and went to the far side of the hotel room. Caleb didn't follow her, respecting her need for distance.

"I can't control them," she told him in a small, frightened voice. "The nightmares."

Caleb didn't speak. He didn't even move. He didn't want to do anything to jeopardize the thin thread of trust she'd offered him. He just waited, willing her to continue.

"I went to therapy. The doctor said that all I had to do was realize they were dreams and then I'd be able to control them—change them. He said that with practice, I'd even be able to get rid of them altogether." She shook her head, and her shiny hair swung above her shoulders. "It didn't work. I tried, Caleb. I swear to God I did. Every night, but these nightmares . . . they aren't just some story my head has made up. They're *real*. They actually happened." He heard her throat tighten with tears, but she turned her back before he could see them.

Caleb had to clench his fists to keep from reaching out for her, to keep from pulling her into his arms to offer whatever meager comfort he could. But he knew that she didn't need that now. She needed his restraint. His control. She had none of her own. It had been stripped from her eighteen months ago, and he knew then that he'd do anything to find a way to give it back. Anything.

It was a scary thought for a man with the kind of resources he had.

He saw her square her shoulders and heard her sniff. When she spoke again, her voice was steady. "The doctor prescribed me some sleeping pills. They didn't stop the dreams, just made it harder to wake up from them."

"Like last night?"

"Yeah. Sorry about that."

"Stop apologizing. It's not your fault."

"I know, but knowing doesn't change a damn thing." She let out a gusty sigh and turned around. Her eyes were red but dry. "Will you drop me off back to my office? I need to get to work on the auction."

"You need to get more sleep. You were only down for three hours."

"It's more than I get a lot of nights. I know myself well enough to know that tonight, three is all I'm going to get. If you don't want to leave, just let me borrow your car. I'll come back and get you in the morning."

Caleb wasn't about to let her out of his sight. He'd made some progress tonight, and he could already see her closing up, trying to revoke the trust she'd offered. "No, I'm happy to take you if you're sure that's what you want. We don't know if your office is bugged, though. You'll have to be careful of what you say."

She looked like she was about to say one thing but changed her mind. Instead she said, "I don't have to worry. I don't have anything to say that anyone would want to hear."

❧

It was dark outside the First Light Foundation office, not quite three a.m. Lana could hear an occasional car drive by, but most of the city was asleep. She took a deep breath, trying to gather the courage to unlock her office door. Monsters waited in there—the mess she had to clean up, the auction that was falling apart, the worry that everything she said or did was being recorded. She couldn't slip, even a little.

Caleb's big warm hand wrapped around the joint of her shoulder. She could see his thick fingers, feel the warmth of them sink through the knit of her T-shirt. She refused to wear the bra that had been handled by Kara, and she wondered if he noticed the missing strap beneath her shirt. Such a silly thing to wonder, but it popped into her head, a welcome distraction from her lack of courage.

"Do you want me to do it?" he offered. She could feel her hair sway under his breath. He was so close. Too close. It wasn't safe for her resolve.

"No," she said. "I'll do it." And she did. She turned the key in the lock, opened the door, and flipped on the lights. Her eyes ached from the searing brightness, but at least now she was no longer in the dark.

Papers were everywhere. Black fingerprint dust coated several surfaces. Blood had dried to a dark brown pool on the bathroom floor. Stacie's blood.

Lana squared her shoulders and prayed for strength. This was not going to be easy.

CHAPTER THIRTEEN

❦

Marcus Lark regretted giving Kara his private number. The woman was growing far too clingy for his tastes.

He lifted the phone from the cradle on his bedside table and shifted his body until he was sitting against the headboard. Elaborate carvings dug into his back, but he ignored the discomfort.

"Yes, love?" he answered in a gentle voice. He'd learned long ago that Kara was more easily controlled with gentleness than fear. She'd grown up alone on the streets of New York and wasn't easily frightened.

Kindness, on the other hand . . . the woman would do anything for the merest scrap of approval or acceptance. That trait made her quite useful on occasion.

"They found my surveillance equipment. I'm sorry. I couldn't finish the job tonight like I told you I would." She was out of breath, almost panicked.

"Calm down, love," cooed Marcus, even as his hand tightened on the phone in anger at her incompetence. "Everything is fine. I've taught you well. Is there any trace of you on the equipment?"

"None. I was careful."

"Good girl. And you wore gloves?" He hoped not. It

would be easy to make her fingerprints available in any one of the American databases. Kara was becoming too reckless, too desperate to please him, which didn't please him at all. He thought letting the CIA overhear that Lana was in danger would be enough to bring them running to save her. They'd find Kara and get rid of her so he wouldn't have to do it himself.

Apparently he'd misjudged.

"Yes. Always."

A stab of frustration made him tense up, and the woman at his side let out a sleepy sigh. Marcus forced himself to relax and lowered his voice. After last night, his bed partner needed her rest. "Good."

"I always do what you say."

Her simpering tone grated on his nerves, but he didn't let his irritation come through in his voice. "You've always been a good girl."

"Did you get the video?"

Marcus did but knew better than to watch it. Kara's taste in entertainment was more . . . undomesticated than his. "It was lovely."

"And the clip at the end?" she asked in a sexy tone. "The one of us together?"

Marcus stilled in shock as her words settled in. She had video of him? With her?

He kept his voice low and even, though inside he was seething in anger. "I'm going to watch it again right now just for you."

He slid from the high bed and walked naked across the room to his private office. A moment later, he found the encrypted e-mail she'd sent and opened it. He sped through images of a young woman's terror—flashes of her twisting in bed with tears streaming down her temples. Her body was contorted in fear and pain, but she didn't wake.

Kara had done that to her. He wasn't sure whether that made him admire her or despise her. But such dedication, as ugly as it was, had its uses.

Then he saw the short clip at the end, which clearly showed his face contorted in the throes of an orgasm. Kara was in front of him on her hands and knees, and the camera—wherever it had been hidden—had a perfect shot of his face.

He couldn't let this video get into the wrong hands. He'd worked too hard to hide himself—to become a man who did not exist—to let Kara ruin everything. Now that the Swarm was destroyed, he was able to operate his business more easily. Profits had never been higher. He was not going to go back to being a hunted man at the head of a condemned organization.

Marcus Lark was tired of being a target.

"You naughty girl," he said into the phone. "You know I don't like my picture taken."

"I know, but I needed something to remember you by. It's horrible being without you every night. At least I have that."

And that video changed everything. If Kara was eliminated now, they'd find the video. "Come home to me, love. I miss you too much to let you stay away."

"I have to finish my work here. I promised you I would."

"Forget the promise. I'd rather have you here." Where he could safely kill her and destroy the video.

"I'm almost done. I'll record the rest of the show for you tonight, and then I'll come home."

"No!" he said, more hastily than he should have. Then more gently, "You can't do it now, love. She's guarded now. It's too dangerous for you. Just come home."

"I'll be careful. I won't let you down. Not again."

Damn it! He'd made too much of her failure in Armenia. He'd rubbed her nose in the fact that Lana Hancock had survived, and now he had to live with that error in judgment. "I don't want anything to happen to you. At least wait a day or two. They'll be expecting you to make a move now that your equipment was found."

A day or two was all he'd need to have one of his men move in and get rid of that video. Then Kara could do whatever foolish thing she wanted.

"You're right, as always," she said. "I can find a good use for the time—punish her for making things difficult and keeping me from you."

"Tell me what you're going to do, love," he coaxed as he sent an e-mail to one of his best hit men containing instructions.

"I'm going to surprise you. I'm going to make you proud."

"I'm always proud of you, love. You know that."

He could hear her soaking up the praise. "After I take care of things here, you'll be even more proud."

After a long, unproductive talk with Stacie Cramer, Detective Hart decided to have another chat with Lana. It was midmorning, and he found her at her office, nearly finished with the chore of cleaning up the mess. The big bruiser, Caleb, was in the bathroom with the door shut, but when the bells on the door jingled, he stepped out, checking to see who was there. Jacob caught the scent of disinfectant and figured Caleb was taking care of cleaning up the blood rather than leaving it to Lana.

Good man.

Caleb nodded at him and continued his work, only this time the door was open. Jacob couldn't see any blood on the tile, not even a stain on the grout.

Jacob left Caleb to finish cleaning and turned his attention back to Lana. She looked tired today, worried, but that wasn't surprising considering what her friend had been through. Her dark hair was pulled back in a short ponytail, but a bunch of the slippery strands had worked their way free and hung around her face. She was pretty in that natural, girl-next-door kind of way. There was nothing exotic in her features, but she reminded him a little of the first woman he'd ever had a crush on. Miss Parish, his sixth-grade English teacher. Although he'd missed most of her lectures, spending the time daydreaming instead, Miss Parish had taught him some interesting things about how his adolescent body worked.

"Morning, Ms. Hancock," he greeted her. She swept a loose lock of hair behind her ear and gave him a fake smile.

"Have you figured out who did this?" she asked.

"I'm afraid not. Do you mind if I ask you some questions?"

She looked like she wanted to say no, but she nodded and pulled up a spare chair for him to sit in.

"I saw Mrs. Cramer this morning. She seems to be doing well."

Lana nodded. "I talked to her on the phone earlier and she asked me to bring her work, so that's a good sign."

"Have you noticed anything missing?" he asked.

"No."

"Anything unusual or out of place?"

She hesitated too long, which meant she was either deciding whether or not to lie or thinking up one. "No."

Okay, so not much intricate thinking involved in that answer, so she must have been debating about lying. Whether or not she had, he wasn't sure. "I noticed the stacks of notebooks on the desks. Is that how you left them?"

"I can't remember. Maybe. Or it could have been something Stacie was working on."

Jacob scribbled down another note to remember to ask Stacie about it. "We found what appears to be a listening device. Do you know anything about that?"

She tensed up but covered it by shooting to her feet. "Would you like some coffee?"

"Sure," he replied as if she hadn't just tried to distract him.

She poured him a cup of coffee that looked like it had been there for several hours—just like he was used to back at the station.

"What about it?" he prodded. "Know any reason why your office would be bugged?"

She gave a shrug that was too stiff to be nonchalant. "We don't do anything top secret here. Our financial records are public, and we certainly don't have a lot of money."

She hadn't said no, just given him an evasive answer. Interesting.

"How long have you been in this office?"

"About six months."

"Did the furniture come with it?"

"No. I bought the desks and chairs. Why?"

"How about the blinds? The artwork?"

She gave him a confused frown. "The blinds were here when I moved in. The posters were free when I bought the desks."

"Where did you buy them?" He sipped his coffee.

"That used-furniture store two blocks down."

"I know the one," said Jacob.

"Can you think of any reason why someone would want to hurt Stacie?"

"She doesn't have any enemies," said Lana.

"That's not what I asked."

"Why would anyone want to hurt her?"

"That's my question," said Jacob.

"I'm sorry. I can't help you."

Couldn't or wouldn't? Jacob wasn't sure which. What he was sure about was that Lana had a bad past. Her office was bugged. A highly decorated soldier was staying nice and close, and she was terrified.

Whatever was going on here was both bigger and uglier than he'd hoped, which meant he had a lot of extra work to do. Between this and the homicide at the drugstore last night, he had his hands full.

"What about you?" he asked her. "Is there any reason someone would want to hurt you?"

"Why are you asking all these questions?"

"Standard procedure."

She raised a disbelieving brow. "I have a ton of work to do."

Jacob nodded and pulled out his business card. "Keep this in case you think of anything else." Not that she'd tell him if she did.

"Thanks." She took the card and set it on top of what looked like a stack of trash on her desk.

Jacob waved a hand at Caleb as he left. He wasn't sure why the man was hanging out with Lana, but he was glad Caleb was here. Jacob wouldn't have felt safe leaving the woman alone. He knew her history, and she'd been through hell. The last thing he wanted was for her to go through it all again.

CHAPTER FOURTEEN

— ⋯◈⋯ —

Lana set the phone back in the cradle and tried not to cry out of sheer frustration. One more thing was swept out of her control, adding to the growing pile. Maybe she was wearing some giant galactic KICK ME sign. That would explain a lot.

"What?" asked Caleb, crossing the office toward her. Concern narrowed his black eyes and made her want to either punch him or beg him for a hug. She did neither, just sat there, trying to stay composed.

"The hotel canceled."

"We don't have reservations for tonight. I didn't want to sleep in the same place twice," he told her in a near whisper.

The bugs. In the flurry of activity, she'd almost forgotten about them.

"No. Not that hotel. The hotel that agreed to host the art auction for free. They canceled."

"Why?"

Lana didn't want to tell him that Oran had struck again. Shame burned bright in her cheeks, she knew, but she didn't want to say it. Knowing she was embarrassed and telling him why were two different things.

Caleb took hold of her hand, his callused fingers gentle. He just held her hand, waiting for her to speak. She hated that about him—that silent patience that urged her to spill her guts better than demanding ever could. It was hopeless to try to fight him. She had to pick and choose her battles carefully, because there just wasn't enough energy left in her to fight them all, or to keep up with all of the lies each battle created.

"I have a friend who runs the place, which is why I managed to convince the hotel to let us use the space in exchange for free advertising. The only catch was that if anyone else wanted to book at least half the rooms in the hotel, I'd have to reschedule my event. Tomorrow was the last day before they couldn't bump me anymore."

"But someone reserved the rooms?"

"Not just someone. Oran."

"Oran? Why?"

"He's throwing his engagement party the same day as the auction. Guess he figured that Brittney was a good candidate for a wife, after all. There isn't room for both events, and Oran is willing to pay big bucks."

"Are you telling me that your ex-fiancé booked his engagement party to interfere with your auction? On purpose?"

Lana nodded, humiliation burning her cheeks. "Probably. I didn't fall all over myself accepting his advances the other day. This is obviously his way of punishing me."

"Give me his address and I'll have a talk with him." The words were steady, but she heard the anger that strung them together.

"No. Don't you dare interfere. I've made my peace about him and that's the end of it. Let him think he's won some imaginary battle. I don't care anymore. I'll figure something out."

"Maybe you should postpone the auction. There's a lot happening right now, and a big public event might not be the best thing."

Lana felt panic well up from deep inside her. If she gave up on the auction, she'd have nothing left to work for. The foundation would crumble, and she'd have to find another reason to get out of bed in the morning. The possibility that she might not be able to find that reason was more than just scary, it terrified her.

"No. I need to do this." She heard the desperation in her voice and wished she could hide her feelings better.

Caleb gave her a slow nod, and she could tell by the carefully neutral expression on his face that he'd seen her panic. "Okay, so we do this. Together."

No, no, no. Not that sweet voice of temptation again. She could not lean on him. He'd leave soon, and then what would she do? How would she get along on her own? It was best if she didn't relax at all. She had so little control in her life that if she let go even a little, she'd never recover.

"Thanks, but I've got it under control."

Caleb knelt down in front of her and reached out. His big hands swallowed hers, the tanned skin of his fingers dark against the paler skin of her wrists. His touch was warm. Comforting.

Damn it, she could not do this. She could not give in to that lure of comfort.

"Let me help," he said, ducking his head so he could look into her eyes. "You have all kinds of volunteers at the youth center. I'll just be one more. What's the harm in that?"

He had no idea the temptation he was, so steady and confident in the midst of her chaotic world. All she had to do was grab a hold and let his strength add to the last dwindling reserves of her own. He was such a dangerous seduction, pulling at her senses as if he'd been made just for that purpose. Everything about him appealed to her—those sinfully dark eyes, the way he used his size to shield rather than intimidate her, his quiet patience. The devil himself couldn't have devised a more appealing temptation.

"I won't get in your way," he said. She felt the callused pad of his thumb rasp over the back of her hand, and it sent little jolts of sensation streaking up her arms. Right to her heart. Just like the rest of him.

Lana closed her eyes in defeat. What use was it to fight him? He'd just win in the end, anyway. She was tired of fighting. She was just plain tired in general. At least if Caleb helped her through the auction, the kids would have the funding they needed. If she had to figure out a way to live without his help when he left, then she'd do it for the kids. When he left, they'd still need her, and she'd still be here to help them. One way or another. She wasn't sure what that way would be, but she'd figure it out later.

"Fine. You can help, but you're taking orders from me."

Caleb gave her a grin. "Yes, ma'am."

"And my first order is for you to never call me 'ma'am' again."

❦

Caleb was pleased with his progress. Lana trusted him enough to let him help with her beloved foundation, which was more than he'd ever dreamed. He knew how much it meant to her, or rather, how much the kids she helped meant to her. He'd seen the way she doted on them at the youth center—the way they cheered and clung to her when she showed up. The fact that she'd allow him to help her keep that love going was enough to put a smile in his heart. He was sure now that she didn't hate him, which was a miracle, but one he was willing to accept with great satisfaction.

Caleb wasn't going to let her down. He didn't know the first thing about charity auctions, but he knew plenty about organizing men toward a common goal.

It was nearly four when the bells on the office door jingled. Grant Kent came strolling in, his long-legged stride casual as a Sunday drive. Sun bounced off Grant's blond hair, which was tousled as if he'd just gotten out of bed. Likely with some willing woman he'd passed on his way into town.

Grant had a way with the ladies that Caleb could only marvel at. It wasn't just that he got a lot of women, it's that he couldn't seem to help it. Ladies flocked to him. It was enough to make a man question his sanity—or at least physics. There was definitely some sort of warp in the space–time–chick continuum around him.

Lana looked up as Grant walked in, the phone plastered to her ear as it had been for the past hour. She was trying to find an alternate hotel, with little success.

For a moment, Caleb felt his gut tighten with jealousy. Never before had he cared that Grant was a ladies' man, but he did now. He didn't want Grant going anywhere near Lana with his magic dick.

Smoothly, Caleb stepped up, putting his body squarely between Grant and Lana. Or at least he thought he'd been smooth. Grant just grinned as he shook Caleb's hand and pulled him into a hard hug. "Possessive much?" asked Grant quietly.

Caleb pulled away from the hug but held his position, blocking Lana from sight. As soon as Grant got one look at her, he'd want to pursue her and all that sweet, classic beauty. What man wouldn't?

"No," he lied.

"So you won't mind if I go introduce myself?"

"She's on the phone," said Caleb, his voice hard.

"She'll get off soon enough." The double meaning of Grant's words were clear, his tone teasing.

"I'll cut off any body part of yours that touches her," warned Caleb.

"Ah, so I was wrong about the possessive thing. Thanks for clearing that up." Grant's golden eyes were glittering with amusement.

Caleb growled.

Grant went on tiptoe and leaned over to see past Caleb's body. "She's cute, but she looks a little stressed. Either you haven't nailed her yet or you're not very good at it. Want some pointers?"

"Fuck off, Kent."

Grant just laughed and pulled Caleb into another man-hug. "God, I've missed you. You wouldn't believe what they've had me doing the past few months, but I'll have to tell you later, when I've cleared this place. All those extra eyes and ears make me nervous."

"Did you bring a team with you?" asked Caleb.

"Just two."

Whoever was watching and listening to Lana already knew they knew about the surveillance, so there was no reason not to discuss the sweep Grant was here to do. Caleb knew better than to ask whom he'd come with when there was still a chance that everything they said was being listened to. The men Monroe sent would not be just any soldiers. They'd be Delta Force, with plenty of secrets to keep, including their names.

"When will you start the sweep?" asked Caleb.

Grant jerked his head toward where Lana chatted on the phone with yet another hotel, trying to find a place to hold her auction. "Depends on the woman's constitution. Think she can stomach watching this?"

Caleb had witnessed the kind of emotions that went along with learning that a person's privacy had been invaded. They felt violated. Betrayed. Angry and afraid. Caleb would have preferred not to subject Lana to that, but he knew the woman never backed down from a bad situation. "She's tougher than she looks," said Caleb.

Grant grunted. "Wouldn't be hard. She looks like she'd fall over if you shouted too loud."

Caleb turned and stared at Lana, trying to see what Grant did. Sure, she wasn't a bodybuilder or anything, but there was a quiet sort of strength about her. A steel beneath the softness that Caleb had seen with his own eyes. Maybe that was the difference. Caleb had seen Lana through the worst kind of hell a person could suffer, and she'd never given up. Grant had no idea what she was capable of, and for some reason, it gave Caleb a little spurt of satisfaction. He and Lana had a connection. Maybe not a fun one, but the kind that was born of pain and fear and survival. Even if Grant did seduce her, there was no way he'd ever be able to match that.

"Let me talk to her," said Caleb.

"Wouldn't dream of doing it any other way, buddy. I'll get the gear and be back."

Caleb nodded absently, still staring at Lana. He loved looking at her—loved the way her shiny dark hair swung around her face, how she'd tuck a wayward lock behind her ear only to have it slip out again a second later. He loved the way her dark lashes covered her eyes when she was trying not to let him catch her watching him. He loved the sweet curve of her cheek and how a real smile would cause those twin dimples to show up out of nowhere.

He wished things between them had been different, but he was glad that he'd had the chance to know her, regardless of their past. Women as strong and selfless as her were rare, and knowing one made him feel like he'd been given a gift.

Lana hung up the phone and was watching him with a suspicious frown. "What?" she asked.

Caleb couldn't keep his distance, even though he knew that was the smart thing to do. Any excuse he could find to touch her, he took advantage of. This was one of those times. Caleb squatted down so he was on eye level with her. She had the most amazing eyes, with so many shades of blue, that for a second he found himself distracted.

Caleb blinked and focused on what was happening. He kept his voice low, though by now, it wasn't a big issue if their listeners knew what was happening. The bugs would be gone within the hour. "In a minute, they're going to do a sweep. You might not like what they find, and I think it will be easier on you if we go grab some food and let them work."

She arched a dark brow. "You think that I'm going to let complete strangers into my office to rummage around? I just got finished cleaning up from the last guy who did that."

"These aren't strangers. They're with me."

"Are you staying with them while they do this sweep thing?"

"No, I'd go with you."

Lana shook her head. "I'd rather stay."

"You sure? This can be hard to watch."

"I'm good at doing the hard stuff," she replied.

Caleb gave her a smile and tucked some hair behind her ear. "I know you are, but that doesn't mean you have to be. Let's get out of here for a while. Go see the kids at the youth center. Get your mind off of it."

She went tense as if he'd slapped her, and the center of her eyes shrank to frightened pinpoints. What the hell?

"What?" he asked her in a low, urgent voice.

She swallowed and blinked, and just like that, the fear was gone, leaving behind a smooth mask of neutrality. "Nothing."

"What are you afraid of?"

Just like that she shut down, and all the warmth in her eyes evaporated. "I'm fine. Going to the youth center is a great idea. I'll meet you in the car." She grabbed her back-pack, tossed him the office keys, and left the building.

CHAPTER FIFTEEN

—❖—

The youth center was stuffed full of kids, their cheerful noise ricocheting off the high ceiling of the gym. The thrum of bouncing basketballs and squeak of tennis shoes filled one side of the gym while the other was quieter. Three long tables lined the space, and several of the volunteers sat with kids, reading to them or helping them with their homework.

Lana just stood in the doorway, drinking in the joy she'd created. It was a happy place, a safe place. At least for everyone but her.

Kara saw her come in and crossed the large room with Phil hot on her heels. Kara wore a starched white shirt under her tailored peach pants suit. Her hair was in an elegantly casual updo, showing off the sparkle of diamond studs in her earlobes. She was such a classy-looking lady, it was hard to believe she was also a killer.

Lana felt Caleb's wide hand smooth over her back as if trying to comfort her. She straightened her shoulders and cleansed her expression of all emotion.

"Back so soon?" asked Phil, giving Caleb a scowl. "We didn't expect to see you today."

"I needed a break from planning the auction," said Lana, praying her voice wouldn't shake.

"I've heard. Anything we can do to help?" asked Kara in that elegantly rich voice of hers that made Lana's skin crawl.

"No, thanks. It's under control."

"That's not what I heard. Is it true the hotel canceled?" asked Phil.

Lana swallowed an ugly word. Bad news traveled too fast, even for a city the size of Columbia. "Yes, but we'll find another one."

The front door of the youth center opened and Lana's sister, Jenny, stormed in, carrying her son, Taylor. Lana flinched and tried to cover it before anyone could see.

She didn't want Jenny or Taylor anywhere near Kara. She needed to get rid of them. Now.

Lana felt panic bubbling up inside her as she tried to figure out the best way to protect her family.

From beside her, she heard Caleb say, "It's under control." His deep, calm voice brushed over her raw nerves, soothing them.

She could do this. All she had to do was act normal—like nothing was wrong. Kara didn't even have to know who Jenny was. Hopefully the family resemblance wouldn't give them away as sisters.

Jenny set down Taylor, who ran eagerly across the room on chubby legs toward Lana. She stepped away from the group and bent down to catch him in her arms, enjoying the solid weight of her two-year-old nephew.

"Kiss?" he asked, angling his cheek for the greeting he expected.

Lana gave him a kiss and he squirmed in her arms,

pushing against her so he could get down. Lana didn't let him go.

Jenny stomped up to Lana. Her dark hair was a mess, as if she'd been running her hands through it. Or possibly trying to pull it out.

"Do you have any idea how much you upset Mom?" Jenny demanded. "I've spent the past two days listening to her cry. You're going to go home and apologize to her if I have to drag you there myself."

"I'm sorry. I really am. I didn't mean for you to be the one to deal with Mom."

"You should have thought about that before you told her you didn't need her."

Taylor pushed hard against Lana's neck in an effort to get down.

"I didn't mean for it to come out like that. I was worried about Stacie, and you know how she is in a crisis. I couldn't deal with her, too."

Jenny rubbed her temples. "Damn it, Lana. You've got to be more careful with her."

"Damn it, Lana," mimicked Taylor as he tried to get out of her arms.

Jenny's face darkened and she let out a weary sigh. "Let him down. He'll be fine playing with the other kids for a minute."

"I like holding him," she countered.

"Yeah, well, I don't want him hearing what I have to say to you." Jenny pulled Taylor from Lana's arms and set him on the floor. He toddled off toward the flurry of activity on the basketball court.

Lana shifted her body so she could keep a careful eye on him. Between him and those tempting basketballs rolling around the floor were Caleb, Kara, and Phil, and Taylor was headed right toward them. Lana tensed. No way was Kara going near her baby nephew.

And if she did, Lana was going to . . . what? Scream at her? Attack her? The only way she could keep Taylor safe was to pretend that it didn't matter.

"Are you listening to me?" demanded Jenny in a frustrated voice.

Lana nodded her head vaguely. Taylor was headed straight for Kara.

Kara saw her watching the boy and gave Lana a smile.

Oh, God. She couldn't do this.

She didn't have a choice.

"I said that I can't keep cleaning up your messes with Mom," continued Jenny. "I've got my own problems to deal with."

Kara took a step to the left and reached out her arms to little Taylor. Her eyes never left Lana's.

It was a test. Kara was testing her to see if she knew who Kara was. If Lana failed, Kara would know, and if Kara knew, Lana's life and the lives of those she loved would be in jeopardy.

Jenny shook Lana's shoulder. "You're not listening to a word I say, are you? What is it with you lately?"

Kara lifted Taylor's compact weight into her arms and cuddled him.

Lana's insides hardened and threatened to shatter. On the outside, she didn't react, not by so much as a fluttering of an eyelash.

Jenny's voice rose a notch. "You don't give a crap

about the rest of the family after everything we did to help you. Mom was right. You are ungrateful."

Lana couldn't have answered if her life depended on it. It took everything she had to keep herself from ripping Taylor out of Kara's arms. Her whole body trembled as she fought the urge.

Kara kissed Taylor's offered cheek, leaving behind an ugly blotch of lipstick. Phil ruffled Taylor's baby-fine hair.

"That's it!" said Jenny. "I'm done trying to help. The next time Mom wants a tearfest, I'm sending her to your place."

Caleb gave Lana an odd look, but she barely registered it. He reached over to Taylor and wiped the lipstick off his chubby cheek and smoothed his hair back in place.

Taylor's arms shot up toward Caleb, and he pulled Taylor from Kara's arms.

Lana had to lock her knees to keep from collapsing to the ground. She pulled in a shaky breath and let it out slowly. Dizziness threatened to make her faint, but she managed to stay upright. "You should leave," she told her sister.

"So now you're sending me away like you did Mom? What the hell is wrong with you?"

"You should go on a vacation. A cruise. Take Mom and Dad. I'll pay." She sounded desperate, but she couldn't help it.

Jenny's anger dissolved into a concerned frown. "You don't have the money for that."

"I'll find it somewhere. Take out a loan."

Caleb set Taylor down and led him by the hand to the

edge of the basketball court. He found an unused ball and handed it to the toddler.

Taylor wrapped his arms around it and grinned up at Caleb.

"You'll take out a loan on what?" asked Jenny. "You don't own anything. I bet you haven't even paid off the Saturn yet."

"Don't worry about it. Just go. Set it up and tell me how much it costs. I'll find a way to pay for it."

"Why?"

"Because I've been horrible to all of you, and I want to make it up to you."

Jenny tilted her head. "You're lying. Why do you want us all gone? Is there something wrong with you?"

"No," she lied. "I'm just dealing with a lot of stress with the fundraiser coming up, and as much as I love you all, it would be nice to have a little space."

Kara gave Lana one last perusing stare before she went to where some of the younger kids were coloring. Phil was right on her heels, and Caleb was splitting his attention between Taylor and Lana.

"So, you want me to take Mom and Dad and spend a week trapped on a boat with them? I can see how much you love me. Besides, Dad would never leave his roses for that long. You're just going to have to suffer. You're stuck with us, sis."

"Then please do what you can to keep them out of my hair for a couple weeks. Please? I need some space. Just until the fundraiser is over."

Jenny's jaw tightened, but she nodded. "You owe me big-time. Once you get back on your feet, I'm going to take you up on that offer to pay for a cruise, only I'm going with Todd. Alone. You're babysitting—both Taylor and Mom."

"Deal," said Lana.

Jenny motioned toward Caleb. "Is he the guy Mom told me about?"

Lana stifled a groan. "She's probably already writing the wedding invitations in her head."

"It's not quite that bad, though I do have to admit that hearing Mom talk about what a nice butt he has gave me the willies."

Caleb saw them watching him, so he picked up Taylor and headed their way.

"Taylor likes him, which is a good sign. Is it serious?" asked Jenny.

"Dead serious."

⌘

Caleb split his attention between Lana's art lesson and Kara. He didn't trust the woman, and Lana's reaction to her was only making him more suspicious.

He phoned Monroe and had him run a quick background check on her. There was nothing out of the ordinary. Her record was clean other than a single speeding ticket.

Still, something was off. Caleb moved to a quiet corner and dialed Grant. "Got any men to spare for surveillance duty?" he asked.

"Sure. Lana?"

"No. Another woman."

"You dog," said Grant.

"This is serious."

"Okay, okay. Give me details."

Caleb gave him Kara's car make, model, and license plate and her address from the background check. "Keep an eye on her?"

"I'm on it." Grant hung up, and Caleb went back to the group.

The finger painting went on in messy glee as the kids smeared globs of color over giant sheets of paper. They were cute wearing too-large men's shirts that hung over their small frames like tents, protecting their clothes. One young girl in particular caught Caleb's eye. Her long braided pigtails reminded him of his sister, Hannah, when she was five. She had a smear of pink paint on one cheek, and she was frowning in concentration as she tried to place one more perfect petal on her flower.

Lana crouched down beside the girl and said something Caleb couldn't hear. The girl listened carefully, as if Lana was telling her the secret of life. A minute later, Lana produced a paintbrush from the smock she wore over her clothes and handed it to the girl. The little girl's eyes brightened, and she took the brush as if it were a delicate instrument. Lana guided her hand over the paper, and after a moment, the flower had a set of neat petals. The girl's smile was wide as Lana left her with the new toy and came to stand beside him.

"Tina has advanced beyond mere fingers," said Lana, grinning as she watched the girl.

"I see. A Picasso in training."

Lana wrinkled her nose. "I see more Monet than Picasso in her."

Caleb felt a smile stretch his mouth. "The kids love you."

She shrugged. "It's easy to love someone who gives you a fun place to play."

"It's more than that."

"Yes, but they don't need to know that. Not at this age. Just let them play."

Caleb watched as Tina carefully dipped the brush in green paint and went after the leaves of her flower with the same intense concentration she did the petals. "Tina looks more like she's working than playing."

Lana's full mouth flattened with sadness. "She's had it rough. Her dad's in prison. She spent the first several years of her life in the room next to the one where her mom turned tricks to make ends meet."

Caleb couldn't imagine doing that to a child, and he was torn between anger at Tina's mother and sympathy that life had backed her into a corner where she thought she had no choice. "And now?"

Lana sighed. "Her mom is still a prostitute, but at least Tina doesn't have to listen."

"That's something, I guess."

"That's what I keep telling myself. I can't fix all the world's problems, but at least I can do some good. I just hope that I get to keep doing it."

Caleb's arm was around her before he even realized it moved. She felt good there, and he was getting way too familiar with the feel of her body against his. "We'll find a way to make the auction happen."

"I don't know how. I can't find any hotel willing to rent us space for what I can pay."

"So why not use this place? It's big enough to hold a crowd, and there's that giant baseball field outside."

"This place isn't swanky enough for the kind of crowd we'll be pulling in."

"So pull in a different crowd. Aim to attract the middle class rather than the rich folks."

"But I need the rich folks and all their nice money," said Lana.

"You can earn just as much money if you attract a larger crowd of not-so-rich people."

"But how do I do that? I'm not a fundraising genius, no matter how many books I read. This is the only thing that's ever worked for me in the past."

"What about a carnival instead of an art auction? You might even be able to draw in more kids if their parents see what good work you're doing."

"I wouldn't know the first thing about setting up a carnival."

"It just so happens that my buddy Grant and I do. We've helped with two carnivals for the families at Fort Bragg, and they both were big hits." They hadn't been large carnivals, but she didn't need to know that. He was sure he could pull this off.

"I don't have the money to rent rides and I'm not entirely convinced they're safe, anyway."

"No rides, then. Just some games and plenty of junk food."

She looked up at him with a hopeful expression. "You really think something like that could earn money?"

"I know it can. If you want, have the art auction be part of the event. Not everyone who's rich is too snobby to show up just because it's not a nice banquet room."

He could see his idea growing on her. Those blue eyes

sparkled as excitement took over the fear that seemed to lurk constantly under the surface.

"Okay, we'll try it."

"What do you have to lose?" he asked.

Lana didn't answer.

CHAPTER SIXTEEN

— ❖ —

Stacie looked stronger today, her color better. Lana came to visit bearing pizza and a stack of magazines she'd seen Stacie reading during her lunch break. Caleb was a silent shadow at her back, and she'd nearly gotten used to having him around. It was dangerous to become accustomed to his company, but she couldn't think of any way around it, not that she'd tried very hard.

"You're an angel," said Stacie, eyeing the magazines. "I've been bored out of my mind today. Well, the part of it that I wasn't asleep, anyway."

Lana pulled the rolling table nearby and helped Stacie raise the head of the bed. "You should be getting your rest."

"Oh, I'm getting plenty of that. They've had me walking around a bit today, and it's worn me out both times."

"Do you know when they're going to release you yet?" asked Caleb.

"Probably not tomorrow, but maybe the day after."

"Do you have anyone who can help you at home?" he asked.

Lana hadn't even thought that far ahead, and she felt

horrible that her head had been so full of her own problems. "I'll come stay with you," offered Lana.

"No, dear. You've got the auction to worry about. Besides, I called my sister, and she's going to fly in for a few days."

"I didn't even know you had a sister," said Lana.

Stacie gave her a sad smile. "We haven't spoken in years. It seems foolish now that I'd let a little squabble get in the way. I figured I'd been stubborn long enough. All Sarah needed was an invitation back into my life and she was on the next flight out."

"You shouldn't have to deal with any uncomfortable family issues on top of your injury."

Stacie took Lana's hand. Her skin felt cool and thin. "If being shot brings Sarah back into my life, it's more than worth it. Sometimes it's the tragedies that bring people together." Stacie's eyes slid to Caleb, just briefly, but Lana saw it.

Lana wasn't sure Stacie was right, but she didn't want to argue with the woman while she was lying there in a hospital bed. "If you need anything, just let me know," said Lana.

"When Sarah gets here, I'll have everything I need."

They shared pizza, and Lana could see Stacie tiring before her eyes. "We're going to leave and let you get some rest, but you'll call if you need anything, right?"

"I will. I promise. Oh, and tell Kara thanks for the flowers, will you? She left them while I was sleeping."

"Kara was here?" asked Lana.

"That's what the nurse said. I felt bad that I didn't wake up for her visit."

Lana could picture Kara standing over Stacie's bed, watching her sleep. Helpless. Alone.

"I'll tell her," lied Lana as she hurried out of the room. Stacie was fine. She kept telling herself that over and over, but it didn't make that sick feeling in her stomach go away.

She had to get out of here—away from the stench of death and pain and hopelessness. She felt Caleb's silent bulk at her back, keeping pace with her rushed steps.

When Lana passed through the automatic doors of the hospital, she pulled in the clean night air, trying to drive out the hospital stench that filled her lungs.

"You okay?" he asked.

Her limbs were shaking, but she managed a weak nod.

As if he'd heard her thoughts, Caleb took her hand and twined his fingers through hers. Such a small thing, but it offered so much comfort. Skin against skin. Human contact.

"I'm worried about her," said Lana, feeling the relief of being able to speak the truth, even if it wasn't the whole truth.

"She seems to be recovering well."

"I know. I mean I'm worried that whoever did this to her will try to come back and finish the job."

Caleb pulled her to a halt and ran his hands over her bare arms. She hadn't realized until now that she was covered in goose bumps. "I can post a guard outside her door if it will make you feel better."

"It would."

Caleb nodded and made a brief phone call. He gave an

order for a guard and said Stacie's room number. As easily as that, Stacie was protected.

"Better?" he asked her.

"Yes. Thank you."

They got into his car, having left hers behind so it could also be checked for listening or tracking devices. "Where to now?" asked Caleb.

Lana's brain ground to a halt. She couldn't go back home, not with the knowledge that the place might still be bugged. She didn't want to sleep in the office, because she knew she'd spend the night thinking about Stacie's attack. She didn't have the money to stay in a hotel, and she wasn't about to sleep in her car. "I don't know."

He hadn't started the engine yet, and inside the car it was quiet. The darkness outside was driven away by the bright lights of the parking lot, leaving deep pockets of shadows over the car's interior. Caleb turned sideways in his seat, adjusting his big body beneath the wheel. "I don't want to leave you alone tonight," he told her. "Wherever you go, I go."

She'd have been lying to herself if she pretended not to be relieved that she wouldn't have to be alone with her nightmares. He'd been with her twice during those dreams and hadn't shown any sign he was disgusted by her weakness. She knew he was a good actor, but she preferred to believe he was being honest. "Maybe Mr. Simmons will let me use another apartment tonight."

"You can go back to your own apartment if you like. We had a team sweep it for bugs, too, and a man's been posted guard to keep it that way."

"Why?" she asked. "Why go to all this trouble when there's nothing I can offer you in return?"

Shadows outlined his wide jaw and accentuated the high ridge of his cheekbone. He was watching her with a hint of sadness in those black eyes. "I know you're scared, but I hope that you'll figure out you can trust me."

Lana ached to give in to the hope she heard in his voice. He wanted her to trust him, and she wanted the same thing, but she knew better. He was only one man. He couldn't possibly protect everyone she cared about, and even if he pulled in whatever resources were at his disposal, Lana couldn't bring herself to trust them. Too many lives were at stake. All she had to do was keep her mouth shut and everyone would be okay.

She just had to pretend a little longer and Kara would go away.

Lana looked away, feigning interest in an older couple getting into their car a few yards away. The little old man opened the door for the little old lady and tucked her into the seat as if she were the most precious treasure on earth.

She wondered if they knew how lucky they were to have each other.

"There's nothing to trust you with," she lied. "I wish I could help you, but I don't know what it is you want me to do or say."

His expression hardened, and she saw that faint hope in his eyes die. "Would you feel safer in a hotel, or would you rather go home?"

At home at least she had work to distract her. "If I go home, are you sure no one will be listening?"

"I'm sure. These men are nothing if not thorough."

"Okay, then. I'll go home."

"At least you trust me about that. It's something, I guess."

Lana realized with a shock that it was true. She did trust him enough to believe he'd take care of the bugs when he said so. Maybe it was foolish to trust so easily, but she couldn't seem to help herself. She prayed she wasn't getting in over her head with Caleb, even as she feared it was already too late.

Grant was sitting outside Lana's apartment on guard duty when Caleb pulled in. He'd managed to avoid getting the two of them together earlier today because she'd been stuck on the phone, but now there was no reason not to introduce her to his womanizing buddy.

Damn it, there was no way he was going to sit by while Grant seduced Lana with his charming smile or whatever it was about him that had women's panties falling off at every turn.

If Lana's panties were coming off, Caleb wanted to be the one doing it.

Grant unfolded his lean body from the car, stretching for a moment before striding toward them. He had the build of a runner, with long, lean muscles rather than the heavier bulk of Caleb's build. They'd been friends for nearly a decade, and Caleb would do anything for the man.

Anything except let him have Lana.

They met on the sidewalk, and Grant had that panty-dropping smile on his face. "You must be Lana," he said, reaching his hand out for her to shake.

Lana gave Caleb a questioning glance as if to ask if Grant was safe. Caleb wanted to hesitate, to give her just a hint of a reason to keep her distance, but he just couldn't do it. Not to Grant. The man had pulled his ass out of more fires than he cared to remember, and he couldn't repay him that way.

Caleb nodded, giving Lana a reassuring smile. "He's safe," he said, wishing the words back the moment they left his lips.

Lana took his hand and Grant did that just-hold-it thing that seemed to make women swoon. Caleb wasn't sure how he did it without coming off as stalker material, but he did. Every damn time. "I'm Grant. At your service."

Caleb waited for the slow smile of feminine approval to dimple her cheeks, but it never came. Instead, she pulled her hand back as soon as was polite and took half a step nearer to Caleb.

He felt like he'd just won the freaking lottery. That small show of trust was worth more to him than every penny he'd ever made. The surprised grin Grant shot him only made the feeling sweeter.

"You two in for the night?" asked Grant.

Caleb had told Lana he was going to stay with her, but he hadn't actually explained to her that he meant to stay by her side. No more hanging out in the car waiting for her nightmares to strike. If she had another bout of bad dreams, he was going to be right there. He owed her that much.

Or maybe that was just a handy excuse to get himself in her door. Either way, he didn't care. He wasn't going to leave her to suffer alone.

Lana licked her lips in a nervous gesture, and Caleb

felt that lick all the way to his toes. Wanting her and not being able to have her wasn't pleasant, but it sure was easy. As easy as breathing.

"Yeah," answered Caleb before Lana had a chance to argue.

"The place is spotless, so feel free to do . . . you know, whatever."

Caleb knew exactly what whatever was, and there wasn't going to be any of that going on. Still, Grant didn't need to know that. "Good night," said Caleb.

"I hope so," said Grant.

Lana looked confused but said nothing.

Caleb shifted his duffel bag and held out his hand. "Give me the keys and I'll go in first."

She hesitated for a second before saying, "No. I need to do this. I can't stand the thought of being frightened out of my own home. Such as it is."

Caleb felt a new spark of pride for the woman. She was no wilting flower, and he loved that about her.

Lana unlocked the door and stepped inside. The apartment was a little worse for wear thanks to the search Grant and his team had done. One of the electrical outlet covers was cracked, and several of her books were lying in a stack on the floor. Her couch cushions were crooked, and her TV was missing.

Caleb shut and locked the door, giving Lana time to absorb her home. She just stood there, still and calm, looking at everything slowly. Tears welled up in her eyes but did not fall.

Caleb couldn't stand to see her suffer. He wrapped his arms around her waist from behind, hoping she wouldn't pull away. She stood in the loop of his arms for a long time. The honeysuckle scent of her skin filled the space between them, and Caleb fought the urge to bury his face in her hair and breathe her in.

Without realizing it, his thumbs were stroking over her stomach as if searching for a patch of bare skin. He stilled his wayward hands and just waited. He'd hold her all night, if that's what she needed, and consider himself privileged to be given the honor.

A few minutes later, he watched her pull herself together. It was a miraculous thing to behold. First the tears that had never fallen disappeared, then her shoulders squared, her chin lifted, and she seemed to grow a couple inches taller. One moment she appeared fragile and delicate, the next she had the stance of a warrior maid bent on battle.

Caleb felt his world shift just then, like the ground beneath him had vanished for a split second. He knew then he was lost. If she'd been weaker or more bitter, he could have resisted. If she'd become cold and cynical, he would have been safe. But she was none of those things. She was selfless warmth and enduring strength, and he couldn't help but love her.

It was the biggest mistake of his life, and there was nothing he could do to stop himself. He'd fallen in love with a woman who could never love him back.

❧

Lana let the hot water spray against her skull and tried not to think about the last time she was in this shower. With Caleb.

Of course, trying not to think of something only made

her think about it more, and eventually her body was aching, her movements jerky with need. Man, what she wouldn't have given for one of those detachable shower massagers right now. She'd have taken care of business and gone to bed with a smile. But instead she just stood there, aching for more than she was willing to let herself have.

Caleb.

His presence was no longer jarring when she'd turn and see him nearby. She'd gotten used to his casual touches—a hand on her shoulder, tucking hair behind her ear, lacing his fingers with hers. She wasn't sure how that had happened. She hadn't been comfortable even with casual touches from anyone but the kids in a long time. He'd ducked under her guard when she wasn't looking, and he'd stayed there. And now she wanted him. There was no denying how she felt—it would only be a waste of precious energy.

The question was, what was she prepared to do about it? Could she really let herself get physically involved with a man she knew would leave soon? Could she find the strength to resist the pull he had on her?

Lana turned the water warmer. She'd heard that a cold shower was better for unquenched lust, but she wasn't a sadist, and no amount of water, cold or otherwise, was going to quench her thirst for the real thing.

"You okay in there?" came his deep voice through the door.

Lana's body heated at the sound, and she briefly thought about asking him to join her. Take up where they left off.

"I'm just getting out now." She turned off the water

and let it drip from her hair. She was going to need every second she could get to pull her defenses back up. A man like Caleb was a powerful force to withstand, but in the end, there wasn't much choice but to try to fight and hope he'd leave before she crumbled.

Chapter Seventeen

It was dark. She knew the moment the nightmare began but was powerless to stop it. The fear came first, followed by the pain, then the fear of more pain. An endless, hungry cycle that ripped at her sanity until she was screaming for mercy.

Then he *was there, light streaming down behind him, casting his features into shadow and forming a halo around his head. He held her in his strong arms and she knew she was safe.*

Or at least she thought she was.

The dream shifted as time reversed. The man with the pipe was dead. Caleb had killed him, but he didn't get them all. Four of them had run and escaped to torment her. It would never stop. The fear. The pain. It would never stop. She was trapped. Helpless. She had no control. No control.

Screams tore at Lana's throat until all that came out was a ragged gasp for air. Caleb tried to shake her awake, but she was apparently trapped in her nightmare. Every light in her bedroom burned bright, and he wondered how she'd fallen asleep at all, much less stayed asleep while he was shaking her, shouting her name.

Then he remembered the sleeping pills. She had trouble waking up when she took them.

Caleb gathered her writhing body and held her against him. He crooned soft words into her hair and stroked his hands over her face and arms, trying to soothe her. He repeated her name over and over, and finally, she opened her eyes.

Caleb sent up a prayer of thanks and brushed the hair off her sweating brow. How had she endured this every night? Had she been plagued by these nightmares when her body was still broken and healing? Had she thrashed around like this?

For months she'd lived alone. No one had been here to wake her and free her from her dreams. No one had been here to hold her. She'd gone through this all alone, and the thought made him long for a reason to do violence.

He felt a killer's cold anger pumping through his blood, and he fought against it, trying to be gentle. It was like stopping a freight train with a feather—hopeless and futile.

She was making sobbing sounds of anguish now, and they ripped at his guts. How could he have let this happen to her? Why hadn't he found a way to protect her?

No new answers came to the old questions, just a familiar aching regret that he hadn't done more to prevent her pain.

Her sobbing halted, and he felt her wake up more fully, felt her pull a heavy cloak of detachment around her. She was drawing away from him, and he'd be damned if he let it happen again. He didn't know how to get through to her, but he knew what he wanted to do, what he'd been craving since the moment he laid eyes on her again.

With a touch more gentle than he felt, he wiped away a wet trail of tears from her temple. She was awake now, closing herself off more with every passing second.

"Don't," he whispered, his throat tight. "Don't pull away from me."

She knew what he meant. He saw the knowledge flash in her eyes. An ocean of blue brightened with understanding. "You shouldn't be here."

"You need me."

"No. I—"

He pressed a finger to her mouth to quiet her. "You need me. There's no shame in needing someone else."

"It's easy for a man like you to say. You don't need anyone."

Grant pounded on the door. "You okay in there?"

"Go away!" growled Caleb.

"Those didn't sound like fun screams. She okay?"

"Yes," said Lana in a breathless voice. Then again, louder. "Yes. I'm fine."

"I'll just be, uh, outside, then. Sorry."

Grant's footsteps faded.

"If I don't need anyone, then why is Grant outside watching your apartment? Why is another man watching your office and another guarding Stacie?"

She tried to turn away, but Caleb held her chin and made her look at him.

"They're out there because I can't protect you on my own. I need their help, just like you need mine. Let me help you. Tell me why you're so afraid."

"I'm not."

"Liar."

Lana's eyes slid shut. "I can't. Just let it go."

"I wish I could, but I can't. Not anymore. I'm not going to let you destroy yourself like this."

"It isn't your choice."

Caleb muttered a caustic curse under his breath. She was right. If she wanted to ruin her life and keep her secret, there wasn't much he could do to stop her.

Caleb started to move off of the bed. Lana's hand stopped him. Her fingers wrapped around his wrist, pale against his tan skin. She hadn't reached out for him since the incident in the shower, and Caleb hadn't realized how much he'd been craving for her to do just that.

He stared at her hand, unable to take his eyes off her slender fingers.

"Will you stay?" she asked. "Just for a while? The dreams . . . they're easier when you hold me."

Caleb's heart filled up with a bittersweet mix of joy that she wanted him to hold her and guilt that she needed him to. He pushed the guilt aside and focused on the joy. He didn't want her accidentally reading anything into his actions that would make her think he didn't want to be right here.

He scooted his body against hers and wrapped his arm over her waist. She snuggled with her back against his front and closed her eyes. His body hummed in delight, happy to be horizontal with the woman he wanted, nagging him to get naked and horizontal. He ignored his desire for her as much as any man could, hoping she'd fall asleep before she'd figure out just how much he wanted her. Another inch closer and his traitorous body would give him away in a big way.

The god of sleeping pills was on his side, and she fell back to sleep in a few minutes. For Caleb, sleep came much, much later.

❦

Caleb remembered hearing on a TV ad that if you had an erection that lasted longer than four hours, it was a bad thing. Of course, that was after having taken some medication. He wasn't sure what it meant for a man who didn't do anything stronger than aspirin.

Just the act of taking a shower had him hard. All he could think about was how Lana had sounded when he pressed her against the tile wall, or how she'd tasted when her demanding little tongue had swept into his mouth. It was enough to make a sane man mad.

He finished in the shower, ending with a cold blast that had him shivering but did little for the lust prowling through his system. Sleeping next to Lana all night had been hard enough, so to speak, but waking up with his hands on her bare stomach and her fingers curled just inside the waistband of his jeans was sheer torture. Not that it had affected her one bit.

She was still sleeping peacefully and would stay that way as long as he had anything to say about it. He'd unplugged her clock and covered her up to her neck before leaving her room. Had things been different between them, he'd have woken her with just his tongue, but that was material best left stored in the back of his mind. His imagination was way too vivid when it came to Lana. He could almost imagine what she'd look like all stretched out and naked beneath him. Her breasts were small, but her nipples stood at attention every time he touched her. Her hips were slim under her jeans, but she had womanly curves that would fit his hands perfectly. She was smooth everywhere he touched, and he already knew the unique taste of her skin, her unique scent. Woman and honeysuckle and miracles.

It was almost enough to make a cynical man believe. Almost.

Caleb dried himself off with a rough brush of a towel. He should have just taken matters into his own hand and come out of the shower with a smile, but he knew that a simple session with his fist wasn't going to do the trick. He wanted Lana. Hot and wet and naked. Nothing else would even come close to scratching his itch.

When he came out of the bathroom, Grant was waiting with coffee and donuts. "Have I ever told you you're my hero?" asked Caleb as he pulled a double chocolate out of the box.

"Get in line. Ladies first."

Caleb shook his head and took a sip of coffee strong enough to make his chest sprout new hair. Perfect. "You can't have her," said Caleb, only half joking.

"I know. Between you and David, the world is losing all the good women."

"There are only two of us, and Lana isn't exactly my woman." The word *yet* seemed to float between them, unspoken but understood.

"You slept with her."

"Fully clothed."

"Harsh," said Grant with a sympathetic wince.

"You have no idea. Gives new meaning to the term *hardship post.*"

Caleb finished off the donut and went for a second. Grant had brought a whole dozen. What a guy.

"Is she still asleep?" asked Grant.

"Yeah. Hopefully she will be for a while."

"Good. There's something I didn't want to tell you in front of her last night. Her car was sabotaged. The brakes had been tampered with."

"Shit. When did that happen? I thought you were watching her car."

"We were. When was the last time she drove it?"

"The morning Stacie was shot."

Grant shrugged. "Could have happened any time between then and when we arrived. It wasn't a professional job, though. I mean, brakes going out on the highway is one thing, but here in the city, the chances of her getting killed in an accident aren't very high."

"No, but it sure would scare the hell out of her."

"You think someone's toying with her?" asked Grant.

"I don't know. Maybe. She's not exactly forthcoming."

"Maybe this will help. There's something I want to show you," said Grant. He flipped open his laptop and pulled up a diagram of Lana's apartment. It was a 3-D model complete with furniture. Several red and blue dots glowed in various locations, along with dotted lines fanning out from each. Caleb had seen diagrams like this before. It showed the location of every bug they found in Lana's apartment and the estimated area each had covered.

Caleb studied the image, frowning. "Is red video or audio?" he asked.

"Video. See anything odd?"

"Hell, yes." For some reason, her bookshelves were covered by two separate video cameras. Those cameras wouldn't have picked up anything more than a passing glance at someone walking by, so why were they there?

Caleb went to the bookcase, looking for the reason behind the unusual setup.

"If you find anything let me know," said Grant. "I looked for over an hour, took out every book and leafed through it just in case one had a hidden pocket. I found nothing. Whatever those cameras were trying to catch, it beats me."

"Maybe Lana would know." Something in the back of Caleb's mind nagged at him.

"And will she also share?"

Caleb sank down onto the couch and took a slug of hot, thick coffee. He didn't even bother to respond to Grant's question. They both knew the answer.

"Anything else I should know?" asked Caleb.

"It was all pretty standard equipment, all up-to-date with no serial numbers to trace. No fingerprints. Everything we found is available in the States."

"What about the shower? Was it bugged?"

Grant raised a golden brow. "Why? Want some footage?"

"Don't be an ass."

"Sorry. Hard habit to break," said Grant with an unapologetic grin. "No, the shower was clean, though there was audio hidden under the sink."

Caleb let out a relieved breath.

"Why? Got something to hide? A little monkey-spank going on, maybe?"

Caleb just rolled his eyes and reached for a third donut.

Grant stared at Caleb for a moment, his grin growing wider until it bloomed into a knowing smile. "You got her in there, didn't you? You had our pretty little lady in the shower and you didn't want anyone to see."

"Fuck off, Kent."

Grant let out a deep laugh. "I'm right. You sly devil you, and here I thought this thing you had for her was all one-sided. I should have known better."

"Mind your own business."

"My friend, your love life *is* my business."

"How, even in the most deranged minds like yours, could you think that was true?"

"Because I need you and David out of the way, all happily settled down, so that I can have my turn. David's done his part, now it's up to you."

"What the hell are you talking about?" asked Caleb, totally confused.

Grant closed the file on his laptop and shut the screen. "I have this theory that since I was the third man to join the team, I'll be the third one to leave. After you and David. If you don't get all domestic and have the little wifey-poo convince you to quit, I'll never get out."

Caleb stared at Grant, struggling not to let his brains spill out his ears from trying to understand such convoluted logic. "How long have you had this *theory*?"

"A couple years before David left. The first time he left, I mean."

"And you've been waiting all this time for us to settle down in suburbia somewhere so you could, too?"

"Yep. Something like that. That job David offered me is looking pretty good. Nice cushy work here at home. No more dragging my ass halfway around the world for months on end."

"Why don't you just quit if you want out?"

Grant shrugged. "I can't leave you without someone to cover your hairy ass, so hurry up and nail you a woman already."

Caleb gave Grant a steady look. "You know there's not enough therapy or antipsychotics in the world to fix what's wrong with you."

Grant waggled his eyebrows. "But the ladies love it."

"Lord help them."

They sat in companionable silence for a while, and that nagging feeling in Caleb's head wasn't going away. "Pull up that diagram again, would you?"

Grant did and handed Caleb the laptop. Caleb stared at the screen, letting his eyes wander, trying to see a pattern. Nothing stood out, but he kept looking at the bookshelves again. Something wasn't right.

Then he remembered. That night he'd rushed her into the shower, he'd seen footage of someone looking through one of her books.

Caleb went to his duffel, took out his own laptop, and pulled up the surveillance footage. He saw Grant's shadow hovering over his shoulder as they watched the intruder come in, replace a bug and pick a single book off the shelf.

"Can you tell which one it was?" asked Grant.

Caleb squinted at the screen. "No." He zoomed in on

the area, but the image was still fuzzy. The only thing he could make out was that the book had a spiral binding.

Grant had seen it too and went to the same shelf, running his fingers over the spines, pulling out three of the books on the shelf. "They're all sketchbooks," he said, handing one to Caleb.

"Why would someone be interested in her sketchbooks? I already checked for hidden compartments."

There was no obvious answer, and Caleb leafed through the book, looking at sketch after sketch. Lana's skill was impressive. Whether she drew people or animals or landscapes, they were all detailed and lifelike.

"Is your book full?" asked Grant.

Caleb flipped to the end. "Yeah. Yours?"

"The first one is, but check this out," said Grant. "The second one is only half full, and the last sketch is dated December before last."

Right before she'd left for Armenia.

Caleb tried to compare the book to the one in the surveillance footage, but he couldn't tell if it was the same one or not.

"Maybe she kept something hidden in the book?"

Caleb felt a cold feeling of dread roll around in his gut. Lana's hand had shaken when she'd tried to draw a puppy. She hadn't put a new sketch in that book since before her kidnapping. All the cameras in her apartment were aimed in such a way that they'd catch the image of anything she drew, whether sitting at her desk or on her couch or on her bed.

Whoever was watching her wanted to know what she drew, and he could only think of one reason why. "Whoever is doing this thinks Lana saw something in Armenia, and they want to know if she puts it down on paper."

"What are you talking about? She was hooded. What could she possibly have seen? And if she did see something, why haven't they just killed her?"

Caleb wasn't sure how much Grant had been told. They'd been briefed on the op separately, and Grant hadn't been there in Armenia. Caleb had been working alone until the very end. "What do you know about Lana's background?"

"Just that she was the only surviving member of a group of hostages taken by a group of loonies trying to get into the Swarm. Her file says she was banged up pretty bad."

"Banged up" didn't even come close to what Lana had endured, and Caleb had to bite back a hostile criticism of Grant's casual attitude. Grant had no way of knowing what she'd gone through.

Grant continued, "A team went in and extracted her, taking down a small group of Swarm wannabes in the process."

Caleb's hands tightened into fists. "There's a lot more to it than that."

Grant's golden eyes widened with understanding. "You were there."

Caleb nodded, unable to speak past the clump of bitterness lodged in his throat.

"That was the op you did solo, wasn't it? The one you came back from all fucked up?"

Caleb stood and turned his back. No way was he going to talk about this with Grant. He couldn't stand to even think about it.

"I can't help if you don't tell me what happened. If she

did see something, then it's going to take more than two of us to keep her safe. You know anyone willing to take innocent civilians as hostages and kill them won't stop until she's dead, too."

Caleb felt like pounding a hole in the wall, like tearing the couch apart with his bare hands. He needed to vent some of this frustration before he did something stupid. "I can't tell you what I don't know. She doesn't trust me, and I don't blame her. She was an easy target before I showed up, but they didn't kill her. They must want something from her—something she can't give them if she's dead."

"Could it be a rival terrorist group—an enemy of the Swarm?"

"As far as we know, the Swarm is gone. At least, they haven't claimed credit for anything since that op we went on six months ago."

Grant gave Caleb a feral grin. "That was fun, wasn't it?"

Satisfying maybe, but not fun. "Let's assume the Swarm isn't gone and they could have something to do with this. She was hooded and kept in a separate cave from those running the show. What could she possibly have seen?"

"Maybe the hood slipped off and she got a peek at plans or blueprints?"

"Or people?" added Caleb. "She could have seen one of them before they managed to get the hood on."

"Maybe she doesn't even know she saw them. She could have had breakfast in the hotel before she was taken. Could have been sitting next to one of them and never known it."

Caleb shook his head. "We thought we got them all, but

those caves were extensive. Someone could have slipped through one of the tunnels."

"Maybe it wasn't someone who was actually there, but someone associated with them. They could think she knows something even if she doesn't, which would match her story."

Except for the fact that Caleb knew she was hiding something. "The bottom line is that it really doesn't matter who is after her, or whether or not the Swarm is still operating quietly. What matters is stopping them—keeping her safe until she trusts us enough to cooperate."

"Any clues when that will be?"

"She doesn't have a lot of reason to be trusting."

"You may be as patient as God, but Monroe isn't. He's going to want results so we can move on. We have a lot of men tied up on this thing right now."

"I don't care what Monroe wants. I nearly got her killed once already. I can't let anything happen to her this time."

"Got her killed? I thought you were the one who brought her out alive," said Grant.

"Yeah, right after I watched them beat her."

Grant's body stilled. "You did *what*?"

Caleb's stomach knotted at the memory. He didn't want to tell Grant what he'd done, but if there was even a slim chance that the knowledge could help Lana, he owed it to her to suck it up and tell Grant his shame.

Caleb's voice was low, and he couldn't look Grant in the eye as he told him. "I watched a man beat her. I stood there and let it happen. I heard every one of her screams. Every one of her bones break. I was right there the whole time and I couldn't do a damn thing."

"God, Caleb. Why?"

He'd asked himself the same thing a thousand times, and all he could come up with was the same pitiful answer. "I was undercover. The Swarm had bombed a school bus the week before, killing three kids and wounding ten more. Their next target was a school. We had to find out which one, so I went in posing as a demolitions expert for hire. One of our teams had taken out the real Miles Gentry, and I took his place."

"And the real Miles Gentry wouldn't have given a shit if they'd beaten a woman to death, since he was willing to blow up a whole fucking school," guessed Grant. His mouth flattened, and Caleb saw something like pity pass through his expression. He hid it quickly, but Caleb saw it anyway, and it made him want to crawl in a dark hole and never come out.

"I should have done something. Killed them all before they hurt her."

"They would have taken you down before you'd had time, and then what would have happened to all those kids? Where would they be?"

"I know. I try to remind myself about that part, but it doesn't make it any easier."

"But you saved her. That's what matters."

"I thought I'd saved her, but I didn't. These nightmares she has, Grant . . ." He swallowed past the anger that burned his throat. "She relives it every night. I kept her from being killed, but I didn't save her."

"You can now. We can find these bastards and take them down. Make sure she knows she's safe. Maybe then her nightmares will go away."

"Whatever I do now it will never make up for what I had to do then."

"Does she know why you couldn't act?"

Caleb nodded. "Monroe told Lana."

"Monroe told me what?" Lana asked as she walked out of the bedroom. She was wearing that giant, droopy robe over her short pajamas. Surgical scars crisscrossed her legs, reminding Caleb of just how much she'd suffered in her struggle to walk again. Her hair was a mess, her eyes were still puffy from sleep, and she had the imprint of her wrinkled sheet on one cheek, but she gave him a warm smile.

Caleb's heart clenched at the sight of her. All this talk had brought back vivid memories of her broken body and battered face. Seeing her whole and alive made him ache to pull her into his arms and beg for forgiveness.

Instead, he waved toward the box of donuts. "Grant brought breakfast."

Lana's blue eyes narrowed at the distraction, but she let it drop. "Save me a couple. I'll be out in a few minutes."

The bathroom door closed behind her, and Caleb heard the water run. His body tightened at the thought of her naked and wet in there, and he wished he could join her. The muscles in his legs were jerking as if they were trying to convince his brain to let him follow her into the shower. He ignored them.

"It doesn't look like she hates you to me," observed Grant.

"She should. For a while, she did."

"But not anymore?"

"Not anymore," agreed Caleb.

"It's a start," said Grant.

"It's not enough. If I can't make her feel safe, she'll suffer for the rest of her life."

"You can't *make* anyone feel safe. All you can do is give her the tools to take care of herself. If this was one of your brothers or your sister, what would you do?"

"Buy them a gun and show them how to use it."

"Sounds like a plan to me. What about teaching her how to fight? It might make her feel better to be able to defend herself, and all that exercise might wear her out enough to keep her from dreaming."

Caleb felt a flare of hope at the idea, which he immediately squashed. "She's too fragile for that."

Grant snorted. "She may look that way, but I have a file full of evidence that proves otherwise. You said yourself she's stronger than she looks, and if you're too much a fool to show her how to use that strength, then I will."

Possessiveness reared its horned head, and Caleb felt his lips pull back in a near snarl. "Don't you dare go putting the moves on her."

Grant held up his hands. "Whoa. Wouldn't dream of it. I swear, you and David get all ugly where your women are concerned."

"She's not my woman."

"Shows just how much of a fool you are. I've seen the way she looks at you. You could have her if you wanted."

"Oh, so I should seduce the woman I let be brutalized so that I can win the World's Biggest Bastard award?"

"I think Monroe has dibs on that prize. The best you could hope for is runner-up."

"This isn't funny, Grant."

"Maybe not from where you're standing, but from

here, it's pretty fucking hilarious to watch you, oh master of self-control, flounder around like this."

Caleb's chest rumbled with a warning growl, and Grant just grinned.

"I think I've overstayed my welcome. I'll be outside if you need me," said Grant, and he left, shutting the door behind him.

Caleb stood in the little living room for a long time, just concentrating on breathing, controlling his temper, controlling his lust. It was an exercise in futility while that shower was running—at least the lust part. There was nothing he could do to stop himself from wanting Lana. Not even his guilt could cool that fire. All he could do was tough it out and hope she didn't notice how he walked around with a constant hard-on.

❧

Lana had managed to avoid another crisis until the unusually late hour of noon. The little bells on her office door chimed, and a walking rainbow stormed through the door. Celia Summers was a young woman dressed in a homemade tie-dyed T-shirt and jeans that looked like they'd been used as a paint palette. Her hair was a vibrant shade of green this week, streaked with pale lavender. Three mismatched hoops dangled from each ear, and the pink crystal stud in her nose glittered in the bright afternoon sun. She was a tiny thing, barely reaching Lana's shoulder, but what she lacked in height she made up for in talent. Forget Armand. Though Celia wasn't well known, she was one of the best landscape painters Lana had ever seen, and that had been when Celia was still in high school. Since then, her talent had only grown.

Celia went straight to Lana's desk and kicked it. "You said he was going to be here!"

Caleb and Grant had been on the phone all morning trying to bring in some of their buddies to help with the carnival. Grant had gone to the back room to make some copies, and Caleb was still chatting quietly on the phone. When he heard the angry young woman shout at Lana, he hung up and started to stand.

Lana gave him a small shake of her head and hoped he'd stay put rather than make things worse by getting involved. Celia was . . . temperamental, but she was the best artist they had left in the dwindling lineup. Lana couldn't afford to lose her, too.

"Who was going to be where?" asked Lana in the calmest voice she had.

"Armand! You said he'd be here, but he's in Italy."

"He canceled a few days ago, but I did send out an e-mail about it. I thought you knew."

"I accidentally killed my computer with a chain saw." Celia waved a hand with five different colors of nail polish on it. "It was a whole thing. I haven't had e-mail in weeks."

"I'm sorry you didn't know. If I'd known your computer was broken, I'd have called you. I know how much you were looking forward to meeting him."

Celia pouted, making the ring in her bottom lip jiggle. "I don't even know if I want to come now."

Rather than throw the contract Celia had signed in her face, Lana tried a more diplomatic approach. "Don't say that. We need you. The kids need you."

"What about all the other artists? You still have them."

"They're not as good as you, Celia. And this is a great way to bring in work. Get your name out there."

"Yeah, but I've already got more work than I can do." Her gaze went past Lana, and something she saw back there made her smile.

Caleb. Celia was staring at Caleb as if she'd just found a new color. Lana didn't even turn around to see if he was looking back at her the same way. She didn't want to know. Celia was cute and fiery and talented, and Lana was no match for her feminine appeal.

"Please tell me you won't back out," begged Lana, trying to ignore the rush of jealousy she felt.

"Who's the stud?" asked Celia, not bothering to lower her voice.

Lana pushed out a sigh of frustration. "My friend, Caleb."

"Not Caleb," said Grant from behind her. "I'm Grant, sweetheart."

Lana turned her head to see the focus of Celia's attentions, and they were most certainly targeted on Grant. She felt herself smiling with relief.

Grant held out his hand, and Celia took it and didn't let go. "Ever had anyone paint you naked?" she asked him.

"Sure have. The brush tickles and the red paint stains," said Grant.

Celia laughed and stepped closer. "Ah, an art critic."

Lana felt Caleb's fingers curve around her arm and gently pull her back. He leaned down and whispered into her ear, "Just sit back and watch."

Lana had no idea what he meant, but she decided to take his advice.

"Never *your* critic. I'd love to see some of your work," said Grant.

"I don't have any with me."

"Then maybe I should go back to your place."

"For a private showing?" asked Celia.

"You show me yours, I'll show you mine."

"I just bet you would, too," she purred.

"I can't help it. I'm a slave to my curiosity."

"Slave? Mmm," she purred. "That has potential, but what is it exactly that you're curious about?"

"Whether green or purple is your natural hair color."

Celia laughed again and turned to ask Lana, "Can I keep him? Just for a couple hours?"

Grant lifted Celia's chin with his finger and made her look up at him. "I'll give you three hours if you promise not to pull out of the auction."

"Done," agreed Celia and grabbed Grant by the front of his shirt, tugging him along behind her.

"The things I sacrifice in the name of art," said Grant with a smile. "See you all . . . later."

Lana just shook her head, staring in awe. "How did he do that?"

"It's the panty-dropping smile."

"The what?" asked Lana, totally confused.

Caleb studied her face as if looking for the joke. "You really don't see it?"

"I guess not."

His smile was all male satisfaction and flashing white teeth. "Good."

❧

For the second time that day, Lana's office bells gave a merry tinkle as another problem walked into the door. This time, there wasn't anything that Grant was going to be able to do to fix it.

Oran flashed her a white smile as if he hadn't personally tried to bring down her fundraiser.

"What do you want?" she demanded.

"To talk, darling. I figured you'd be about ready to listen by now."

"You mean now that you've done your best to stop my fundraiser from happening."

Oran shrugged his athletic shoulders. "I'm desperate to get you back."

"I can tell by the way you're sparing no expense for your engagement party to *another woman.*"

"I'm just looking for the right time to let her down easy," said Oran.

"Like you did me?" she asked with false sweetness.

Caleb came out of the back room, where he'd been making copies for her. He looked from Oran to Lana. "Everything okay here, Lana?"

"Oran was just leaving," said Lana.

Oran's gaze slid to Caleb, and something he saw there startled him enough that he dropped his smile. "I guess I misjudged," he said. "I figured you'd be happy to see me."

"After you tried to destroy my careful planning? Not likely."

"I wasn't trying to destroy your anything, darling. I just wanted to open your eyes to a better way of doing business."

"Yours?"

"Well, yes," he said, sounding shocked that she had dared ask.

Lana felt rage swell inside her, threatening to spill over. She really wanted to punch Oran in the eye and leave him one hell of a shiner for the media. Knowing him, though, he'd press charges and Lana would end up in jail for assault. "I'm only going to ask you to leave one time. After that, I'm going to go in the bathroom and let Caleb deal with you as he sees fit. With no witnesses."

"Really?" asked Caleb with almost childlike glee.

Oran frowned at her as if she'd done something naughty. That look used to be able to make her blush with humiliation, but now it just pissed her off. "Leave, Oran."

Technically, it wasn't a request, but Lana was done giving Oran even another second of her time.

Caleb stepped up beside her, doing nothing more than merely standing there. It was enough that Oran straightened his tie with a nervous gesture. "If I leave now, I'm never coming back."

"Promise?" she asked in a sickly sweet voice.

Oran turned on his heel and left, the little bells chiming in his wake.

Lana looked up at Caleb. "I shouldn't have used you to intimidate him like that. I'm sorry."

Caleb slid a slippery strand of hair behind her ear. "Don't ever be sorry for needing a little backup. I want to help you, even if that means scaring off slime like Oran."

Lana shook her head, sending the hair Caleb had tucked away flying again. "I'm ashamed that I used to love that man."

Caleb's voice dipped to a deeply serious tone. "We can't help who we love. You should try to remember that."

꿍

"What time does the youth center close?" asked Caleb as he fired off the last of the e-mails he needed to send.

"Seven. Why?" asked Lana.

Caleb looked at his watch. It was nearly nine, and he could see Lana was struggling to keep herself going. She'd worked nonstop all day, not even pausing while she ate the Chinese food he'd had delivered. Grant still hadn't come back yet, but Caleb had seen the black sedan pull into the lot about an hour ago. The night guard for the office. Caleb hadn't recognized the man, but if Grant had brought him in, that was good enough. Grant might appear casual and careless, but he never fooled around with the important things.

"They have floor mats over there, right?"

Lana nodded, but her brows drew together in a curious line. "A few we use when I can get one of the local gymnastic coaches to donate some lessons."

"And you have a key."

"Of course. Caleb, what are you getting at?"

"I was just thinking about something Grant said to me today he thought I should try with you."

Caleb saw her eyes darken and a pretty blush spread up her throat. "I'm, uh, not sure that we should be doing anything Grant suggests at the youth center."

It took Caleb a minute to realize that she thought he meant sex. Possibly kinky sex. Which, of course, made Caleb's mind go there, too. What a lovely place that was.

She hadn't said no to the idea, just no to doing it at the youth center, and if that wasn't enough to make a man's blood boil, Caleb didn't know what was. "It's not what you think. I just wanted to show you a few self-defense moves."

"What for?"

"Just in case."

"In case of what?"

"In case those secrets you're keeping come back to haunt you. I don't want you to be completely defenseless."

Any sign of sexual interest he thought he'd seen vanished. "I've taken self-defense classes," she said, her voice even.

"Not from me."

"And what makes your teaching special?"

"Because in my class, the best defense is a good offense."

CHAPTER EIGHTEEN

———— ❖ ————

An hour later, Lana was sweating and breathing hard, and only partly from the strenuous moves Caleb had her practicing. He'd stripped out of his shirt, leaving that glorious expanse of muscled chest and abs on display. And she got to touch him, too. Not just little passing touches, but hard holds that taught her just what the man would feel like if she ever got him in her arms for real. It was more than any red-blooded woman should have to take, and yet it wasn't nearly enough.

"That was good," he said as he pushed himself back to his feet. He'd let her knock him onto the ground to show her how it felt to follow through the motion. Of course, once she'd knocked him flat on his back, she wanted to climb aboard and stay there for a good long while, but that wasn't in the cards.

"This time when you get me on the ground, I want you to follow through with that stomp kick I showed you."

"I don't want to hurt you," she said, her voice light with breathlessness.

His black eyes were glittering in the bright lights of the gym, and his skin glowed as if it had been oiled.

"Aim just to the side of my head, but don't hold back on the force of the kick. If you get too close, I'll just dodge."

"What if you're not fast enough?" she asked, taunting him. She knew full well he was. She'd seen him move tonight and was astonished that a man his size could be so quick.

"I'll be fast enough if you're not trying to hurt me. Come on," he said, motioning her toward him with his fingertips. "Let's go."

Lana took a deep breath as she waited for Caleb to come toward her. She went through a series of moves he called "nothing fancy," using his own momentum and a kick to the back of his knees to bring him down. Something went wrong, and a second later she found herself on top of him with her nose in his crisp chest hair.

Lana's laboring lungs pulled in the scent of his skin, felt the firm bed of man beneath her, and she felt the liquid flow of desire pooling low in her belly. She tried to hold in a low groan of need, but her breathing was too ragged to control it.

"You okay?" he asked, sounding a little winded himself for the first time tonight.

Lana nodded and tried to push herself up. Her arms shook with effort as her mind tried to take control of her wayward body, which wanted to stay right here and taste the salt of his skin.

Her weight shifted as she worked to move off Caleb's body, and pressed against her stomach she felt the unmistakable length of his arousal. Lana went still, trying to make sense of what she felt, trying to figure out if it was all in her head or if he really was hard and hot against her belly.

"One of us should move," he told her in a thick voice. "And if it's me, I swear to God I'm going to slide you under me and do something that would make even Grant blush."

The words went into her brain and rolled around in an indecipherable pile. Blood raced along her skin, making the gymnasium air feel cold. Something deep inside her melted, and her muscles went weak. She wanted to stay right here—to force him to do whatever it was he had in mind. She wanted it. Needed it. She'd been too long without pleasure in her life, and she knew on an instinctive level that Caleb had what it would take to make her body sing.

She must have stayed still too long, fighting for the right decision, because she felt Caleb shudder beneath her. His powerful muscles clenched and shifted, and when they stopped, she was lying on the cold vinyl mat and Caleb was gone.

She looked up and saw him with his back to her a few feet away. "I'm sorry, Lana. I shouldn't have said that, shouldn't have put that pressure on you."

She tried to tell him it was okay, but words lodged tight in her throat. She wanted to tell him to come back and bring back the warmth he'd given her, but all that came out was a choking sound of unsated lust.

"I'll, uh, be back in a sec," he said and headed toward the men's room.

Lana flopped onto her back and looked up at the steel beams and bright lights overhead. It was better this way. No ties between them, nothing to rip her apart when he

was gone. Some things weren't worth a night of pleasure, and watching Caleb walk away with her heart was
one of them. And there was no doubt that he could walk
away with her heart. No matter whom he'd pretended to
be in the past, she saw him for who he was. Noble. Honorable. Dependable. A freaking Boy Scout's pledge full
of things that Oran had never been. He was the kind of
man a woman wanted to keep, and that was the problem.
His days with her were numbered. She didn't know how
many, but eventually, Monroe would find some better
use of Caleb's time and talents, and when that happened,
Caleb would leave.

The world needed its few remaining heroes, and Lana
needed to keep any more people from getting tangled up
in her mess of a life. She had nothing to offer him but
secrets and lies and night after night of being woken by
her screams.

He deserved more than that.

❧

"Did you do as I asked?" said the metallic voice on the
other end of the phone.

Denny felt himself start to sweat—a cold, sour sweat
that made his stomach turn with the stench. "I couldn't.
There was some guy watching her place."

"One man and you couldn't handle it?" asked the
voice, mocking his ability.

Something about that man had made Denny think
twice about taking him on. There was nothing particularly special about him, just this air of confidence

that made Denny hesitate. The guy was no amateur. "It wasn't the right time. That's all. I'll try again tonight."

"Don't bother. She's got a guard dog now, and there's no way you'll get in while she's sleeping."

"What do you want me to do?"

Silence reigned on the other end of the phone long enough to make Denny shake. He was sure he wasn't going to like whatever his boss was going to have to say. He never did.

Denny had pulled all the blinds shut, hoping that the nagging sense of being watched would go away. It hadn't. He still felt the silent gaze of his boss heavy on the back of his neck.

"I want you to obtain a set of blueprints for the First Light youth center. The file number is listed along with the location of the file in a letter in your mailbox."

"What do you want those for?" he asked before he could stop himself. He'd drunk too much tonight. His wits were slow, and now it was going to cost him. He braced himself for the reaming, but it didn't come.

"Shame on you, you naughty boy." The words were almost singsong, grating discordantly against one another in the robot's voice.

"Sorry."

"That's a good boy. Now get some coffee to clear your head, and have the prints sitting on your kitchen table by morning."

"Where do you want me to take them, then?"

"Nowhere. I'll come get them."

"In my house?" Oh, man. The thought of having this guy come into his home made him sick. There was something off about him—something that was more fucked up than even Bruce's love for breaking guys' legs.

"You won't even know I was there. You never have."

The phone went dead, and Denny started shaking, and not from the booze. His boss had been here before and he hadn't even known it? What else didn't he know?

Before the thought could scare him stupid, he got up and made a pot of coffee, feeling his boss's eyes on the back of his neck the whole time.

❧

Lana showered the sweat from her body, letting the hot water run over her tired muscles. Even through the physical weariness, she felt a new kind of strength flowing through her. Despite the embarrassing episode on the mat, Lana realized that she'd learned more in the hour of training from Caleb than she had in weeks worth of self-defense classes in college. There was something about the brutally effective moves he'd taught her that gave her a thin strand of confidence to grab on to. It made her feel powerful, safer somehow. She just hoped that the end of their lesson tonight didn't mean the end of lessons altogether. If she could keep her libido in check, she might actually manage to fight back some of the fear she'd been living with for so long.

The notion made her giddy with hope.

Now if she could only convince Caleb to continue the lessons without the two of them ending up naked, she'd be set.

Yeah, right.

Caleb had frozen up and stayed frozen from the moment he'd walked out of the men's room. He was the picture of walking regret, and she knew that her lessons were over.

Lana pulled on her pajamas—a knit T-shirt and matching shorts set that was cool and comfortable. She came out of the bathroom and Caleb's black gaze slid up and down her body, making her nipples tighten to hard points against her shirt. Lana licked her lips and tried not to read anything into his stare.

"Those hurt?" he asked, nodding toward her legs.

Lana looked down the surgical scars and saw a few shadowy patches of skin where their mock combat had bruised her. She wasn't sure which he'd referred to, but the answer was the same. "No."

"Good. You sore?"

She would be tomorrow, but for now, she was just pleasantly tired. "No."

He ran a wide hand over his face and pulled in a deep breath. "I'm staying here tonight," he told her in a tone that gave away his displeasure with the notion.

Lana felt a zing of excitement race through her but tried to hide it. "You weren't invited."

"I know, but I'm still staying."

"Why?"

He stepped forward until he was close enough she could reach out and touch him.

Lana clenched her hands to keep from doing just that. He was so solid and safe. Real and warm. For some reason he could anchor her to reality when the nightmares came, ward away all that darkness.

She was so tired. Worn down.

He reached out and slipped a thick finger over her ear

to tuck back damp tendrils of her hair. "Because I can't stand the thought of leaving you alone."

Lana looked up at him, losing herself in the warmth of his concerned gaze. "I'm a big girl."

"You're all woman. Don't think I haven't noticed. But that doesn't mean you should be alone."

"It's easier that way."

"Liar." He closed the remaining distance between them, making Lana back up against the wall.

She felt the heat of his body, the unyielding slabs of muscle over his chest pressing against hers. His cheeks darkened, and his nostrils flared as if drinking in her scent. She was caged against the wall by his body, unable to tell if she was more worried by his odd behavior or excited by it.

"What are you doing?" she asked. Her voice wavered and her lungs sucked in air, pressing her breasts more fully against him.

He leaned down until she could feel his lips move against her neck. "Tell me you want me to stop," he dared her.

Lana couldn't. Her hands pressed against his chest, but she couldn't find the strength to push. Instead, her fingers curled against his hot skin in an effort to drag him closer.

He opened his mouth and flicked his tongue just below her ear. A jolt of heat shot through her, making her body clench hard. She sucked in a shocked breath, and it came out as a hiss of pleasure.

"There's no one watching us this time. No one listening." He slid his fingers into her hair until his big hand covered the back of her head. "Nothing to stop us."

Lana's lips parted in an effort to find something to say to that. Nothing came out, and Caleb took advantage of her speechlessness by kissing her.

Just the touch of his lips on hers was enough to make her sway. Caleb kept a light hold on her body with one arm while his fingers were firm and warm against her scalp, giving her no means of retreat.

Not that she wanted any.

When he held her like this, kissed her, there was no room for fear between them. He drove everything from her thoughts but excitement and pleasure.

Lana kissed him back, sliding her tongue along his bottom lip. His breathing sped, and she could feel the air around them heat.

He pulled his mouth free of hers and kissed his way over her cheek, down her jaw, until he reached her neck.

"God, Lana," he breathed, "I can't take much more of this."

"Me, either," she told him and clung to his wide shoulders to steady herself.

"Just tell me." His teeth nipped her skin, sending a zing of pleasure to her core. "I don't want secrets between us. Or lies."

The words buzzed around in her brain until they finally made sense. He was seducing her for information.

"Tell me what you're hiding and all this will be over. I'll keep you safe. I swear it."

Lana froze in outrage. Humiliation. Once again she'd been swept away by his touch, his kiss. But it was all an act. Part of his job.

Caleb must have felt her go stiff. He stopped kissing

her and straightened his body so he could look at her. Concern and lust tightened his features

Tears burned Lana's eyes, and she knew if she so much as blinked, they'd spill over. She was so sick of crying, so angry that he could hurt her like this.

It was the anger that saved her, burning away her tears.

"I can't believe you'd use me this way." Her clenched teeth made the words come out tight and bitter.

"I have to keep you safe. Whatever you're hiding might get you killed. I won't let that happen."

"So you thought you'd try fucking the information out of me?"

She shoved him, but he didn't budge. His body was hard and immobile under her hands.

The glow of lust that had lit his eyes brightened to angry determination. "Whatever it takes. I played by the rules last time and you nearly died. I don't make the same mistake twice."

"You think you're that good? That a few minutes with your cock inside me is going to make me throw all my deep, dark secrets at your feet?" Sarcasm made her voice ugly and hard.

Something hot flared in his features and he shifted closer, crowding her with his big body. His voice was low and velvet soft. "A few minutes, a few hours, a few days. Whatever it takes."

Yes! shouted a feral voice inside Lana, but she held her ground. "So you admit that it would be manipulation."

"I'd rather see you live by manipulation than die by honesty. Besides, there's not a whole lot of that between us, anyway. Is there?"

Lana looked away from him, ashamed of all the lying she'd been forced to do. "There's nothing between us."

"That's not true and you know it. You and I are tied together by the past. There's no escaping that and no escaping me."

"Unless I tell you whatever secret you think I'm keeping. If I did that, you'd be gone within the hour."

He hesitated for a moment and some faint hint of indecision glided over his features. He slid a blunt finger along her cheekbone, down to her jaw, along the line of her throat. Lana bit back a rough gasp of pleasure.

His pupils expanded, making the golden chips in his eyes dilate. "You think you know me. You think you know what I want. But you're wrong."

"I know exactly why you're here," she argued without much heat.

"Yes, but you don't know what I want."

"Then tell me."

He said nothing, just bent his head over her hair and pulled in a deep breath. His body shuddered, and his arms tightened around her. "I want to believe in second chances, Lana. In miracles."

She had no idea what he meant, but something desperate inside her wanted to give him whatever he wanted. Second chances, miracles, secrets, the truth. Everything.

It was at that moment that she realized just how close she was to breaking, to spilling out all the lies and secrets and half-truths she'd been keeping inside. Maybe he could keep her and her family safe. But maybe not. Lana couldn't take the risk—not with the people she loved.

With an effort of will that left her exhausted, Lana pulled herself away from Caleb, both physically and emotionally. She slipped away from him and crammed her expression into a hard mask. "Sorry. Can't help you. There's no such thing as miracles. Or second chances."

⊰✲⊱

Caleb woke fully from a dead sleep in the space of a heartbeat. He kept his eyes shut, listening to his surroundings. Something had woken him, and he strained his ears to figure out what it was.

The sound came again, a slight sigh of shifting fabric, the faint squeak of Lana's bed frame.

She was having another nightmare.

Caleb shoved up off the couch and went into her room without knocking. Sure enough, she was thrashing on the bed, her body bowed into a tight arc, her skin glowing with sweat.

He had to make this stop. He couldn't leave her knowing that she'd go through this alone every night. And eventually, whether she remained silent or not, he'd have to leave. There was no future for them, not with the past they shared. She'd said herself there were no second chances. At least not for him.

Caleb lay down and pulled her up against him, giving her soft, soothing words of comfort. He didn't know if she'd taken sleeping pills again tonight, but he tried to wake her anyway.

Ragged sounds of pain gurgled in her throat, and Caleb's hold on her tightened to the point where he had to focus on relaxing so he wouldn't hurt her.

"Wake up, Lana. Come back to me, honey."

She let out a stuttering sob and lashed out at him with her fists. Caleb caught her hands and tucked them under the blankets so she wouldn't hurt herself. He rocked her and urged her to wake up, suffering right along with her.

"You're safe," he told her. "I won't let them hurt you again."

He felt it when the nightmare released her, slowly, painfully. Her sobs deepened, and he felt the hot wetness of tears against his bare chest.

He would have given anything right now to take her pain away, to free her of this torment. He would have given his honor, his career, his life, anything to make this stop.

Her struggles slowed and weakened until she was clinging to him, her body shaking with the aftereffects of the nightmare.

Caleb murmured soft words into her hair and rocked her in a steady motion until he felt her pull away. Her eyes were red and shadowed with fatigue. They pleaded to him to help her, and Caleb wanted to howl at the unfairness of her life. She didn't deserve this. No one did.

"You're okay now," he told her, hearing his rioting emotions thicken his voice.

She wiped her eyes and sniffed. There was still a wildness in her expression—a sort of frantic panic he'd seen on the faces of men who knew they were cornered. Trapped.

He wanted to soothe her, protect her, but he had so little to offer. He smoothed the cobweb of dark hair away from her face, trying to tell her without words how he felt, that he would do anything to make the bad parts of her life go away.

"I don't know how much longer I can stand this," she whispered to him, as if saying the words too loud would hurt. She rested her forehead on his bare chest, and her breath fanned out over his skin, making his body tighten. He gritted his teeth and ignored it. He stroked her hair, down her delicate spine, pushing away the covers as he passed. She should have been pushing *him* away instead. He should have been walking away from the temptation she posed, but he wasn't man enough to leave her. Not yet. Not until she calmed down and could rest again.

She lifted her head and looked into his eyes. He could see the fear from the nightmare lingering in those blue depths, begging him to help. "Make me forget. Just for a little while. Please."

Caleb knew it was a mistake—one more on a giant pile—but he didn't care. She'd given him something he could do, and he was damn well going to do it.

He took her mouth in a soft kiss, a mere brushing of lips. Such an innocent thing, but it nearly turned his body inside out with a wave of raw lust. He felt himself harden in a painfully swift rush and couldn't keep from grinding his hips against her to show her just how much he wanted her. Warning her just how he planned to make her forget.

Lana's arms freed themselves of tangled sheets and looped around his neck, holding him in place with a fierce grip. She wasn't letting him get away.

Her lips parted under his, opening herself up to him. He couldn't wait another second to taste her. He licked just inside her upper lip, teasing her, trying to hold back in case she changed her mind. He hoped she wouldn't. He no longer cared whether loving her was right. It was necessary.

Lana made a low sound of relief and sucked his tongue into her mouth. Caleb felt the kiss all the way down to the soles of his bare feet. Her fingers speared through his hair, holding his head still while she gave him deep, devouring kisses. He gave her leave to show him what she needed, show him what she liked.

His hands slid under the hem of her shirt, finding skin as soft and warm as sunlight. Her supple spine arched in response, pushing her hips against him in a maddening gyration. Caleb's restraint broke and there was no more holding back. He was going to love her tonight, no matter how much of a mistake it might be.

Caleb's mouth pulled away from hers, and he rained hot, open-mouthed kisses along her neck, sucking and biting as he went. He was sure he was leaving marks behind for anyone to see, and part of him cheered a primitive response. He wanted everyone to know she was his. Only his.

His teeth bit gently along the joint of neck and shoulder, and Lana hissed and her nails scored his back. "Like that?" he asked, already knowing the answer.

She gave an incoherent noise of appreciation, and Caleb swirled his tongue to soothe the sting his teeth had left behind. His hands slid around to her front, splaying over her pale tummy and ribs, brushing away the barrier of her soft knit shirt. Caleb's stomach did a slow, lazy roll as he watched his hands moving over smooth, perfect skin. Lana's skin.

"I want to see you," he told her, his voice rough and

demanding. "See your naked breasts all puckered and eager for my mouth. Like they were in the shower."

Lana's fingers tangled with his as she tried to rid herself of the shirt. They managed to get it off, and it flew somewhere across the room, lost and forgotten.

Caleb found her hands and held them away from her body so he could look his fill. She was so beautiful with her skin flushed and her nipples tight and begging for his mouth. He'd seen a lot of naked women, but no woman before Lana had made his hands shake. None had made him wish he was a better man, more deserving of her.

No longer able to resist, Caleb released her hands and drew a finger over the lower curve of her breasts. She jerked and wiggled, trying to coax him to touch her more fully, but he held back. Lana was a once-in-a-lifetime woman, one who had to be savored, and he was going to do just that.

She grabbed his wrist, trying to move his hand to cover her breast, showing him how she wanted to be touched, but she was no match for his strength. She couldn't make him budge from the slow, lazy path he drew over her smooth skin.

Lana quit fighting him and started to wage her own war. Her clever little hands slid down between them until she found the rigid length of his penis. Slim fingers wormed their way under the stretchy waistband of his sweats and wrapped around him in a bold caress.

It was Caleb's turn to hiss out his pleasure, and he closed his eyes, enjoying the feel of her hand on him, the feel of her fingers stroking and teasing. He wasn't going to last two minutes if she kept that up, and he had more in mind than a hand job. "None of that yet," he told her, pulling her wayward hand out of his pants. "When I come, I want it to be deep inside you, right where I belong."

She shivered and her eyes darkened, driving the deep blue to a thin ring of color. Her tongue slid out over her bottom lip, and Caleb couldn't stop himself from tasting her mouth again. She tasted like home, sweet and warm and his.

How was he ever going to let her go?

Caleb shoved the thought away before it could taint the time they had now. She was half-naked and willing, in his arms, and that was enough. It had to be enough.

He spread his hand wide, covering her breast so that her tight little nipple speared up into his palm. Lana whimpered into his mouth and he felt her slim hands clench his shoulders. She fit perfectly in his hand, the soft, womanly curve of her breast making his mouth water.

He slid his fingers over her skin, tugging at her nipple, feeling it lengthen and tighten against the calluses of his fingertips. Lana let out a ragged moan of approval that made Caleb's head spin. He loved her responsiveness, all the little noises she made and the way her body quivered and strained to get closer to his.

He pulled his mouth from hers, needing to feel her nipples against his tongue. He cupped her breast in his hand while his lips closed over her nipple. She let out a strangled cry, and Caleb felt her flesh vibrating with his possessive growl. She was his. Too far gone to stop. Too wild. And he loved it.

Maybe he should have pressed the advantage and tried

to question her again, but he couldn't bear the thought of her pulling away from him. Not now. Maybe not ever.

He suckled her breasts, loving them evenly, using lips and tongue and teeth to drive her into a frenzy. She didn't even notice when he slipped those flimsy shorts off her legs and spread them wide. The scent of her arousal sent streamers of need shooting through him, but he held himself back, just a little longer. He knew she was turned on, but he wanted her desperate, unable to think of anything but getting him inside her.

His mouth moved down her body while his fingers tugged and rolled her nipples. He kissed her ribs and lingered on the sweet curve of her stomach, running his tongue around the rim of her belly button. That had her arching her hips off the bed, and he fit his hands under her, gripping the firm cheeks of her ass in his palms.

She knew what he was going to do now. He could feel it in the way she went still, in the way her legs vibrated against his shoulders. He wasn't sure if it was something she wanted, but he wasn't going to give her a chance to protest, not before he got to taste her.

His tongue flicked out, barely grazing her flesh. Her thighs tightened, but his shoulders held them open wide. The second touch was more firm, more direct. Her fingers raked through his hair, holding him, not pushing him away. It was all the encouragement Caleb needed.

He slid one finger along her folds, parting the delicate skin, feeling the slick heat of her arousal. It was nearly enough to make him come, knowing she wanted him like that, feeling the proof of her want for him against the tip of his finger.

He pressed into her just a little, just enough to let her

feel the invasion. Her body clamped down on his finger as if trying to pull him deeper inside.

Caleb choked on a raw groan of need that bubbled up out of him, giving away his own desperation. He wasn't going to last much longer, and he wanted to make it as good for her as possible.

He opened her folds so that he could see the little pink button hidden inside. Lana stiffened at his intimate inspection and she started to sit up, so he pushed his finger deeper, giving her what her body had begged for only moments ago. Lana's hands fisted in the blankets, and she flopped back down onto the bed with a soft sound of pleasure.

Caleb grinned as he flicked his tongue lightly over her clitoris. Lana pulled in a shocked breath, but he didn't give her time to let it out before he licked her again. He felt the flesh around his finger pulse and become slicker. She was tight, maybe too tight to take him easily, and as much as that tightness thrilled him, it also made preparing her that much more important.

He wrapped his lips around the sensitive flesh, being careful to gauge her reaction, not wanting to do anything that would hurt her. But whatever she was feeling wasn't pain. She was panting, and the skin on her chest had deepened to a pretty pink blush that spread up her throat.

Caleb slid his finger out and back while he licked and nibbled. Her breathing was growing more ragged, and her head was thrown back. She was getting close to coming, and he forced her forward with eager determination. With each passing second her back arched higher, until he felt her climax take over her body. She let out a sweet cry of pleasure as the lower half of her body trembled against the orgasm. He locked his lips around her clitoris and suckled her as he had her nipples, driving her right through her release. He felt the liquid response of her body and the rhythmic pulsing of her muscles. Caleb waited until the waves of her orgasm had started to fade and then pressed a second finger inside her slick body, stretching her.

The pressure drove her back up and over the crest of a second climax and made Caleb moan into the sensitive flesh between her legs. He felt her orgasm rock him to the marrow of his bones, making him feel like a freaking superhero. Making her come was the world's greatest high, and he wasn't sure how long he'd be able to go without doing it again.

She came back down, breathing hard and limp on the bed. Her legs were splayed wide, and in the bright lights of the room, he could see the shiny proof of her release slick on his hand and her thighs.

A wave of lust hit him so hard he couldn't breathe. His fingers were still buried inside her, feeling the tiny quivering twitches that remained of her orgasm. He pulled them from her body and heard her answering whimper of loss.

He should have just walked away from her, leaving her sated. He'd made her forget, which had been his goal, but now that he was here, with her body laid out before him like an offering, there was nothing he could do to resist. He needed her. Needed the soft strength of her body to enfold him, ease him. He'd never needed anything more.

Caleb shucked his sweats and lowered his body over

hers. As the weight of him pressed against her, her eyes snapped open, revealing more than just the aftermath of passion. She was afraid.

Caleb bit back a violent word and eased himself away. No way was he going to take her with that look on her face. He'd sooner blow his own head off.

CHAPTER NINETEEN

———— ❧ ————

Lana saw Caleb's face, the desperate set of his jaw, the way it bulged as he gritted his teeth and backed away from her. He'd seen her fear. He'd been about to make love to her, and he'd seen that momentary flash of panic she'd gotten in her eyes.

Lana wanted to kick herself for letting him see it, but she hadn't been able to predict how panicked she'd get with his bulk holding her down. She hadn't been with a man since Oran—before her abduction—and this reaction slammed into her from out of the blue, completely unexpected.

Her body was humming with satisfaction, her limbs languid and slow, but she was fast enough to stop his retreat. She grabbed his wrist and forced him to look at her. "I want you, but I can't be on the bottom," she explained, her voice hoarse. "It makes me feel . . . trapped." Bound, helpless, out of control. She couldn't think straight with those memories of being held captive still too near her waking thoughts, so she shoved them away, focusing on Caleb's beautiful body.

He looked unconvinced, and she saw the muscles in his jaw bunch.

"Please," she whispered. "I need you." She didn't want him leaving yet, not until she'd felt what it was like to hold him inside her body, to be as close to him as a woman could be.

"Give me ten seconds." He raced out of the bedroom and returned in less than that, ripping a condom package open with his teeth. She watched as he rolled it over his erection, wishing she'd had the fun of doing that herself.

"Lie down," she urged him, tugging at his arm and moving aside so there was an empty swath of bed to hold him.

Caleb lay down, and his body swallowed up all the space on the double bed. Lana gave him what she hoped was a seductive smile and straddled his naked body, sitting over his stomach with the heavy length of his penis just behind her. He was glorious. There was no other word for it. His limbs were thick with muscle, the veins standing out under the strain of his racing heart. The dark hair on his chest tempted her to touch, to explore the springy texture with her fingers and breasts. His eyes were black with desire, and a dark stain of lust highlighted his cheekbones.

Lana pressed her palms to his bare chest and leaned down to kiss him. He didn't move. Didn't reach for her, didn't urge her on in any way. His lips were firm and hot beneath hers, and she ran her tongue along the seam, asking him wordlessly to open for her. When he finally did, Lana sucked his lower lip into her mouth.

Caleb finally responded. He took hold of her head, angled it slightly, and swept his tongue into her mouth. Lana's recently sated body flared back to life and returned the kiss with open abandon.

This was what she wanted, what she needed—this human connection that drove away everything but the quest for pleasure. He drove away the darkness and set her body ablaze, leaving no room for worry or doubt or fear. Her whole world collapsed down to the space between them, the brush of his hair over her nipples, the slick warmth of his mouth, the rough caress of his callused fingers over her skin. Nothing else mattered.

Her fingers grazed his shoulders, moving down, kneading the thick slabs of muscle over his chest. Caleb made deep, rough sounds that could only be taken as masculine satisfaction, but Lana wasn't done with him yet. Not even close.

She lifted her body and wrapped her fingers around his erection, just like she had before. And just like before, Caleb let out a slow hiss of pleasure that made her feel like a goddess. Her touch had done that. She'd made him feel good. And she was about to make him feel much better.

Lana positioned him and pressed her body down against the tip of his erection. The blunt thickness sent zingers of electricity racing along her nerves until they ended right where they'd begun. He was big, but she was wet and ready for him. Man, was she ready.

His hands wrapped around her hips, and his fingers opened and closed almost involuntarily, pressing into her flesh. She managed to sink down a couple inches, feeling her body stretching to take him. It didn't hurt, but it was . . . intense. He took her breath away.

She moved back up, descended again, this time farther than before. Caleb's hands tightened, and Lana felt her body spiraling upward toward another climax. He wasn't even fully inside her yet and she was already fighting off the need to come.

A few more slow, torturous movements of her hips and she had taken as much of him as she could. She was filled up, stretched, her body vibrating with pleasure.

Caleb gave her a fierce smile. "I wasn't sure I'd fit inside that tight little body of yours," he told her.

"Perfect fit."

Caleb did something that made his erection twitch inside her and Lana felt her world tilt.

"If you don't move, I'm going to have to move you," he said.

Lana braced her hands on his ribs and lifted her body, then slid right back down. Moving was nearly more than she could stand, and it left her feeling weak and boneless. Caleb came to her rescue and lifted her up with a strong grip of his hands on her hips.

He slid out of her only to fill her again. Lana was dying. The pressure inside her was too much so soon after he'd given her the best orgasms of her life. But Caleb didn't relent. He lifted and lowered her over and over while his strong hips worked beneath her. She heard his breathing speed, felt the way his skin heated and his hands were hot against her hips. Lana steadied herself, kept her balance, but that was all she could manage. He'd driven the strength right out of her, and she was just along for the ride. And ride she did, until her head was spinning and her body was vibrating so hard she thought she'd shatter.

She leaned forward, and the angle caused his penis to press against something magical inside her. Raw feeling expanded through her body, radiating out from where his erection filled her. Her mind shut down, and she let the pleasure wash over her, giving in to the need to cry out. She didn't care if anyone heard—all she cared about was living inside that shimmering pleasure as long as she could, surrendering to it with shameless abandon.

The jolts of feeling subsided after endless moments, and just outside her orgasmic haze, she heard Caleb let loose a raw cry of his own. She felt him swell and throb inside her, stretching her farther as he came. It was perfection, feeling his pleasure inside her. Sweet, potent perfection.

Lana toppled down onto his chest, enjoying the remnants of her orgasm, the faint buzz of her limbs, and the internal spasms that lingered. Caleb's arms wrapped around her and his wide hands stroked down her back. His hands were shaking.

She pressed her cheek over his heart and let his deep breathing lull and calm her. He didn't bother with pillow talk, and she was grateful for the silence. Words would only make reality intrude and ruin what had been the best sex of her life. His hands kept stroking and his heartbeat evened out. Lana closed her eyes and let herself drift.

For the first time in eighteen months, she slept without dreams.

❧

Caleb smiled up at the ceiling. He could have ripped apart mountains with his bare hands if she'd asked him to. He felt like some sort of ancient god, powerful and immortal. Lana had done that to him. He held her, reveling in the feeling. It had been more than just sex, at least for him. It was proof of her forgiveness, proof of her trust.

He wasn't going to let her down.

He wasn't above using sex as a tool to pry her secrets from her, but not because he was under orders. He didn't give a damn about his orders compared to Lana. But he knew that as long as she held back, as long as she kept her problems secret from him, she'd be in danger. He couldn't stand to let that continue. He'd find a way to get her to trust him enough to share her burden. And then he'd kill it. Whatever it was.

He stroked his fingers lightly over her back, just barely touching her. He still couldn't get over the way it felt like he was stroking sunshine. He figured he'd never get over it.

Caleb pulled in a deep breath and let it out. Lana's weight lifted atop him, but she didn't move, and he wasn't going to encourage her to. He liked her right there, all soft and replete, warm and satisfied. She was perfect just where she was.

❧

Denny waited as long as he could for the older couple to leave. Didn't they have jobs to go to? Grandkids to see? Something—anything—to make them leave before it was too late?

He checked his watch again. He only had fifteen minutes left before the job had to be done. The stench of gasoline was making him sick, not to mention the thought of roasting Grandma and Grandpa alive.

Why the hell didn't they leave?

The air in the garage was suffocating him. Not that there was much of it. The place was packed floor to ceiling with junk, which was why he'd chosen it to start the fire.

A pile of lumber. An old couch. Too many cans of paint. This place was going to go up like a torch.

Denny eyed the exit again, ten feet away. All he had to do was light a match, drop it, and run. His car was a couple of blocks away—a short dash through overgrown back yards. No one would see him.

It would all be over soon.

Sour sweat slid into his eyes. He wiped it away with a shaking hand.

They were still in the house, puttering around. He could hear the TV. The morning news was blaring.

Denny checked his watch again. Time was up. For all of them.

He sucked in a deep breath that burned his lungs, lit the match, and let it fall into the gasoline-soaked lumber. Flames roared up as they burned off the fumes in the air, then settled down to a nice hot glow.

Denny watched from the door just long enough to see he'd done his job, then took off at a dead run.

CHAPTER TWENTY

————— ❧ —————

By the time Caleb and Lana pulled into the First Light Foundation office, the four men Caleb had called in to help were already waiting for them. He was glad to have the distraction from the thoughtful silence Lana had been giving him all morning.

She hadn't been cold toward him, but neither had she thrown herself at him this morning when she'd woken up to find him still in her bed. She'd blushed and headed for the shower, leaving him wishing he'd offered to soap her up and see where it took them. Like he didn't know just what would happen if he got her back under that hot spray of water. He'd give a repeat performance of the first time, only this time he'd keep going until they were both too tired to stand.

Instead, he shoved his morning erection into an uncomfortable pair of jeans and pretended like she hadn't spun his world off its axis last night. He'd give her time to digest what had passed between them and pray she didn't think it had all been a mistake. He wasn't sure he'd survive knowing he'd never get the chance to make her come again while he was so deep inside her he could feel her heartbeat.

With that thought in mind, he got out of the car and gave the man who had guarded Lana's office last night the signal to go get some rest.

"Who are they?" asked Lana.

"Friends. Guys I've worked with before and know I can trust. Let's go inside and I'll introduce you."

Lana slung her backpack over one shoulder and eyed the men warily while Caleb clasped hands and gave his thanks to each man for coming.

They filed inside with the cheerful chime of bells tinkling in their wake. All four of these men had worked with Caleb at one time or another, and besides being good in a bad situation, they had volunteered to take some time and help out with the carnival. He couldn't have asked for a better group.

"Lana, I'd like you to meet my friends," he told her, motioning to the first man. "This is Brent Collins."

Brent was the youngest of the group and had a baby face that had fooled more than one bad guy. He looked like someone's kid brother, with messy brown hair and a few freckles. He had a slim build that was a hell of a lot stronger than it looked, but it was his almost unnatural technical ability that had earned him a place in Delta Force.

"Good to meet you, Lana." Brent shook her hand, giving her that boyish smile that Caleb knew would put her at ease.

"This is Jack Langston," said Caleb, introducing the next in line. Jack was the kind of man you wouldn't look at twice. He blended in wherever he went, as long as he was wearing dark glasses or contacts. He had the palest blue eyes Caleb had ever seen—almost silver—which caused him to keep his eyelids down as if to hide them. The effect was that he looked sleepy, which was a dangerous assumption to have about a man as deadly as Jack.

Jack said nothing, just nodded in acknowledgment, keeping his hands in his pockets and leaned against the wall.

Next in line was Riley. He stuck out his hand and gave Lana's hand a warm shake—the kind presidential candidates use to win votes, with both hands—and a wide smile full of straight white teeth. "Riley Seaton, ma'am. So glad we could come help you and the kids."

Riley could have been a professional model had the urge struck him. He was drop-dead handsome, and Caleb felt himself tense as he waited for Lana to swoon or fall all over him like the women Riley met usually did. Instead she just smiled, released his hand, and took a step back to Caleb's side.

He felt a thrill of satisfaction and pride at the simple action. He loved how she could do that—make him feel like he was invincible, the luckiest man on earth.

"And this is Madison Parker," said Caleb. "We call him Mad for short, 'cause it makes him so happy."

Brent and Riley laughed.

"Mad?" she asked, looking at Caleb.

"Yes, ma'am," answered Mad in that steady, even voice that Caleb had never once heard raised in anger or joy.

Mad was a bit shorter than Caleb, but with plenty of muscle. They all teased him about his tendency toward emotionless stoicism, but when someone needed the impossible done in a hurry, Mad was the man to call. Which made him perfect for this job. Caleb still wasn't sure how they were going to pull it off.

The carnival was in a few days, and there were a million details to cover. Good thing these were some of the most detail-oriented men on the face of the planet. Doing the impossible with whatever resources were available was what they did best.

Caleb pulled Lana aside and lowered his voice. "If you don't need me, I'm going to brief the men on the situation, and we'll get started pulling the carnival together."

She looked up at him like she wanted to say something different but changed her mind a moment before the words came out. "Are you sure about this? About . . . them?"

"The men?"

"Yes. They're kind of intimidating, don't you think? Won't they scare the kids?"

Caleb couldn't stop himself from tucking a stray strand of hair behind her ear. He needed to touch her again, to feel her skin heat under his hands, but he settled for what he could get away with in public until he could get her alone again. "Trust me, honey. We know what we're doing. We've done things like this for the kids on base, and none of them have run screaming."

"Are you sure? This fundraiser is important to me. If it fails . . ." She trailed off, and he saw something frightening flash through her eyes—something dark and powerful—a desperation so intense he could almost feel it rushing through her.

"I won't let you down," he promised. "This is going to work. You'll see."

"We only have a few days." That hopeless look she wore nearly brought him to his knees. He didn't care who was watching or what his men thought. He pulled her into his arms and kissed the top of her head.

"Twice as many as we need. Trust me."

He felt her nod under his lips, but he could tell that she didn't quite believe him. Didn't quite trust him.

The knowledge made his chest ache, but he knew he couldn't force something like that. She trusted him with her body, but it wasn't enough. He wanted her to trust him with her life, her future. He wanted to prove to her that no matter what had happened in the past, he'd never let her down again. He wasn't sure why this fundraiser was so important to her, but he didn't really care. It was important to her, and that was all he needed to know.

Caleb released Lana before he did something that would embarrass them both in front of the room full of men. He gave her a quick kiss on the forehead and a reassuring smile. "Just trust me."

❧

While the men were having their powwow, Lana ducked out of the office, intent on going to visit Stacie. She'd been sent home yesterday, and Lana wanted to make sure she and her sister were settling in okay.

Lana had just reached her car when Caleb caught her. The sun blazed down, casting his face into a deep shadow. That jolt of feeling coursed through her as she was thrown back in time to the day he'd carried her out of that cave. Lana closed her eyes and braced her weight against her car door.

"You okay?" he asked while his hands wrapped around her upper arms to steady her.

Lana felt the heat of his touch warm her more thoroughly than the hot sun overhead. She stifled a little shiver, remembering just how his hands had felt as he'd touched her last night, how much pleasure he'd given her with just the stroke of his fingers.

"I'm fine. Just feeling a little crowded in there."

"It's a lot of people to cram into such a tiny office. Why don't we go for a drive?"

Lana stared at his big feet rather than risk getting hit by the force of the memories that lurked in his silhouette. "I'd rather be alone for a while."

"Let me come with you," said Caleb. "It's not safe for you to be alone. Not after what happened to Stacie."

She needed some time to herself—some space away from Caleb so she could think. Regroup. "I need this, Caleb. Just let me go. Please."

He stood quietly for a moment, and she wasn't sure if he was trying to think of another argument or trying to convince himself he didn't need one. "Would you prefer one of the other men go with you instead?" There was a quality in his voice that she hadn't heard before. If she hadn't known better, she would have thought it was insecurity, but that didn't make any sense. No one was stronger or more courageous than Caleb.

"Of course not. I don't know those men. I just need some time alone. I need to go see Stacie. I need to visit the kids." She hid the spike of anxiety she felt at the thought of going back to the youth center. Kara seemed to always be there.

His hand cupped her cheek, and he fought the urge to lean into his touch. "I don't want to let you go, but I guess it's not my choice."

There was a deeper meaning to his words, she could hear it in his tone, but she didn't dare try to figure it out.

As it was, she was using every bit of willpower she had to keep from begging him to make her life go away again. He'd given her a precious gift of solace in a world that had revolved around fear for so long she'd forgotten what it was like not to be afraid.

He'd shown her what it was like to be normal again, and waking up to her real life had felt like a crushing blow. Nothing had changed. She still had to stay silent. It was the only way to protect those she loved—a group that was well on its way to including Caleb.

"I'll be fine," she told him. "Trust me."

❧

If she hadn't thrown his own words back at him, he might have forced the issue and pressured her to let him come, but instead, she'd asked him to trust her. How could he expect her to trust him if he didn't do the same?

Damn, he wished he just had something to blow up rather than having to deal with all this psychological shit.

He watched her drive away and called Grant on his cell phone. He answered with a sleepy, " 'lo."

"Tell me you planted a tracking device on her car when you swept it for bugs and fixed the brakes."

All sleepiness vanished, and Grant sounded wide-awake. "Of course. What's up?"

"She needed some time alone."

"Got it. I'm already on the way to the car. I'll have her in sight in less than five minutes."

Caleb pushed out a relieved breath. "Thanks."

"Does that mean you trust me not to seduce her away from you?"

"Not if you like your smile on the front side of your head."

"Yeah, yeah. I get it. You're big and mean, and you'll beat the shit out of me if I so much as touch her."

"I always knew you were a smart man." Caleb hung up and went back inside to finish nailing down the final plans for the carnival. They weren't going to try for anything fancy, but there was plenty they could do without spending much money. A lot of that hinged on the men being willing to humiliate themselves, but that was all part of the fun.

Three hours later, Caleb rubbed his ear, which was sore from too much exposure to the telephone. He'd made some progress, but not nearly enough to suit him. He didn't want anything else to go wrong with Lana's fundraiser. He'd told her to trust him, and he was determined that when all was said and done, she would know she could.

He'd just set the phone back in its cradle when it rang. Lana still wasn't back, so he answered it in her stead. Sixty seconds later he was nearly in a panic, rushing out the door to find Lana. He was done playing games now. The stakes had just gone up, and he didn't want to let her out of his sight again.

⤜⊱⤛

Lana was sitting on the edge of Stacie's bed, chatting quietly with her about her sister when Caleb came into the room. The look on his face nearly stopped her heart. His jaw was set at a grim angle, and his black eyes had darkened with anger to the point they reflected no light.

"What is it?" she asked, knowing something was wrong.

He took her hands, and she could-feel rage vibrating though his limbs. "I'm sorry, Lana."

"What?" she demanded, fear uncurling inside her until it was a nearly living thing.

"Everyone's fine. You need to know that first, but there was a fire at your parents' house. It was totally destroyed."

"A . . . fire?" She couldn't digest the information. It was too surreal.

"Your mom and dad are safe. A little shaken up, but fine otherwise."

"Oh, Lana," said Stacie, starting to rise from the bed.

Lana held out her hand to stop her friend from getting up. She still wasn't strong enough yet to be moving around much.

Caleb pulled her against him, hugging her, but Lana was a statue in his arms. She couldn't let him comfort her. If she weakened even a little, she would lose control. Mom and Dad were going to need her. "What happened?" she asked him.

"Police and firemen are there now. It will be a while before they know anything."

Lana pushed away from him and took a step toward the door—away from Caleb, away from Stacie, too. She had to get away from both of them and their soft words of comfort. "And you're sure they're okay?"

"Yes. I spoke with your mother briefly. She says they're both fine."

Lana nodded. A fire. Was this what was next on Kara's list to destroy her life? First her peace and any sense of security were destroyed, then Stacie was shot, and now a fire? What was next? *Who* was next? Which of the people she loved was going to be the next target of violence?

Caleb reached for her, but Lana jerked away. She couldn't let him get near her again. It wasn't safe. She had to break things off with Stacie, too. Fire her. Shove Stacie out of her life. It was the only way.

Lana turned around, ignoring the worried voices behind her. She couldn't stay here. She had to go see if her parents were really okay, see it with her own eyes. Only then would she believe it was true.

She had already pulled out of Stacie's driveway by the time Caleb came running out of the door. She had to get away from him. What if he was the next target?

The streets blurred by her as she took the familiar path to the home where she'd grown up. It was nestled back on a little plot of land her father had worked two jobs to buy. She remembered her dad helping erect the frame of the house when she was five, remembered her mom poring over carpet samples and paint chips. She'd had sleepovers with friends and birthday parties there. She'd woken up many Christmas mornings to a festive tree and a pile of presents, her fat stocking hanging from the fireplace. She'd had her first kiss on the back porch and cried after her first breakup at the kitchen table.

It was home.

And now it was gone. Lana cleared the corner and the road was still clogged with rescue vehicles. Dribbles of black smoke wafted into the clear summer sky, and the smell of that smoke choked her lungs. She got out of the car, not even sure if she'd left it running, and walked like a zombie up the street.

Everything was gone. There was just a big black pile of charred concrete and brick where her home used to be.

She knew it was her fault.

Her mother ran over to her, wrapped in a dirty blanket. She had smudges of soot on her cheeks and a lost look in her blue eyes. Her mom's arms wrapped around her, covering them both with the blanket, and it was all Lana could do not to shove her away. It wasn't safe to show her love like this in public. She was probably being watched.

Lana wondered if the tears rolling down her mother's face brought Kara as much sick pleasure as her screams had.

"Where's Dad?" asked Lana. "Is he okay?"

"He's with the fire chief right now."

"Show me."

Madeline Hancock led Lana over puddles and through a crowd of neighbors. Carter Hancock was standing near the front of the fire truck, staring over the ruins of his house.

Lana hesitated for only a moment before going to him.

"Dad," whispered Lana, choking back her tears. She couldn't stop herself from hugging him. He looked so shaken, so devastated.

"Lana," he said, as if he was surprised to see her.

Lana checked him over for visible signs of injury but found none. He was pale and shaking but looked unhurt. She knew that didn't mean a damn thing, though. For all she knew he was screaming on the inside, rough, ragged screams of pain and loss. She knew what that was like all too well.

"I think the roses may survive," he told her as if it

was the only thing holding him together. "They were far enough away from the house that the fire didn't get them. If the water didn't rip them apart, they may be okay."

Lana wiped away a soot stain from his wrinkled cheek. "I'm sure they'll survive."

He gave her an absent nod.

Madeline took her husband's hand, and together they stared at the charred remains of their home.

Lana turned away, unable to stand witnessing the suffering she'd caused for even one more second. Standing behind her a few feet away was Caleb. He was watching her, looking invincible and strong, and she struggled against the urge to go to him and let him take away this nightmare, too. But unlike last night, this was real, and she had to face it.

Lana ripped her eyes from him and just looked at the soggy ground. "What are you going to do?" she asked her mom. "Do you want to come stay at my place?" She regretted the words the moment she said them. No way could her parents stay at her place. That would make them even more of a target than they already were.

"We'll go stay with Jenny and Todd. They have more room, and little Taylor will take our mind off this mess like no one else could." Taylor was their one and only grandchild, and they doted and fussed over him as if he were the only child on earth.

"Is there anything you need? Anything I can do?" asked Lana.

"No. Jenny's on her way, and I know you've got your fundraiser coming up. You concentrate on that and don't worry about us."

Lana nodded. Her parents held each other. She turned away.

Lana pulled herself together as tight as she was going to get and marched over to Caleb. "I want you to put a guard on my sister's house. And Stacie's."

Caleb's eyes narrowed. "Does this mean you're ready to talk to me?"

"Will you do it or not?"

"I will."

"Even if I have nothing to say."

"We both know that's not true," he replied.

"Answer my question. Will you do this or not?"

"Yeah. I'll do it."

"No strings attached?"

"Is that what you want?" he asked her, and she knew he was talking about more than just her request for help. He was talking about them—about what they'd shared last night.

Lana shoved the thought away before it could take root. One night of killer sex did not equal a relationship. She couldn't let herself think otherwise, no matter how much she wanted to. "Yes. That's what I want."

Caleb's expression hardened, closed up. He pulled out his cell phone and pressed a button. "Assign guards at the Cramer residence as well as her sister's house." He paused. "Yes, twenty-four/seven. Don't let them know you're there." He hung up, looking at her with that same cold expression. "It's done. No strings attached."

Lana's eyes closed in relief. At least she'd managed to get her family and her friend that much help. It wasn't much, but it was something. More than she could have done alone. "Thank you."

"This isn't going to end here," he told her. "Whatever is causing this is only going to get worse."

Not if she cut everyone out of her life. Kara only wanted to hurt the people Lana loved, so all she had to do was pretend she didn't love anyone. She was good at pretending, and she was going to start with Caleb. "I don't want you following me around anymore."

"Tough shit."

"I mean it. I'm tired of having you trail after me like a puppy dog. Go home. Send someone else if you have to, but stay out of my way."

He stepped closer, and she had to tilt her head back to look into his eyes. "I know what you're doing, and it won't work."

"You don't know anything," she told him, using the bitchiest voice she could muster.

"I know you're scared."

There was no way she could fool him with a lie about that. He'd been right by her side through the nightmares—both the real thing and now the ghostly remnants of it. He would see right through her lies.

She turned and walked away because there was nothing else she could do. The farther away from Caleb she got, the safer he'd be.

CHAPTER TWENTY-ONE

———— ✦ ————

Caleb let her go, knowing Jack was on her trail like a shadow to watch her back. He'd seen Jack's dark sedan slip out behind her, unnoticed. She'd never see him, but he'd keep tabs on her and make sure she stayed safe.

For now, that's all Caleb wanted. Or at least that's what he tried to tell himself. The lie didn't work any better than Lana's had.

He surveyed the damage to her parents' home. Whatever she was hiding was getting bigger every day.

Maybe something here would clue him in to what Lana was hiding. He scanned the crowd for the person in charge and found Detective Hart looking right at him. He was as good a place to start as any.

"We meet again," said Detective Hart as Caleb approached him.

"You investigate arson as well as robbery?"

"Who said it was arson?" asked Hart, his hazel eyes glittering with intelligence.

Caleb shook his head. He must not be thinking straight to be trapped as quickly as that. "What do you think?" he asked.

Detective Hart glanced over at the house and gave a

shrug. "I think it's more than just a coincidence that two properties connected to Lana Hancock have been singled out in the same week in a very dangerous way."

"You got a theory?"

Hart laughed. "Not one that will beat yours, I'll bet. Care to share?"

"Sorry. Can't help you." Caleb almost wished he could. There was something about Hart's quiet competence that reminded him of David. Man, what he wouldn't give to have David at his back right now. Not that he begrudged his friend time with his new wife. Caleb would be doing exactly the same thing that David was—doting on his bride—if he'd been given half a chance.

As if.

"The doctor next to Lana's office keeps reporting a suspicious man sitting outside. When our patrol car shows up, no one's there. I'm assuming he's one of yours?"

Caleb didn't confirm it but said, "I wouldn't worry about him if I were you."

"Wouldn't want to waste precious resources," said Hart with more than a hint of sarcasm in his voice. "I realize that you've got a job to do, but so do I. I won't step on your toes. I just want to know what we're up against. These events aren't just some punky kids on a crime spree. It's more than that."

"Is it?"

"Don't give me that secretive shit. I know that you're military, and based on the limited information available, you're probably Special Forces. You wouldn't be here if this wasn't big."

"It's illegal for me to operate inside the United States.

I'm just a guy on leave protecting my girlfriend from some pranksters."

"Yeah, and I'm the fucking tooth fairy. Drop the crap and tell me what I can do, even if you don't want to tell me why. Miss Hancock's been through hell enough already."

Caleb hadn't expected the detective to know about her past, though he guessed he should have. She was something of a local celebrity. Thanks to the press, everyone knew she was the girl who was taken hostage and lived to tell, the girl who came back and devoted her life to helping kids.

"That's why I'm here."

"It's also why I'm here. I don't want to see a sweet girl come to a bad end. Let me do my job."

Caleb didn't want to bring anyone else into this mess. He had enough men already, and no matter how much Hart reminded him of David, he wasn't David. Didn't have David's training or history. "Sorry. Wish I could help."

Hart uttered a caustic string of curses, stomped off a few feet, ran a hand over his face and came back. He was like a freaking bulldog, refusing to let it drop. "I hear there's a big shindig going down at the youth center," said Hart calmly as if his little fit had vented off all that frustration.

"In a few days," said Caleb.

"Gonna be lots of kids there, from what I hear."

"You heard right. Is that a problem?"

"Not for me. In fact, plenty of us on the force think what Lana's doing is great. We'd love to come out and lend a hand."

Caleb finally pulled his head out of his ass far enough

to figure out what Hart was offering. Police protection. "I suppose we can always use the help," he told the detective.

"That's good to know. I like a cooperative man," he said with no lack of sarcasm.

Caleb just grinned, liking Hart more by the second.

"Who should I contact?" asked Hart.

"Me. Lana's got enough on her plate with the art auction, so some of my buddies and I are helping run the carnival side of the fundraiser."

"Buddies. You mean coworkers."

Caleb confirmed nothing. He didn't want to draw any attention to the fact that there was a team of former and active Delta Force operators hanging out in the middle of Missouri.

"Whoever they are, I'd love to meet them. When's our first meeting?"

There was a little more than a week until the carnival, and Caleb figured Hart would need some time to organize things on his end. "How about right now?"

Hart raised his dark eyebrows. "Don't you need to follow Lana home?"

"No. It's covered," said Caleb with more disgust in his voice than he would have liked.

"Ah, I see. Trouble in paradise."

Caleb felt his fists clench. "You wanna be part of this or not?"

Hart held up his hands. "Point taken. Don't talk about your love life. Or lack thereof."

Caleb shot Hart a glare. "I'm going to regret working with you on this, aren't I?"

Hart just grinned. "Without a doubt."

☙

Kara kept a close eye on Caleb as he spoke to the police. She couldn't make out what they were saying from this distance, but Caleb's manner was not that of a man with an immediate sense of urgency. Whatever they were talking about, it had nothing to do with her or the fire.

Good. She didn't need any more of Caleb's interference.

The stench of smoke in the area was stifling, but Kara ignored it as she snapped photos of the scene. Lana's parents sat huddled together under blankets, like refugees. Their fingers were laced together as they stared at the smoldering remains of their home. The sun sparkled off the tears streaming down the woman's soot-smudged face.

How touching.

Kara froze the image on her digital camera so she could save it with all the rest. She knew it was risky to have this kind of evidence on her, but she couldn't help that. She had to show Marcus what she'd done. He was going to be so proud of her.

After snapping a few more pictures with her zoom lens, Kara moved her car several blocks down the street so it wouldn't be spotted. She pulled over and got out to retrieve her laptop from the trunk so she could download the images and e-mail them to Marcus.

She opened the trunk and her laptop wasn't there. The trunk was empty.

Kara had put her computer in her trunk only a few hours ago. She'd been out of her car for no more than five minutes when she went in to get a cup of coffee.

Apparently, that five minutes had been enough for it to be stolen.

A sickening suspicion rose up inside her. Kara scanned the area as she made her way back behind the wheel. She saw nothing. Whoever had taken it was gone, but she was pretty sure she knew who had done it—or at least who had ordered the laptop to be stolen.

Marcus hadn't been pleased about that video of him. He would have been livid if he'd known she had a backup of the video hanging from her keychain. She should have kept the whole thing to herself, but when it came to Marcus, she had so little self-control. She wanted to please him too much.

Maybe that was a mistake. Maybe she was trying too hard.

Maybe she wasn't trying hard enough.

Yes. That was it. He'd taken her in, fed her and clothed her, and protected her when no one else cared. And now she had to show him just how grateful she was. She had to try harder.

If she couldn't take care of Lana with Caleb guarding her, then she'd have to take care of him, too. Get rid of all of her guard dogs at the same time in one nice, neat bundle.

The bigger the explosion, the better.

CHAPTER TWENTY-TWO

Lana sat on her living room couch waiting for Caleb to show up. Her fingers had a mind of their own as they doodled over the paper. It wasn't until they stopped that she realized what she'd drawn. The face of the man who had beaten her. The man Caleb had killed.

With a jolt of panic, Lana tore the sketch up into tiny pieces and flushed it down the toilet. She was going to have to be more careful. If that mindless drawing had taken place where someone could see, she might be dead before she had time to flush the evidence.

Lana set the paper out of reach and curled up on the couch, hoping Caleb would hurry. She wanted this over with.

It was nearly midnight, but she knew he would come here. What she hadn't expected was for him to let himself in as if he lived here. He stepped through the door, pocketing a key. How he got it she had no idea, but he wasn't leaving here with it.

His dark eyes slid over her, taking in her floppy robe and the bare feet sticking out beneath it. "You're still awake."

"I was waiting for you," she said.

A relieved smile curved his mouth, and Lana's heart sped at the memory of just how good that mouth could make her feel. "I was hoping I'd given you enough time alone."

"That's not why I was waiting. I wanted to make sure you understand that what happened between us last night was a onetime thing. You're a great guy, but I'm just too busy for any kind of relationship right now. Even just sex."

She saw his abdomen tighten abruptly as if she'd hit him. The smile faded from his face, and he gave her a hard, black stare. "Is that what it was to you? Just sex?"

Make it a clean break. It's better that way. "Great sex, but yeah. Just sex."

He moved closer, as if stalking her. He towered over her, and Lana had to stand up from the couch to help even the playing field. Ending things with him was hard enough as it was without the added disadvantage.

"I don't believe you," he told her. "You came apart in my arms last night. You can't tell me that something that good is a one-shot deal."

"I needed that kind of release last night, but not anymore. I appreciate that you think you have to protect me, but I think we'd both be better off if you just left."

"Not against orders I won't."

"Then convince Monroe that I don't know anything. Tell him you believe me."

"You want me to lie for you?"

Lana's mouth clamped down tight before she could say something she'd regret. She knew better than to think that a man as noble as Caleb would ever lie to his commanding officer. No matter how desperate she was, she couldn't ask that of him. "Fine. Then tell him it's hopeless. You even seduced me and I still couldn't tell you anything. Tell him whatever you want, just leave. Please."

He settled one big hand at the base of her throat, stroking over her collarbone with his thumb. Shivers of remembered pleasure flooded her, making her bones go soft. She tried not to make any noise, but she failed; a soft sigh escaped her lips before she could stop it. Her eyes fluttered shut, and she tried to regain control over her hormones. "I'm not going anywhere."

"Please, Caleb," was all she could manage to say before her voice broke. She swallowed hard against the tears that clogged her throat but didn't fall.

His finger glided along her skin, warm and slightly rough. "If I leave, who will hold you when the nightmares come?"

Lana had been trying not to think about that all day. Caleb had given her peace, and now that she had to push him away, that peace would go with him. "I don't need you or anyone else to hold me. I'm a big girl."

"Someone should be there for you. You shouldn't have to do this alone."

"It's easier that way."

She heard anger sharpen his words, but his hand remained gentle. "So you're just going to suffer? Push everyone out of your life so that you won't care if one of them gets hurt because you're too stubborn to see you need help?"

It was her turn to get angry. How dare he accuse her of not caring? "You have no idea how I felt when I saw

Stacie was shot, when I saw my parents' home burned to the ground."

"Don't I? How do you know? How do you know I haven't been through exactly what you have? You've never asked about my life, my family, my friends. Not once. Was it because you didn't care or because you didn't want to?"

He'd nailed her motives so completely that Lana was stunned silent. She backed away, stumbling against the couch. She had to put some distance between them before she was stripped bare of every one of her secrets.

Caleb followed her, backing her into the little kitchen. She realized her mistake in choosing the kitchen when she realized there was no place left to run.

His skin had darkened with anger, and his nostrils flared as he followed her, backing her against the counter. "You can't run from me. You may not give a shit about me, but I don't feel the same about you. Push all you want, I'm not going away until I know you're safe. I nearly got you killed once, and I don't make the same mistake twice."

This was a side of Caleb she'd never seen. She'd seen him angry. She'd seen him furious when he'd killed the man that had hurt her, but she'd never seen that anger turned on her. "You may not want me in your life, but I'm staying until the job is done. You don't have to let me in your bed, but that's the only choice I'm giving you."

"It's not your choice to give. It's my life. You're not welcome in it."

"And yet here I am, sticking around. Get used to it. As stubborn as you are, I may be here for a while."

"Caleb, please don't do this."

"If you want to get rid of me so badly, then tell me what I want to know."

"There's nothing I can tell you."

He stared at her for a long time, his mouth pressed into a hard line. "Who's going to be next, Lana? Your sister? Her son? When are you going to learn that we aren't meant to do the big things alone?"

She almost believed him. She almost caved under the weight of her secret. What if he was right? What if her silence was causing the people she loved to be hurt?

Then again, what if he was wrong? She knew what would happen if she ever let on what she knew. For now, Kara could only guess. If Lana pretended long enough, Kara would believe she knew nothing and go away. If she told the truth, Kara would know she was a threat. Even if Lana went into protective custody, Kara or one of her goons would rip through her family, killing every one of them until they found a way to destroy her. Or maybe just to torture her for hiding from them for so long.

Her choices were limited, but the possibility of violence was better than the guarantee of violence. She had to stay quiet, but she also knew now that she had to leave. The fundraiser was in a few days, and after that, she'd disappear. If she wasn't around to watch her family suffer, it would no longer amuse Kara to do it. She'd have to focus on finding Lana instead. She hated the idea of leaving her home and family, but she had no choice. Not anymore.

Lana looked up at Caleb, knowing he was one of those people she'd have to leave behind. Part of her wanted to open her arms and let him give her what little bit of joy she could squeeze out of life, but the smarter part of her knew that would be a mistake. She'd never asked any personal questions, because she knew that if he became a real person in her eyes, she'd have no defenses left. Right now, he was just a hero that had saved her life and made her body sing. He was larger than life—not truly human—and she needed him to stay that way. If he became human to her, she knew she'd fall in love with him, and walking away would be only that much harder.

"Give me back my key," she demanded.

Caleb pulled in a deep breath that made his shirt stretch over his chest. What she wouldn't have done to possess half his physical strength. Too bad she wouldn't be able to continue the self-defense lessons he'd given her. That would have gone a long way toward making her feel safe.

"No. I'm keeping the key."

"It's not yours to keep."

"Maybe not, but when you start screaming tonight, I'll be able to get in without breaking your door down again."

The idea of him holding her, making her forget her dreams, was potent. Blood surged through her body, making her tremble at the memory. "If I start screaming tonight, I don't want you anywhere near me."

"Tough shit. I can't just stand by and let you suffer. Not ever again."

"I've been doing fine without you for a long time. I don't need or want your help."

"Yes, you do. Eventually you'll figure that out, but until then, I'm not going to let you suffer."

Too late, she thought. Her suffering was just getting

started. Once she was on her own, that's all she'd have left.

⚜

Denny's head was pounding. There wasn't enough beer in Germany to make it stop. He knew because he figured he'd been through half that much today without relief.

He could still smell the gasoline clinging to his hands no matter how many times he washed them. He could still feel the heat of the flames on his face. This was one job he'd never forget. Or repeat.

His phone rang, and it took his shaking hands three tries to hit the talk button. "What?" he barked into the phone, then instantly regretted it when the loud noise spiked through his head.

"I have another job for you."

Denny had come to hate that robot voice. "No. I'm done."

"Not until I say you are. Unless you'd like me to have a chat with Bruce."

"I've got enough money to make him back off for a few days. I'll get the rest some other way."

"How?" asked the metallic voice. "With your keen intelligence and charming personality? I'm sure there is a line of employers at your door waiting for the privilege of hiring you."

He was right. God knew Denny didn't have a lot going for him, but he'd find a way to make money that didn't hurt so many people.

He'd watched the news and seen Madeline Hancock sobbing, clinging to her husband. She didn't look anything like Denny's mother, but there was something about Madeline that reminded him of her all the same—some mannerism, or maybe that deep, sorrowful look he'd seen his mother wear every day until the day she died.

Denny wasn't sure he was ever going to get that image out of his head. Not enough beer in Germany.

"We're done," he insisted, though his voice wavered.

Silence filled the line for a moment. "You know, Dennis, Bruce is not the only one who knows how to use his hands. If you don't want my money, I'm sure I can find someone who does."

Denny got the underlying threat. His boss would use that money to tutor Denny in the most basic way—by beating the shit out of him.

Denny's head pounded harder, and he struggled to clear it. He didn't want anything more to do with this nut job, but he'd backed himself into a corner. He could either play nice or take his punishment. Just like old times with Dad.

"What do you want me to do?" he asked, knowing he had no choice.

"There's a package on your front porch. Open it. Take everything out and lay it on your kitchen table."

Denny waited for more instructions, but none came. "That's it?"

"That's it," confirmed the voice.

"Why?"

"Just do what you're told and be a good boy."

Denny hung up and got the box off his front porch. He shoved everything off his kitchen table into the trash, making beer bottles clang and pummel his aching head.

He slit the tape open with a steak knife and pulled out everything inside, placing it all carefully on the table.

Denny had never been the brightest lightbulb in the box, but he was smart enough to know the makings of a bomb when he saw them.

CHAPTER TWENTY-THREE

———❖———

Caleb wanted to break something out of sheer frustration. For nearly a week, Lana did little more than acknowledge his existence. She'd even wedged a chair under the door to her apartment to keep him out. Caleb could have blasted through it, but that wouldn't have helped his efforts toward getting her to trust him. Besides, he knew that part of him only wanted to get in hoping that she'd beg him to make her forget her nightmares again. Just the thought of a repeat of that night was enough to have him sweating and shaking with unsated lust.

She'd been polite to his men, thanking them for helping with the fundraiser, but other than that, she'd kept her distance from everyone.

Except Grant.

Every evening after the youth center closed, Grant had been training with Lana, teaching her the brutal, deadly moves they'd all learned in unarmed-combat training. From the bruises on Grant's body, Caleb was pretty sure she was learning quickly. If it hadn't been for that raw gnawing of jealousy in his gut, Caleb would have been comforted to know she was learning how to protect herself.

Grant spun a chair around backward and straddled it. They'd turned Lana's office into a war room of sorts so that they could have a place to coordinate their efforts. Lana had taken to using the tiny storage room at the back of the office for her own work space, likely to keep from having to see Caleb more than necessary.

The thought pissed him off, and his mood wasn't improved by Grant's smug smile.

"How is she?' asked Caleb. His only source of information about Lana was Grant, and as jealous as he was of the time they were spending together, he knew better than to cut the man off.

"Same as yesterday and the day before. Working herself ragged all day making the auction happen, and working out the frustration of doing that on my poor abused body."

"Yeah, it must suck to have a beautiful woman rolling around on the floor with you like that. You poor bastard."

Grant gave a laughing grunt. "She's got one hell of a punch. Check this out." Grant pulled up the front of his shirt and showed Caleb a new bruise along his ribs.

The purple mark made Caleb smile.

"I told her not to hold back, but damn. She's stronger than she looks."

Thank God for that. Caleb wasn't sure how well she was holding up, but he knew she wasn't a wimp or a quitter. Once this fundraiser was over, she wouldn't have anything to distract her from him, and he'd move in for the kill, so to speak.

Assuming Grant didn't beat him to it.

"Did you sleep with her last night?" asked Caleb. He hadn't been able to stick around after Grant had been invited inside. Instead, he'd gone to an all-night gym and beat his frustration out on the heavy bag. His knuckles were sore today, but that's all he'd managed to accomplish.

"No, I didn't sleep with her last night. Or any other night. Relax. She may be giving you the ice-queen treatment, but under all that frost, the woman's still got the hots for you."

Caleb tried not to get too excited by Grant's statement, even though he wanted to lurch out and grab on to that hope with both hands. "Is that so? Guess it's that way she has of looking right through me like I'm the Invisible Man that had me fooled."

Grant ran a hand through his blond hair in frustration. "God damn, you can be an idiot. I swear, you act like you've never been around a woman before."

"What's that supposed to mean?"

"It means you're a jackass if you just sit there and let her do this. You think she and I are all buddy-buddy, but you're wrong. She's a freaking zombie. No emotion. Not even when she's fighting. She's holding all of that in for some reason."

"Why?"

"Hell if I know. All I know is that every time I bring up your name, I see a little crack in the ice. She's got it bad for you, man, and if you don't do whatever you can to fight for her, you don't deserve her."

Grant walked off leaving Caleb reeling. Was he right? Had Caleb done the wrong thing when he'd given her space? He'd done it out of respect. He'd been raised to respect a lady's wishes, and it was just second nature to him. Maybe that was where he'd gone wrong. Maybe this was one of those rare times when the rules had to be bent if not completely broken in order to obtain the goal. And Caleb definitely had a goal. He wanted Lana untangled from whatever mess she was in so that she'd be able to take back her life. He wanted more than just casual sex with her, and she wasn't going to be in a position to make those kinds of decisions if she was still constantly looking over her shoulder, praying her life wouldn't spiral out of control.

He had to find a way to give her back control. He wasn't sure how, but he had to try. He loved her too much not to.

❧

Caleb knew it was bad news when he saw the private number on his caller ID. That was the way it always showed up when Monroe called.

He stepped away from the other men before answering the call. "Hello."

"This is taking entirely too long," said Monroe without preamble.

Caleb didn't ask him what he meant. He already knew he'd been here too long. "It takes as long as it takes, sir."

"From what I hear, you aren't even trying anymore. I didn't send you out there to lounge about and play with kids all day."

Caleb wasn't sure just how Monroe knew he'd been spending most of his time at the youth center, teaching the kids general safety precautions, but he had a good idea. He was going to have to kick Grant's ass for this prank. "She's too worried about her fundraiser to focus on anything else."

"You've got enough men to pull off ten fundraisers and you know it. This is child's play—literally—and I'm not letting you use it as an excuse. Finish the job, or I'll send someone who can."

"I thought there wasn't anyone else, sir."

"Are you *trying* to piss me off?"

"No, sir."

"So you can piss me off without even trying, but you can't gain the confidence of one woman with an entire team to back you up while you do? What the hell are we paying you for?"

Caleb focused on breathing and not saying how he really felt about Monroe's opinion. "I need more time, sir."

"You've got three days. Get it done or move aside for someone who can."

"The fundraiser is in two days," explained Caleb.

"Then that gives you a whole day after the damn thing to get the girl to talk."

"Yes, sir," grated out Caleb. Had he tried to say anything else, it would have been the end to his career. Then again, maybe that wasn't such a bad thing.

"Good. Check back in every twenty-four and give me a progress report." With that, Monroe hung up.

Caleb stood there for several minutes, trying to get his frustration under control. It wasn't going to help anyone if he couldn't pull himself together and focus.

Three days. It might not be enough, but there was only one way to find out. Caleb was done being nice. Lady or not, Lana was about to meet the side of Caleb that had earned him his career in Special Forces. He didn't like playing dirty, but it was for her own good.

❧

Kara rushed into the motel room and locked the door behind her. Her heart was pounding, her breath coming in ragged gasps.

Someone was following her, and in her line of work, that was a death sentence.

She'd slipped her tail about an hour ago and stolen a car before holing up here for the night. It was as safe as she was going to get for now.

Marcus was angry. She didn't blame him for that. She'd failed him and deserved to be punished. But killed? Kara thought he loved her more than that.

Maybe she'd been wrong all along. Maybe he didn't love her at all. He wouldn't kill someone he loved, would he?

This was all Lana's fault. If she hadn't survived, none of this would have happened. And she wouldn't have survived if it hadn't been for Caleb Stone.

The two of them had ruined Kara's life, and she wanted them dead—blown into so many pieces there would be nothing left to bury. No one would question her presence at the youth center. She could plant the bomb herself—make sure it was done right.

Once Lana and her guards were dead, Marcus would no longer be angry. He'd forgive her for her failure and she'd finally be able to go home and be with him again.

❧

Lana entered the gym at the same time she had the past three nights, only this time, Grant wasn't waiting for her. Caleb was. He stood with his feet braced apart, looking like he was ready to come sprinting after her if she tried to run.

She let out a weary sigh and tossed her backpack along the wall. Running away wasn't an option, but neither was allowing Caleb to take over her lessons. "Is Grant sick?" she asked, striding forward. The sight of Caleb in that snug T-shirt and shorts made her stomach tighten. His thick legs were layered with muscle, and the dark hair dusting them made every ridge stand out in stark definition.

"No," was all he said.

Lana stepped onto the mat, pulling together her strength to face him. "I'll wait for him, then."

"He's not coming."

"Then I'll call one of the other men. Jack has been following me everywhere I go. Maybe he's sitting outside." She turned to go check, but Caleb's hand stopped her. His fingers wrapped around her arm, and the contact of his skin on hers drove the breath from her body. She dangled there at the end of his arm, unable to free herself, too stupid to even try.

His thumb slid over her arm as if he couldn't help himself. Little skittering bundles of nerves scampered through her system until they settled low in her belly in a writhing pile. Six days without his touch had been too much. And not nearly long enough.

He pulled her toward him, and she had no choice but to go. She didn't have the will to fight him, knowing it was a losing battle.

She looked up into his face expecting him to be angry

for shutting him out, or at least gloating that she hadn't been able to walk away. Instead he gave her a solemn, steady look—the same one he'd worn when she'd first woken up in the hospital. It wasn't exactly pity on his face, because that she could have resisted. It was something more—a kind of yearning that went beyond sorrow. She could see that he wanted something, but not for himself. For her. He wanted to save her. Protect her.

Lana couldn't breathe. It was too much, seeing him like this, knowing that he'd stop at nothing to keep her safe even though he had no idea what he was up against. It didn't matter to him what he had to fight or even if it killed him. This was what he did. He saved people.

A second later, that devastating look was gone as if he hadn't just turned her world upside down. His hand slid down her arm, leaving a wake of goose bumps behind.

"I won't let you shut me out. I'm done playing nice."

Nice? His ruthless determination to stick by her side until he wore her down was playing nice? Even when he wasn't with her, he was nearby, watching her.

She must have had one hell of a look on her face, because Caleb let out a rough laugh. "I can see you finally believe me. Well, that's something, at least."

"I don't know what you mean."

He stopped laughing, but his eyes were still glittering with amusement. "Yes, you do. We're done playing games."

"I wasn't playing any games."

"No? You weren't just pretending you didn't want me around? You really can't stand me?"

She couldn't bring herself to say the word, so she just nodded.

It was a mistake to taunt him like that.

Caleb leaned closer, and Lana was frozen in place. Her heart was racing like a rabbit's, knowing she was caught. He reached out and swept a lock of hair behind her ear with a single finger. His voice dropped low, stroking against her nerve endings like velvet. "Do you really hate it when I touch you?"

She couldn't even nod. She was too busy wishing he'd touch her again.

He bent his head to her neck, his warm breath fanning out over her throat. "Does that mean you don't want me to kiss you?" He pressed his mouth at the joint of her neck and shoulder, swirling his tongue over her skin.

Lana grasped his arms to keep her balance and sucked in a breath.

His teeth grazed her neck while his hands slid around to her back. His fingers spread wide, holding her in place. "Does that mean you don't want to feel me inside you again, filling you up over and over until you come?"

Her knees gave out, and Caleb was the only thing holding her up. Ribbons of sensation shot through her body, and she felt herself growing wet and ready for him to do just what he'd said. She couldn't remember ever wanting anything more than to feel the hard length of him slide inside her.

His lips worked up to nibble along the line of her jaw. She tried to turn her mouth to kiss him, but he evaded every attempt. "No answers for me, Lana?"

She managed to shake her head just a little, hoping he'd felt it against his mouth.

Caleb pulled back enough to look into her face. His eyes were black, and the signs of his own lust stained his cheeks. "I'm done playing. I just wanted you to know that I meant what I said. No more pushing me away. I won't allow it."

Lana swallowed and nodded. She would have agreed to almost anything right now without argument, just as long as he kissed her mouth. But he didn't. He held her up by her arms, hovering just out of reach.

Lana blinked in confusion and tried to close the distance, but he held her back.

"Not now. Not here," he said. His thumbs stroked the skin under the edge of her sleeve, making her shiver. His voice dipped until it was deep and so quiet she had to strain to hear. "When I take you home, you're going to let me in. I'm going to make love to you until you're too tired to think. Too tired to lie."

"But what if I don't—"

He cut her off. "This isn't a negotiation. I'll make you want it. We both know I can."

"You don't get to make me do anything."

"Your silence has given me no choice. I have to keep you safe, and I'll do whatever it takes. Even if you can't stand me when it's over."

"You can't make me tell you something I don't know."

"No, but I can make you forget to keep lying. But first, we have some work to do." He toed off his shoes and kicked them off the mat. "Come on, Lana. Show me what you've learned."

The abrupt shift from sex to combat left Lana grasping for a foothold in reality. It was a strategy to keep her from arguing with him, she knew, but she couldn't get her blood-deprived brain to function well enough to figure out how to outsmart him.

Before she could step back and take the time to figure out what to do, he rushed her in a mock attack.

Lana reacted on instinct, using every bit of frustration to give her strength. Her body went through a series of short, brutal moves Grant had taught her, and when she was still, Caleb was on his back, grinning up at her, rubbing his chest.

"Good," he told her. "Now we're getting somewhere."

❦

"Is it done?" Marcus asked his second-best hit man, John. His first choice was already occupied, but that couldn't be helped.

"I got the computer," came the quiet reply over the secure phone line. "Melted it into a pile of slag, just like you asked."

"And Kara?"

"She's being careful. Staying hidden."

Meaning John hadn't managed to kill her yet.

Marcus ground his teeth together and barely managed to not throw his phone against the wall. "This needs to end."

"We both trained her. She's good."

"You're supposed to be better."

"I am. I know where she'll show up. When she does, I'll be there, waiting."

There was only one place Kara was sure to appear. Near Lana, where she'd have a front-row seat to the girl's torment. It was the only thing about Kara that was predictable.

John would stalk Lana, knowing Kara wouldn't be able to stay away for long. It would work. In fact, he could kill Lana, as well, while he was there and tie up all the loose ends.

"I want you to take care of both of them," said Marcus.

"It'll cost you double."

"Do it in twenty-four hours and I'll pay you triple."

Marcus could almost hear the greed thicken the hit man's voice. "Deal. I'll call you when it's done."

※

"Told you she was stronger than she looks," said Grant out his car window. He'd taken his shift keeping an eye on Lana's apartment to prevent anyone from planting more bugs. Or worse. With twenty-four/seven guards on her home, car, and apartment, and the occasional sweep, Caleb was fairly certain Lana's infestation had been stopped.

Caleb rubbed the swelling under one eye. "She caught me off guard."

"You mean you got distracted by that sweet little ass of hers."

"Don't go looking at her ass," warned Caleb.

Grant just smiled wider. "Sorry. It's a sickness."

"I know the cure."

"Yeah, yeah. Enough with the macho crap. What did you think? She's not bad, eh?"

Caleb was actually impressed. He'd expected her

to hold back, to pull her punches, but she didn't. Lana fought with a kind of desperate determination that he'd rarely seen before. "Not bad at all."

"Too bad she's scared shitless. Poor girl needs a break."

And Caleb was just the man to give it to her. He could hardly wait to see how she was going to react when she found out that he'd meant every word he'd said. He was staying the night with her, and although he'd never force her to have sex, he wasn't above using every bit of seductive skill he had to make her want it as bad as he did. He wasn't going to let her freeze him out. Not anymore.

"You can go get some rest. I've got her covered tonight."

Grant's golden eyes twinkled. "I just bet you do. Have fun." He handed Caleb a stack of paper.

"What's this?"

"Surveillance report on Kara McIntire."

"Anything odd?"

"She likes to go slumming once in a while, but that's all."

"Slumming?"

"She's got a boyfriend who lives in a crappy part of town. He's much younger, and she only goes there long enough to get a quickie."

"Anything else?"

Grant grimaced. "She slipped our tail last night."

"How did that happen?"

"She got lucky with a freight train. Brent didn't think it was intentional."

"We're still watching her, right?"

"Yeah, but with the additional duties on Lana's family, we're getting spread a little thin."

"Do what you can," said Caleb. "Lana's family takes first priority."

"Got it. See you in the morning. Sleep well. Or not." Grant was grinning when he drove out of the lot, no doubt to find his own female companion. Or three.

Caleb was already planning on just how he was going to enjoy Lana first when he tried to open her door. His key had unlocked it easily enough, but it didn't budge more than a couple of inches. The chair was wedged under the handle again.

Like that was going to stop him.

"Back away from the door," he said, giving her a minute to comply. He used a burst of strength and a jerk of his shoulder to crumble the flimsy wooden chair. The door swung open, but Lana was nowhere in sight. Caleb closed and locked the door behind him, pushing the remains of the chair out of the way with his boot.

That's when he heard the shower running.

A wide grin stretched his face, making the skin under his eye twinge where she'd hit him. He briefly wondered if she'd try to knock him on his ass when he stepped into the shower with her. And whether or not she'd succeed.

Of course, sitting in the bottom of the tub had as many possibilities as standing up, all of which were fine with him.

CHAPTER TWENTY-FOUR

L ana heard the bathroom door open, which should have startled her but didn't. Part of her had expected him not to be stopped by the chair—that hopeful part of her that she kept scolding for its idiocy.

She'd just finished washing her hair, grateful that she didn't have soap in her eyes when he stepped into the small, steamy room and shut the door. The clear plastic shower curtain blurred his image, but didn't protect her from his view. She saw his gaze fix on her naked body, and he started stripping out of his clothes. Her body heated as more and more of him was revealed. For the first time in her life, she realized what men saw in the whole striptease thing.

"You shouldn't be in here," she told him. Her arms were wrapped around her to shield her body, even though she knew he'd seen it all before.

"Of course I should. I know how much you like the shower. I figured I'd finish what I started the other night."

The image of his body pressing hers against the wall flared in Lana's mind. A lethal rush of desire nearly drove her to her knees.

He was naked when he pulled the curtain back. Naked
and hugely erect, already wearing a condom.

Lana's mouth went dry, and she couldn't stop staring
at him, couldn't move. Water sprayed out of the tub as it
bounced off her.

Caleb stepped into the tub, forcing her to step back and
give him room. He pulled the plastic shut behind him,
closing them in.

"This time I won't stop until you come. I promise." He
bent down and took her mouth in a kiss.

His lips were gentle and hot. His hands pressed against
the tile, caging her inside his arms. She could smell the
sweat from their workout and the sweet fragrance of her
shampoo. Every stream of water seemed to make her skin
more sensitive.

He teased her mouth open until she could feel the
stroke of his tongue against hers. She clung to his shoulders for support and went up on tiptoe to deepen the kiss.
She no longer cared whether or not sex with Caleb was
smart. It was necessary.

Caleb pulled his mouth away and picked her up, sliding her up the slippery tile wall until her breasts were on
level with his face. He made a low, rumbling sound of
need and closed his mouth over one nipple.

Lana gasped and shoved her fingers through his wet
hair to hold him in place. With every rhythmic tug on
her breast, sweet fingers of fire stroked inside her belly,
making her ache to get him inside her. She wrapped her
dangling legs around Caleb's torso to help hold on to her
spinning world.

He shifted his attention to her other breast while his
arm wrapped around under her bottom to support her

weight. He let her slide slowly down the cool tile while his free hand guided his erection unerringly into her body, just a little. The first feelings of being stretched made her cry out, her voice echoing off the walls.

Her progress down stopped, and Caleb leaned his head so his forehead met hers. "You okay?" he asked in a strained voice.

She nodded and held his head while she kissed him, showing him without words how frantic she was for this. How much she needed it.

Caleb eased her weight down farther until she could think of nothing else but the length of him inside her, pressing against nerve endings she'd never known she had. He used his weight to hold her against the wall while his hips rocked away from her, then back.

Another slow thrust made her skin tingle both inside and out, and she leaned her head back on the wall, letting the feeling wash over her. She knew she was getting close, and by the steadily increasing pace of Caleb's breathing, so was he.

Lana pulled herself back up, letting her nipples rub against his chest. A quiver started deep inside her where Caleb slid in and out, and she heard him groan as her muscles clamped down on him. She tried to speed things up, wanting to find that shimmering completion she knew lay just ahead, but Caleb held her to a steady pace, not allowing her to rush things.

His lips brushed her ear, and she felt his tongue swirl on a sensitive patch of skin just below her earlobe. "You're close," he whispered to her. "I can feel it. Let go, Lana. Give me what I want."

Any part of her mind not directly responsible for plea-

sure was shut down. She sensed that he'd meant more
than he'd said, but she couldn't figure it out, nor did she
bother trying. That shimmering heat that pooled inside
her was building to a vibrating flame that leapt through
her in a merciless wave. Her arms locked around Caleb,
and she held on to him while her world exploded and collapsed down to pure sensation. Her orgasm tore through
her, ripping a loud cry from her lungs and making her
body contract around him.

He pushed her hips down, sealing them together as his
own deep shout added to hers. She felt him jerk as he
came in time with her own release.

Caleb eased her to the floor, where he sprawled in a
boneless heap with her. Water sprayed over their heads,
but every little drop was like a caress over her sensitized
skin. She shivered and Caleb shifted her so that his erection pulled from her body.

He cradled her while their breathing calmed, then
reached for the soap. By the time he was done washing
her, there wasn't a bone left in her body.

❧

When her nightmare started, Caleb woke her with his
hands and mouth, gently easing her from the dark mist of
her dreams into the solid, tangible pleasure of his touch.
When he was sure she was fully awake, he covered himself with a condom, curved his body behind hers, and
pushed into her warmth. She arched against him, urging
him on. He took her slowly, letting her set the languid
pace. His hands were free to caress her, and he stroked her
from her scalp to her knees and back again.

Lana sighed when he slid his hands down her arms and sucked in her breath when he rubbed her nipples against the palm of his hand. Her noises taught him what she liked best, and by the time he'd driven her to her first release, he knew her body better than he ever had any other woman's. By the time he surged inside her, joining her in her third climax, he knew her body better than his own.

※

John waited until the men guarding the youth center changed shifts before he made his move. The sun was a blinding glare on the horizon when he crept up onto the roof, ensuring that he was less likely to be seen.

He watched the ladder leading up to the roof long enough to be sure he wasn't going to have any visitors before he went to set up for the job.

A few minutes later, his rifle was ready, and he was barely visible behind the giant air handler. His view of the front parking lot wasn't great, but he had a clear shot of the lawn where the carnival was going to be held—where all the action would be happening today.

All he had to do now was wait for the women to arrive. He'd have only a few seconds to take them both out before he was spotted, so his best bet was to take them both out at once—line up the shot.

Neither one of them was big enough to stop a round—at least not the firepower he'd be sending their way. And if he couldn't get both of them, he'd take whichever one he could get and leave the second one for later.

John still had ten of those twenty-four hours Marcus had given him to eliminate both women. There would be plenty of time left to get the job done and earn his triple pay.

·❧·

The youth center was crawling with volunteers by the time Caleb and Lana arrived. Grant was directing the troops as they assembled game booths and tents to shade tomorrow's carnivalgoers from the worst of the hot sun.

Out of the corner of Caleb's eye, he saw Lana's reaction to the busy scene. She was staring in open-mouthed shock. "How did you manage all this?"

Caleb's chest swelled with pride that he'd impressed her. "I pulled in a few favors and got permission to borrow some gear. Grant and the guys did the same thing, and between all of us, we managed to get everything we needed to throw one heck of a party."

Lana fumbled in her backpack and shoved on a battered pair of sunglasses, but not before Caleb could see the sheen of tears wavering in her eyes.

He leaned over and smoothed a swath of dark, glossy hair behind her ear. "Teamwork, Lana. No one of us could have pulled this off alone, but together, we're all but invincible. You should give it a try."

He felt her freeze up, going rigid. "I appreciate what you've done here, Caleb, but not every problem is the kind of thing you share."

He stroked a finger down her cheek and along her jaw, urging her to turn and look at him. He couldn't see much behind those dark glasses, but he'd come to know that tense, fearful quality in her voice. There wasn't much he wouldn't have done to free her of that, if only she'd given him the chance. "Don't know until you try," he said. "If I can't help you, I'll be the first to admit it. I swear."

She hesitated for a moment before she pulled away and reached for the door handle. "We've got a lot to do today. I need to get to it."

Caleb grabbed her arm, forcing himself to be gentle when he really just wanted to shake some sense into her. He had until tomorrow to pry out her secrets. It wasn't nearly enough time. Then again, a lifetime with her wouldn't have been enough to suit him. "Don't run away from me. Let me help you."

"You are helping me." She waved a hand out at the men working. "You've helped me more than I ever thought possible. Let that be enough, Caleb. Please."

He feared that nothing would ever be enough when it came to Lana. The longer he was with her, the longer he wanted to be with her, like some sort of sick joke. How the hell was he going to walk away from her, leaving her to whatever interrogation measures Monroe would subject her to next? Monroe wouldn't stop until he'd gotten what he wanted out of her.

Maybe that was the safest thing for her. As long as Lana was silent, she'd be in danger.

Caleb released her and watched her get out of the car. Her easy glide over the pavement still amazed him. She'd gone through so much, and all he wanted for her was to be happy. With him.

He wasn't sure where that thought had come from, but there it was, glowing brightly in his brain, blocking out all other thoughts. He wanted to stay with her—to be with her—and not just because he had a job to do or because she was in trouble. He wanted her all for himself, all that courage and strength, all that stubborn sweetness.

He knew a lost cause when he saw one, and that's exactly what this was. No way would Lana even consider being with him on anything more than a temporary basis. Sure, they had chemistry and the sex was great, but that was all just a trick of hormones. Relationships were based on trust, and Lana didn't have enough for him.

Caleb unfolded himself from the car, shoving the unwanted thoughts away. A few hours of hard labor would help him refocus on what was important—keeping Lana safe. As long as she was safe, there was hope that one day she'd come to trust him.

Yeah, right, because trusting the man who watched as you were beaten was such an easy thing to do. Happened every day.

He'd never known what false hope felt like until this very moment, and he decided it sucked.

"You're cheerful this morning," greeted Grant. Sweat darkened his shirt and made his blond hair look almost brown.

"Nothing a good swift kick in the ass wouldn't cure," muttered Caleb.

"Then I'm your man," he said, handing Caleb a set of tent spikes. "Get to work."

Caleb did. He lifted and hammered and hauled until his muscles were burning and sweat rolled off his body. The bright sun sank into his black hair, making him hotter.

Across the field where they were erecting tents and booths, Caleb spotted Lana talking with a few people, and something about her posture set off warning bells in his head.

He broke into a jog, crossing the hard ground quickly, trying to figure out what was wrong. There wasn't any one thing that alarmed him, just this impression that she was terrified. Her spine was rigid, her chin up, and though everyone else in the group shifted from one foot to another, or gestured with their hands as they spoke, Lana was eerily still.

Caleb didn't even stop to think what he was doing—he just came up behind her, said, "Excuse us," to the group and pulled her away by her hand.

When they were far enough away not to be overheard, he bent his head over her, wishing he could see her eyes behind her sunglasses. "What's wrong?"

She swallowed visibly. "Don't look, but there's a man with a gun on the roof."

CHAPTER TWENTY-FIVE

Caleb resisted the urge to glance up. Instead, he stepped to the left to shield Lana's body with his own. "Where's the roof access?"

"Back of the building. By the employee door."

"I want you to get the women and Phil inside. I'll take care of it."

"What about your men?"

"I'll call them on my way."

"You can't go alone."

"Don't worry. I've got plenty of backup. I won't do anything stupid."

"I'll call the police."

"No. We'll deal with this our way. Sirens might scare him away."

Lana nodded. She pulled in a breath, and just like that, all the terror melted from her features. She turned to the group standing a few feet away, and in a calm, steady voice she announced, "It's too hot out here. Let's move this inside."

Caleb dialed Grant, even though he was only fifty feet away. Grant, being the smart guy he was, didn't even bat an eye or let on how odd it was that Caleb was phoning him.

"Yeah?" answered Grant.

"Sniper. Rooftop," whispered Caleb. "I'm going up."

"You armed?"

"Not as well as I'd like to be, but well enough."

"I can take him out from down here."

"Once he knows we've seen him, do you think he's going to wait while you set up your rifle?" asked Caleb. "We're going to do this quietly. I want him alive for questioning. I need you to scan for more men. He may not be alone, and you know all the best sniper tricks."

"I'm on it. I'll get the others to back you up."

Lana and the civilians disappeared behind the doors, and Caleb ignored the wave of relief he felt. His adrenaline was pumping hard, putting his senses on high alert. The phone was suddenly too loud, the scent of the grass and asphalt too strong as he made his way to the building.

"Make sure no one tips him off. And get the men behind some concealment," ordered Caleb. "I don't want him to start picking us off because he can't get to his real target."

"I got it covered. Stay on the line. I'll be right behind you with my eyes open."

Caleb left the phone on and clipped it to his belt. The knife he carried wasn't designed for combat, but it would do in a pinch.

He climbed the scalding metal ladder and peered over the edge. At first he saw nothing, but then he heard a faint scraping sound and smelled hot male sweat.

Someone was definitely up here.

Caleb eased over the ledge. It was hot up here, the sun searing his skin from above and waves of heat bouncing off the roof below. There were only a couple of places a man could hide, and Caleb headed for the first—the one that had the best view of the carnival area.

The sniper was there, tucked against a humming HVAC unit. His body was tight with anger and frustration, likely because his target was now hidden inside, out of reach. He peered through his scope at the field below.

Something feral inside Caleb reared its head. He didn't normally enjoy killing—it was just something necessary that had to be done. But this time was different. Fuck questioning. This man had intended to hurt Lana, and now Caleb was going to kill him.

He crept forward on silent feet, mindful of his shadow and the scent of his body on the slow breeze. When he was three feet away, the sniper sensed him somehow and turned. He swung the rifle around, knocking the tripod over. Caleb rushed him, closing the distance so that the rifle was no longer effective. He batted the weapon up and out of the way and swiped at the man's belly with his little knife. Fabric gave way under his blade, and the man gave a satisfying grunt of pain.

The sniper slammed the butt of his rifle into Caleb's shoulder so hard it made his arm tingle. The knife fell to the roof with a muffled thump. Caleb balled his fist and hammered the man in the stomach with the full power of his body.

The sniper let out a whoosh of air but didn't go down. Instead, his foot lashed out and caught Caleb just below the knee. Caleb sagged but caught his weight and forced his knee to hold him up.

Whoever this man was, he was professionally trained. Lana would have no chance against him if Caleb failed.

Rage fired through his veins in hard pulses. He was not going to give this asshole another chance to strike.

The sniper tried to pound Caleb with his rifle again, but Caleb ripped it from his hands and flung it away.

Knuckle to knuckle, Caleb was better than nearly any man out there, and something in his gaze must have warned the other man it was true. The sniper reached for a pistol at the small of his back, and Caleb charged. He knocked the man to the hot roof, pinning his weapon and one arm under him. A sickening crunch and a high-pitched scream from his enemy told Caleb he'd damaged something under the force of their fall.

A vicious smile stretched Caleb's mouth. He could feel his skin tighten, see the man's eyes grow wide with fear.

His legs flailed, trying to kick Caleb away, but he was too massive a target to budge. Caleb pinned his free arm and shoved his chin high and to the side, yearning to hear the sound of breaking bone.

"Stop, Caleb," came Grant's voice. He was on the rooftop, only a few feet away. "We need him for questioning."

"Let them question him in hell." Caleb kept pushing. The man made gurgling sounds.

"Lana won't talk. We need him to."

Grant's strong hand landed on Caleb's shoulder, and he nearly shrugged it off. He didn't want to stop. "He was going to kill Lana."

"I know, but what if he's not alone? What if he knows

something that can help Lana?" The voice of reason, calm and sure.

And right.

"Shit," growled Caleb, and he eased off the pressure.

"It's best for Lana this way."

"I know," said Caleb. Then he punched the man in the side of the head so hard his knuckles split open.

The sniper's lights went out, and he sagged awkwardly around his damaged shoulder. Caleb found the man's pistol and handed it to Grant so he wouldn't be tempted to finish the job.

"Have Mad take him in," ordered Caleb. "Monroe will want to question him."

"I'll deal with it. You go clean up."

To hell with that. He was going to find Lana—make sure she was okay and hold her for about a year just to convince himself it was true.

"Did you see anyone else?" asked Caleb.

"No. The men are checking the area again, just to be sure."

"I want to know if he's alone," said Caleb. "And why he was trying to kill her."

"Our guys will find out what he knows."

Caleb waited until Mad appeared on the rooftop before he left Grant. His knee was throbbing, but he ignored it. Nothing a little ice wouldn't fix.

Then again, if he was injured, he could take some time off with Lana and heal. A month or two of R & R with her sounded good. Too good. He'd take her home, where he knew he could keep her safe. Not her home. His—that big sprawling ranch house in Texas where he'd grown up, where his brothers could help him guard her and where he knew the land so well he could hide her for days if he needed to.

He found her and the others near the finger-painting station. She was tense, but a sniper would tend to do that to any sane woman.

Her eyes caught his as he came through the doors. She sagged a little and clenched her hands at her sides as if trying not to reach out for him.

When he crossed the space and was standing in front of her, he couldn't help but touch her. He laced his fingers through hers.

"Everything okay?" asked Kara.

"Fine."

"You're limping."

He thought of a quick lie, not wanting to scare the other women. "One of the folding tables fell on my foot. It's no big deal."

"Your hand is bleeding, too," said Lana. "Come on and I'll get the first-aid kit."

He followed her down the hall. She grabbed a plastic box out of the break room and led him to an office.

The small room was mostly empty, with just a few boxes of files stacked to one side and a broken office chair in the corner. "This will be my office when the lease on the other one runs out," she told him. "No one will bother us here."

The fluorescent lights flickered on with a low buzz, and Lana shut and locked the door behind her. They were all alone.

Caleb felt that consuming need to touch her again. His fingers slid up over one bare arm. She gave a delicate shiver but didn't try to stop him. No matter what lies were standing between them, in this, she was honest. Her reaction to his touch was without guile or secrecy.

"Are you really okay?" she asked.

"I am now."

"Did anyone else get hurt?"

"No."

"Good. That's good."

"Do you know who he is?" asked Caleb.

"No," she said. "I saw his face for a second. I didn't recognize him."

Caleb sensed she was telling the truth. "He's unconscious. Do you want to get a better look? A second isn't very long to identify someone, especially when they're armed."

Her body tensed, and she nearly dropped the bottle of disinfectant she was holding. "No. I don't want to see him. My memory for faces is good, and I don't want to start seeing his when I close my eyes at night."

Caleb didn't push. He'd be able to get photos for her to look at if she changed her mind. It would be easier on her than looking at the man himself. "He won't be able to hurt you now."

Lana nodded but said nothing. She swabbed disinfectant over his cut knuckles. Caleb ignored the sting and watched her tend him in silence. Her fingers shook, but she didn't falter.

"I think you can stop. I'm not even bleeding anymore."

She swallowed and nodded again. "Anyplace else hurt?"

His blood was still hot with adrenaline, his body ready for a fight. Or sex. That would work, too. In fact, it sounded like a great idea. "Depends. Are you going to kiss it and make it better?"

"Don't joke."

"Who's joking? I want you. Right here. Right now."

Her eyes darkened, and she swayed toward him. "You could have been killed."

"I wasn't. We're both safe."

Caleb stepped closer, pulling her body against his, heedless of the dirt and sweat of combat on his torso. Lana wasn't complaining, either. Her skin was warm from the sun, making the honeysuckle and woman scent of her rise up to his nose. Caleb breathed in, holding her essence inside him for as long as he could before letting it out.

"I shouldn't be turned on right now."

"Survival instinct. Perfectly normal." He couldn't even form a complete sentence anymore, and he had to kiss her. He pinned her against the door and lowered his mouth to hers. Lana's lips parted without hesitation, and his tongue swept inside her mouth to taste her. Home. She tasted like coming home felt. Sweet and warm and inviting.

He told her with his lips and tongue how much he wanted this. Wanted her. His kiss was hard and demanding, giving her no room to back away.

Lana melted inside his hold and returned his kiss with a sense of desperation, though whether she was desperate for more of him, or desperate to forget the killer on the roof, he couldn't tell.

Lana's hands slid up under his shirt over his abdomen. Slender fingers twined through the hair on his chest, pressing into the muscle beneath. "I love the way you feel," she told him in a rough whisper against his mouth.

The L-word left him reeling, making his hopes soar. He wanted her to love him, needed it. Needed it so bad he thought his skin would ignite.

Caleb kissed his way over her jaw and down her neck, swirling his tongue as he went. He'd used every one of his powers of observation to gauge her reactions to his touch so that he could learn her most sensitive spots. He wanted to please her like no other man ever had, and he put his monumental force of will behind the task of learning her body. It hadn't taken long, because Lana was such a responsive woman. She didn't hold back telling him with her sighs and moans and shivers what she liked best, and right now, Caleb wanted to show her just what he'd learned.

His lips teased the joint of her neck and shoulder—the exact spot he knew drove her crazy. He let her anticipation build, let her know with the light scraping of his teeth what he was going to do, let her want it. Then, when she was panting and clutching at him, Caleb pressed his teeth against her skin, reveling in the hiss of pleasure she gave him.

"More," she breathed. "I love that."

There it was again. The L-word that he wanted to hear with a longing so deep it left him aching.

Caleb smiled and licked away the sting of his teeth. He pulled back enough to look into her eyes. They were the rich blue of deep ocean water, heavy-lidded with desire.

Lana tugged at his shirt, unable to get it off without his help. He swept it off over his head and tossed it onto the broken chair. "Your turn," he told her as he reached for the hem of her shirt.

She let him strip it off of her and reached behind her to unhook her bra. Caleb's jeans tightened as he watched the guileless striptease. Finally, her perfectly shaped breasts were bare to him, and he lowered his mouth to one tight pink nipple, unable to resist.

Lana's body arched toward him, and her hands wrapped around his dark head to hold him in place while he loved her with his mouth. He suckled gently, then harder, figuring out what she wanted, what would give her the most pleasure.

He thrust one thick thigh between her legs and lifted her up so that her center was pressed hard against him, her feet barely reaching the ground. His knee complained, but he didn't listen. Lana's hips shifted, grinding herself against his hard muscles as he moved his mouth to her other breast. The sight of her nipple, red and wet and distended from his attention, made him groan aloud, and he cupped her bottom to pull her more firmly against his leg.

Lana's fingernails bit into his scalp, and a dark flush rose up over her breasts and throat. She was making soft little mewling noises that drove Caleb crazy. He had to get inside her, had to feel the wet heat of her body surround him and drive away his insanity.

Caleb attacked the button of her jeans and tugged the zipper down with a jerk. His hands slid inside her clothing, caressing sunlight-soft skin.

Lana breathed out a jagged sigh and pulled his head up for an open-mouthed, devouring kiss. Caleb moved his leg from between hers so he could get the offending jeans off her body. His hands cupped her ass for a moment before moving down, taking jeans and panties with them. Her shoes were a nuisance he quickly rid himself of, and in seconds, she was standing in front of him gloriously naked.

Caleb let himself stare, enjoying the chance to see her in the bright office lighting. Her slim body was scarred, especially her legs, but that didn't detract from how beautiful she was to him. The scars only emphasized her strength, her resilience. He loved her soft, pale skin and the gentle curves of her hips and stomach. He loved the feminine strength that flowed through her limbs and the way she couldn't hide the blush of arousal that spread up her torso. He loved the way her breathing sped as he watched her and the way she had to clench her fists to keep from reaching for him. She was perfect—everything he could have ever wanted in a woman, and right now, she was all his.

"I love you," he told her, unable to hold it in any longer.

He watched as that sensual smile fell from her face, as that deep blush of arousal faded and she went pale. He watched as she covered herself with her arms, trying to shield her naked body from his sight. "No," she whispered in horror.

It wasn't the kind of reaction a man wanted to see in a woman when he confessed love, and Caleb felt her rejection like a physical blow.

Lana scrambled for her clothes, her hands shaking as she slid her jeans up over her hips, not bothering to zip them so she could look for her shirt.

"Lana," he said, trying to figure out what she was

thinking, what he'd done wrong. He reached for her arm, but she jerked away.

"Don't touch me," she snapped, and then calmer: "Please don't touch me."

Anger glowed in Caleb's gut. He'd told her he loved her, and she acted like he'd just said he was a child molester. "What the hell is wrong with you?" he demanded.

"You're wrong," she told him in a clipped voice. She pulled her shirt on over her head, not taking time to put her bra back on. "You don't love me."

"How do you know how I feel?"

"I just do. It's your hormones talking."

"Like hell. I've had hormones for a long time, had plenty of sex, too, but you're the first woman I've ever loved."

She flinched as if he'd hit her. "Please don't do this," she begged.

"Do what? I can't help that I love you. Most women would be happy to hear those words." And then he belatedly realized, "At least they would if they cared anything about the guy saying them."

Lana looked up at him with her blue eyes full of guilt, and Caleb knew the truth. Suddenly, he felt every ache in his battered body, every stinging cut. "That's it, isn't it? I'm just a convenience for you, aren't I? Just a casual fuck to help you sleep at night?"

"Caleb, it's not like that."

"The hell it isn't. If you gave a shit about me, then it wouldn't be like that, but you don't. You don't want me to love you, because you know you can never love me back."

"Caleb, please."

"Please what? Please leave? Please don't stop fucking you? Please what, Lana? Spell it out for me."

She bowed her head in defeat, making him ache to take her into his arms. He loved her, wanted to soothe her, but it was his love that had made her need comfort in the first place.

What a joke that was. A fucking riot.

"I just want to . . . forget about this," she told him. "Just let it drop."

"I tell you I love you and you want to forget about it?" That made him feel like the world's biggest loser.

"I don't mean to hurt you, Caleb. But I can't give you what you want."

"What do you think I want?"

"A future. Hope." She let out a heavy sigh of regret that vibrated with a restrained sob. "I don't have any hope to spare. You deserve a woman who does."

He didn't want another woman. He wanted Lana, and knowing she didn't want him was tearing him apart. His heart was in shreds, and there wasn't a damn thing he could do about it. Lana didn't want him.

He should have known better than to hope that she would. He'd warned himself about this very thing happening. Don't get too close, don't care, she can't ever have feelings for the man who helped ruin her life. The man who let her be brutalized.

Caleb wanted to blame her for her rejection. He wanted to be furious at her and tie her down until she gave in and professed her undying love for him. He wanted to go back in time and relive the past—find some way to prevent her torture.

But he couldn't do any of those things. All he could do

was let her walk away and pray that someday she'd find a man she could love—a man she could trust.

∽❦∾

Caleb didn't love her. Lana kept telling herself that over and over as she hid in the bathroom stall, trying not to cry.

He was just infatuated. It was just the sex talking. Or the adrenaline rush. It was just pillow talk that all men gave women to keep them interested in sex.

It had to be, because the possibility of anything else was just too frightening.

Caleb didn't love her. He felt guilty over being powerless to protect her in Armenia. He felt protective of her now because it was his job. He was just confused.

It would pass. He'd realize he was wrong, and things would be fine again. No harm, no foul.

Yeah, right.

Lana knew the damage was already done. He'd said the words, and they couldn't be taken back. He couldn't unring the bell.

"Damn it!" she cursed at the stainless-steel door. This couldn't be happening. How was she going to protect herself from all the feelings his confession of love gave her? How was she going to resist letting herself daydream about happily ever after when reality was so freaking bleak?

As long as he didn't love her, there was no way she'd let herself love him back. She'd protect her heart, keeping it safely locked up in the cage that pain of loss and rejection had constructed. Nothing could get to her as long as she protected her heart. She wouldn't be vulnerable. She'd be safe. She'd be in control.

She had to keep hold of what little control she had left in her life, protect it ferociously. She couldn't let Caleb, or any man, barge into her life and force her to feel things she wasn't strong enough to feel. Like love.

As long as he didn't love her, she didn't have to fear loving him back. At least, that's what she kept telling herself.

CHAPTER TWENTY-SIX

———❧———

Did you do what I told you?" asked the modulated voice of Denny's boss.

Denny wiped the acid taste from his mouth and prayed he wouldn't puke again. "Yeah," he said in a voice made rough from retching into the toilet for the past twenty minutes. The combination of too much alcohol and his boss's bizarre instructions had turned his stomach inside out.

He still couldn't get the sloppy crayon drawings out of his head. Flowers and dogs and race cars, all scribbled in with garish colors. The building he'd broken into—First Light Foundation—was plastered with them, along with gloppy paintings that made no sense and crooked clay sculptures formed by clumsy little hands.

"Good boy. Now there's only one more thing I need you to do."

A sickening wave rolled over him, and he swallowed hard to keep from throwing up again. He was sweating and shaking and could barely hold the phone to his ear. "What?"

The voice gave a metallic laugh. "Nothing so dramatic

as you're thinking. I just need you to go pick up your last payment."

Denny sat silent, waiting to hear the catch. The money his boss offered him was enough to pay off Bruce, which meant he'd have no hold on Denny any longer. With the threat of broken legs gone, there was nothing that freaky robot could do to convince Denny to keep working for him. "Where?"

"Meg's Diner. Be there in five minutes."

"But that's a fifteen-minute drive!"

"I suggest you get moving, then. If you're late, the money will no doubt be found by someone else."

Shit! Denny ignored his twisting stomach, grabbed his keys and flew out the door. He ran six stoplights getting there, but he made it in time. The money was sitting in a little paper sack behind the toilet. Denny opened it with trembling hands and counted the money. It was all there. His nightmare was over. Bruce would be paid off, he'd never work for Mr. Robot again, and he was going to pick up and move the hell out of this place—so far away no one could find him.

❧

Caleb sat down on the grass next to Grant. The evening air was still hot, but at least the sun was no longer overhead.

"Any word on the sniper?" asked Caleb.

Grant swallowed a bite of one of the sandwiches that the foundation's cook, Sharon, had provided to all the workers who had stayed to finish setting up for tomorrow. There was still plenty to be done before nightfall, but they were on schedule. "CIA's working on him. They either haven't gotten him to talk yet or they're not sharing."

"Gee. That's helpful."

Grant shrugged. "The job is the same either way. Keep her safe."

"Nice and simple," said Caleb with more sarcasm than he'd intended.

"Where is she?"

"Inside. Avoiding me. Jack's with her. Everyone is on high alert."

"Which is why I'm surprised you're not at her side."

"I don't want to make her cry again." God, he sounded pitiful.

"What happened?"

Caleb hesitated. He wasn't one to talk about things like this, but if anyone knew what was going through a woman's head, it would be Grant.

"What does it mean when you tell a woman you love her and she acts like you just threatened to murder her kitten?" Caleb asked Grant, trying to sound more casual than he felt. Inside, he was twisting with a mixture of anger and regret that he couldn't shake.

Grant raised an amused brow. "Are you sure you didn't accidentally say you have herpes?"

Caleb rolled his eyes at the lame joke. "Pretty sure."

This time Grant was completely serious, not even a glimmer of amusement in his golden eyes. "She's not ready for that kind of pressure, man."

"What pressure? It's supposed to be a good thing."

"Maybe to a woman who hasn't had her life turned up-side down, but not for Lana. The woman's been through hell, and she's not out yet. She's too scared to even tell you what she's scared of, she's got this fundraiser riding her ass, her friend was shot, her parents' house burned down, a sniper on the roof, and you go dumping confessions of love on top of that pile. How do you expect her to react?"

"Something other than that look of horror would have been nice," said Caleb. Truth was, he hadn't really thought about it like that. He felt it, so he said it. Simple. Stupid, but simple.

He should have kept his feelings to himself, but it was a little late for that.

Caleb fisted his hand, watching the broken flesh over his knuckles stretch.

"She'll come around. Back off on the Romeo routine and let her get through this thing tomorrow. Once that's over, maybe she'll have the space to process what you said. Maybe she'll even say the words back."

Caleb grunted his skepticism. "Not in this lifetime. Besides, my time here is almost up. Monroe is reassigning someone else to the case if I can't get her to talk by tomorrow."

Grant's face wrinkled in a pained expression. "That's harsh. Any idea who he's going to replace you with?"

"Why? You looking for a broken face?"

Grant laughed and held up his hands. "No warning needed, man. I just thought that you might appreciate knowing that the next man won't be putting the moves on her."

"Like you wouldn't. When have you ever been able to keep your dick in your pants?"

"Have patience. I'm learning a new skill. Besides, Celia is rough on a man. Woman made me sore."

"I do *not* want to know how that happened."

"Like I'd ever kiss and tell."

Caleb laughed, considering how Grant loved to awe the team with the stories of his female conquests. "You still seeing her?"

Grant shrugged. "While I'm here. When there's time. It's nothing serious."

"You make that sound like it's a bad thing. I thought you were all about no serious relationships."

"Never mind," said Grant, waving it off. "Just hurry up and get this thing with Lana straightened out, will you? A man can only wait so long for his turn."

"Your turn at what?"

"Love, my friend," said Grant.

Caleb scoffed. "You get more action than any man I know—hell, more than any three men I know put together."

"Yeah, and look where it's gotten me. I've got paint stains on my ass and a sore dick."

"Poor baby. Maybe you should try telling Celia you love her. That'll scare her off."

"Don't I wish," said Grant with a sigh. "Knowing her, it would probably turn her on. Everything turns that woman on."

"Even watching paint dry?" teased Caleb.

Grant winced as if a memory stung. "Especially that."

⌘

Lana couldn't hide any longer. She'd spent the day avoiding Caleb, but they'd shared a ride here, and as much as she wanted to continue to avoid him, she knew it was the coward's way out. He deserved better. He deserved an explanation about why she'd reacted the way she did to those three little words. She knew her reaction had to hurt him, and it killed her inside to know that she'd given him pain in exchange for such a precious gift.

Lana locked up the building and found Caleb lying on the hood of the car, waiting for her. Everyone had left an hour ago when the final prep work was done. It was nearly ten, and the sky was dark, the air still hot as it blew over the sun-heated ground. She could hear crickets singing in the bushes nearby and the hum of traffic along the street. Swarms of bugs hovered in a cloud around the light overhead.

Caleb was leaning back against the windshield with his hands stacked behind his head. Muscles in his thick arms bulged beneath the sleeves of his shirt, which was stretched tight over the ridges of his chest and abdomen.

Lana's chest tightened at the sight of him lounging there so casually in an elegant male sprawl. Part of her wished she was a normal woman with a normal life so she could just give in to the fantasy life his love could create for her. He would be an easy man to love, so caring and gentle. A true hero.

He deserved better than Lana, and she deserved better than pretending she was a normal woman when she was anything but.

"You waited," she said as she approached the car. Her pace was slow as she tried to gauge his mood.

"I still have a job to do," he told her in an even voice. No accusations.

Lana felt herself relax a little. She should have known

he wouldn't throw a fit. He was better than that. "I'm sorry about . . . today," she told him.

He didn't seem inclined to get up, just stayed where he was, staring up at the stars. "What part are you sorry about? The part where I said what I did, or the part where you ran away?"

"Both, I guess."

He let out a heavy sigh. "I can't take it back, Lana. I would if I could, but I can't. We can either get past it or not. Your call."

For a second, she resented him putting that burden on her, until she realized that he didn't see it as a burden as much as he did a choice. One he was letting her make. No pressure. No pushing. She didn't deserve to be treated so gently after what she'd done.

Lana lifted herself up onto the hood, being careful not to touch him. "I can't be the kind of woman you want. I don't have room in my life for romantic complications."

"Is that what I am? A complication?"

"I didn't mean it like that. I just meant that there's too much going on right now, and I don't have the energy left to put effort into a relationship."

"You have plenty of energy left for sex."

"Yeah. It's selfish, I know, but so far that's the only thing I've found that lets me . . . forget." A wave of grim memories threatened to crash into her, and she stuffed them down before they could. Just talking about forgetting made it impossible to do so. "When I'm with you I don't have to think. I just get to feel."

"And that's a good thing?"

"The way you make me feel, yeah."

That earned her a twitch of a smile.

She had to make him understand that her inadequacy had nothing to do with him. She was the one who was broken inside. She was the one who was warped. "It's hard being afraid all the time."

He turned his head and she could see him watch her out of the corner of her eye, compassion flattening his mouth. "You don't have to be. You could let me help."

"You really want to help me?"

"That's all I've wanted since the moment I laid eyes on you."

That statement made her stomach knot. How hard must it have been for him to watch all that brutality and not be able to do anything about it? She often wondered if he didn't carry as many emotional scars from that ordeal as she did. Maybe more. "Promise me that whatever happens between us, you'll protect my family, Stacie, and the kids at the foundation. Promise me you'll keep yourself safe."

He turned, propping himself up on his elbow, his black eyes searching her face. "You make it sound like you expect something to happen to you. What aren't you telling me now?"

Panic fluttered, but she controlled it with a force of will. She didn't want him to see her plans to run away in her eyes. "Nothing, I just don't want your anger toward me to make them suffer."

"First, I'm not angry at you. Second, even if I was, I'd never let that stop me from doing the right thing and protecting the innocent."

Lana was quiet for a while, listening to the crickets. "You should be angry, Caleb. What I did today was inexcusable. I shouldn't have walked away from you like that after what you said."

"It was an honest reaction—probably more honesty than I've gotten from you since I showed up."

That stung, but she tried not to let it show. She'd told him plenty of lies, but she'd had no choice—no more than he'd had a choice about letting her abductors beat her. She'd forgiven him for that and could only hope that if the truth ever came out, he'd do the same for her.

Lana pulled at the strands of her resolve, needing to explain why she'd shunned him. It wasn't going to be easy to admit all her shortcomings. "You deserve a lot more than I can give, Caleb. You deserve a woman who can love you back. One without so much baggage." She swallowed a lump of regret. "One who can give you children."

He reached for her but let his hand fall before he touched her, as if fearing she'd reject that, as well. "If you're trying to tell me you're not good enough for me, then we have some things to straighten out. I've never met a stronger woman than you. We all have our own baggage, and you've handled yours fine, as far as I'm concerned. And if you're holding back on me because you can't have kids, don't. The same could be true of any woman out there. I don't love you because you'll be a good brood mare. I love you because of who you are, not what you can give me."

Tears burned her eyes, and she had to turn away. So much for being strong. She couldn't go one damn day without crying. "I don't want you to love me at all. It's too hard."

"Grant said I should just back off and give you time to

let things soak in. That's not going to help, is it? Not even if I wait a lifetime."

Lana shook her head, feeling the silky sway of her hair over her shoulders. She couldn't give him any hope, because it would only be another lie. "I can't be with you like that. I'm sorry, Caleb."

She wanted to give him what he wanted, but she couldn't. She wasn't nearly as strong as he thought she was. Not nearly as strong as she wished she could be for him.

"Then how *can* you be with me? Because I'm not giving up on you. I won't let you just walk away."

Did he know her intentions? She didn't think she'd given anything away, but Caleb was smart. "I know. You have your orders."

"To hell with my orders. They have nothing to do with this." He motioned between them. "I want to be with you—take whatever you're willing to give."

Lana knew tonight would be her last night with him. She didn't want to spend it alone. As he said, there were no second chances. This was the last night she'd ever have in his arms. She couldn't deny herself one final moment to forget her troubles, even though she knew the risk it posed. "I'm willing to share my bed, my body."

"But not your heart," he said, his jaw bunching.

Lana was dying inside, crumbling under the weight of his stare and the desperate need within it. "I'm sorry."

"Not as sorry as I am, but I'll take what I can get."

"And it will be enough?"

Finally, he touched her, running the tip of his finger over her cheek. "I guess it will have to be."

CHAPTER TWENTY-SEVEN

———❖———

Lana woke long before dawn, too anxious to sleep. Caleb had made love to her with a relentless, driving obsession that had nearly frightened her with its intensity. He'd told her that if all he could have was her body, then he was going to take everything she had to give, and he did, leaving her reeling.

She'd fallen into an exhausted sleep and enjoyed another dreamless night. She wasn't sure how she was going to go back to living through those nightmares without him.

He'd done so much for her and the foundation, and in return for his kindness, she would repay him with betrayal—sneaking off without even saying good-bye.

Under her bed she'd stowed a suitcase full of a few things she knew she'd need. She wanted to bring the sketches she'd done of her family, or even a few photos, but she didn't want anything with her that could connect her to them. She forced herself to stick to the necessities, and she scoured those for anything that might link her to her home. She'd even ripped the prescription label off her sleeping pills, just in case.

After the fundraiser, while the chaos of cleanup was

going on, Lana would slip away. She'd written notes to her parents, her sister, Stacie, and Caleb, begging them not to look for her. She'd been harsh in those letters, saying that she needed time alone without her family to interfere. She'd thanked Caleb for his help but had worded his letter so that there would be no question about the fact that she'd ended things between them. It was over. Period.

That one had hurt the most, had forced her to lie in the most heinous way of all. She pretended she didn't care about him, that what they'd had was just a way for her to get some sleep, blow off some steam. She'd used him. That was all it had been.

Lana blinked back hot tears. She would not cry. She couldn't give Caleb even the slightest hint that she was planning on leaving. He'd find a way to follow her, and she wasn't sure she could leave him twice.

He shifted in his sleep, and the muscled weight of his arm crossed over her stomach, pinning her in place.

There had been a time not so long ago when that weight would have made her panic. Even the slightest hint of being restrained had swamped her with memories of her abduction. But that time was gone. Caleb had healed her somehow, driving away her nightmares with the quiet strength of his presence.

God, she was going to miss that.

Lana stroked his arm with her fingertips, trying to soak up every last bit of him she could. She wasn't sure if she was strong enough to learn to live without him again, but she knew she had no choice.

Caleb made a sleepy sound of contentment and pulled her beneath him, parting her legs with expert ease. A spear of longing stabbed right through Lana at the feel of his weight atop her, the tip of his erection nudging at her opening.

She was ready for him, wet and relaxed, her body aching to feel him slide inside her just one more time. Lana arched her hips toward him, taking him into her body in a long, slick thrust.

Caleb's groan mixed with a sound of surprise, as if he hadn't quite intended this to happen. His eyes were half-open, slumberous and sexy as hell. "Lana."

She wrapped her legs around his waist, allowing him to sink deeper. The feeling of being filled and stretched tumbled through her, and she let out a soft sound of delight. Bright little spots danced in her vision, and she wrapped her arms tight around Caleb, trying to steady herself.

His powerful body moved over hers, sliding in and out with the kind of strength that made her feel weak and protected all at the same time. "I'm on top," he whispered into her hair.

"Yes," she hissed out as he thrust deep once again. He hit that magical spot high inside her that made her world shrink down to a pinpoint of feeling between her legs.

"You okay with that?"

She could hear the concern in his voice but couldn't respond. The sweet friction of his body inside hers, the grinding pressure against her clitoris, was too much. She gave herself up to the explosion of pleasure, let it become her whole world, where nothing could scare her or hurt her or take her away from Caleb.

It was perfect. She had one perfect moment to take with her into her bleak future, and she was grateful for the precious gift he'd given her.

As she came down, she heard Caleb's deep chuckle, felt it inside her. "Guess you are okay with it," he said, grinning at her.

He kissed her forehead, her eyes, her cheeks—little gentle, soft kisses over her sensitized skin that made her feel cherished.

"Thank you," he told her, his face once again solemn.

He was still thick and hard inside her but remained still. "For trusting me. At least enough for this."

She did trust him. More than she'd ever thought possible.

He moved, and Lana's eyes fell closed. She was no longer able to concentrate on anything but the feel of his body riding hers, and she no longer cared that she couldn't.

Caleb set the pace, a steady, deep rhythm that had Lana climbing toward climax once again. She had no idea how he did it. Sex had never been like this with Oran. It was like Caleb had an owner's manual for her body and knew just what to do to drive her higher with every stroke.

Lana clung to him, her fingernails biting into his muscled back. He growled his approval at her rough treatment and eased a hand down between them, so he could toy with her nipples. It took no more than a slight pinch to have her arching off the bed into his thrusts.

"I'm not going to last much longer, honey. And I'm taking you with me." Caleb's mouth found that spot on her neck that drove her wild and swirled his tongue over her hot skin. His hips sped, and he changed his angle so that he was hitting that magic spot with every powerful motion.

Lana felt her orgasm coming and reached for it, wanting to feel that perfect pleasure one more time. Caleb moaned as if trying to hold back, and his teeth tightened over that place where her neck and shoulder met. Wild sparks spread out from that bite, cascading down through Lana's body until they lit a fire inside her womb. She crashed headlong into pleasure, giving out a ragged cry of completion just as she felt Caleb's erection thrust deep and pulsed hot and hard inside her.

His jagged shout vibrated her spine, lengthening her release until her whole body was trembling with effort of sustaining it. Slowly, the intensity faded, and she stroked her hands over Caleb's back.

He relaxed all those hard muscles and his weight pressed limply onto her, but she reveled in the feeling rather than fearing it.

He said something that was muffled by the pillows.

"What?"

He lifted his head and looked down at her. Into her. He was still lodged inside her, jerking every time one of the after-spasms of her orgasm made her quiver around him. He hadn't worn a condom, and she could feel the slick heat of his semen inside her. The intimacy of eye contact combined with the presence of his body so deep inside hers made Lana tremble. She'd never been this close to anyone before, and it was almost too much to take.

His eyes slid over her features, studying them. "It was nothing," he told her.

But it was something. He'd said he loved her again. She could see it glowing in his eyes. He loved her but wouldn't say it, because she had told him not to.

Lana couldn't do this any longer. She couldn't keep

him at arm's length. Couldn't keep lying to him. Not after everything he'd done for her. He deserved better.

And Lana was tired of feeling alone, tired of carrying her burdens by herself.

She pulled in a deep breath, praying she was doing the right thing. Like his confession of love, once she said the words, they could never be taken back. She lowered her voice, still uncertain whether the words she'd kept so tightly caged inside her would even come out.

"Kara was there," she whispered. "In Armenia. She was the one who had my friends tortured. The one who had them killed. She was the one who ordered my death."

CHAPTER TWENTY-EIGHT

———⟡———

Caleb was stunned silent, but his arms tightened around Lana as she spoke in a voice so low it was hard to hear.

Kara? That elegantly dressed, seemingly normal woman had ordered Lana's death? He knew something about her was off, but he'd never expected this. It didn't seem possible, but it explained everything. It explained why Lana was so jumpy every time she went to the youth center. It also explained why Kara's perfume had tugged at his memory when they first met.

Caleb had been in that cave not long after she'd been there. He'd smelled her perfume lingering in the air, along with the stench of blood and death. He'd never seen her—she'd been one of the terrorists who had carefully concealed their identities and never let a peon like him meet them face to face—but he'd smelled her.

Lana shuddered in his arms. "I couldn't tell you because I thought if I pretended not to know her long enough, she would just go away. I thought if she had no reason to suspect I could identify her, she'd leave me in peace. It was the only thing I could think of to protect my family."

Caleb wasn't sure if her plan was more brave or ignorant. "You didn't tell anyone? Not even your mom?"

"No one. When you found all those bugs, I thought she'd go away—that she'd know I hadn't told you or anyone else."

"I'm surprised she hasn't already killed you."

"Why would she want to kill me if I couldn't identify her? It would just draw more attention, which I doubt she wants. Besides, she liked the torture best. She made them film it so she could watch over and over." Her voice trembled over the words.

Caleb wanted to be gentle, but there was no easy way to tell her. "Your death was part of Kara's initiation into the Swarm. She can't let you live, even if you hadn't seen her."

He felt her stiffen in his arms. "Monroe said the Swarm was gone. Wiped out."

Caleb pressed a kiss against her slippery hair. "It doesn't matter. Even if she's not working for them, she'll have a reputation to uphold."

"I know she wants to hurt me, but if she kills me, her fun will be over."

When he thought of all the times that woman had the chance to hurt Lana . . . it made his blood run cold.

"Maybe that's why you're still alive," he said. "She's enjoying watching you suffer. But eventually, she'll get bored. In fact, she probably already is, which is why there was a sniper on the roof yesterday, waiting for a shot at you."

She sat up, gripping the sheet over her breasts. Panic had drained the color from her cheeks. "I'll never be safe, will I?"

"Like hell you won't. I'm going to have Kara taken

into custody, for starters. Then, if all goes well, she'll die in prison. Soon."

"And if it doesn't go well? If Kara has some way of pulling in help from outside prison? Then what? You can't do that. You can't let her know I told you who she is—that I'm a witness to what she did. She'll hire someone to go after my family."

"She won't have the chance, Lana. I'll make sure she has no outside contact."

"How? How are you going to make sure? I won't let you put my family at risk."

"We've got to stop her. You trusted me enough to tell me who she was, now I'm asking you to trust me enough to get rid of the threat she poses."

"That means you can't be there when they capture her. If you are, she'll know it was me."

Caleb squirmed under Lana's desperate gaze. She looked so vulnerable right now, so afraid. He wanted to do whatever it took to wipe away every trace of fear from her life. If that meant giving the pleasure of capturing and questioning Kara to someone else, then that's what he'd do.

"Okay. I won't go. I'll have Monroe send in a clean team to bring her in—men she's never seen before."

Some of the tension eased from her rigid posture. "Promise me she won't have any reason to think I'm behind this," demanded Lana.

Caleb smoothed a hand over her mussed hair. "I promise."

"Promise me my family will be safe."

"They're all being carefully guarded by men I trust. Stacie, too."

She was silent for so long, he wasn't sure she'd heard him. Finally, she pulled her guilty gaze away from his and said, "There's more."

Caleb wasn't sure he wanted to hear it, but he knew he had to. "Tell me, Lana. I need to know everything so I can keep you safe."

She nodded, but he could see how hard this was for her—how fear was making her limbs shake. "Kara wasn't alone. I saw others, too."

Caleb bit back a curse, keeping his expression neutral. He didn't want her to stop opening up to him now, even though he wanted to scream at her for holding onto this information so long. "How many?"

"The man you killed. Kara. Three more who may or may not still be alive."

"Can you identify them?"

Rather than answer, she reached into her nightstand drawer and took out a sketchbook. Her hands moved slowly as if compelled, opening the sketchbook to an empty page. Her knuckles turned white under the strain of gripping the pencil so hard. Lines flowed onto the page as if she'd drawn them a thousand times before. One by one, three faces appeared on the page, each one sketched with photographic detail.

Lana ripped them carefully out of the book and handed them to Caleb. "Will this help?"

"Yes. Thank you."

Lana covered his hand with hers. She was trembling. "I need this to be over, Caleb. I'm not sure how much more I can take."

Caleb gave her the most confident look he could muster. "Let me make a phone call. I'll be right back."

Caleb closed himself in the bathroom to make the call. The less Lana heard about the details the better. Monroe answered before the second ring. "This had better be good."

"It is. Is this line secure?"

"As secure as any can be in this day and age. There's always some snot-nosed punk out there cracking the latest security."

It would have to be good enough. "Kara McIntire was the woman who headed up that whole mess in Armenia."

There was a brief, shocked pause before Colonel Monroe said, "I'll have her in custody within the hour."

Caleb knew it was illegal for Monroe to have men operating inside the U.S., so he didn't bother asking any questions about why he had someone so nearby. He really didn't want to know, even if Monroe would have told him. "Make sure you use a clean team so Kara won't connect her capture back to Lana. Also, there are three more people you need to locate. Lana drew sketches."

"I'll send a man for the sketches right away. We'll find them, too."

"Thank you, sir."

"I'll call you back and confirm when it's done. Until then, stay on guard."

The line went dead, and Caleb let out a relieved sigh. It was almost over. She'd trusted him, and now he could keep her safe.

⚜

Marcus got off the plane, already regretting his decision to come here, no matter how necessary. He hated the Midwest. All the smiling people and their intrusive questions grated on him. The stifling heat and humidity ate at his patience until there was none left. Not that he'd had much left since finding out just how badly Kara had messed things up.

She'd been captured like some kind of amateur. So had John, which was a shame. John had always been useful. Kara had her uses, too, but she was a serious liability. If she talked, Marcus's days of blissful, profitable anonymity were over.

John would keep his mouth shut. Not that he knew anything of value about Marcus's operation. Kara, on the other hand . . . if she held true to form, all it would take was a little kindness to get her to open up. One gentle interrogator could ruin all his hard work.

Marcus had to get to her first. Good thing he had an inside source who knew where the CIA was holding her and when she'd be moved to a more secure facility.

He wasn't fond of wetwork himself, but if he wanted a job done right, he had to be willing to get his hands a little dirty now and then.

The sooner he got out of this hellhole and back to the coast, the better.

꧁꧂

The sun was just coming up over the horizon when Lana heard Caleb's phone vibrate. He ducked into the bathroom to answer it, and Lana gripped her coffee mug harder as she stared out the window.

She prayed she hadn't made a mistake. Caleb promised

her that her family was safe, but so many things could go wrong.

Then again, so many things already had.

Caleb came out of the bathroom a minute later. He was smiling. "It's over. She's in custody."

Lana crumpled to the floor in a boneless pile. Coffee sloshed over the rim, staining the carpet, but she didn't care. It was over. Her nightmare was over.

Caleb's arms wrapped around her and he pulled her into his lap. She leaned into him and saw her tears make dark spots on his shirt. "Are you sure?"

"Do you want to see it for yourself? I can arrange for you to make a positive ID."

The thought of facing Kara again sickened her. "No. I trust you."

Caleb kissed the top of her head. "Thanks."

"So, what now?"

"Now we get over to the youth center and pretend like nothing's happened."

"I'm good at that."

He gave her a solemn look. "You need to know that Monroe told me I have to leave tomorrow. I've got another assignment waiting for me."

Lana's throat tightened, but she managed a nod. "You've done your job here. Of course you have to move on."

He was watching her carefully. "I'm going to tell Monroe you're not ready for me to leave. I'll take some personal time."

She wasn't sure how she was going to be able to watch him walk away, but she knew she had to. "No, Caleb. You have a job to do. People need you."

"So do you."

Lana couldn't deny it. She was done lying to him. "I'll be fine." Which was the truth. She was always fine.

"Will you?" He tilted her chin up so she was looking into his eyes. "What about your nightmares?"

"I'll go back to counseling. Maybe it will work this time now that I know for sure Kara isn't out there anymore."

"You may still have to face her. Testify against her."

Oh, God. She wasn't sure she could do that. She wasn't sure she could be in the same room with that woman ever again. Not even to put her behind bars. "I will?"

"It's possible. There are only two of us who know you are a witness—me and Monroe—and for now, I'd like to keep it that way. You'll be safer if you're not listed as an official witness."

Safer, but not safe. Even with Kara in custody, she wasn't safe.

But maybe her family would be.

"I could stay," offered Caleb, "but if you don't want me to stay, then you should go into protective custody or the witness relocation program."

She wanted to beg him to stay with her, but she couldn't do that to him. She knew it would hurt his career. She wasn't willing to let him make that sacrifice. "I don't like either of those options, but I promise I'll think about it. For now, I just want to get through today, okay?"

A disappointed look darkened his face, but he nodded. "Okay, but once the carnival is over, we're going to talk about your options. Deal?"

Lana nodded. "Deal."

CHAPTER TWENTY-NINE

———⋱∘⋰———

Lana couldn't believe the turnout at the fundraiser. Hundreds of families showed up, and she wondered how they all fit. The baseball field outside the youth center was packed with kids playing carnival games, trying to knock over bottles or shoot rubber ducks with water guns, but the biggest attraction by far was the dunk tank, where kids and adults alike lined up for a shot to soak one of Caleb's friends.

She hadn't seen much of Caleb all morning, but every once in a while, she'd catch a glimpse of his head towering over the crowd and her heart would speed. She forced herself to focus on the fact that Kara was behind bars and not think about how she'd feel when he left.

Lana ducked into the next tent and stopped short in shock. Grant was on one side of the tent, allowing six young girls to play dress-up with him. A local theater had loaned them bits of old costumes, and right now Grant was wearing donkey ears and a tutu over his jeans. In his right hand was a stuffed carrot, and his left held a magic wand coated in glitter. Another volunteer snapped Polaroids for the girls who had dressed them.

Standing on the other side of the tent was Caleb, surrounded by a flock of giggling girls. Each one had some sort of garish makeup in hand—lipstick, eye shadow, blush—and they each took turns painting Caleb's face. She expected him to wear the same long-suffering look Grant wore, but instead he was smiling into a mirror. "You missed a spot," he told a girl who couldn't have been more than six.

She giggled, and he leaned down so she could add a bright blue splash of glittery eye shadow to Caleb's face. It really brought out the purple in the bruise under his eye.

Lana watched as the girls finished with Caleb and went after Grant with their cosmetics. She walked up to Caleb and pulled his head down to her for a hard, quick kiss.

Caleb gave her a warm smile as he wiped lipstick from her mouth with his thumb. "There's something wrong with this picture," he said. "You're supposed to be the one leaving lipstick on me."

Lana's smile widened. "Having fun?"

"To be honest, I would have preferred dunk-tank duty, but I wouldn't be much of a leader if I ordered my men into situations where I wouldn't go myself."

"Cover Girl country is dangerous territory," she agreed.

Caleb grabbed a box of wet wipes and went to work removing the makeup. "It's for a good cause."

Lana had to kiss him again. She couldn't stop herself. "Thank you for this," she told him.

He discarded the now rainbow-colored wet wipe and pulled her against his body. He was just leaning down to take a serious kiss when a new group of girls filed into the tent, announcing themselves with a series of gagging noises and high-pitched screeches. "Eeew!" shouted one of the younger girls, and the others broke into uncontrollable giggles.

Caleb sighed and let her go with a wink instead of a kiss. "Back to work. I'll come find you before the auction starts. We're closing most of the tents so you'll have more people attend the auction."

Lana left him to the girls, unable to quit smiling. The auction was scheduled to start in an hour and would be held inside the gymnasium. If only half the people attending showed up, she was sure they'd do well.

Lana entered the youth center, letting the cold rush of air-conditioning wash over her. Sweat cooled on her skin and she lifted her dark hair off her neck to help the process along. She could smell popcorn and freshly baked chocolate chip cookies. People lined the cafeteria tables, having snacks or just taking a few minutes to cool off. Most of the gym was partitioned off and set up with chairs for the auction. All of the paintings were hung on display above the height of sticky little fingers, and dozens of people strolled around, looking at them.

"Lana!"

She turned at the sound of her name and saw Stacie sitting at the registration table. Her long graying hair was in a loose bun and her crisp white shirt was perfectly pressed. Her cheeks were pink with excitement, and she gave Lana a warm, happy smile.

It hit Lana then that Stacie really was going to be okay. Intellectually, Lana had known it, but until now, she hadn't *felt* it. Now that she did, the weight on Lana's shoulders seemed to lighten.

Lana took the opportunity to give Stacie a gentle hug. "What are you doing here?" she asked Stacie.

"I couldn't stay away today. I had to come help."

"You shouldn't be pushing yourself."

"I'm not. I'm supposed to be getting exercise, not that sitting here counts as that. I want to start back to work next week."

"What does your doctor say?"

"That I should decide what I can and can't handle for myself. I'm a big girl." That last was delivered with the maternal frown Stacie was so good at.

Lana shook her head, grinning. "Point taken. You know I'd love to have you back as soon as you're able."

"I could come back now, but my sister isn't leaving for another couple days and I want to spend that time with her."

"Take all the time you need."

Stacie looked at her watch. "Speaking of time, have you seen Kara today? She was supposed to be taking my place about an hour ago."

Lana's face was a carefully neutral mask. "No. I haven't seen her."

"That's odd. She's usually very punctual."

❦

Kara wasn't sure where the authorities were taking her, but she doubted she was going to like it. She eyed the armed guard in the back of the van with her. He was young, or maybe she was just getting old. Either way, her time was nearly over, and somehow, that was okay.

She'd stayed loyal to Marcus and protected his identity even when they'd offered her her freedom if she gave him up. Thankfully, she'd seen the men coming for her in time to drop the thumb drive containing the video out her car window. She didn't think they'd seen her do it, but even if they had, it would probably be a useless mess of crushed plastic, thanks to the heavy traffic on I-70. She could die proud of herself knowing she'd saved the man she loved from harm. And she was going to die. After they finished using her, they'd get rid of her. No records. No paperwork. No trace she'd ever existed.

At least Marcus would remember her. She took comfort in that.

The van lurched hard to the right. Tires squealed. The van tilted and finally tipped onto its side. Kara's head slammed into the metal wall several times, and she shook it to clear her vision. The guard caught himself before he could fall into her. The chains shackling her to the van rattled, and outside, she could hear short, sharp bursts of gunfire. The van slowed to a screaming halt as the side slid over asphalt.

The guard recovered and drew his weapon just as the back doors of the van opened. Another armed guard was there. "We gotta get her into one of the cars. I'll cover you."

The too-young guard fumbled for the key. Gunfire slowed but didn't stop. It seemed to take forever, but he finally managed to unlock her cuffs.

Kara scurried out of the van. The guard covering them staggered backward, taking a hit.

She was momentarily stunned and looked up in shock to where the shot came from. Marcus was there, crouched behind a thick tree not thirty feet from the isolated road.

He'd come to rescue her! He was going to take her home.

A broad smile stretched her face. Marcus smiled back and raised his weapon, pointing it right at her.

Disbelief froze her in place. Marcus wasn't here to save her or bring her back home. He was here to silence her. To kill her.

"I didn't tell them anything," she yelled, betrayal making her voice weak and hollow.

"I know," he said. "And you never will."

Kara saw the tendons in his arm shift, saw his finger move on the trigger.

The too-young guard saw it, too. He shoved her hard, pushing her to the side.

A gun went off, then another. Two more shots.

Kara expected to feel a bullet slice through her, but the pain never came. She didn't wait around to see what happened. She raced for the closest car—one of her armed escorts' cars. The keys were in the ignition and the motor was still running. She slid into the driver's seat and gunned the engine. The tires shrieked, but she didn't relent.

Her eyes shot to the rearview mirror every two seconds, but no one else was there. Not the CIA. Not Marcus.

A shard of grief stabbed through her at the thought. If she hadn't failed him, he wouldn't have had to come after her. Everything had gone terribly wrong.

This was all Lana's fault. Kara could torture her for lifetimes and it would never be enough to make up for what Marcus had done. Never.

No more playing. It was time for Lana to die.

The art auction was at two. The youth center would be packed. Lana would be there. So would her doting, supportive family. One call to the cell phone attached to the bomb Kara had planted and Lana would be shredded into so many bits they'd never find them all.

It was better than she deserved.

❧

Caleb's phone vibrated against his hip, and he had to dig through the grassy layers of a hula skirt to find it. When he saw the caller ID list a private number, he excused himself from the girls who were using him as a mannequin and stepped out of the tent.

"Stone here."

"We searched the place where Kara was living. I think we've got a situation," said Monroe.

"What kind?"

Monroe was silent for so long Caleb thought he wasn't going to respond. Finally, he said, "The kind Miles Gentry might cause."

A bomb. Miles Gentry was an expert in explosives, which was why Caleb had taken the man's place—he knew his way around a detonator.

The sun beat down on Caleb's black hair, but all he felt was cold.

"What did you find?" asked Caleb.

"Not much. Tools. But the place was so clean otherwise, they stood out. We've got men and dogs on the way to help you sniff out any problems."

"I understand." Caleb's mind whirled through what he needed to do to deal with the threat. He wanted to find Lana, but there wasn't time, and everyone here was in as much danger as she was. All these kids were in danger. "But on the way isn't good enough. I'm not waiting."

"Be careful," said Monroe.

"Yes, sir."

Caleb hung up the phone and ducked back into the tent, where Grant was being painted by a group of little girls.

"Gotta go, Kent," he told Grant.

Grant looked up, and Caleb could see that he knew this was business. He didn't ask any questions, just extracted himself from the girls, grabbing a handful of wet wipes to clean his face.

"We need to clear the entire area. Round up the men. Set up a perimeter. Have everyone spread out, and disperse the crowd as quickly and quietly as possible. I'll clear the youth center."

"I'm on it," responded Grant, and he took off at a jog.

Caleb ran for the youth center and Lana.

He entered the building and spotted her standing near the podium. His heart started a heavy, hot pounding. God, he loved her. He didn't want to leave her even for a day. How the hell was he going to live a lifetime without her?

There was time to worry about that later, if he was lucky. Now he needed to get everyone out of the building.

As if sensing his gaze, she looked up, and all the color drained from her face. She came toward him, meeting him along the center aisle of chairs that had been blocked off for the auction. A crowd circled the outer edge of the seating, but they were separated from that crowd, as alone as they were going to get.

"What's wrong?" she asked him, her voice shaking.

"We need to clear the building. There may be an explosive device in here."

"A bomb? Oh, God, no! The kids! We've got to get them out of here. It's not saf—"

Caleb clamped a hand over her mouth as people began to turn and stare. "Listen to me. I'm going to deal with this. I need you to stay calm and do exactly what I say. Do you understand?"

Lana gave a shaky nod.

"Good. Now, I need a microphone."

Lana ran to the podium, where the auctioneer's microphone was ready and waiting. Caleb was right on her heels.

Lana flipped the microphone on with a shaking finger and handed it over to Caleb. "Can I please have your attention?" His voice was even and calm, without a hint of the panicky fear that was racing through him.

"The kids have been working hard with me on something for the past few days, and I thought all of you would like a little demonstration. Kids, are you with me?"

A scattering of young cheers went up, and parents smiled in anticipation.

Caleb pressed a button on his watch. "Okay, kids, your record is sixty-eight seconds. Let's see how much your folks slow you down. Go!"

Immediately, kids started making blaring noises like car horns or alarm clocks and headed for the door, pulling their parents behind them.

Lana gave Caleb a questioning look.

"Fire drill," he explained. "The kids added the noise on their own. I just taught them to get out of the building in an orderly manner. After what happened at your parents' house, I thought it might come in handy if there was ever a fire here."

"Thank God you're such a Boy Scout."

"I want you out of here, too. Get behind the perimeter

the men set and stay there. I can't afford to split my attention right now."

Lana didn't argue, but before she went, she pulled him down and gave him a brief kiss. She handed him a set of keys that opened all the doors in the building. "Stay safe."

He gave her a feral warrior's smile. "Promise me more of that sweet mouth and there's nothing that will take me down."

CHAPTER THIRTY

—— ❧ ——

Disarming the bomb wasn't going to be the hard part for someone who was as good with explosives as Caleb. Finding it was another story.

Caleb would have given his right arm for a dog trained at sniffing out explosives right now. His sense of smell was good, but not that good, and the bomb squad hadn't arrived yet.

The only consolation he had was that he was alone in the building and the crowd was clear and out of danger. Grant and the other men had seen to that. If Caleb messed up, he would be the only one paying the price, which was about as good as a situation like this could get.

He started at the rear door, figuring the private office area was a more likely location to leave something someone didn't want noticed. There was no way to know if opening a door would trigger the device, but he sure as hell couldn't see through them. Slowly, one by one, he opened each office with the keys Lana had given him. He started sweating on the first door. By the third, he was drenched.

But his hands remained steady, and that was the important part.

The offices were small and most were empty, making them easy to search. One of the rooms had been converted into an employee lounge, though it was hardly bigger than the offices. The faint scent of coffee clung to the walls. He opened each of the three cabinets over the counter, as well as the one under the sink, and found nothing but coffee, filters, dishes, and cleaning supplies. There was a large metal supply cabinet next to the refrigerator that he didn't remember seeing before, but he'd been in here only once, to get some ice for one of the kids who twisted his ankle.

Caleb approached the cabinet cautiously. He could see gouges in the vinyl flooring where the cabinet had been scraped across it. The gouges hadn't had time to collect any dirt. It definitely had been moved recently.

He picked up a chair and used the metal leg to push the lever that opened the door. Nothing happened. The door inched open, but nothing exploded. Which was a good thing.

Caleb definitely wanted all his fingers intact when this mess was over. He liked the way Lana's skin felt under his hands too much to give up even a little of that tactile sensation.

He leaned close and peered inside the cabinet. He could see only one side, but it looked empty. Again, using the chair, Caleb nudged the cabinet door open. Again, nothing exploded.

He could see inside the cabinet easily now, and it was, indeed, empty.

He turned to go to the next office when the refrigerator kicked on and the stench of urine and fear was pushed up to his nose. He paused, sniffing the air to figure out where the smell was coming from.

He moved to where the scent was stronger. It was coming from behind the cabinet.

Caleb leaned over until he could see behind the cabinet and found a door. The handle had been removed so the cabinet wouldn't stick out from the wall—so that the cabinet would completely obscure the door.

Bingo.

He checked for any triggering devices connected to the cabinet, and when he found none, he carefully picked it up and moved it out of the way. The door behind it was painted the same plain white as the walls. An empty bulletin board hung crookedly from a nail in the door.

The hole where the door handle should have been had been taped over with a strip of duct tape. Caleb pulled out his small multi-tool and used the knife to poke a tiny hole in the tape so he could see inside. The storage room, or whatever it was, was dark inside. Of course.

With a deep breath to steady his nerves, Caleb slowly pulled the tape away from the hole. The sticky sound was too loud in his ears, and he realized he'd slid into adrenaline-induced hyper-awareness. Everything slowed down and stretched out, giving him more time to react. He prayed he wouldn't need it.

A muffled, frantic noise came from the other side of the door. Someone was in there.

Caleb forced himself to stay steady and keep his movements controlled. Now was not the time to get hasty. "I'm coming," he told whoever was in there in a calm voice. "Just hold on."

The person didn't quiet. Instead he grew more frantic, and Caleb could tell now that it was a man from the deep, panicked grunts.

"Is there a bomb in there with you?" asked Caleb.

A broken sob from the man confirmed his suspicions.

"Okay. I can deal with that. No problem." His voice was as steady as his hands. His pulse, on the other hand, was fast and hard. He didn't want to die here, not when there was still a chance he could have a life with Lana. She wasn't convinced they should be together yet, but she'd trusted him enough to tell him about Kara. That had to count for something. He wanted to stick around long enough to find out what that something was.

Caleb slid a finger through the hole and felt around for any sort of triggering device. His movements were necessarily slow, but he wanted nothing more than to blast through this door and get this guy out of harm's way. When he felt nothing, he poked the leg of a chair through the hole and used it to pull the door open.

Still no explosion. Thank God.

The room was dark, but the light spilling in from the employee lounge was bright enough to see by. The bomb was hidden near the gas line going into the kitchen, where the explosion would result in a nice, big fire. It was attached to a cell phone, which wasn't good. Caleb had seen setups like this before, and unless the phone was a decoy, one call would set the thing off.

Opposite the bomb sat Oran, bound and gagged, and living proof that karma existed. Tears streamed down his face, and his pants were dark where he'd wet himself. Caleb was man enough to pretend not to notice.

He crouched beside Oran, checking him for any connection to the bomb.

"I thought you were supposed to be at your engagement party today," said Caleb conversationally, as if they had all the time in the world. The last thing he needed was for Oran to panic and blow them both to hell.

Oran gave him a furious grunt.

"Bet you'd like that tape off your mouth," guessed Caleb. "I'll get to it in a minute. Just want to make sure you're not wired to set that thing off if you move too much."

Oran went completely still.

Caleb saw nothing that led him to think Oran could trigger the explosion with a shift of his body weight, so he eased a corner of the tape up and ripped it off the man's face.

Caleb wasn't a petty man, but the gasp of pain Oran gave him made him smile all the same.

"What's going on? How did I get here?" Oran asked.

He cut the tape around Oran's arms and legs. "You don't know?"

"The last thing I remember was coming here this morning to talk to Lana. My head's killing me. Someone must have knocked me out."

Caleb did not ask him what he was going to talk to Lana about. He was pretty sure that whatever it was would only piss him off, and he didn't need the distraction right now.

"Can you walk?" asked Caleb.

Oran nodded. "I think so."

"Good. Get the hell out so I can disarm this bomb."

"By yourself?" asked Oran, horrified.

"You see anyone else standing around?"

"You should wait for the bomb squad."

"And risk it going off in the meantime? I don't think so. When they get here, I'm happy to share the fun. Now, unless you want to help, get out. I don't have time to carry you out."

Oran was gone before the echo of Caleb's voice in the empty storage room settled.

Caleb pulled in a deep breath and went to work.

CHAPTER THIRTY-ONE

— ⋙✦⋘ —

The press arrived at the youth center within minutes of the evacuation, their cameras trained on the building. Lana was inundated with questions, and microphones were thrust into her face.

"Is it true there's a bomb inside?" asked one reporter.

"We have reports of a release of nerve toxin. Can you confirm that?" asked another.

"Have you received any threats before today?"

"Can you think of any reason why your foundation would be targeted?"

They kept coming at her with questions, some of the same ones over and over. Lana spent what seemed like forever answering questions when all she wanted to do was find Caleb and make sure he was safe.

The only break she got from the reporters was when Oran stumbled out of the building, looking like he'd wet his pants. Reporters swarmed him. Cameras flashed, capturing Oran's appearance in embarrassing detail. Those pictures were going to be popping up for the rest of Oran's career, she was sure of it.

The bomb squad arrived in a blast of sirens. A team

had gone into the building, but minutes crawled by, and no one had come out yet.

Some of the reporters left Oran to come back and attack Lana with more repetitive questions. Lana finally had to resort to "No comment."

Detective Hart came to her rescue, fending off the reporters. He pulled her beyond a line of police tape where the reporters couldn't get to her. "I got word from a man inside that Caleb disarmed the bomb. They're checking the place for more, but with any luck the threat is over."

Lana kept her knees locked to prevent herself from crumpling to the ground.

The detective's hand gripped her arm and steadied her. "You okay?"

"I will be if everyone gets out of this alive." Worry crushed her, making it hard to breathe. She'd brought this danger here. She'd put the lives of so many people at risk. Whatever it took, she could never let this happen again. If she had to go into protective custody, that's what she'd do. Her freedom was nothing compared to the lives of the kids at the youth center and their families.

It was nothing compared to Caleb's safety.

He had put himself in so much danger by going in there alone. She knew his job was dangerous, but knowing and witnessing it were two different things. And this danger she'd brought down upon him herself. If only she'd told him about Kara earlier, maybe they could have avoided this. Maybe he would have been able to stop Kara, take her into custody before she could have planted the bomb.

It was too late for that. The mistakes she'd made were set in stone, but that didn't mean she had to make more. She was going to take responsibility for her role in this disaster. Publicly. She didn't know how she would find the strength to do it, but she would. Somehow.

❧

"We're clear," said Grant.

"Tell them to do another sweep with the dogs, just to be sure," ordered Caleb.

"They've done two. They're sure. Bomb squad's moved outside to start checking cars. No one's going home until they're sure the exterior is clear, too."

"Good. You and I can follow a lead, then."

"What lead?" asked Grant.

There were still way too many ears around for Caleb's peace of mind. "Not here. Outside."

Caleb and Grant slipped out through the crowd without tipping off the press.

When they were out of earshot, Caleb said, "Monroe traced the cell phone used to trigger the bomb to a man named Dennis Nelson."

"Not Kara?"

"No. I've got his address."

"This is Kara's boyfriend, or so we thought. I'm coming with you."

Caleb didn't argue. He was too glad Grant was here to lend a hand and make the job safer so he could get back to Lana in one piece.

They geared up on the drive over, donning vests and headsets to keep them in constant communication. They were both revved up, tense, and on edge as they neared the Nelson residence.

The man's house was a run-down little place that

matched all the others on the block. The cracker box had been built right after World War II and looked like it hadn't been painted since. A flower box full of weeds graced the single front window.

Grant circled around back while Caleb let himself in through the front door. The place was a wreck, with newspapers and beer bottles and pizza boxes thrown everywhere. The smell of stale sweat and old beer filled the air, forcing Caleb to breathe through his mouth.

"The back is clear—I'm coming in," said Grant over the headset Caleb wore.

Grant was at his side an instant later.

There wasn't much to the house, just a small kitchen, a living room, and two bedrooms with a bathroom between. Caleb motioned for Grant to take the bedroom on the right.

Weapon in hand, Caleb went to the bedroom on the left. He nudged the door open and saw a man lying facedown on the bed. A soft snore gave away that the man was alive, and Caleb felt his mouth pull back in a fierce smile.

"Clear," whispered Grant over the headset.

Caleb felt Grant's shadow beside him, covering him while he entered the room. Caleb woke the sleeping man up by pressing a knee against his back to hold his body immobile against the mattress.

The man came awake with a frightened shriek and thrashed under Caleb's knee. Caleb pressed more of his weight into the man's spine until he stopped fighting. "How do you know Kara McIntire?" he asked.

"What the hell? I don't know any fucking Kara. If your old lady is sleeping around on you, that's not my problem."

"Wrong answer. Try again. We found your cell phone on the bomb."

The man tensed beneath Caleb's knee. "It couldn't have been mine. Mine is on the dresser."

Caleb heard Grant take a step toward the dresser, but he kept his eyes on Dennis.

"No phone here," said Grant.

"I'm only going to ask you one more time, Mr. Nelson. How did your phone end up on the bomb at the youth center?"

"I don't know. I swear it. My boss must have come in and taken it last night."

"Your boss?" asked Caleb.

"I don't know his name. I swear to God. He contacted me by phone, using this freaky thing that fucked up his voice so I couldn't recognize it."

"Are you sure it was a man?"

Dennis hesitated for a moment, then said, "Sounded like a man, but like I said, it was all fucked up, like a robot or something."

It could have been Kara using a voice-modulation device. He'd have Monroe add that to the list of questions to ask her. "What did you do for your boss?" demanded Caleb.

"I didn't plant the bomb. I swear."

"Your fingerprints were at the youth center," lied Caleb. It would take a while for the results of the fingerprints they'd lifted to come back, but it was a good guess—one designed to get Dennis to talk.

"I picked up some stuff for my boss. He wanted me to bring back a bunch of photographs of the kids."

"What photos?" asked Caleb.

"They were on a bulletin board in the break room. It was just a bunch of kids at some swim party or something. He came here and got them when I was sleeping. My boss is the pervert, not me. I don't go for kids."

"What do you know about the bomb?"

Dennis swallowed hard. "I saw the parts. My boss had me take everything out and lay it on the kitchen table. I have no fucking idea why. The guy's a psycho. You should be looking for him."

Caleb knew exactly why Dennis had been ordered to do that. Whoever had really made the bomb—probably Kara—wanted to make sure that there were nice, clear fingerprints on all the components. No doubt Dennis Nelson had a police record and his prints were on file. The police would track him right back here and find trace evidence that there had been explosives in his kitchen. They'd probably also find photographs from the youth center hidden around his house, with his prints all over them. Dennis would be blamed for the bomb, and the real culprit would walk away.

It was a good plan. Too bad for Kara they already had her in custody.

"Did you ever meet your boss in person?" asked Caleb.

"No."

"What about a woman named Kara? Know her?" asked Grant.

"No."

"She came here several times. Let herself in with a key."

Dennis went pale. "My boss was a woman? That's fucked up."

"Is there anything else you were told to do? Anything at all?" Caleb let all his anger come though in his voice. He used it as a weapon to scare Dennis, to make the bastard talk.

"I broke into a couple places. He, or she, I guess, wanted me to find some drawings or something."

"Drawings?" A chill flooded Caleb's stomach.

"Yeah, like sketches. She wanted to see every new drawing this one chick did, but I never found any."

Lana's sketchbooks.

"What was the woman's name?" asked Caleb in a lethally quiet voice. Out of the corner of his eye, he saw Grant move closer to the bed, as if preparing to pull Caleb off if he did something stupid, like beat Dennis to a pulp.

The thought had crossed Caleb's mind.

"I don't know," said Dennis.

"Tell me." Caleb grabbed a fistful of hair and pulled the man's head back at an awkward angle.

"Laura something. That's all I know." Dennis's voice gurgled from the extreme angle.

"Lana?"

"Yeah, that's it. Lana. Please let me go. You're breaking my neck."

Caleb only wished. He loosened the pressure just a bit. "Did you break into Lana's office?"

"Yeah."

"You shot her coworker." It wasn't a question. Caleb knew the man had.

"I didn't mean to." Dennis started crying, his voice ramping up to a high-pitched whine. "It was an accident. The gun just went off, and then there was all this blood . . ."

Caleb let go of the man's hair, shoving his face toward the mattress in disgust. He took some plastic flex-cuffs from Grant and bound Dennis's wrists behind him, then did the same with the man's ankles.

"Call Hart," he told Grant. "Tell him we've found Stacie's shooter, and have him hurry the hell up. I want to get back to Lana."

CHAPTER THIRTY-TWO

———❖———

It took only a few minutes for Detective Hart to arrive. Trailing behind him were half a dozen cops who immediately began to secure the scene, though they were carefully staying away from Nelson's private property until the search warrant arrived.

Caleb sat Dennis at the curb so Hart would be free to arrest him without stepping foot on his property. He didn't want anything messing up this arrest.

"You sure this is the guy who shot Stacie?" asked Hart, his hazel eyes sharp as he looked at the man.

"He confessed," said Caleb. "The gun is in the top drawer of his dresser, so you can do the ballistics match. Arrest him or detain him or whatever you're going to do, but I need to get back to Lana."

"I want protection," pleaded Dennis.

"Does that mean you admit to shooting Stacie Cramer?" asked Hart in an even voice.

"Yes. Just get me the hell out of here. My boss is probably watching right now."

Hart gave Caleb a questioning look. "Is he sane?"

"Far as I know. I suggest you do as he says and get him

somewhere less out in the open. He may have more information about the bombing attempt at the youth center."

Hart read Dennis his rights and hustled Dennis to the nearest patrol car. "Thanks. Lana and Stacie will be thrilled to know we found the guy."

"You'll find his prints all over the bomb, but I don't think he's the one who built it."

Hart helped Dennis ease into the backseat without hitting his head. "On the way here, I had his record checked. He was photographed running several red lights last night. All on the street leading away from the youth center."

"My boss said I had to hurry or my money would be gone," wailed Dennis.

Caleb waited until Hart shut the car door and lowered his voice so it couldn't be heard inside the patrol car. "He's being set up for the bombing. I think the real bomber is already in custody."

Hart gave Caleb a skeptical frown. "How the hell do you know all that?"

"Just putting two and two together. Finally came up with four, though it took long enough. How's Lana holding up?"

Hart shrugged. "She took off as soon as she knew you were safe. I made sure she got out of the danger zone. Told her to go home and get some rest."

"Thanks."

Caleb's phone vibrated. When he answered it, Monroe was on the other end. Without preamble, he said, "Kara escaped."

"What?" bellowed Caleb.

Lana was alone. Unprotected. Caleb felt his skin ice over with fear.

"We were transporting her to a more secure location. Her transport was attacked. Two guards were killed. Three more injured."

"Where and when did this happen?" Caleb was already heading for the car.

"She took one of the guard's cars. The authorities are looking for it, but most of them are still at the First Light Foundation. Kara's had plenty of time to make it back to town, and she'll want to eliminate her as a witness, so don't let her out of your sight."

"Too late for that," said Caleb as he hung up the phone.

Caleb tried not to panic, but it was a close thing. Lana was alone, and Kara was free to hurt her.

"Everything okay?" asked Grant, hot on his heels as Caleb reached the car.

"No. Kara escaped. She's going after Lana."

"Let me drive," offered Grant. "I've got gear in the trunk."

By "gear" he meant weapons. Knowing Grant, lots of them.

Caleb dialed Lana's house and got her voice mail.

He prayed to God she'd stopped for groceries or got caught in traffic or something—anything—to keep her from getting home before he did.

꙳

Lana unlocked her apartment door and went inside. It took her eyes a second to adjust from the brightness outside, and when they did, she saw Phil slumped on her couch with a ragged bullet hole in his temple. Blood and pulpy chunks of brain were splattered across the framed sketches of Lana's family.

Her mind ground to a halt as she tried to make sense of what she saw. Lana turned her head toward a blinking light that caught her attention. A small video camera sat on a tripod, angled so that it could capture the small living area. A red light flashed on and off, indicating it was recording.

Kara leveled a gun at Lana and gave her a cold smile. "I think this has gone on long enough, don't you?"

CHAPTER THIRTY-THREE

———◦❧◦———

Marcus knew exactly where to find Kara. She was nothing if not doggedly determined to finish what she started.

It took a bit of time to find Lana Hancock's address. The woman protected her privacy and had an unlisted number. His well-paid computer genius hacked into her medical records and solved the problem with only a short delay.

Marcus abandoned the car he'd used while disrupting Kara's transportation, just in case one of the guards lived long enough to ID it. He was now behind the wheel of a distressingly average four-door sedan, blending in with all the others.

His face was nothing special, and even though he kept his body in peak physical shape, his specially tailored clothing helped conceal both his size and build. He could hide in plain sight. No one would look twice at him. No one would suspect he was a man headed to murder two women and anyone else who got in his way.

◦❧◦

Fear made Lana clumsy. Slow. She reached behind her for the door, but Kara stopped her.

"Oh, no you don't. No more running. This is where you and I finish things."

"You're going to kill me." Her heart was pounding so hard she was sure Kara could hear it.

"Of course. That's the way it has to be. You should be happy."

"Happy?" She wished she had a cell phone. Maybe she would have been able to call 911 or Caleb.

"You've had a year and a half longer than you were meant to have. That's got to count for something."

Lana's eyes darted around, looking for a weapon. All she found nearby were bits of wood that had once been a chair—the one Caleb crushed when he forced his way in.

She was going to miss him so much.

"I promise not to tell anyone who you are. Just leave. Disappear."

Kara laughed. It was a rich, elegant sound that made Lana's skin crawl. She steadied the gun with her left hand. "It's too late for that."

"Just tell me why," pleaded Lana, stalling. She needed more time to figure out what to do. How to get out of this. She didn't want to die.

"Why what?"

"Why me? Why did you want to kill me in Armenia?"

Kara frowned as if truly puzzled. "What makes you think I need a reason to kill?"

"Because you like to watch people's torment too much to end it without a reason. If they're dead, you can't enjoy their suffering."

"You make me sound like some sort of lunatic. Torture is an art. Do you think that any of your friends would have suffered nearly as much if they hadn't known they were going to die? Hadn't had proof?"

"So, each death was only for the purpose of making the next person more afraid?"

"And to isolate them." Kara cocked her head to the side and dropped her voice as if trying to seduce a lover. "Tell me, how did it feel to be the last one alive? To know you were all alone? In the dark. No one was coming to save you. No one was there to hear you cry. You were the last. Destined to suffer and die all alone."

Lana found herself speeding back to that place against her will. She could smell the stench of decaying bodies, feel the rough cloth over her face.

Black, suffocating terror swelled up inside her, spilling out until she could feel it crawling along her skin, inching up her nose, leaking into her mouth.

Kara let out a low, pleased moan. "Yes. That's right. You were the best work I've ever done."

Lana's body tensed up. She struggled to pull herself back to the here and now.

"Sometimes," said Kara, "I think there will never be another like you. So helpless in your fear. So consumed by it. Maybe it's genetic. Maybe your sister has the same trait."

"Jenny." The word slipped out in a nearly desperate plea.

Kara shuddered in pleasure.

"And she has a son. A husband. So many people to lose. So much pain to bear."

No! Lana couldn't let that happen. She couldn't let her family endure the torture she had. She loved them too much not to fight. This evil had to end, and Lana was the only one here to do it. That thought gave her the strength to crawl back to reality, shrug off the terror of her past, and face Kara without fear for the first time.

She was just a woman. Sure, she was a woman holding a gun, and Lana still hadn't found a weapon, but she couldn't let that stop her.

It was going to end here. Now. She had *not* fought her way back from the grave and lived a life of fear and torment, struggling to survive, just so she could die now. As long as she was alive, there was a chance she could keep her family, Stacie, and Caleb safe. As long as she was alive, there was hope.

Kara had tried to steal her life in Armenia. She'd tried to ruin it by moving here to torment Lana. It was not going to end like this. She was not going to end up like Phil, lying on the couch with a bullet in her head. *She was not.*

Lana lashed out using one of the brutal moves Caleb and Grant had taught her. It was no graceful motion of limbs like some accomplished martial artist—it was violent and ugly and effective. She went for Kara's eyes, sweeping the gun out of her way as she moved inside her reach.

Kara didn't expect her fearless attack, and she was thrown back on the floor. Lana came down hard on top of her and pressed a forearm against Kara's neck, bearing down with all her weight and fury. Kara gurgled and slammed the gun into the side of Lana's head.

Bright spots flared in Lana's sight, but she didn't stop fighting. Adrenaline made her stronger, faster. Eighteen months of anger made her ferocious. She screamed as she pummeled Kara's face with her fist, still choking off her air.

Kara's body heaved in a desperate attempt to dislodge her, and Lana was rolled to the side, her back slamming hard into the bookcase. Air rushed from her lungs, and she couldn't pull any back in, but she didn't care. Her rage was burning too bright to be put out by something so seemingly trivial as oxygen. She tried to push to her feet but only made it to her knees. Her hand found something heavy and hard on one of the lower shelves, and she bashed it against Kara's head.

Kara let out a pained yelp and instinctively curled her arms over her head. The gun went flying, but Lana didn't bother wasting precious seconds to look for it. Instead, she forced herself to her feet and gathered every scrap of anger and pain and terror Kara had forced on her. She saw the face of every friend she'd lost, heard their pain-filled cries for help. She couldn't do anything then, but she could now.

Lana shoved all that emotion into a tight ball and let it explode inside her in a frightening rush of strength. The giant bookcase moved easily as she ripped it away from the wall and pushed it over.

The tall furniture toppled and books slid out, landing in a heavy pile over Kara's torso. Kara let out a high-pitched scream, but Lana could not find even a sliver of pity for the trapped woman. Kara deserved whatever she got.

All Lana felt was a giddy wave of victory and a terrifying need to finish the job. She wanted to kill Kara—to watch the light of life flicker and die behind her eyes.

The door slammed open and Caleb appeared, his big body outlined in sunlight. He had a gun in his hand, which he carefully lowered with slow, precise movements.

He turned and shouted over his shoulder, "We need an ambulance!"

Caleb stepped inside, his eyes roaming over the scene, taking it in in a split second. He pulled her against him in a desperate hug that made breathing even more difficult. It lasted only a heartbeat before he released her and bent his knees, making himself short enough to look right into her face. "You okay?" he asked, his voice even.

Lana was too out of breath to answer, but she gave him an unsteady nod. Kara's gun lay on the ground at Lana's feet. She reached down, picked it up, and aimed it at Kara's head.

Caleb's voice was low and gentle. "You don't want to do this, Lana. You don't want her death on your hands."

"She tortured and killed my friends. She tortured me. She ordered my death. She threatened my family. She deserves to die."

"Yes, but you don't deserve to be the one to pull the trigger. Killing someone is a heavy responsibility. You've already suffered enough because of her. Don't let her cause you any more pain."

"She would have killed hundreds of people today, and if she lives, she'll try to do it again. She already escaped once."

"She won't get away again. Look at her. She can't move. Her back is probably broken. She's finished."

Lana looked down at the woman. Really looked at her. Her face was bleeding from various scratches Lana had gouged into her skin. Her left eye was swelling shut. Her nose looked crooked and was bleeding heavily. A thick, purple bruise was darkening over her throat where Lana had choked her. Her limbs were unnaturally still. She was trapped. Helpless. Broken.

Just like Lana had been in Armenia when Kara had ordered her death.

"Please don't kill me," begged Kara.

Lana felt no pity for her. None. She would have killed those children today if Caleb hadn't stopped her.

All Lana had to do was move one finger a scant inch and it would be over. Sure, there were other terrorists out there, but this one would be dead. Lana would know it for a fact. No more worries that Kara would see the fear in her eyes and know. No more nightmares about the elegant voice ordering her death. All she had to do was pull the trigger and take back a sliver of control. All she needed was a tiny sliver. It wasn't asking for much after what she'd been through.

Kara gave Lana a defiant stare burning with hatred. There was no question that Kara would try to kill her if she got the chance—if Lana let her live.

All she had to do was twitch. Just a little.

Sweat rolled down Lana's temple, stinging the cut there. Her whole body was quivering from the rush of adrenaline, and her breathing seemed too loud.

"You can't do it," urged Caleb.

"Yes, I can. Watch me."

"You're not a killer. You're not like her."

In that moment, Lana knew exactly what she had to do. She had to take back control of her life—recapture it from those who had tried to steal it away from her. And there was only one true way to do that. She had to let her anger go before she turned into one of them.

Lana lowered the weapon, sliding it back into Caleb's big hands. "You're right. I'm not like her."

She felt Caleb's muscled body behind her relax fractionally. He took the weapon from her hands just as Grant came rushing into the apartment.

Kara tried to scream, but it came out as more of a wet gurgle. "You bitch! I should have killed you a dozen times over. I should have made you watch your family die one by one."

Lana couldn't stay here and hear this. She had to get out.

"Grant, stay with Kara until the paramedics arrive, then contact Monroe," said Caleb.

"I'm on it."

Lana was halfway down the sidewalk when Caleb caught up to her. He shoved the disk from the video camera into his pocket and pulled her to a stop. "Hold on a minute, honey," he said, his voice so gentle. "You're in shock," he said as he rubbed his hands up and down her arms.

Lana couldn't seem to make sense of his words. She blinked up at him. The sun was behind him, casting his face in shadows, just like it had been that day he'd carried her out of the cave. He'd saved her then, and with a sudden realization, she knew that he'd done it again.

He'd kept her from killing Kara. Proved to her she was in control of her life. Her decisions. No one could take that away from her, no matter what Kara or anyone else did to try to tear her life apart. It was her life, and no matter how much evil she'd been forced to face in the past months, she couldn't let it define her. Not anymore.

"Sit down." He guided her to a step and lowered her

to the warm concrete. "Give yourself a minute to let the adrenaline wear off. I can hear an ambulance now, and they can take a look at your head."

"My head?" Somewhere in the dim haze of crazy signals her body was giving out, she realized that her head hurt. She reached her hand up to that spot, and it came away red with blood. "She hit me with her gun."

"You still took her down." She heard the pride in Caleb's deep voice.

"I didn't kill her," stated Lana, as if he hadn't been right there.

"I knew you wouldn't."

His faith in her was humbling.

The ambulance pulled into the parking lot, the siren making Lana's head feel like it was going to split open. A young EMT hurried to her side and started poking at her, flashing a light in her eyes, pressing a bandage over the wound. She wanted to leave, but Caleb held her in place while they patched her up.

"We should take her to the hospital," said the EMT.

"No hospital!" said Lana, feeling panic rise up inside her. She couldn't stand the thought of being confined in a stark room that reeked of death and hopelessness.

"I'll look out for her," said Caleb.

The EMT gave Caleb a strange look she couldn't understand—some sort of silent male communication. "Keep an eye on her, and if she gets worse, bring her in."

"The woman inside needs your attention more than Lana," Caleb told the man.

The EMT left to go inside, and Lana needed to get away before he came back and changed his mind. If he tried to take her to a hospital, she might just find a use for a gun.

She tried to get to her feet, but her legs were too weak.

"Just sit. I won't let them take you to the hospital. You'll feel better once you give yourself a few minutes to let the shock wear off."

"I'll feel better when this is over. Really over."

❧

Marcus shoved the limp, nearly naked body of the paramedic into the ambulance. The man's clothes were a little snug, but they would have to do. Cleaning up this mess wouldn't take long if he hurried. Doubtlessly, police would be arriving soon, but they were a bit occupied with the recent bomb scare at First Light Foundation.

Thank you, Kara.

He grabbed what looked like a tackle box to complete his disguise and headed toward the apartment building.

❧

Caleb held Lana close, thanking God she was still alive.

Grant was on the far side of the parking lot, where Lana couldn't hear what he was saying to Monroe. It was probably best that she had as little involvement with Kara as possible. Until the trial.

That wasn't going to be any fun, but Caleb was going to be right there by her side the whole time, supporting her. No matter what it took.

The second paramedic came up the sidewalk.

"Your partner's inside," Caleb told him, motioning toward Lana's apartment.

"Thanks."

He veered around them. Sunlight bounced off his highly polished shoes, revealing a few drops of blood.

"You've got some blood on your shoe," said Caleb.

The man didn't even slow down enough to look. "Last call was messy. Hazard of the job."

Caleb didn't want to know. He pulled Lana closer, ready to interrupt him if he decided to share any stories.

Lana clung to him, and it felt good. He wasn't sure how he was ever going to let her go.

She looked up at him, her eyes a bright, sorrowful blue. "Can we go?"

The apartment door clicked shut behind them.

Why would they have done that? Her apartment was dark. Wouldn't they want the extra light?

Caleb turned around and looked at the closed door, and a feeling of dread started to swell. Something was wrong here.

The shoes.

Since when did EMTs wear expensive dress shoes on the job?

They didn't. That man wasn't an EMT.

Caleb prayed he was a reporter hunting for the inside scoop, but he didn't think he'd get that lucky.

Two muffled pops sounded from the apartment, followed by one more. Silenced shots.

No luck today.

"Get in the car," Caleb told Lana.

"What's wrong?" she asked.

Caleb didn't have time to explain. "Grant!" he bellowed as he charged up the sidewalk, drawing his weapon.

Grant looked up from his conversation, saw there was a problem, and started toward them.

Caleb couldn't wait for him to catch up. Lana was still too close.

The apartment door flew open. The imposter EMT held a Sig Sauer like he knew how to use it. He fired.

Caleb's body jerked, and he spun to the left. He felt like he'd been hit in the chest with a sledgehammer, and he had to struggle to stay on his feet.

The man leveled his weapon, but this time he wasn't aiming at Caleb. He was aiming for Lana. And she wasn't wearing a bulletproof vest like he was.

Caleb was not going to let her get hurt again. Never again.

Rage filled him up, making him stronger, faster. He forced his body to move despite the pain in his chest. He fired his weapon, even though he knew he'd have to get lucky to hit anything while at a dead run. The man flinched, distracting him for a split second. It was all the time Caleb needed.

He lunged at the man, putting the full force of his anger into the motion. He slammed the man into the wall of the building with a satisfying thud.

Another sledgehammer drove the breath from his body. His arm went numb for a moment, and he heard his weapon clatter to the ground. In the back of his mind, he recognized he'd taken another round.

Better him than Lana.

Caleb had him pinned to the wall, but the man was

strong and managed to free his weapon enough to bring it up toward Caleb's head for a fatal shot.

Lana screamed. Grant shouted at her to get back. From his voice, Caleb could tell he was still too far away to help unless Caleb could separate their bodies enough for him to get a clear shot.

Caleb hammered a fist into the man's side, rocking him, making him grunt in pain. The blow cost Caleb his precarious balance and opened him up for a solid punch to his face. As he toppled, he caught a hold of the man's weapon hand and pulled him to the ground.

The man tried to roll out of it, but Caleb outweighed him and used brute force to hold him down. He locked a strong hand around Caleb's throat and squeezed. Caleb ignored everything but the gun. He couldn't risk a stray shot hitting Lana. The man gripped Caleb's throat harder. He couldn't pull in any air.

The pistol went off again, firing past Caleb's head into the air.

Lana screamed. She was still too close.

Caleb felt his body giving out due to lack of oxygen. Bright spots were bursting over his field of vision. He wasn't going to last much longer. He had to get that weapon away before he passed out, or he was a dead man.

Caleb squeezed the hand around the weapon. Hard. Used every bit of his strength to crush the man's hand against the unyielding metal contours of the pistol.

The man screamed, his voice rising an octave in pain. Caleb felt bones snap.

A vicious kick landed along Caleb's back. The edges of Caleb's vision were fading to gray. He could hear Grant shouting at Lana to stay down. Hear his boots pounding nearer.

He figured he had another few seconds of consciousness at most and willed Grant to hurry.

Weakness started to flow into him at an alarmingly fast pace. He turned the gun toward the man who had wanted to hurt Lana. Used his fury to keep him awake another second. Two.

Another bone cracked. A strangled noise rose up from the man beneath him. Caleb angled the weapon until the silencer was pressed against his enemy's flesh. He didn't know what part it was, because he was totally blind now, but he guessed it was going to hurt, all the same.

The man gave a panicked grunt. Caleb found the trigger beneath the man's own finger. The gun gave a silenced bark and jerked in their hands.

Hot blood sprayed up over Caleb's face, and the man beneath him went limp.

Caleb hadn't realized he'd blacked out until it was over and he was waking up again. It was the sound of Lana's frightened voice that got his attention. "Is he hurt?"

"He's okay," he heard Grant say. "Both rounds hit his vest."

Caleb opened his eyes, a little shocked he could see again, breathe again. The first thing he saw was Lana's tearstained face. She was hovering over him, holding his hand. "God, you're beautiful," he told her.

She laughed and new tears leaked out of her eyes. "You're awake."

"Just needed a quick nap." Talking hurt. Breathing wasn't much fun, either.

Caleb pushed himself up. That hurt, too, but he didn't

think anything was broken. His shirt had been shoved up, and he could see two bruises forming over his ribs. The vest had stopped the bullets, thank God.

"Asleep on the job again," said Grant. "What a slacker."

"I'm a slacker? You're the one who took your sweet time lending a hand."

"I figured you weren't interested in learning about friendly fire up close and personal. Besides, I didn't want to make you look bad in front of the lady."

Lana took his face between her palms. "How do you feel?"

"I'll survive." An ambulance pulled into the lot, sirens blaring.

"You'd better," said Grant. "Monroe said they've located the other men Lana saw in Armenia. A chopper will be here to pick us up in ten minutes. If you whine, he won't let you in on the fun of hunting them down."

Like hell. Caleb was going to finish this. End Lana's nightmare. And then he was coming back for her. Whatever it took.

❧

Caleb had been gone six days, and Lana's life felt bleak without him. Barren.

She'd chosen to go into protective custody in order to keep everyone else safe—at least until the men she'd seen had been found and brought to justice. Once the trials were over, she would go back to her regular life.

At least they'd allowed her brief contact with her family via phone, so she was able to keep tabs on them. Let them know she was okay.

She tried to be happy about all the good things in her life. Kara had been killed and could never hurt anyone again. The money from the carnival had been more than enough to put the youth center back in the black, and with all the press from the bomb scare, all kinds of donations were coming in. Stacie was up and about. She and her sister were taking a trip to Europe in the fall. Lana's parents were already working on plans to rebuild their house. Her mom was thrilled to be able to pick carpet and wall colors all over again, especially since their insurance was paying for everything. Her dad had already started designing his new gardens and a greenhouse he could use all year round.

Brittney broke off her engagement with Oran as soon as the embarrassing photos of him started popping up in the daily paper and on the news. Rumor was he'd abandoned his political aspirations.

The papers depicted Lana as some kind of hero, which bothered her a lot. No matter how many times she told them that she was a coward and that she should have come forward sooner, people seemed to wave that part off as unimportant. Especially her family.

Caleb was the real hero. He'd disarmed the bomb, saved her from being shot, and was hunting down terrorists while she sat in her well-guarded room, praying he was safe. Hoping he'd come back. Not that she'd given him much reason to. She'd been painfully clear that they had no future together. Why would he bother to come back?

If only she'd said something—anything—to let him

know how much she cared about him, how much she wanted him to come back to her. But she hadn't. He'd stepped onto that helicopter, and all she could think to say was, "Good-bye."

She wished she'd at least kissed him.

The late-night TV show she'd been trying to watch was over, and she couldn't remember seeing any of it. Even though her nightmares were mostly gone, she still didn't like going to sleep alone. She missed Caleb so much.

Loved him so much. It was easy to see that now that she was no longer consumed by fear. She finally had room in her life to love, and she prayed it wasn't too late. As soon as it was safe, she was going to hunt him down and tell him how she felt. She only hoped he'd have a better reaction than she had to the words.

A knock on the door made her jump. It was after midnight, and she wasn't expecting anyone. A kick of fear froze her in place. She knew she was safe, but all those months of terror had not yet let go of her completely.

Lana took a deep breath, forcing herself to relax. She was safe here. Only Monroe and his men knew where she was.

She opened the door, and Caleb stood there. He looked tired and dusty, like he'd been dragged behind a truck for a couple of miles, but he was here. Alive.

Lana's heart squeezed, and she ran into his arms. He stumbled back under her impact, but he held on to her like he'd never let go. Lana held him back just as hard.

"You're safe," she said against his shoulder.

Caleb kicked the door shut. There was an odd mix of fury and resignation in his tone. "And so are you now. It's over. For good this time. You can go home."

Lana understood what he meant. What he hadn't said. There wouldn't be any trial. Kara was dead, and now those men were, too. She didn't let herself dwell on why that was or how it had happened. She simply accepted that each and every one of them had deserved whatever fate they'd met. That was justice enough for her.

"You look worn-out," she told him.

"I am. Dirty, too. But I needed to see you. I didn't want to wait to tell you, you don't have to be afraid anymore."

That was her Caleb. Always the hero, thinking of others first.

Lana offered him a smile that came straight from her heart. She had no idea how to tell him how she felt. All she could think to do was show him. "I'm glad you didn't wait. The shower is big enough for two."

A hot glow lit his eyes and highlighted his cheeks. "You're killing me, woman."

"No, I'm loving you."

Caleb's body took on an unnatural stillness. "You mean that?"

"Yes."

"Then say it." His tone was hard, unyielding.

Lana went up on her tiptoes and looked right into his dark eyes. She let him see every bit of hope and love and desire she felt for him, holding nothing back. She'd never hold back from him again. "I. Love. You."

Caleb's big body shuddered at her words, and his arms crushed her against him. "I'm not going to push you. I know you still have a lot of things to deal with. But I'm not going away, either."

"No?"

"Not a chance. I'm taking that job David offered me so I have more time to spend with you."

Lana pressed a light kiss to his mouth, grateful that he was choosing a safer line of work. She wasn't sure how much more worry her poor heart could take. "How much time?"

"As much as you can stand. I want you in my life, Lana. Permanently. I'll wait until you're ready for that kind of permanence, but you should know I'll be waiting nearby."

"How close?"

"As close as you'll let me get."

That sounded wonderful. She could think of nothing she wanted more than to be with him without the taint of violence hovering over them. "I have the feeling you won't have to wait long."

"No?" he asked, sounding hopeful.

"No," she replied. "Now let's get you out of those clothes and into the shower."

A hungry sound rumbled from Caleb's chest. "I'm too tired for the kind of loving I want to give you."

Lana gave him a sultry smile full of promise. "That's okay. It's my turn to take care of you for a change. I guarantee you'll like it."

ABOUT THE AUTHOR

After spending too many years as an industrial engineer, Shannon learned to write from her husband, bestselling author Jim Butcher. She learned writing craft in order to help him with his stories but found the idea of writing her own too compelling to resist. She lives in Missouri with her husband and son, where conversations at the dinner table are more often about things someone made up than about anything that's actually happened. Feel free to contact Shannon via her Web site: www.shannonkbutcher.com.

THE DISH

Where authors give you the inside scoop!

♥ ♥ ♥ ♥ ♥ ♥ ♥ ♥ ♥ ♥ ♥ ♥ ♥ ♥

From the desk of Shannon K. Butcher

Dear Reader,

Some things are innately sexy: Long, slow kisses. The warm glide of skin on skin. A man in pain.

Okay, maybe I'm a little warped, but I really love to make my heroes suffer—a fact I'm sure my husband can attest to. Caleb Stone in NO CONTROL (on sale now) was a particularly engrossing project for me. Poor guy.

The idea of forgiveness has always intrigued me, probably because I make so many mistakes. It's almost magical the way something we can't see or touch can change people's lives. And the fact that it's a gift involving no physical construct or action seems counterintuitive. How can something that illusive be so powerful?

The little things are easy to forgive—like forgetting to put the milk away. No sweat. It's the bigger mistakes that give us pause, but usually, as long as we know they're mistakes, we can let those slide by, too. But what about the things we do purposefully? The decisions we make knowing someone is going to get hurt? The decisions we would make exactly the same way if we had to do it all over again?

Those are the questions that drove me to create Caleb. I knew from the moment he sparked to life inside my head that he was destined for a very special kind of hell—one of his own making. He was designed to be a walking, talking example of action meeting consequence in a messy collision, like the ones they show you as a warning in Driver's Ed class.

Thankfully, Caleb is tough and never complains, no matter how much I heaped on him. Which was why I had to give him a second chance. If anyone deserved one, it was Caleb, and there was only one person in the world who was capable of giving it to him.

But it couldn't be that easy, right? I mean, what fun would that be? So, Lana had to have her own heaping helping of suffering, just to make things interesting. I believe in equal opportunity, so it was only fair that I share the torment equally.

Not many people would have been strong enough to survive what Lana has. Terrorists abducted her and tortured her for days while she watched her friends die one by one, knowing she could be next at any time. Caleb was there. He saw it happen and did nothing to stop it and that decision has haunted him ever since. He knows he doesn't deserve forgiveness—not because what he did was too terrible to forgive, but because if he had to do it all over again, he'd make the same hard choices—but that doesn't stop him from wanting it all the same.

He gets his second chance with Lana, but even that is its own kind of hell. Being forced back into the life of the woman he nearly killed is not a comfortable place to be—for either of them. But they don't have a choice. Lana is hiding something and it is Caleb's duty to find out what it is before it can get her killed again. He refuses to fail her a second time.

Writing the book was great fun, which, I guess, makes me a sadist. I'll leave you to judge for yourself. I'm still intrigued by forgiveness. I'm not sure exactly what makes it so powerful even after spending way too much time thinking about it. In the end, I don't think I learned much, because I'm off to torture some more characters and I don't feel bad doing it at all.

Shannon K Butcher

www.shannonkbutcher.com

♥ ♥ ♥ ♥ ♥ ♥ ♥ ♥ ♥ ♥ ♥ ♥ ♥ ♥ ♥

From the desk of Robin Wells

Dear Reader,

The idea for my latest romantic comedy, BETWEEN THE SHEETS (on sale now), came to me while reading the tabloid headlines standing in a grocery store checkout line. Those poor celebrities, I thought; how awful to be humiliated in front of the whole world! And then a worse scenario occurred to me: What if a totally innocent woman suddenly found herself on the front page of one of these scandal sheets? What if she simply had been at the wrong place at the wrong time, but the whole world thought she had done something horrifically scandalous— something, like, say, giving the president-elect a heart attack in the sack during an illicit tryst? And what if she tried to rebuild her life by moving to the small town where her grandmother lived, and falling for a handsome, straight-arrow DA, a man who absolutely, positively, could not afford to have his name tainted by scandal? The story was off and running!

Unfortunately, it limped to a halt when Hurricane Katrina hit Louisiana. I live just outside New Orleans and many of the scenes are set there, so the catastrophe impacted the novel as well as its author. Lots of unexpected things were affected. Where would Grams and Harold get a wedding license, for instance, since New Orleans' city hall was destroyed? Could I mention the streetcar or would it still be out of commission? Would I ever be able to write funny stuff again?

It took a while, but the story finally started rolling once more, and then the characters took over and began misbehaving. Emma turned out to be a lot more smart-mouthed than I'd originally thought, Max had issues with his grandfather, and Grams was impossible to control. Louis was a late arrival to the story, he didn't show up until the last draft, and in typical Louis fashion, he caused problems all around. As for Katie, she might just need a book of her own. (Let me know if you agree!)

The secondary romance between the elderly couple was inspired by a true story. My late mother-in-law, Barbara Mix Wells, found new love in her eighties with a man who had mild Alzheimer's. They met at an assisted living center and lit up each others' last years. Here is a poem Barbara wrote about their late-in-life romance:

How can I stay in this moment of bliss?
A time I never dreamed
Would happen in my elder years.
I found and was found by another soul of my vintage
Who needs me as much as I need him.
We are tuned alike, parted from our mates
After giving loving care for a lifetime.
And now, alone, have found a company of two
To enrich the years that are still ahead.
                                        —Barbara Mix Wells

Sigh. How sweet is that? Just goes to show, it's never too late for love.

I'd love for you to drop by my Web site—www.robinwells.com—to read a sample chapter of my next novel, share your thoughts, or just say hi!

Happy reading and all my best,

Robin Wells

Dear Reader,

I hope you've enjoyed reading Caleb and Lana's story as much as I enjoyed writing it! Both of them are close to my heart and I hope to go back and revisit them every once in a while, just to see what they're up to.

If you'd like to see what I'm up to, I'd love for you stop by my Web site. It's www.ShannonKButcher.com. In addition to finding out about me, my books, and scheduled appearances, there's almost always a contest running with all kinds of fun prizes. There's also an e-mail link, making it easy for you to contact me. It's great to hear from readers and I'd love to hear from you!

Best wishes,

Shannon K Butcher

Want to know more about romances at Grand Central Publishing and Forever? Get the scoop online!

❧

GRAND CENTRAL PUBLISHING'S ROMANCE HOMEPAGE

Visit us at www.hachettebookgroupusa.com/romance for all the latest news, reviews, and chapter excerpts!

NEW AND UPCOMING TITLES

Each month we feature our new titles and reader favorites.

CONTESTS AND GIVEAWAYS

We give away galleys, autographed copies, and all kinds of fun stuff.

AUTHOR INFO

You'll find bios, articles, and links to personal websites for all your favorite authors—and so much more!

THE BUZZ

Sign up for our monthly romance newsletter, and be the first to read all about it!